ARCTIC
DAWN

KARISSA LAUREL

Arctic Dawn
The Norse Chronicles™
Copyright © 2016 by Karissa Laurel. All rights reserved.
First Print Edition: May 2016

ISBN-13: 978-1-940215-74-7
ISBN-10: 1-940215-74-9

Red Adept Publishing, LLC
104 Bugenfield Court
Garner, NC 27529
http://RedAdeptPublishing.com/

Cover and Formatting: Streetlight Graphics

For my Myrtle Beach Girls

Some say the world will end in fire,
Some say in ice.
From what I've tasted of desire
I hold with those who favor fire.
But if it had to perish twice,
I think I know enough of hate
To say that for destruction ice
Is also great
And would suffice.

—Robert Frost (1874-1963)
Harper's Magazine,
December 1920.

CHAPTER ONE

O NEIDA LAKE LOOKED ALMOST THE same as I remembered. The water was dark and glassy, the perfect mirror for a giant or a god. Late fall had come to northern New York. The surrounding trees had shed their fiery fall cloaks and encircled the lake as skeletal sentries, silent witnesses to what happened there all those weeks before. A blast of wind sent the trees swaying, and they creaked and groaned but gave away no secrets. They told me nothing about what had happened to Skyla.

The bits of detritus scattered throughout the Ramirez family's cabin maintained the silence as well. Our sleeping gear and luggage lay undisturbed. Empty wine bottles adorned the counter, and dishes collected dust in the drying rack. I ignored the cooler squatting on the kitchen floor. The ice had certainly melted over the past five weeks, and whatever was left inside had probably bred several mold cultures I was happy to never know about. *If only mold could talk.* Then again, the stuff growing inside that cooler probably could.

Outside, in the front yard, a smear of burnt grass indicated the place where I had gone stellar, transmuting into that *other* state, but no rusty stains showed where Inyoni had bled out from a fatal cut to her throat. No remains proved Khalani, the Valkyries' Mistress of the Blade, had existed. No ash pile signified the gravesite of Hati, the mythological wolf who'd killed my brother. No monument to my vengeance, no memorial to commemorate the place where I'd fulfilled my promises.

I had found Mani's killer and brought him justice. Still, a hollow place lingered inside me: the hole that had formed after Mani's death. Killing Hati had not healed it. Perhaps it restored some sense of balance, though, because I no longer felt so much like a broken-keeled ship, listing to one side.

1

I had never killed anything other than the occasional spider or mosquito. Hati was a man, a wolf, a monster, and I had snuffed his animating spark, or his spirit, or whatever it was that had brought him to life. Did it matter whether he was myth or real, magic or flesh and bone? I had wanted him dead, and the result was the same. I kept asking myself if I regretted killing him, if I felt bad about it, but I never did. I still don't. Was that wrong?

At the end of the day, I managed to look myself in the face without cringing. Nothing else mattered.

I crouched in the yard and studied my hands, my smooth palms, which had held fire and flames and bent them to my will. The transmutation had drained me, and in the days since, I had managed nothing but a pitiful glow from my fingertips. A cold ball of dread resided in my gut and would likely stay there until my fire returned to its full potential. I had no idea how long that would take, how long I would be vulnerable and defenseless.

Not a question you can answer today, Solina. Quit wasting time. Every minute you stay here, you're putting yourself in more danger.

To satisfy my need for diligence, I circled the lot one more time. I didn't want a doubtful voice whispering in my ear when I left the lake: *Are you sure you didn't miss something? Are you* sure...? After my second inspection, I realized the big black truck was gone, the one Thorin had left at the Aerie for me, the one Skyla, Inyoni, Kalani and I had driven on a cross-country sprint from Mendocino to Oneida.

In the end, Thorin had provided resources, supported my decisions, and honored my wishes. A cooperative Thorin was hard to dismiss and even harder to resist. Letting him get close meant trusting he wouldn't compromise my independence or manipulate my plans in ways that best suited him. It meant believing he had not only his own interests at heart but mine, too. *Not sure I'm willing to take that chance on him. Not until I know myself better. Not until I can stand on my own and face him as an equal.*

Maybe Nate McNairy had taken the truck to remove evidence. Maybe Thorin had managed to track it, despite having insisted the truck was a ghost, untraceable. Maybe Skyla had used it to escape from

Nate, and she was on the run, same as me. The idea of Skyla as a fugitive was a hopeful one, and I clung to it because it meant she had survived.

Other than the absence of the truck, I found nothing worth noting. After shushing the questioning voice in my head, I returned to the driveway and climbed into the backseat of the cab that was waiting for me—meter running, of course—while I conducted my investigation. A rental car would have been more economical, but it required identification and paperwork. Coming back to Oneida Lake was dangerous enough, but Skyla was worth that risk. Coming back to Oneida Lake and leaving a trail would have been suicidal. Sacrificing myself to save the world was a noble idea, but dying because of lazy mistakes was just plain wasteful.

And I don't want my life—or my death—to be a waste.

"Where to now, miss?" the driver asked.

"Take me back to where you got me," I said.

The taxi had picked me up from a bus station in Syracuse, the closest depot on Greyhound's route.

The cab driver fiddled with his GPS and said, "Okee dokee. You got money to burn, I guess?"

"Not a lot of money. Just a whole lot of worry."

CHAPTER TWO

Five weeks later...

THE SOUR ODORS OF ALCOHOL and sweat infused my work shirt. My deodorant and body wash had fought gallantly on my behalf, but the arrival of a celebrating men's softball team and a spilled glass of cheap gin had struck the conquering blows. Spills and stains had defeated me before and probably would again unless my fairy godmother showed up and worked a miracle on my behalf. In my experience, magic was rarely so benevolent. I was better off relying on myself.

The bar smelled nothing like my family's bakery with its signatures of vanilla, yeast—the bread kind, not the beer kind—cinnamon, butter, and warm sugar. Even the cleaning solutions and rubber floor mats supplied their own distinct notes. I missed my bakery, but not as much as I probably should have, considering I had once been resigned to spending the rest of my life there, pinned under the weight of my parents' expectations. A lot had changed since then. Metamorphic things. Immortal things.

I swiped a rag over the old wooden bar top, clearing smudges and spills. Then I reached for a nearby mop and bucket to do the same for the floors, another chore added to a long and exhausting day of doling drinks, fencing grabby-handed advances, and placating obstinate drunks. A glance at the overflowing tip jar cheered me up, though.

"Hey, Sabrina," Nikka said as she passed me on her way to the front door.

Her casual use of my false name felt like nails on a chalkboard, but the precaution was necessary for not just my safety but hers, too.

"You gonna be much longer?" she asked.

"Nah," I said. "Just finishing up."

"Five, ten minutes?"

"Something like that."

"Then what?"

"What do you mean?"

"Then what are you going to do?"

"Uh." I racked my brain for items on my to-do list that I might have overlooked, but mopping up and totaling the register receipts were the last chores in my nightly routine. "Then, nothing, I guess. I'll go to bed."

"You always go to bed." Nikka pursed her lips into a pretty pout.

"I don't think the boss would be too happy if I passed out from sleep deficiency during my shift tomorrow night."

"The boss isn't happy that you go home rather than going out with her when she asks you to dinner." Nikka winked, and her bright smile contrasted beautifully against her Mediterranean skin.

Nikka's father had bequeathed Stefanakis Spirits and Suds to her before his death several years before. As far as I could tell, she kept the bar alive and thriving with a little know-how and twice as much hard work.

"The boss should get used to disappointment."

Nikka's smile drooped. "C'mon, Sabrina. Today makes a month since you came to work for me. We should celebrate. I mean, what's the big deal?"

The big deal was the hundreds of pounds of psychotic baggage I lugged around. If Nikka knew about the hot mess that was my life, she'd run away screaming. I was doing her a favor. I was an anathema to friendships. Skyla would have testified to that if I could find her.

"Bacon and waffles at that all-night diner down the street, my treat," Nikka said. "We don't have to do any friendship bonding rituals or anything."

"Nikka—" I started.

She raised a hand to stop me. "Don't say it. I've heard it already. See you tomorrow, Sabrina." Nikka started for the door.

I almost let her go, but regret and loneliness welled up from the empty places in my heart. The emotions were so overwhelming that I responded before my common sense could kick in and counteract them. "Wait," I said.

Nikka froze but didn't look back.

"Just breakfast, right?"

"And a coffee or two."

"They do chocolate-chip waffles?"

Nikka pivoted on her heel and let loose a brilliant smile. "They will if I have anything to say about it."

<hr/>

At the diner, Nikka sat across from me and guzzled her coffee. She set down her mug, burped, and patted her stomach. Then she smiled in a self-satisfied way.

"Okay," I said, laughing, "I totally apologize for not agreeing to this sooner. I think I needed a good sugar high."

Nikka leaned forward and grinned. "You should trust my wisdom more often."

"Oh, I trust your wisdom."

"You do?"

"Of course. Anyone who gives a homeless girl a job without any references or proof of experience must be a really wise woman."

"You proved yourself," Nikka said. "What you lacked in experience, you made up for in effort."

"But you didn't know that I wouldn't just rob you blind and head for the hills."

"This isn't my first rodeo, and I also have great intuition."

If that were true, she wouldn't have wasted her time trying to befriend me. But for whatever reason she wanted to attribute, Nikka had provided a much-needed job and a place to lie low while I recovered my powers. Nikka didn't ask for a driver's license or social-security card. She set me up in the apartment over her bar for next to nothing. I told her my name was Sabrina Moody—close to the real thing so I would remember to answer to it—and Nikka never asked for proof. She paid me in cash and respect. I hated lying to her, but what other choice did I have?

Nikka probably suspected I was running from a bad relationship.

She was right if one could call the thing between Skoll and Helen Locke and me a relationship—an apocalyptic hate triangle, more like.

"It's only been a few weeks, Nikka. I could still make my getaway."

"Nah," she said. "You got Pacific Ocean in your veins, I can tell. Just look at you—blond hair, that bronze skin. You look like an advertisement for the ideal California Girl."

"Maybe. I do like it here. A lot."

Nikka nodded in a knowing way. "So, you're hooked, and you're not going anywhere, which brings us to the next question: What are you doing for the holidays? You worked through Thanksgiving, and I thank you for that, but I always shut down the bar for Christmas. So, you'll have no excuse. You *cannot* spend Christmas alone."

"Don't tell that to this crowd." I motioned to the ragtag group of late-night diners around us. "Besides, I was looking forward to a grand-slam breakfast with Joe."

"Who is Joe?"

"I don't know for sure, but if you wander around Chicano Park long enough, you'll probably find a guy named Joe camped out under the Coronado Bridge. And I bet he likes chocolate-chip waffles at least as much as I do."

Nikka rolled her eyes upward and talked to the ceiling. "She's been in San Diego four weeks, and she's already as cynical as me."

I laughed and sipped coffee from my cup. Outside the restaurant, San Diego was waking up. The rising sun had turned the sky from black into an enchanted lilac. The gloaming hour suggested weakening barriers and the surge of possibility—as though anything could happen. I closed my eyes and imagined that when I opened them again, I would see my brother standing on the sidewalk outside the diner. He'd be laughing about something with a buddy or tapping his foot, impatiently waiting for me.

When I opened my eyes, my gaze fell not on Mani, but on a tall, dark-haired stranger standing under a streetlight near the front window. He stepped out of sight before I got a good look at him, but something about the way he suddenly turned away—or the way the hairs on the back of my neck stood up—made me think he had been watching me.

7

"He was checking you out the whole time you had your eyes closed," Nikka said.

"Who?" I drained the rest of my coffee.

"That guy out there." She flung a hand in the direction of the stranger, who had disappeared. "Don't act like you didn't notice."

"Hmm." I shrugged and looked away.

The incident made me uneasy, but Nikka didn't need to know that. She might have asked why I was so jumpy, and that was not a story I wanted to tell.

Nikka leaned forward, intent on making her point. "Totally intense. Like he knew you or something."

"I don't know anyone here except you and Tre," I said, naming the San Diego police officer who worked security for Stefanakis in his off-hours.

"Maybe you just look like someone he knows. Or maybe it was love at first sight. You should go after him. Give him your number. If you're going to make new friends, you could definitely do worse than him. He was… spectacular."

Cold waves rippled over my shoulders. I shivered and shrugged off the chill. *No making friends with handsome strangers.* Letting Nikka into my life had been risky enough.

Nikka must have sensed my mood change. She frowned and tossed a couple bills on the table, enough to cover my check and a tip. We slid out of our booth and headed for the door.

"We should do this again," she said. "Soon."

No. No, we shouldn't. Routines and habits and friends made a person comfortable. Comfortable people made mistakes like letting down their guards and trusting. Trusting opened the way for betrayal and broken hearts.

CHAPTER THREE

"Faster," said Tre Hobbs, my sparring partner. He raised a padded strike shield to chest height. "You've got to bring up that left. It's not about technique right now. It's about speed."

I sucked in a deep lungful of air and caught my breath. The krav maga gym smelled like sweat and stale body odor—the perfume of hard work, pain, and tenacity. I nodded. Tre nodded back and readied for my assault.

Hit, hit, hit—left, left, right. I pounded my fists against the pad. Hit, hit, hit—right, left, left. Tre had me focused on my left strike, working to strengthen my weaker arm.

"Good," he said. "Much better. Now, let's see that speed again but with a little more control."

"Uh," I said, voicing my exhaustion.

We had sparred off and on for nearly half an hour and spent the last few minutes on intense upper-body work. I had maybe one round left in me before my arms melted to Jell-O and my lungs self-combusted.

"One more time, Sabrina. You're fighting for your life. Exhaustion means defeat."

After weeks of steady eating, routine sleep, and a semiregular schedule, my fire had mostly rekindled, but that stint of powerlessness had showed me the danger of depending on the fire as my sole weapon. My supernatural abilities were depletable resources. When the flames were gone, my fists and fierceness remained. Damned if I wouldn't learn how to use them.

Two intense weeks of training among the Valkyries had knocked off the dust and awoken my survivor instincts, but I was far from mastering proficiency in combat. My so-called fight against Skoll had enumerated my many inadequacies, and Hati's incineration was the result not so much of skill but of blind and incoherent rage.

I welcomed any tool, any asset that increased my odds of survival—no waiting for others to save me, no more helpless human. Fists, fire, or cunning, I would stand firm and retain a position of strength, even among gods and monsters.

I closed my eyes and drew in a deep breath. Then I nodded but kept my eyes shut and waited for Tre's assault. Tre used that technique, the blind attack, to hone my reaction time. "Your attacker won't usually give you a warning," he said the first time we had trained that way. "No 'Here I come, better get ready' speeches."

Tre pounced, soundless and sudden, like a cat—one of the large panther varieties. He nearly knocked me off my feet when he shoved the strike pad against me, putting all his weight behind the assault. I stumbled and opened my eyes. Strike, strike, strike—left, left, right. Tre shifted toward me, and I struck again—right, left, left. The last hit fell short, and I faltered and fell to my knees.

"Oh," I wheezed. "Oh, that's done it. I'm just going to stay down for the night. Tell the staff to sweep around me when they close up." To emphasize my meaning, I slumped to the floor.

Tre's chuckle sounded like a grizzly growling. He reminded me of a large brown bear, minus all the fur. "I guess that's enough for one night."

"Maybe I should call in sick tomorrow. How can Nikka expect me to pull a beer tap or shake a martini?" I wagged a shoulder, and my arm slid to the floor. "See? Limp noodles."

Still laughing, Tre shook his head and leaned over. He extended a hand to me. "You'll leave a grease stain on the mat, and I'll have to revoke your guest privileges."

I snorted. "Okay, okay."

Tony, the owner, kept his studio meticulously clean and threatened to kick out anyone who messed it up. It wouldn't do for Tre to lose his membership because of me, and I couldn't afford to train in that gym on my slim paycheck. Also, I tended to avoid membership forms—they asked too many personal questions.

I took Tre's hand and let him tug me to my feet. "Can you meet me again tomorrow? I have to work, though, so it'll have to be earlier in the afternoon."

Tre's brown eyes widened, and his mouth fell open. "What are you? A robot? Take a break. You've been at this for a week straight. Those ghosts you're trying to fight will still be there when you come back."

I blushed. "That obvious, is it?"

Tre shrugged, and his massive shoulders strained against his T-shirt. "It's just the way it is with these sort of things. Most women aren't proactive about self-defense. In my experience, they are *reactive*. They train to make up for the shortcomings they realized after it was too late."

I crossed the room, grabbed a clean towel from the shelf, and dabbed at the sweat on my forehead and neck. "It's not too late for me. But it was a near thing." And that was the most I would say about it to Tre or to Nikka. Let them think what they would: abusive boyfriend, a random stranger attack. The possibilities were all as terrible and horrifying as anything that had happened to me in reality, but with the addition of that whole apocalyptic, end-of-the-world thing. *Yes, let's don't forget about that.*

"If you want, I can ask one of the other members to work with us next time," Tre said. "It'll be good for you to change your opponents from time to time."

What I really needed was a sparring partner who fought on four legs. Tre should have lent me a German shepherd from his PD's K-9 unit. "Makes sense," I said instead. "Maybe we'll do that."

"Need me to drop you off at home?" Tre asked. The sun had set an hour before, and I lived several blocks away. Usually, we met in the afternoons before my shift at the bar, but I'd had the day off, and Tre had met me after he got off work.

"If you don't mind?"

Tre nodded. "Just let me grab my things."

At home, in the relative safety of my apartment, I bolted the door, threw the latch, and went to the shower for a long, hot scrubbing. Afterward, I stood before the fogged-up mirror and studied my ghostly shadow. I reached to wipe away the condensation but stopped and pulled my hand back. *Nope, nothing to see here, folks.* Skin and bones, some bruises from krav maga, eyes that reflected the many disturbing things that had happened to me.

Shaking my head, I stepped away from the clouded mirror and hung up my towel. I shrugged on a loose T-shirt and slipped into a pair of raggedy old pajama bottoms. Faded yellow suns and moons dotted the worn blue flannel. My mother had given them to me for Christmas many years before. I doubted she knew the relevance, doubted she thought I'd be standing in California so many years later, laughing at the irony woven into a pair of drawstring pants.

I brushed my teeth, combed out my hair, and turned out the light. Streetlights bled through the window blinds, dimly lighting my way as I padded to the bed that shared the same space as my couch and most of my kitchen. *Welcome to efficiency living.* I eased onto my mattress, tucked my feet beneath me, and stretched out my hands, palms up. Closing my eyes, I sank inside myself. The font of my fire glowed steady and bright, a comforting thing, indeed. A little at a time, I let the flames loose, and hot flickering light filled my palms.

Ever since my transmutation, my control had improved, but I hadn't tested it under emotional duress: wolf attacks, angry goddesses of the underworld, manipulative gods, the usual. When had those things become "the usual" in my life? If I was any good at lying low, I would never have to fight for my life again.

And Jesus and the devil might stroll arm in arm along a moonlit beach.

After my failure to find a lead on Skyla's whereabouts at Oneida Lake, I had traveled to San Diego for several reasons. First, it was far away from home, and I had no connections to it. No one would have a reason to track me there. Additionally, I had found a hint in an older newspaper article from Skyla's hometown in upstate New York. The article had briefly discussed her graduation from basic training. It had also mentioned her father, Sergeant Major Neron Ramirez, a retired Marine who had finished his career at Camp Pendleton. If Skyla were on the run, she might have come to San Diego looking for his help. So far, though, I had found no whisper of Skyla or Sergeant Major Ramirez.

Determined and unrelenting in my hunt, I had stayed in the city to recuperate and continue my search for Skyla in the safety of total anonymity. If and when I faced Helen and the gods again, I meant to do it as an equal, or as equal as possible, considering my mortality. I rolled my hand over, and the flames enveloped me from fingertips to elbows. No, I wouldn't stay there forever. I missed having a place where I belonged, fit in, and had a purpose. This tatty little apartment, Stefanakis, Nina and Tre—they wouldn't last. Superman had his Fortress of Solitude; Batman had his Batcave; Wonder Woman had Themyscira. Sure, they all had to leave their sanctuaries and go to the real world to fight the good fight. And so would I. But at the end of it all, if and when I succeeded against Helen and Skoll, I had no safe place to take off my mask and hang up my cape. Where would I park my invisible jet and hang my lasso of truth?

I meant to find that safe place, though. I meant to find a home in the new world and claim my right to it. And, if I was fortunate, I wouldn't have to do it alone.

I released my fire and tucked it away, safe in its internal hidey-hole. My body whined, complaining about the rigors I had put it through. *Shut up*, I told it. *You hate me now, but you'll thank me later.*

Snugged up under the covers, I reached over to my nightstand and flicked on my lamp. I tugged a dog-eared old spy thriller from beneath my pillow, where I had stashed it the night before. No romance novels for me.

I no longer had much sympathy for the damsel in distress.

———◆———

All my recent turmoil had mixed my emotions into a toxic lather that seeped into my subconscious and distorted my dreams into strange and disturbing experiences. When I woke sometime before dawn, sweat had coated my sheets and pillows despite the cool nighttime temperatures.

The same dream had disturbed me for weeks: apples, a whole orchard—row upon row of shiny fruit, all golden, none red. In the dream, I picked a few and munched them as I strolled through rows of trees. The apple's crisp flesh snapped and gave way under my teeth, and juices filled my mouth, sweeter and richer than any apple I had eaten before.

A flicker of movement glinted in the shadows between the trees.

A distant light flashed—not a reflection, nothing manmade like a flashlight. The glow was warm and natural, the light of a fire. The tang of acrid smoke spoiled the air, and an intense heat baked away all moisture. Ash coated my skin and hair. Unable to resist the fire's allure, I reached to touch the flames. Like a witch's cat, fire was my familiar spirit. But in my dream, the blaze was not my ally. When I stroked them, the flames burned me. I drew back a hand, blackened to the bone.

I woke up gasping, strangling on a scream.

The vision probably meant something important, and my subconscious wanted me to pursue it. Without Skyla as my kickass Hermione, mythology research had fallen to me, and I had read everything I could get my hands on. I had developed a theory that my dream signified the legendary apples tended by the goddess Idun. In the legends, the Aesir gained all their eternal youth and longevity from Idun's magical fruit. But my dream was too vague, or the legends were too limited—or some of both—to explain what portent these recent visions meant to convey. If fate wanted me to solve this latest puzzle, it would have to be a lot more direct.

Hot, annoyed, and frustrated, I gave up on going back to sleep. I slid out of bed, padded to the window, raised it, and crawled out onto my fire escape. The cool night air dried my sweat and erased lingering odors of smoke and fire.

I closed my eyes and leaned into the breeze, sending my stress out in a whoosh of breath, but the sharp caw of a protesting bird startled me from my moment of Zen. I yelped and recoiled from the railing where a huge black bird perched. It clacked its beak at me, and the streetlight reflected in its beady black eye.

"Shoo!" I threw my hands out, waving it away.

The bird cawed again, flapped its wings, and leapt from the railing. It rose toward the sky in a steep ascent before turning to plummet toward the ground. Instead of crashing in a feathery heap, the bird silently dissolved into the street's shadows.

I backed against the brick wall behind me and pressed a hand over my racing heart. I inhaled several steady, deep breaths and waited for my composure to return.

"What the hell?" I asked, but no one answered.

14

Curiosity towed me back to the fire escape's edge. I peered into the alley, looking for signs of the crow. For a moment, the whole world was still and silent. Then a man-shaped shadow separated from the darkness. The figure ambled to the end of the alleyway, turned onto the sidewalk, and passed out of view.

I raised my hand and formed a fireball in my palm. Its presence comforted me as I contemplated the shadowy figure. After four weeks in San Diego, a week of traveling on the road, and four weeks lost to transmutation, I should have been a ghost. I had been so careful.

How did they find me? And who are "they"? Friend or foe, enemy or ally?

I spun on my heel and ducked back inside my room. From my closet, I dug out my duffel bags and chucked in piles of clothes—clean, dirty, crusty, it didn't matter. The fight-or-flight instinct was saying *Go! Now!* But a cooler, calmer voice cut through the panic: *You just saw a blackbird that could change shape. How do you run from that? Slow down and think.*

After sinking to the floor beside my bed, I hugged my knees, buried my face in my lap, and inhaled several deep breaths. Running was pointless when I had no idea what I was fleeing from or how best to get away from it.

I raised my head, rubbed my face, and crawled back to my window. When nothing ominous appeared, my shoulders slumped, and I heaved a sigh. *Time to start forming an exit strategy.* Until then, I would stand my ground and stay aware and on guard. *And why is Thorin's face the one I see whenever I think about where to run?*

CHAPTER FOUR

THE SUN WAS HALFWAY INTO its workday by the time I rolled out of bed. I had slept later than usual because my disturbing encounters had kept me up until the wee hours of dawn. I paced the living room throughout the night, waiting for someone to break in or for a wolf to show up on my fire escape. Was it coincidence that the crow had appeared a day after Nikka caught a stranger staring at me outside the diner? Perhaps he'd been checking me out simply because he had a thing for blondes. Exhaustion eventually sent me back to bed, and I squeezed in a few hours of restless, dreamless sleep.

I started a pot of coffee and stumbled into the bathroom to wash my face and brush out my bed-head hair. When Mr. Coffee chimed a few minutes later, I drooled like Pavlov's dog. After adding a dab of sweetener and a touch of half-and-half to my cup, I sank into my bedraggled sofa cushions, clutching my mug, careful not to spill a drop. It was the kind of sofa that molded around me, sucked me in, and held me in its seductive embrace. The couch was ugly, but our love for each other transcended surface appearances.

Beyond my window, the San Diego traffic rushed by. Someone yelled. A car horn honked. The outside world fell away as I sipped my coffee. Amazing, how a simple cup of java could have that kind of power.

With my coffee pot emptied and caffeine buzz securely in place, I checked the time on my alarm clock—four hours until my shift started, plenty of time—and exchanged my PJs for jeans, a T-shirt, and a plain gray hoodie. I wound my hair into a tight knot, pulled up my hood, and slipped on a pair of sunglasses.

A few minutes later, I stood at the stop around the corner from my apartment, waiting for an MTS bus to pick me up and carry me across town to a random branch of the San Diego Public Library. In an effort to cover my trail, I picked a different branch every time. When the bus arrived, it lumbered up to the curb, its brakes hissed, and the doors opened. I climbed aboard behind a woman toting a collapsible shopping cart and a grumpy preschooler, and I paid my fare in cash. I paid for *everything* in cash. No one aboard the bus seemed to notice me. No one raised his or her head or looked me in the face. I settled into a seat near the front and slouched against the window for the entirety of the trip.

After a long ride extended by multiple stops, the bus wheezed to a halt outside the University Community Library, and I slipped out onto the sidewalk. As I scanned the parking lot, double-checking for signs of pursuit or surveillance, I pulled a prepaid burner phone from my pocket, reconnected the battery, and turned it on. I had bought and activated it when my cross-country bus had stopped in Iowa to refuel at a truck stop doubling as a shopping mall.

I had watched enough true-crime shows to know, at least in theory, about triangulating location based on cell-tower signals. I never turned on the phone near my apartment. Even with all my precautions, using it was still a risk but one I needed to take.

I punched in a memorized phone number and waited.

Two rings later, a familiar voice answered and said, "Thorin Adventure Outfitters, Hugh Rabe speaking."

Hugh. Val Wotan's roommate. Exactly the person I'd hoped to reach. If Val or Thorin had answered, I would have hung up. The thought of hearing either of their voices again, even after all we had been through… It pained me. In a way, I missed them—even Val. He was an oaf, overbearing and manipulative, but I refused to believe he was unredeemable. He was complicated and screwed up, but we all were. And Thorin… *Gah!* I couldn't wrap my brain around him, much less my heart.

"Hi," I said, trying to flatten my southern accent into something less distinguishable. "I was wondering if Skyla Ramirez was around. I did a kayaking trip with her a while ago, and I wanted to talk to her about planning a group outing for me and some friends in the spring."

"Skyla is on an extended sabbatical," Hugh said.

That was the same excuse he had given me when I called the week before and asked to speak to her. That time, I had posed as a journalist wanting to interview Skyla for an article about women making a living in the sporting industry. I had made up some excuse every week, for the past four weeks, to call Thorin's store and ask about her. In all that time, Hugh's story never changed. Thorin Adventure Outfitter's official statement on Skyla's whereabouts may have meant Thorin thought she was alive but missing. Or maybe he thought she was dead but wouldn't admit it without official evidence.

"Do you know when she'll be back?" I asked.

"I don't, but I can take a message."

"No," I said, throwing a little annoyance into my tone, the better to fool him into thinking I was a disgruntled customer. "Maybe I'll just try to find another guide."

After I hung up with Hugh, I disassembled my phone and went into the library and logged onto a public computer. Logging in required a library account number. Library account numbers required photo IDs and physical addresses, but in my experience, librarians were a softhearted bunch who easily succumbed to young women bearing sob stories about broken California dreams and unstable living conditions. The librarian on whose shoulder I cried had offered me a temporary account number that would last until I brought back my credentials and registered for a permanent account. Until then, they wouldn't lend me books, but I could access the Internet.

Just as I did every week, I conducted an exhaustive online search for anything that might lead me to Skyla—or as exhaustive as could be performed in the hour the library allotted for computer use. So far, I had found nothing but old history: a brief mention of Kara North's marriage to Neron Ramirez in the *San Diego Tribune*. Vital records showed Skyla and her brother, Paul, had been born there too, but military families moved around a lot, and I lost track of the Ramirezes in New York. I had already followed my few New York leads to dead ends in conjunction with my visit to Oneida Lake. After those fruitless searches, I backtracked the Ramirezes' trail to its start with hopes of finding a new thread.

Paul Ramirez, Skyla's brother, had disappeared after high-school graduation, and he seemed to have no social presence online. Skyla's parents, Neron and Kara, had vanished similarly. Was the cause of their disappearance magic, malice, or something more common, such as sickness or death? Asking questions while constructing an in-depth investigation was difficult when trying to remain anonymous. The United States military and government-records offices tended to shrug off young women who wouldn't give contact information or personal details.

My searches resulted in more of the same disappointments, and I was running out of ideas.

In the past weeks, I had discovered plenty of news about my own disappearance. Not long after my transformative experience at Oneida Lake, my parents had issued a missing-person notice, and the Siqiniq Police and Alaska State Troopers circulated a press release asking for information about my possible whereabouts. No one had put as much effort into locating Skyla, but she deserved better treatment than that. She had saved my life. Searching for her was the least I could do in return.

An hour later, my time ran out on the computer, and the system logged me out. I leaned back from the screen, rubbed my eyes, and stretched. Then I slipped on my hood and sunglasses and went outside to catch the bus back across town.

Another day of fruitless searching had confirmed what I'd already accepted in the depths of my heart. I wasn't going to find Skyla by hiding out in San Diego any longer. I had recovered the majority of my fire, and I would have to hit the road again soon. Helen was probably the most direct resource for information on Skyla, but I wasn't brave enough, or *dumb* enough, to face her alone. I needed backup for that kind of confrontation. *So, back to Alaska and the Nordic deities who contest my every move? Or return to the Aerie and take my chances among the potentially compromised Valkyries?*

I had gone to San Diego because Skyla's family had established its foundations there, and it seemed like a good place to search for new leads. It was far away from my home in North Carolina, no one had reason to look for me there, and I had needed a place to hide while recovering my strength. If I admitted I had done all I could on my own, and my search required my making a more... *public* nuisance of myself, then the time had come. But if I reached out and reconnected,

I'd have to decide whom I most trusted to support my goals. Thorin's image appeared in my thoughts—the look in his eyes when I'd last seen him, when he had told me he was not like Val and would not make his mistakes. At the time, I thought Thorin meant he wouldn't force his affections on me, but in the weeks that had passed, I wondered if Thorin meant he wouldn't make the mistake of getting close to me or letting me get close to him.

Good thing I didn't need his intimacy. I only needed results. Of all the supernatural beings in my life who could help me find Skyla, Thorin was the one I most believed in, a man not much on words but big on action. *Guess I just made up my mind.*

<hr />

Back in my apartment, I spent my remaining free time washing dishes and packing my paltry laundry in tote bags so my things would be ready to go at a moment's notice. In the late afternoon, I tossed aside my cleaning rag and donned my bartending armor, a psychological shield constructed of layers of patience, humility, and a healthy sense of humor. I also put on a bowling shirt printed with the "Stefanakis Spirits and Suds" logo and a dark pair of jeans that hid spills and stains. I tied my hair up in a messy knot and headed for the door. Successful bartending relied on a careful balance of being attractive but not too attractive. After too many beers or bourbons, customers sometimes developed possessive inclinations toward me. I did my best to discourage them in advance.

The commute from my apartment to my office took all of thirty seconds, the time required to lock my door, jog down a short flight of stairs, and step through the bar's back door into the storage room.

"Sabrina," Nikka said in greeting.

"Nikka," I said in return. She had brought racks of clean glassware from the dishwasher to the bar, and I helped her stock the shelves.

"You ready for tonight?" she asked.

"You think it will be as bad as last Friday?"

Nikka nodded. "The band I scheduled for tonight has a pretty dedicated fan base."

"Rock?" I asked, trying to predict the crowd.

"Nah, more like folk."

"So, more PBR and less Bud?"

"Yes," Nikka said and rolled her eyes. "I can't stand assholes who drink beer ironically" —she rubbed her fingers together— "but I have to love them because they drink so damned much of it."

Nikka and I hustled to restock well liquors and inventory the premium brands. She filled ice wells and opened several beer taps to release air from the lines while I sliced limes and oranges for our garnish trays. The first few regulars trickled in: two old guys who drank shots of ouzo between glasses of an imported Greek beer I had never heard of until I started working at Stefanakis.

Nikka's bar attracted an eclectic mix: old guys from the nearby Greek community loyal to Nikka's dad and his bar; professionals stopping in for a drink before they headed home for the night; and a trendy, younger population who came to Stefanakis looking for an "authentic" experience. Nikka and I slipped into our routines without the need for chatter. In our four weeks together, I had learned most of the steps to the bartender's dance, and Nikka and I made pretty fabulous partners.

Tre showed up for bouncer duty around the same time the band arrived to set up. I poured him a glass of sweet tea, a delicacy in those parts. He swore I made it like his grandma had when he was a kid in Alabama, so I made a point to brew a fresh batch for him whenever Nikka put him on the schedule.

Tre took the glass from me, chugged down half, and smacked his lips in a show of appreciation. "What do you know about banana pudding?" He handed the glass back to me for a refill.

"I know everything there is to know. Why do you ask?"

Tre made puppy-dog eyes at me. "I can't even tell you how long it's been since I had a real homemade banana pudding."

"Oh, yeah? If I made you one, what would be in it for me?"

Tre's eyes narrowed. He chewed his bottom lip and considered what bargaining chip to offer.

The band's guitar and drums kicked in as their technician tweaked the sound system's idiosyncrasies. Dissonant notes reverberated around the room, and microphone feedback stabbed my eardrums.

Tre winced and yelled over the noise, "We'll settle this later."

I winked at him and turned to greet my latest customer. He was no Greek patriarch or trendy college kid but a dark-haired, blue-eyed stranger. He settled his tall frame onto a stool near the register and ordered a black and tan.

"You want to start a tab?" I asked.

He rolled a shoulder. "Sure."

"Under what name?"

"Rolf Lockhart."

"Rolf? That's not a name you hear every day."

"No. It's old—a family name."

"Haven't seen you in here before, Rolf." I made friendly chitchat because that's what bartenders did and because something about the man drew me in. My immediate, visceral response to him upset my careful composure, and not in a good way. My defenses snapped into place, and my suspicion flipped into high-alert mode.

"Haven't been here before. I'd ask how long you've been around, but I can tell by your accent that it hasn't been very long. You're a southern girl, yes?"

"Yes," I said and cursed my ingrained twang. If I concentrated, I could neutralize my accent, but Rolf had caught me off guard. I finished pouring his beer, careful to stack the Guinness above the paler Bass without mixing the two.

"Whereabouts?" Rolf paused to sip his beer. "I have family in Mississippi."

"Uh, no. I'm not from Mississippi."

A woman beside Rolf yelled for a Heineken. I drew a cold bottle from the cooler and poured it into a frosted glass. She gave me a ten and I passed back her change.

"But I'm sure it's nice," I said.

Rolf's lips twisted into a wry grin. "That's debatable."

I shrugged and scooted past him, heading for a customer waving at me from farther down the bar.

"You still haven't told me where you're from," Rolf said when I returned to pour a pint for another customer.

Sure, I had a fake back story, but explaining it to Rolf only invited him to ask more questions. I humored Nikka and Tre's inquiries to an extent because I needed them, and they had befriended me. But that guy... I owed him nothing, and my instincts said to push him away quickly. I remembered a quote in my latest spy thriller, the words of Eugene V. Debs: "'I have no country to fight for. My country is the earth. I am a citizen of the world.'"

The bar's population swelled after that, and Nikka and I hustled to keep up with the increasing orders. Too harried to maintain our idle chit-chat, I put Rolf out of my thoughts and focused on work.

Later, near midnight, Nikka grabbed me and pulled me aside during a lull. "I knew that guy down there looked familiar." She nodded at Rolf. "It just hit me where I saw him last."

I snatched a couple of empty glasses off the bar and set them in a bus tray. "Where?"

"The diner. Remember I told you some guy was staring you down like he knew you... or wanted to eat you... or both, maybe?"

My gaze shot to Rolf, who looked back at me as though he knew he was the topic of our conversation.

"Him? Are you sure?" I asked.

"Does he look like the kind of guy I would easily mistake for someone else?"

Rolf's black hair hung in a glossy sheet, almost brushing his shoulders. He had the pale skin of a northern European rather than the darker tones I was used to seeing around that area, especially with hair like that. His eyes were so vibrantly blue they seemed purple in the neon bar lights. Elizabeth Taylor had had eyes like that. "What the hell, Nikka? How did he know I was here?"

"Luck?" She shrugged. "Coincidence."

"Coincidence and I don't get along very well."

A shiver rolled up my spine and broke in cold waves across my shoulders. Coincidence equaled monumental trouble in my world. Compounded by the strange incident on my fire escape the night before, the appearance of this would-be stalker set my nerves on edge—not that they weren't there already.

"Nikka, can you handle things here for a second? I need to go talk to Tre."

Nikka shrugged. "Sure. I got it."

I rounded the end of the bar and pushed my way through the throngs of fans swaying to the jam band's music. I tuned out the distractions and set my sights on Tre's hulking dark figure, guarding the entrance to the bar. A smile lit his face when he saw me coming. Outside, the crowd's roar dropped to a dull murmur.

"How's it going in there?" Tre asked.

"Not too bad. Mostly, they're behaving."

"So you just came out to visit me?"

"Not entirely. I came to tell you I thought of a way for you to earn that banana pudding."

Tre's bright smile widened. "Oh yeah?"

"There's a guy in there. He's been polite and well behaved, but he gives me the creeps."

"You want me to tell him to get lost?"

"No." *No need to draw any more attention to myself or this odd situation.* I described Rolf to Tre and said, "Just watch him for me, will you? In case he tries anything?"

Tre nodded. "I'd do that for you anyway. It's my job. But I'm not going to look a gift banana pudding in the mouth."

Rolf had drained the last of his second beer by the time I returned. I refilled his drink without comment and spent the rest of the night trying to avoid him. At some point I looked up and found an empty space where he had been sitting. I let out a breath I hadn't realized I'd been holding, and a coil of tension eased in my chest.

Tre parted the crowd and caught my eye. When I finished serving my latest customer, I stepped down to the end of the bar where Tre waited. I leaned close so I could hear him.

"Your buddy took off down the street. No trouble. Didn't look back. Still, I'd like to walk you up to your apartment tonight—check it out and make sure you don't have any unwelcome guests waiting for you."

My heart plunged into my gut. "You think...?"

"Better to be safe than sorry. Come get me when you're ready to leave."

Tre was settled on a bar stool, sipping a to-go cup of sweet tea when I finished my close-up duties. Nikka said goodnight and headed out the front. I locked up behind her and clenched my keys in my fist. "Ready to go?" I asked.

Tre stood and followed me through the bar, into the storage room, and out to the alleyway behind the building. I had climbed halfway up the staircase to my apartment before realizing Tre wasn't behind me. I turned around, intending to ask him about the hold up, and found him crumpled at the foot of the stairs. Something cold and hard crawled up my throat. I covered my mouth before a scream escaped. Realizing panic was useless, I swallowed my fear and stiffened my shoulders. Something was coming for me, something undoubtedly bad, and I had to be ready for it.

Before I could descend the stairs, a man stepped from the shadows into the glow of the Stefanakises' backdoor light and crouched over Tre's limp body.

Ice water chilled my veins, but fire simmered beneath the surface of my skin. "Rolf," I said, "or whoever you really are…"

Rolf stood, looked up at me, and smiled. "I'm of no consequence. I am merely a pawn, like you."

"Helen sent you?"

He shrugged.

"How did you find me?"

"You've been very clever. I'm sure if I was merely a mortal, your attempt at anonymity might have been successful. But we are not human, are we? And the gods have their ways."

"Where's Helen?"

Rolf shook his head and stepped forward. "You'll see her soon enough."

I raised a hand and let my fire erupt around it. I kept the other hand, the one clutching my key ring, behind my back. "Don't come any closer."

"No?" Rolf sneered at my measly fireball. "And what are you going to do with that?"

"Whatever it takes."

"Convert yourself into a star again? Lose yourself for another month?"

My heart seized up like a piston without oil. "H-how do you know about that?"

Rolf laughed. "I *know* everything, Solina. I *remember* everything. There is nothing that happens outside my knowledge."

"Then tell me where I went," I said, challenging him. "Tell me where I was for that four weeks. Who was I? *What* was I?"

"You were Sol. You were her essence, the pure power that is her soul."

"How did I come back?"

Rolf shrugged and stepped closer, moving around Tre's lifeless body. "It's not important."

"You don't know, do you?"

"I just said I know everything. I didn't say I would share all the secrets of the world with you. I am not here to be your tutor; I am here to take you to Helen."

"Not without a fight." I made my way down the stairs, fast but cautious. Tripping or falling meant losing the fight before it started.

My fire flickered in Rolf's eerie eyes. The light reflected on his gleaming teeth. He looked demonic and possessed by evil. "This should be fun," he said.

"You need to find a new definition of fun." I lowered into a fighting stance, ready to hit, hit, hit. Strike, strike, strike. Kick, claw, bite, anything to defend myself and prevent him taking me to Helen. Or at least make him *think* I was ready to fight.

"I know the secret for dealing with you," Rolf said. "If I avoid you long enough, you'll burn out, and I'll take you when you're exhausted and vulnerable."

"I don't plan on giving you the chance to wait that long." I lunged forward, aiming a kick for his knee.

Rolf danced aside and laughed. "Ha ha, Solina! You weren't joking."

I gave him no time to reassess but brought out my other hand, the one holding my key ring, the ring on which I kept a tiny can of pepper spray. Misdirection was not a technique reserved solely for the use of magicians. Pickpockets, con artists, and smart women fighting for their lives depended on it, too. I thumbed the pepper spray's trigger and pointed it at Rolf. The stream struck his face, and he screamed. Blinded and in obvious pain, he stumbled away. I dropped my keys, rekindled my fire, and attacked—kicking, hitting, yelling, *burning*. The pepper spray coating his hair and skin ignited. Rolf roared, and the scent of his charring flesh and hair filled the space between us.

I leaned in for another punch, but my fist met air. My ears popped as they did whenever the air pressure changed. The alley felt empty, devoid of Rolf's animosity and ominous presence. I raised my flames higher, encouraging them to light the scene. The fire's glow revealed nothing more than the still and silent figure of Tre, crumpled at the bottom of my stairs. I peered into the darkness overhead, searching for the dark figure of a man or a crow or anything out of the ordinary. Maybe Rolf had changed shape and appeared as that crow on my balcony, or perhaps he had other agents spying on me. Either way, he had disappeared, and the alley seemed empty except for me and the police officer at my feet.

I snuffed my fire, crouched beside Tre, and searched for a pulse in his neck. It thumped, slow and weak, beneath my fingertips. I blubbered in relief and dashed into the bar, where I grabbed a phone, called 9-1-1, and told the operator about the wounded police officer lying in an alley behind Stefanakis Spirits and Suds. Nikka kept a list of San Diego taxi companies by the phone so we could call a ride for our overindulgent patrons. I chose the first number on the list and told the dispatcher to have a driver pick me up at the diner down the street, the one where Nikka had bought me chocolate-chip waffles.

Before the ambulance and a whole throng of SDPD showed up and started asking questions I couldn't answer, I raced up the stairs to my apartment and grabbed my prepacked tote bags. On my way out, I patted my ugly old couch. "Sorry, girl. Don't think you'll fit in the trunk, or I'd bring you along."

Nikka deserved a call from me or a note, at least—some words of good-bye and thanks. If I didn't tell her I was going, she couldn't give a precise indication of when I had left if anyone thought to ask her.

Muddy the trail, Mundy. Skyla's voice was urging me into action. Thinking of her made my heart hurt.

One tote bag slung over my shoulder, a duffle bag in one hand and another tote in the other, I started for the door and steeled my emotions against regret and disappointment. *Damn Rolf Lockhart, whoever he is. Damn him and Helen and the entire Norse pantheon for screwing up a perfectly good life.* I stifled another sob. Indulging in self-pity was a tempting but pointless waste of energy.

I passed Tre on the way out. He moaned and made an effort to move that ended in another painful groan. I felt like a humongous jerk for leaving him like that. Actually, *jerk* wasn't a big enough word for how I felt. No word in my vocabulary properly conveyed my self-loathing at that moment.

A distant cry of sirens cut through the night, telling all the neighborhood help was on the way. I crouched, pressed a kiss to Tre's forehead, and left him moaning behind me. *There's probably a special torture awaiting me in hell for leaving him like this.*

I hurried down the sidewalk, checking over my shoulder for signs of pursuit. Storm clouds had moved in, and lightning lit up the night sky, followed by the ominous rumble of thunder. I thought of Thorin and his lineage—God of Thunder. Had he retrieved Mjölnir during our time apart? Helen wouldn't have given it up without a fight.

The taxi was waiting for me when I reached the diner. I ducked into the backseat and asked the driver to take me to the nearest bus station. Greyhound and I were getting to be fast friends. *I should probably buy stock.*

The taxi pulled away from the curb, and I turned to look out the rear window. Across the street from the diner, centered under a ring of light from a dim streetlamp, stood Rolf Lockhart, looking pristine and untouched by my fire. He raised a hand and waved a two-fingered salute. I gasped and ducked down. *Quit being stupid. He already saw you.*

When I looked for Rolf again through the rear window, he was gone. The place where he had stood under the streetlight seemed a little darker than the space around it. I let out a heavy sigh, and the taxi driver glanced at me in his rearview mirror. Rolf had let me get away. *After his earlier threats, why would he let me go? Hmm. Not sure I want to find out.*

CHAPTER FIVE

AT THE GREYHOUND STATION, I bought a bus ticket, and my destination was anywhere that got me out of town quickly. That meant I ended up in the back of a bus traveling north on Interstate 5. Sometime near dawn, the bus stopped at a depot in Sacramento, and I reserved a room at a nearby motel. With paint peeling from the exterior trim and fraying carpet on the outside walkways, the motel looked like the kind of accommodation that attracted truck drivers and traveling construction crews. The parking lot smelled like old pee and ancient hamburger grease. Maybe that was a good thing. Maybe no one would think to look for me there.

In the privacy of the motel room, I settled on top of the bed's polyester comforter—no way was I touching those sheets—and powered on my little burner phone. For so many weeks, I had remained purposefully disconnected, theorizing that my anonymity equaled safety, but Rolf's appearance had refuted my beliefs, so I had no reason to hold on to them anymore. I sent a text to Nikka, set the phone on the bedside table, rolled over, and let my thoughts drift until I fell asleep. I dozed off and on until my ringing phone brought me fully awake sometime near noon.

"Oh, thank God," Nikka said when I answered. Panic sharpened her tone. "I didn't know what happened to you. The police came by and told me Tre had been attacked behind the bar, and then you were missing…"

"I know, Nikka. I was there."

"What happened?"

"It was that guy at the bar. Rolf Lockhart. But I'll bet you anything that isn't his real name." I rehashed the story of the fight, leaving out my

29

fire and giving credit to Tre for keeping Rolf distracted until I chased him off with the pepper spray.

"Who the hell is this guy, Sabrina? I thought you didn't know him."

"I *don't* know him, but there are a lot of people looking for me that I don't know. I think it's safe to say I won't be back to San Diego. I'm sorry I couldn't tell you in person."

"Let me help you. I'll call the police or the FBI, or—"

"No. No, Nikka. Just, please, stay out of it."

"But if something happened to you, I don't think I could live with myself."

"And I'd feel the same way if something happened to you because you got yourself mixed up in my mess. Tre was already hurt because of me. How is he? Is he okay?"

Nikka sighed. "He says he's all right. Not that he'd admit it if he wasn't." A moment of uncomfortable silence passed over the airwaves. "I'm so sorry this is happening to you. You seem like a nice girl. You probably don't deserve this kind of life."

I laughed, but it wasn't warm or friendly. "I *am* a nice girl, and I totally don't deserve this life."

"What do you want me to do with your paycheck? Can I mail it somewhere?"

I shrugged even though Nikka couldn't see it. "Donate it to charity. Put it back into your operating accounts."

"I won't hear from you again, will I?"

"No, probably not."

Nikka sighed. "I'm going to miss those brownies you make."

"I'll mail you the recipe, someday. Thanks for everything, Nikka."

"Try to stay out of trouble, Sabrina."

"Ha. Too late for that."

Nikka and I said our good-byes and ended the call. I got out of bed, showered, and changed into fresh clothes. My little black phone sat on the nightstand, daring me to pick it up again and make the call I dreaded most of all. With a huff, I snatched the phone, flipped it open, and hit the button preprogrammed to dial Thorin's store.

The phone rang once, and I hung up.

I cursed at myself. *What stupid game am I playing?* I dialed the number again and let it ring until someone answered.

"Thorin Adventure Outfitters, Hugh speaking."

"Hugh?" I said, not aiming to disguise myself this time.

"Not Jackman, Grant, or Hefner, but sexier than all three combined. How may I please you this afternoon?"

"Hugh, it's Solina Mundy, Mani's sister."

Silence.

More silence.

Then a noisy gasp of breath. "Solina? Where in the holy *hell* have you been?"

"Um, I was on vacation." I poised my finger over the End button in case things got weird. Weirder. Whatever.

Hugh muffled the receiver on his phone, yelled something unintelligible, and came back on the line. "It has been like the hunt for the Holy Grail around here, looking for you. Then you call the store out of the blue like you're wanting to know if we carry your size in climbing shoes or something. Thorin is going to lose his mind."

"What else is new?" I muttered.

A growl of background voices carried over the line. "Hold on a sec, Solina. Someone wants to talk to you. I'm going to transfer you to the Boss Man's office line."

Hugh hung up, the phone beeped once, and someone picked up on another line. "Miss Mundy?"

My jaw clenched, and my breath stuck in my throat, but I managed to squeak out a thin "Yeah?"

"What in the hell..." Thorin's voice faded into nonsensical, angry muttering. I swiped my thumb over the End button again, not pressing hard enough to make it work, but close, so close. *Let him say one nasty word to me.*

"Is it really you?" Some strong emotion crackled in Thorin's voice— anger, probably. Murderous rage. Volcanic fury. "How can I be certain?"

"You want me to prove it?" I asked.

"Yes. Tell me, what was the last thing I said to you?"

Heat bloomed in my cheeks when I thought of Thorin's last words to me, and I desperately did not want to repeat them.

"Sunshine," Thorin said, sing-songing his nickname for me. "What did I say?"

31

I grunted and spat the words out, rapid as a machine-gun. "You said you weren't like Val. That you wouldn't make his mistakes."

Thorin cleared his throat and said, "Ah. It *is* you."

"You also said you didn't waste time playing games. I'm not your mouse, and you're not my cat, so let's stop screwing around."

Thorin growled. "You got a lot of explaining to do, Miss Mundy."

I ignored his formal use of my name. He was doing it to rile me, and I refused to take the bait. Instead, I rose to my feet and paced the short space at the foot of my bed. "I don't have a lot of answers, unfortunately."

"But you're safe for the moment? Whole? No wolf nipping at you?" Thorin held his tone even, his voice low, but that cool demeanor didn't fool me for a second.

"Safe as houses." I didn't fully understand the expression, but Val had used it once.

"Tell me where you are. I'll come get you."

And that was what I wanted, right? "Where's Skyla?" I asked instead.

Thorin made a hacking noise in his throat. "The last I knew she was with you."

"So, she's still missing?"

"Yes, Miss Mundy. She is."

"Damn." Thorin had been one of my last hopes for leads on Skyla's whereabouts. His lack of knowledge meant I had one card left to play, but only when the time was right.

"I assumed you two were together somewhere—that Helen had taken you—but after she failed to make her move, we all started to wonder. Tori told me about your dream. What the *hell* were you thinking?"

There it was—the animosity I had expected. "I was thinking about saving your life."

"By putting your own at risk?"

"You've all but pounded it into my head that your—how'd you put it—your *perpetuity* is the most important thing to you. I don't know how you expected to perpetuate with Odin's spear piercing your heart. You can call it a lie if you want, but I saved your lives. You and Val both."

"Only to put yourself right back in the middle of the situation we have all risked so much to keep you away from." Something banged on

Thorin's end of the line, probably his fist on the counter. "You should have told me. I do my own fighting."

"I know you can fight. I'm aware you are a freaking superhero, but how can you protect me if you're dead?"

Thorin roared, "How can I protect you if you *keep things from me?*"

"Skyla—" I started.

"Skyla is human, and what good did that do for any of us?"

"The Valkyries—"

"Inyoni and Kalani are dead. We found their bodies eviscerated and—"

"You found their remains?" I asked. "What did you do with them?"

"Brought their bodies back to the Aerie and let the Valkyries do with them what they saw fit."

"How did you know to look for us at Oneida? There's been nothing in the news about what happened out there, and the only people who could tell you where we were are dead or missing. You said that truck you gave us was a ghost. I knew you were lying about that."

"It *was* a ghost... for all intents and purposes other than my own."

"So you tracked the truck and found it at Oneida. Good for you. Shall I call you Sherlock?"

Thorin grunted. "I want you to tell me exactly what happened out there."

And I want to think about anything but *that night.* The events of Lake Oneida had created more problems than solutions, and Hati's death was the only worthwhile consequence of that confrontation. Perhaps Thorin sensed my reticence and sympathized because he softened his tone. "Tell me, Sunshine. You didn't come back from the dead and call me for no reason. I can't help you if I don't know everything."

I shook my head and chewed on my lip while I tried to think of something to say, but no words came to mind. I shook my head again, stopped, wobbled around on my heel, and lurched toward the bed. A great big ice ball had settled in my stomach, and it chilled my blood. I curled up on the comforter and hugged a pillow close. "I don't know what happened. It defies my ability to explain. Nate was there, and he said—"

Thorin cut in. "Nate? What was he doing there?"

"Helen's bidding, I assume. Being Helen's lover must have its perks."

"They're not lovers."

"But they were all over each other that night we met them in Juneau."

"They're family."

I gagged. "Eww!"

"Nate was once better known as Nott, son of Narfi. Narfi's father was Loki, and Loki, as you know, was Hela's brother. That makes Nate Helen's nephew."

"Still," I said. "Ew."

"Who else was at the lake?" Thorin asked, ignoring my commentary.

"Hati and Skoll. Skoll was in wolf form, and Hati... Hati was a man." Slowly, haltingly, I told him the story of that night, of how I'd killed Hati and transformed into a shooting star.

"Hati's dead," Thorin said. "You're certain?"

"He was all but charcoal when I saw him last. Do the wolves recover from that kind of thing?"

"We found no wolf remains."

Neither had I, but I wasn't going to tell Thorin I had gone back to the lake, not unless my confession was utterly necessary. "Maybe Nate took his ashes. Better than thinking Hati regenerated."

Thorin scoffed. "I assure you he's a wolf, not a phoenix. You're certain he died?"

"I didn't stick around to take a second look, but yes. I turned him to ash and bone. I'm sure of it."

A moment of silence filled the line before Thorin exhaled and said, "Unbelievable. The original Sol could do such things but no one since then."

"I doubt there's been a need for it. Seems the real sun has been getting along fine without my help."

I put down my pillow, relieved by the catharsis of sharing my story. I could have made a life with friends like Nikka and Tre, but it would have been hollow, based on lies and misdirections. Living a common life would have meant ignoring an elemental part of myself. *How can I be happy having to hide myself like that?* I had spent only a few minutes on the phone with Thorin, someone with whom I didn't have to pretend or lie, and I already felt more like my real self than I had in weeks.

"What about Val?" My heart danced a panicky beat at the thought of reuniting with my brother's best friend and my former... something. "Where is he?"

"Looking for you. We parted ways after following your trail to Oneida Lake. He's had his nose to the ground, sniffing for clues."

"Did he find anything?"

Thorin grumbled again. "Not even a whisper."

I pumped my fist in victory. *Off-the-grid Solina—sign me up for black ops, and kiss my grits, James Bond.* "Thorin, I think *someone* knows where I've been." I told him about Rolf Lockhart.

Thorin put steel into his voice when he said, "Where are you right this moment?"

"At a hotel in Sacramento." I gave him the street address and my room number.

"Sacramento? What the *hell...?*" He stopped and cleared his throat. "Never mind. Stay put. I'll be there in a couple of minutes." He paused and added a final warning. "And wherever we go from there, from now on, you won't leave my side. I thought I could trust the Valkyries to protect you. I thought I could trust *you* to know better than to go out on your own."

"You want something done right, you gotta do it yourself?" I asked, my words thick with derision. "I'm not going to run from you, Thorin. If I were, I wouldn't have called you in the first place."

"You could always change your mind."

"I could, but I won't. You'll have to take a chance on me whether you like it or not. I'm guessing you will." I thumbed the End button and cut off the call before Thorin replied. He would show up for no other reason than he couldn't stand to let me have the last word. And because he liked to think he was in control.

I chuckled to myself. *He's going to be so disappointed.*

CHAPTER SIX

WAS I GLAD FOR THE impending reunion, or was I scared, or apprehensive? When the door of my motel room shuddered under the pounding of Thorin's fist, I felt a little of all three at the same time. I inhaled a deep breath, drew open the door, and there he stood: God of Thunder with his hands shoved into the pockets of worn jeans. His pale hair hung loose, softening his austere expression—so surreal yet so unassuming. Even in scuffed boots and an old flannel shirt, Thorin's magnificence made my heart dance an eager jig.

I stepped back, and Thorin crossed the threshold. His movement stirred the air and brought a whiff of late summer sun showers. Thorin and I faced each other in the small area between the foot of the bed and the dresser. Part of me wanted to scurry away, but I pushed the urge aside and met the full weight of his gaze. Darkness showed in his eyes, but not the depthless black of rage or other intense emotions. Maybe that meant he would be reasonable.

"So, Sunshine. I've reconstructed a timeline from what I already know, but I'd like to hear from you just exactly how long you've been hiding from me."

"No 'Good to see you. How's it been?'" I asked. "Just straight to the inquisition."

Thorin said nothing but glared at me.

I sighed and slumped down on the corner of the bed. "I wasn't hiding." *Big fat lie number one.*

"How *long*?" he growled.

"I *wasn't* hiding, not from you, anyway." *Big fat lie number two.*

"From who, then?"

I arched a brow in a meaningful way. "Do you really need me to make a list?"

Thorin grimaced and waved for me to continue.

"As far as anyone knew, I was dead. And regular dead is a way better alternative to being chewed up by a wolf to fulfill some cataclysmic prophecy, no?"

"You can see how well that worked out."

"I made it five weeks," I said. "I was on the road for one week and in San Diego for four before that Rolf guy showed up and started making threats. How can you not know who he is? Only so many of you survived Ragnarok."

"Reincarnation, a Jötunn, or simply a well-connected human who has deep pockets and access to high-level technology—he could be anyone or no one."

"He wasn't no one. And he wasn't simple."

"There were nine worlds," Thorin said as his phone rang. He tugged the device from his pocket and peered at the screen. "He could have come from any of them."

Thorin swiped his thumb over the screen and put the phone to his ear. An animated voice on the other end rattled on for a bit before Thorin replied with a casual, "Yup. She's here." And a moment later, "Yes, she's fine." After the caller spoke again, Thorin said, "I don't know yet. I'll give you a call when we figure it out."

"Who was that?" I asked when he hung up.

"Val."

I blanched. I would have rather faced the wolf than deal with Val. Skoll wanted to kill me, and I harbored a steadfast and unequivocal loathing for the wolf. Val, however, wanted to own me and had used heavy-handed methods to get his way. I didn't hate him, but I wasn't eager to face him yet, either.

"Where is he?" I asked.

"North Carolina."

My pulse skittered. North Carolina was home, the place I most wanted to protect and keep separate from the strange and dangerous world of magic and monsters. "Did he really think I was dumb enough to go back there?"

"Weren't you?"

"Dumb? No. Incognizant? Yes. I left there fast. I knew what a danger it was."

"Well, it's as good of a place to look for your trail as any."

Thorin was right, which is why I hadn't stayed. Not wanting to talk about home anymore, I moved on to my next question. "How about Baldur? Where is he?"

Thorin's brows drew down into a contemplative look. "Back in New Breidablik. Why?"

Instead of answering, I asked another question. "What were your plans for me once you got here? When you heard my voice on the phone and you knew it was me, what did you think would happen next?"

The furrow in Thorin's brow deepened. "I thought I'd come and make sure you were safe."

"Then what?"

"Then I planned to take you back to Alaska, regroup with Val and Baldur, and put you somewhere safe. Being out in the open, as you've discovered, is too dangerous."

"So, lock me in a cage. That's your answer?"

Thorin's jaw clenched. He folded his arms over his chest, and darkness—the cold, angry kind—glinted in his eyes. "I'm sure if I say yes, you'll tell me all the reasons why that would be a bad idea."

"You're a smart guy, Thorin. I'm sure you could figure them out for yourself."

"Why did you call me? If it wasn't my protection you were seeking, then what do you want from me?"

"I *do* want your protection," I said.

Thorin's eyebrow flickered upward, and his expression changed from antagonized to intrigued.

"I want your brawn and your might. I want your experience and knowledge, too. I want all these things for several specific reasons, and none of them have to do with you locking me up in a cage. How would that work, anyway? Your conscience is appeased because you saved the world—and yourself—without having to kill an innocent woman. Meanwhile, I rot away in captivity. Is that how you see it going?"

A-a-and here comes the animosity again. But no, quite the opposite.

Thorin's severe posture relaxed. He slumped onto the bed beside me and rubbed his eyes. "Is that really how you see me, Sunshine? It's true I'm an immortal being and a god, and it's my nature to command and expect submission, but I have also lived as a man for a very long time. It has tempered me, some, believe it or not."

Thorin scratched his jaw. "When I left you at the Aerie, the last time I saw you, I thought we had established a trust between us. I thought we had an understanding. I had proved myself capable of compromise, but then you took advantage of my goodwill. You used it to deceive me, so forgive me if I'm less inclined to reason with you now."

Thorin's argument made more sense than I wanted to admit. All the ire and self-righteous pomp I had built up in preparation for confronting him seeped out like air from a leaky balloon. I stared at the blank TV screen and said, "It would be easier if you were just the Thor stereotype. Angry. Rash. Obstinate. Not too bright."

Thorin snorted, but a smile played on his lips. "Then you could dismiss me and not take my opinions or feelings into consideration."

"Yes. It's easier to keep you at an arm's length that way."

"It's no surprise that building walls would be your tendency, Sunshine. You've been hurt. Badly. That's not a thing anyone easily overcomes." He spoke truth.

I didn't want to let Thorin in, didn't want there to be more between us than an agreement, a compact based on our mutual need for survival. His last words to me at the Aerie had indicated he wanted the same thing: distance, objectivity. But there he sat, slumped beside me in a dingy motel room in Sacramento, offering compassion. His presence felt like a lot more than a cold business agreement.

"I didn't deceive you on purpose. At the Aerie. I was trying to protect you."

Thorin exhaled a heavy breath. "I know that, and I should probably express my gratitude."

I chuckled. "I'm sure that's not really in the nature of a god, either, is it?"

Thorin looked at me, his eyes warm and brown. "Not so much." His expression turned serious again. "I am immortal, Solina, and not so easy to kill. Going forward, I need to know you appreciate that fact.

You should never make the choice to risk yourself for me or Val or any of our kind."

I opened my mouth to say something, but the words didn't come. I shook my head, cleared my throat, and started again. "I understand. I do. But in the short time you've known me, you must have realized I'm not the type to sacrifice others to save myself. Which brings me to the reason I called you."

"It wasn't because you were longing for my companionship?" Thorin waved in a dismissive gesture. "Don't worry. I won't make you admit it."

I laughed, thankful for the offering of his humor. "I do welcome your company, but you're right, it's not the reason I reached out to you. What I really want is to have your help in accomplishing two things." I held up my index finger. "First, I want to stop running and hiding. I want us to be more proactive about our approach to Helen and Skoll. Get them before they get us."

"And the second thing?"

I raised my middle finger, making a pair. "I want you to help me find Skyla."

Thorin's jaw slackened, and he blinked several times, obviously overcome by surprise. Then he recovered his composure and said, "I can agree with being proactive, but I don't see how hunting for Skyla would be the best use of our time and resources right now. Why should we make finding her a priority?"

"Why? Because if you don't help me, I'll make sure you spend the rest of my life chasing me down and hoping you find me before the wolf does."

That got him. Thorin sobered and rubbed his jaw. He raised his chin and peered down his nose at me, but a twinkle shone in his eye. "That's not being proactive. That's just wasting time."

"Chasing me is a waste of time? You're probably right, but chasing Skyla wouldn't be. She's my number-one ally. She didn't abandon me when I needed her most, and now it's my turn to not abandon her. Don't tell me you don't appreciate loyalty, Thorin. I know how you feel about Baldur."

"*If* I were to agree to your demands"—Thorin's eyebrow arched high in skepticism—"how would we even begin? She could be anywhere. Or nowhere. You should be prepared for the worst."

"I *know* that." I had, in a weak moment, admitted to myself that Skyla might be dead, but I wouldn't abandon her until I had verified her death. No amount of reasoning would change my mind. "But I have to know, either way."

"Should I call Nate and ask him to tell us what happened? Schedule a meeting and demand proof of life?"

"Do you think he would respond to that?"

Thorin gave me a what-do-you-think look.

I shrugged. "Well, if you don't think Helen or Nate would be willing to just hand Skyla over, assuming they took her in the first place, then I might have another idea about how to track her down."

Thorin's head tilted, and his brows drew together. "What's that?"

"Baldur. He's an expert in searching for missing women, no?"

Thorin nodded.

"And how does he do that? Cross his fingers and pray for good luck?"

"He's created an extensive information-gathering network," Thorin said. "He's always had such a thing, in one form or another. He's always used it to find Nina."

"Information-gathering network?" I laughed. "How come, when you say that, I picture courier pigeons and tin cans strung between bedroom windows? How's his Morse code?"

"Don't be so critical," Thorin said. "You'd be surprised how well we've adapted over the years."

"Okay, then. You've proven my point. Baldur is our best chance for finding Skyla. Let's get to Baldur, plug Skyla into his system, and see what turns up. At the same time, we can track down Skoll."

"And then what?"

I rubbed my hands together and grinned. "Then we kill him."

<hr>

Thorin had arrived via Aesir Interdimensional Expressway, and he didn't offer to take us to New Breidablik on the same route. *One of these days, I'm going to find out how they move around like they do.* Instead, Thorin whipped out his cell phone and made a call, to order a car to come pick us up. After securing our transportation, Thorin called Val and shared our plans to reunite with Baldur at New Breidablik.

"If you want to know the details," Thorin said, "meet us at the Executive Airport in Sacramento... Yes, Sacramento... Don't ask. I'll tell you later."

"We're taking your jet?" I asked after Thorin ended the call.

"No. It's booked. We'll charter a private flight."

God of Thunder *and* Lord of Deep Pockets. The Aesir's wealth was a handy resource for funding the prevention of the apocalypse. Sometimes, I felt a little guilty about all the money the Aesir spent on my behalf, but my logical side overruled my shame. It would've really sucked to have to say, "Sorry world, could have saved you, but I was too short on cash."

After a while, a sleek black car rolled up to our door and honked. Thorin escorted me from the motel room and opened the car's rear door. I eased into the buttery leather interior, all plush and full of new-car smell. Maybe I swooned a little. Thorin tossed my tote bags in the trunk and slipped around the car. He slid into the seat beside me and gave me a smug smile.

I waved in a gesture that encompassed the whole car. "Are you for real?"

"What do you mean?" Thorin asked as the driver reversed out of the parking lot, shifted into drive, and pulled onto the highway.

"I thought these were the cars the villains were supposed to drive."

Thorin smirked. "Who says I'm the good guy?"

"You're one of the few *not* trying to kill me. Makes you a good guy in my book."

"Have you never been in a car like this before, Sunshine?"

I snorted and thought of the plain white Civic sitting in my driveway at my parents' house. I'd had that car since high school, and I had bought it already used and well worn. "I don't really roll with the *Jag-you-wah* crowd," I said, pronouncing the name in a bad British accent.

Thorin winked. "Then you've been missing out." He barked something in a foreign language, and the driver stomped the gas pedal. The car leapt forward like a thoroughbred eager to run. My pulse took off along with it.

"What about cops with radar guns?" I asked, breathless. "I thought you said police complicated things."

Thorin stared out his window as the highway roared past us. "Do you trust me, Sunshine?"

That was a loaded question if ever there was one. I closed my eyes, leaned back against the headrest, and tried to loosen my choke-hold grip on the door handle. "Yes," I croaked. "Why do you think I called you over anyone else?"

Thorin's response came after a lengthy pause. Maybe my frankness confounded him. *That would be a first.*

"I'm not going to let anything happen to you," he said. "Try to relax and enjoy the ride."

Val Wotan met us in the entrance hall of the Sacramento Executive Airport, a small annex for private jets near the larger, commercial airport. The moment I sighted Val's familiar face, my emotions jumped up and took off in a confusing swirl. Anger partnered with affection and spun a dizzying waltz. Antipathy and longing locked eyes and stalked around each other like partners in a hostile tango.

Val set his mouth in a thin line. His jaw jutted, and blue sparks glinted in his narrow stare.

"This is going to be a long trip if you're going to insist on brooding all the way to New Breidablik," I said as I passed him on my way into the airport's small lobby.

"I'm not brooding," Val said through gritted teeth. He stalked behind me, and I imagined him panting and growling like an angry bear. "You lied to me, and I am trying desperately hard not to shake you until your teeth rattle."

I hacked a derisive laugh and spun around to face him. "You haven't learned anything, have you? Don't you know by now that I don't respond well to threats?"

Val sneered. "Maybe I need another lesson."

"You're being a humongous jerk about something that isn't that big of a deal."

Val's face shifted, and something pained and frightened showed in his expression. He stepped closer and loomed over me. He didn't touch me, but he had to know his superior height and size intimidated me. Except

43

for a desk clerk, whose attention Thorin was currently occupying, the tiny airport lobby was empty. No one noticed Val's hostility. *So much for airport security.*

"You were gone for *nine weeks*," Val said in a strained voice. "We didn't know what happened to you other than you lied to us and ran off from the Aerie's relative safety with three women of disputable loyalty. There was no one to fight, no quest to undertake to bring you back, no oracle to consult.

"Just... *poof*"—Val spread his fingers to mime smoke disbursing through air—"you were gone. And you think I'm supposed to act like nothing happened? You think I'm being unreasonable? Get a clue."

Well, when he puts it like that...

Val leaned down, and his eyes bored into mine. "You might hate me, Solina. But every moment you were gone was agony for me. Don't ever do that again." Without giving me an opportunity to form a rebuttal, Val dropped his gaze and turned his back to me.

I didn't hate Val, but I didn't like him a whole lot, either, and I refused to placate him or soothe his ego with apologies and self-justifications. *I shouldn't have to. I haven't done anything wrong.*

Thorin finished checking in with the counter clerk and returned to the waiting area, where Val and I stood in a cold and stifling cloud of silence. Thorin glanced between us, rolled his eyes, and motioned for us to follow him outside. A sexy, lustrous charter jet awaited us, and it brought to mind glossy Tag Heuer and Polo advertisements. In the commercial playing in my head, some exotic creature, a leopard or a panther, descended the airplane's steps wearing a diamond-studded collar.

She was no slinky jungle cat, but the flight attendant who greeted us was close enough. She introduced herself with, "My name's Samantha, but please just call me Sam," and purred over Thorin and Val. She moved about the cabin with preternatural grace despite her three-inch heels. I didn't hate her for her sophistication and elegance, but man, I really wanted to.

While the guys settled into their seats, I went to the galley and searched for something to drink. The flight attendant tried to intercept me, insisting she would provide the refreshments.

"I got it under control," I said. "I'm professionally trained and everything."

She arched a manicured eyebrow, shrugged, and turned away. I passed beer bottles to the guys and sat down with my own tumbler of ice and Diet Coke.

"I know you've already explained everything to Thorin," Val said. He leaned back in his seat, folded his hands in his lap, and kept his face arranged in a pleasantly neutral expression—neither apologetic nor critical. "But I'd like to hear it for myself. Tell me everything that happened from the moment I last saw you at the Aerie."

I closed my eyes and let my head drop against the headrest. "I'll tell you, but let's be clear about one thing."

"What's that?"

"I am not defending myself. I stand by every one of my actions, every one of my decisions. The fact that we are all still alive today has a lot to do with the choices I made, and I will not apologize for misleading you."

"For lying."

If that's not a donkey calling a mule ugly... I opened my eyes, leaned forward, and glared at Val. "For doing whatever it takes to ensure that Helen does not win."

Val winced. Then he nodded. After that, I told him everything: of the dream about Helen attacking the Aerie and killing Thorin with Odin's spear; of going to Oneida Lake; of losing Kalani; of Inyoni's betrayal; of my fight against Skoll and my transformation. I told him about waking cold and wet on the banks of Lake Norman, about the park ranger finding me and taking me home. About my days on the road and getting a job in San Diego before I had to run away again.

"Why San Diego?" Val asked.

"It was as far away from home as I could go."

"Why didn't you call us right away? Why didn't you come back to Alaska or go back to the Aerie?"

I huffed. "I couldn't go back to the Aerie alone because I don't know who to trust there anymore. Helen has infiltrated at least some of the Valkyries, if not all of them. As for going anywhere else... I was hoping I could just be a ghost. I was bankrupt—no powers, no fire, no way to protect myself. Letting everyone think I was dead or gone was the safest thing for me at the time. Or so I thought. I have since discovered it's impossible to completely disappear in this world. *Someone* always knows how to find me."

Val's face softened. He leaned forward, and his blue eyes peered solemnly into mine. "You don't get it, do you? Helen is intent. With or without you, Solina, she intends to rule this world. If she can't recreate Ragnarok, she'll find another way."

I turned away and stared out the window. "I can't control Helen, and maybe I can't stop her. Not yet. But at least it wouldn't be all my fault."

"Your parents are worried sick about you. They've opened up a missing-person case. They believe they've lost both their kids. Don't you think you should call them?"

I had put my parents out of my thoughts, purposely refusing to think about them or consider the pain I must have caused them. If I thought about them too much, my resolve might have faded. I might want to go home again or call them and tell them I was okay, but that was too risky. "Do they think I'm still alive?"

Val shrugged. "I don't know what they think at this point. It's been two months since anyone knew where you were."

"I think it's better they believe I'm dead. I think it's better if everyone does. If things go badly in the end, then they won't have to mourn me twice." Saying that aloud sounded coldhearted, but the weight of my parents' expectations inhibited my freedom. Their continued involvement in my life made things harder and more dangerous. A ghost could move about freely, so it made sense to keep playing dead.

Thorin cleared his throat, disrupting the morose atmosphere that had settled over our group. He rose to his feet. "I'm going to get another beer."

Val raised his empty bottle. "I'll take another one, too."

Thorin glanced at my drink and raised a questioning eyebrow.

I studied the last few inches of Diet Coke in my glass. Then I wrapped my lips around my straw and sucked up the remaining contents in a rude and prolonged slurp. When I had to stop and let out my breath, I smiled, handed him the empty glass, and said, "Thanks, Thorin. You're a real sweetheart."

CHAPTER SEVEN

AN HOUR OR SO INTO our flight, Thorin's phone rang. He tugged it from his pocket, swiped his thumb over the screen, and put it to his ear. "Yes," he said to the caller. "We just left Sacramento. We should be back in Siqiniq by—"

The caller cut him off. Only one person could interrupt Thorin without igniting his immediate irritation: Baldur.

"Why, what's happened?" Thorin asked.

I sharpened my hearing after noting the concern filling Thorin's voice. Baldur said something, and Thorin's expression darkened.

"Okay. I'll talk to the pilot," Thorin said. "I'll see if we can change our flight plans. I'll call you and let you know our ETA."

"What's up?" Val asked after Thorin ended his call.

"Baldur," Thorin said.

"What's he want now?"

"He's got a lead on Nina, so change of plans. He wants us to meet him in Vegas."

Ah, Nina, Baldur's wayward soul mate. I should have known. I had mostly forgotten about her over the past few weeks, but of course Baldur hadn't.

Val exhaled a noisy breath. "And the Allfather always gets his way, doesn't he?"

Thorin went to talk to the captain but returned a few minutes later wearing a grim expression. "The captain can't change our itinerary. He already has a return flight booked on the other end. The best he can do is drop us off in Salt Lake. We'll arrange something from there."

Thorin and Val spent the next several minutes focused on their phones, searching for transportation from Salt Lake City to Vegas.

"I'm having déjà vu," I said.

Val looked up and arched a questioning brow.

"Feel like I've done this before," I said. "Gone off on the Legend of Nina quest. I wasn't terribly fond of the idea last time we did it. I'm even less game now."

Thorin glanced up from his phone. "Have you got urgent plans that I'm not aware of?"

"Finding Skyla, getting rid of Helen *and* the wolf, saving the world..." I said, flicking up a finger for each point. Then I waved those fingers at Thorin. "I've got *four* urgent items on my to-do list, and you *should* be aware of them already." I pointed to my unextended thumb. "You'll notice that, once again, Baldur and Nina are nowhere on my list."

Val watched our exchange, wearing a carefully neutral expression, although I suspected he sided with me.

Thorin's nostrils flared, and he huffed. "Baldur has as much interest in locating Skyla as you do in tracking down Nina. If you expect him to do you a favor, then maybe you should do one for him, too. Quid pro quo."

I sighed. When had Thorin gotten so good at making reasonable arguments? If assisting Baldur meant having his help in return, I could make hunting for Nina a temporary priority—emphasis on *temporary*.

"Okay," I said. "Let's go to Vegas. I mean, it worked out so well for us last time. What could go wrong?"

When we touched down in Salt Lake City, Samantha-just-call-me-Sam escorted us from the plane. She lavished her charm on Thorin and Val, passing them her business card and assuring them of her eagerness to accommodate them anytime they should need her services. For me, she offered a perfunctory smile and a brief "Buh-bye."

We disembarked and headed toward a black Yukon parked nearby. Thorin and Val marched behind me like wardens transporting a dangerous prisoner, Hannibal Lecter style. *Wonder how their livers would taste with some fava beans and a nice Chianti...* I tolerated their behavior because airports were notoriously bad places to exercise displays of agitation. One tends to end up in secret federal detention centers when one starts setting things on fire.

"Come on, Solina," Val said when he noticed my lagging pace. "You can stretch out in the back. It won't be so bad."

He opened the door for me, and I sank into the supple leather of the Yukon's backseat.

A yawn cracked my jaw as I settled into a mostly horizontal position. "What's the point of owning a private jet if you can't use it when you need it?"

"Seemed like it made good business sense." Val shrugged. "Sometimes I question whether that's true."

<hr/>

Val's tight grip on my knee jolted me awake. "C'mon Solina. We're here."

He shook my shoulder until I cracked an eyelid. The Yukon had stopped, the doors were open, and darkness had fallen outside, but the SUV's bright interior light stung my eyes.

I grumbled, squeezed my eyes shut, and tried to ignore Val, but the aroma of coffee wafted through the air, and the powerful scent could have raised the dead. Against my will, I sat up. My body had gone zombie, and coffee was the *braaains* it craved. Val's shadowed figure loomed in the Yukon's doorway, but the interior lights shone like God's heavenly light on the jumbo white cup in his hand.

"You want it?" He waved the cup before my face. "Come and get it."

"Jerk," I mumbled, but his enticement got me out of the Yukon, onto my feet, and shuffling in the right direction—a donkey chasing a carrot. My cognizance returned in bits and pieces, bringing awareness of my surroundings. "The Bellestrella?" I asked, recognizing the familiar neon lights. "Won't Helen know we're here?"

"We're not staying," Thorin said, startling me from behind.

I flinched and spilled searing hot coffee over my hand.

"We're just swinging by to pick up Baldur."

"Then what?" I asked and licked coffee from my burnt fingers.

Thorin stopped our group outside a door, presumably one leading to a villa like the one we had stayed in last time we were in Vegas. "I don't know. Baldur said he would give us the details when we got here."

Thorin knocked, and Baldur opened the door a moment later. As soon as he saw me, Baldur wrapped me in a hearty hug. He smelled fresh, like crocus blooms and cool spring mornings, but the images his touch inspired were nothing so pleasant. In a flash as brief as a blink, I saw a murky room that might have been a cavern, or it might have been a mansion. Stalagmites and stalactites stretched from floor to ceiling like cathedral columns intermingled among lush carpets and drapes and gilded furniture. At the end of the huge, open room, a woman sat on an elaborate throne carved from ivory—*or is it bone?*—and she looked like death incarnate. *Hela?*

The vision dissolved, and I shivered, but no one seemed to notice my discomfort. I refrained from mentioning what I had seen because it was irrelevant and possibly upsetting to Baldur, and people generally disliked knowing I could sometimes see into their heads. Besides, what I had seen was just a memory, something he already knew. Baldur chattered about how glad he was to see me and how happy he was that I was okay, but when the door closed behind us and we spread out around the living room, Baldur dropped the banter and dove into business.

"We'll have to act fast, before this lead on Nina goes cold," he said. "Helen's holding her."

"How do you know this?" Thorin asked.

"I've been working on getting to someone on the inside."

"Who? How do you know this person can be trusted?"

"He's an employee of Helen's private security firm, and he's greedy and lecherous. I greased his palm until he finally gave me some useful information. It's all I've got, but I have to take it."

"Does Helen know we have Solina back?" Thorin asked.

Baldur shook his head. "Not as far as I know."

"She *does* know," I said and told Baldur about Rolf Lockhart and his intentions of taking me to Helen. "Unless he was lying about his connections to Helen, and why would he do that?"

"I don't know who he could be," Baldur said. "Rolf is based on an old Germanic name, Hrolf, and the Old Norse Hrólfr. It's a conjunction of Norse words meaning *notorious wolf.* But whether he means the name in a literal way or not..." He shrugged and held his hands out as if apologizing for not having any more information.

I huffed. "I find it hard to believe there are so many of you still

50

roaming around out there that you could have lost track of someone. Didn't Ragnarok make the Aesir an endangered species?"

Val sniggered but cut off his laugh when Baldur glared at him.

"He may not be Aesir," Baldur said. "Some of the other realms escaped Ragnarok's destruction. This mystery man of yours could be any one of Helen's dozens of bastard cousins and kin."

I blanched. "Sorry I asked."

"It's important we know these things. We must consider all possibilities when conceiving a plan."

According to Baldur's corrupt information source, Helen kept a woman held in secure locations and moved her on a regular basis to make her difficult to track. Helen had assigned Baldur's informant to guard Nina during the next transfer, which explained how he knew any information worth selling. The possibility of it being a baited trap to bring in Baldur did not escape any of us.

"They're transferring her tonight," Baldur said. "They're driving her from a holding in Vegas to some of Helen's warehouses in Mojave County, over the Arizona border."

The three amigos converged around the coffee table to study satellite images on Baldur's laptop—what looked like warehouses, Helen's, I presumed. I tiptoed out of the room and headed for the bathroom, intent on taking a lengthy and overdue shower.

The hot spray washed away hours of delirious travel, soothed my nerves, and went a long way toward restoring my good mood. A day of rest and a night of solid sleep might rid me of any remaining complaints, but I suspected I wouldn't be that fortunate. *Miles to go before I sleep...*

I had just finished drying my hair when a knock rattled the bathroom door. Thorin's deep voice carried through the thin barrier. "Let's go, Sunshine."

I set down the hair dryer and opened the door. "Not that I want anyone to suffer the likely inhumane treatment of Helen Locke's hospitality, but I can't see how going along with you on this rescue attempt is anything but a very bad risk."

Thorin gestured, implying he wanted to come in. I moved aside, and he stepped into the bathroom and closed the door.

"Any other day, I'd leave you here," he said, "but I've got no idea what's going down tonight or if we'll be able to come back here. We might have to run for it. We can't take the risk of being separated."

"I don't have a good feeling about this. It's like walking into the middle of the enemy's camp."

Thorin frowned. "Aren't you the one who said we needed to be proactive? What if Helen's there? Maybe this is our chance to end things."

"Proactive means gathering information and making a plan. That's not what this is. This is running in blind."

Thorin's eyes darkened, but not in anger. A muscle worked in his jaw. He scraped his fingers through his hair and cursed something under his breath, a word from his ancient tongue, if I had to guess. The tenseness in his shoulders and the way he pressed his lips thin indicated frustration and uncertainty. His promises to protect me and his loyalty to Baldur must have been tugging him in opposite directions, and I felt a little sorry for him. But only a little. An immortal being who possessed the power to subject thunder, rain, and lightning to his will didn't need much pity.

"I *have* to do this thing for Baldur," he said. "My vows—"

"I know," I said. "So, how about we compromise?"

Thorin raised an eyebrow as if to say, *"Oh? And how does that work?"*

"I'm going to cooperate with you. No, don't give me that look. I mean it. Whatever you want us to do next, I'll do it, and I won't give you a hard time. In return, I expect you to make a complete commitment to helping me find Skyla."

Thorin's lips thinned. "I said I would. I don't go back on my word."

"All right. Then we have an understanding."

Thorin leaned closer and lowered his voice. "Have you had any dreams about this? You know… *premonitions* like the one you had about your brother's death? Have you had some forewarning about Nina and Baldur or Skyla that you've been holding back because you think it will protect someone?"

I huffed and waved a hand, dismissing his question. "I'm not Zoltar the fortune-telling machine. It doesn't work that way. I've had some dreams, but there's no context. They don't make sense."

"Tell me about it?" Thorin took my hand.

Maybe he meant it as a sympathetic gesture, but my fingers burned against his. Could he feel it, or was it all in my head? I hesitated, expecting one of his thoughts or memories to overcome me, but the moment passed, and my awareness remained firmly in the present. *What does that mean?*

To avoid invading Tre and Nikka's thoughts, I had shunned prolonged physical contact. When Tre and I trained together, I focused on his instruction and my technique and refused to dwell on the occasional unwelcome mental image. At most, I saw flashes of things probably inspired by Tre's experience as a cop. I never lingered on those visions or made opportunities to explore further.

I was in no way prepared to go spelunking in Thorin's head. For whatever reason, the contents swirling through his gray matter remained locked behind his skull. And for that, I was immensely grateful.

I swallowed and cleared my throat. "I, uh, there were apples." I told Thorin the rest, the bit about the orchard and the fire and how it had burned my hand.

"It sounds a little like Idun's orchard," Thorin said.

"I thought so too." When he quirked an eyebrow, I shrugged. "What? My research assistant is missing, and I had some time on my hands. Would you have preferred that I stick my head in the sand?"

Thorin grinned. "That makes for an interesting mental image."

"Not helpful." I poked his shoulder. "Do you have any idea what it means? It makes no sense to me."

Thorin shook his head. "I don't know what it means either, but I assume we'll find out soon enough."

For a moment, Thorin and I stood in silence, my hand still gripped in his, but I blinked, and the moment passed. I pulled loose from his hold and backed away, eager to breathe air that didn't smell like him. When I opened the bathroom door, Thorin took my hint and strode out to the living room.

I followed him out and found that Baldur and Val had changed into a matching set of Commando Ken outfits. They wore black cargo pants, black T-shirts, and black caps—possibly in an attempt to blend into the darkness outside. I had failed to notice before, but Thorin was dressed in similar attire.

"Here." Thorin grabbed another black T-shirt from the kitchen

53

counter and shoved it at me. "Put this on and meet us out front at the truck."

I snatched the shirt and marched into the bathroom. The fabric had molded to every plane and angle of the men's physiques, but if I knotted the hem around my hips, it looked slightly less like a trash bag on me. I braided my hair and pulled up the hood of my black sweatshirt. "Good as it's going to get," I said to the mirror. My reflection didn't disagree, so I turned off the lights and hurried to catch up with the guys.

CHAPTER EIGHT

AFTER AN HOUR-AND-A-HALF RIDE AND a brief geography lesson from Baldur, I learned Helen's warehouses were situated near the Mojave National Preserve, a federally owned wilderness composed of 1.6 million acres near the border of Nevada and Arizona.

"That's neato and all," I said, "but why would Helen take Nina to some warehouses out on the edge of nowhere?"

"It's not an easy place to stumble on by accident or run away from on purpose," Baldur said. "Desert for miles around. If you escaped, you might succumb to the elements before you lucked into an ATV or a hunter who was willing to help you out. It makes a good prison."

"It makes a good place for us to die without anyone noticing, too. I learned that lesson at Oneida Lake."

Speaking of the lake had the effect of naming an evil spirit. Everyone fell silent, and gooseflesh broke out on my arms. I wondered again about Skyla—where she was and if she was okay.

"Seriously," I said. "All you're going to achieve by this is to gratify Helen's desires. The only things waiting for you at the end of this road are empty hopes or a trap. Probably both."

Thorin slowed the SUV and turned it off the dirt path we had followed into the desert. The truck rolled to a stop behind a thatch of cacti and desert brush, and Thorin killed the engine and turned off the headlights.

"We've considered all that," Baldur said. His flashlight bobbed in my direction as he bailed out of the truck. "But it's a chance we have to take. This is the first solid lead I've had on Nina in decades."

"You guys could be putting yourselves in danger—"

"Solina, don't worry," Val said, cutting into my objection. "We know the risks. We'll be smart about it."

Smart? Hardy har har. But I bit my tongue and took a fortifying breath. "Okay, what's the plan?"

Thorin grimaced. "It's one thing to keep you close, Sunshine, and quite another to lead you into the heart of the lion's den. Stay here, be safe, and if we don't come back—"

"Run for your life," Val said.

No valid reason existed for me to insist they take me along. Immortal blood did not flow through my veins. Some goals and schemes might have been worth the risk of losing my life, but walking into semiobvious traps laid by Helen was not one of them. "All right. I'll wait here. But this is the part in the movie I always fast-forward through. I hate the anticipation."

Val squeezed my shoulder. "We'll be back before you know it."

Thorin hung back as Val and Baldur started down the pathway. Without a word, he dangled the SUV keys before my face. I snatched them and stuffed them in my pocket. He winked at me, turned on his heel, and caught up with the others.

The three men's figures moved away from the truck and dissolved into the darkness. I climbed into the Yukon and pulled the door closed, making sure to lock it before stretching out across the bench seat. After a few minutes of staring up through the aptly named moon roof, my stomach growled, and I cursed myself for not having asked for a food stop on the way. I had eaten nothing since... I couldn't remember, exactly. The ghost of a low-blood-sugar headache haunted my temples. When the scheme ended, if we all lived through it, I intended to insist on a burger stand or a taco truck or a freaking 7-Eleven hot dog, even if it meant we had to drive all the way back to Vegas to get it.

"Solina, wake up!" Val pounded on my window and jolted me from my daze.

I hadn't slept—too much worry kept me from dozing off—but I had zoned out, staring into the sky, looking at the moon and thinking of Mani and tacos.

"Solina!"

I popped the lock, and Val flung open the door. "What happened?"

56

I scrubbed my eyes and peered into the darkness behind him. "Where is everybody?"

"It's gone to hell." Val scrambled into the driver's seat. He riffled through the glove box and flipped down the sun visor.

"What are you doing?" I crawled over the center console into the passenger seat. "What do you mean it's gone to hell?"

"Helen's guards were waiting for us when we got there." Val leaned down between his legs and rolled up the floor mat. Then he reached over and rolled up mine.

Well, duh! I didn't say. "What happened to Thorin and Baldur?"

"They've been taken. I'm going to get you out of here *if* I can find the keys."

I had the keys but wasn't going to give them to Val without getting the full story from him first. I scrutinized the darkness again, looking for signs of pursuit. "Are they chasing you?"

"No, Thorin and Baldur got ahead of me. I stopped to take a piss. By the time I caught up, they were already out. Helen's guards had used something on them. They were knocked out."

I threw open my door and jumped out. "So, you think they used a tranquilizer? Like they were wild animals or something? Is that even possible? It's so, so... *absurd*." The Valkyries had done the same to me, but I was mostly human, and they had wanted to take me alive. Helen would most likely prefer to dispose of Thorin. Baldur, however, she would keep, so maybe drugs made sense, for the time being. I had to get to Thorin before Helen changed her mind and utilized something deadlier, such as Odin's spear.

Val leaped from the truck and jogged around to my side, using his body to block my forward progress. "C'mon, Solina. We've got to get you out of here."

"We can't leave them." I shoved past Val, went to the Yukon's back end, and opened the rear hatch to dig through stacks of luggage and a toolbox. Eventually, I found a tiny LED flashlight in a roadside emergency kit.

"They're big boys." Val positioned himself in my way again. "They can handle themselves. They knew the risks. Thorin would want us to leave."

"If the roles were reversed, he wouldn't leave us behind."

Val stiffened, and his voice took on a harsh edge. "He wouldn't leave *you* because any time you're at risk, he's at risk. He protects you out of pure self-interest. If you think he'll love you for this..." Val didn't finish the thought, but I got his meaning.

Not for Val, but for my own sake, I paused and thought about my motives. If my softer feelings for Thorin, whatever they might have been, were inspiring my actions, then I had to stop. Val was right. I couldn't risk my life on the expectation of receiving some future preference from Thorin. My motives had to be mine alone.

I wouldn't go out of my way to help Baldur find Nina, but I wouldn't feed him to Helen, either—same for Thorin. My reason for going into the desert was no longer about participating in a simple treasure hunt for a pot of gold I had no desire to find. My motives were now about the lives and deaths of people I cared about—circumstances that did not tolerate apathy. "That's not what this is about. It's about right and wrong. If they die because of my indifference, that would be wrong."

Val shook his head. "You don't know what you're talking about. There's a compound full of armed men up there. Thorin and Baldur took out a handful of them barehanded before someone put them down with a dart gun, as if they were beasts. How do you expect to do any better than them?"

"I *cannot* stand by and let someone die simply to save my own hide," I said. Losing Thorin meant losing my greatest ally against Helen. Val had demonstrated strength and fortitude when it suited him, but his chances of defeating Helen on his own inspired little confidence in me. He needed Thorin as much as I did.

Val gritted his teeth. "You are the stubbornest, most pig-headed—"

"I'm going, Val. Stay here or come with me and do your best to keep me safe." I held up a flat palm in his direction. "So help me, if you stand in my way, I will char your ass." As Val dithered, I went in for the kill. "I would do it for you, too. I wouldn't leave you behind if they had taken you."

In the glow of my LED flashlight, Val's eyebrow arched. "I wouldn't ask you to save me."

"I'd do it anyway."

Val's lips thinned, and his nostrils flared. He folded his arms over his chest and glared at me. When I didn't back down, he finally nodded. "Okay. But at the first sign of trouble, I'm grabbing you up and throwing you over my shoulder. You can burn me to ashes if you want, but your life comes first."

Security lights illuminated several guards on patrol inside an industrial compound made up of seven or eight large corrugated-metal warehouses. The sentries—all toting mean black rifles—walked the inside perimeter of a huge chain-link fence topped by three strands of barbed wire. Crouched in the darkness behind a convenient patch of prickly desert vegetation, Val and I watched the guards stroll back and forth along the fence.

I pulled my hood up and balled my hands together in my hoodie's kangaroo pocket. The desert was surprisingly cold at night, and it smelled of dust, horse manure, engine exhaust, and wood smoke.

"Did you learn anything useful about this place before you came back to get me?" I whispered to Val.

He motioned farther down the fence line. "I don't know where they're being kept. The place is full of guards, so whatever we're going to do, we gotta do it fast."

"How did Baldur and Thorin get past this fence *and* all those guards?"

Val peered at me from the corner of his eye. "They have their ways. Ways not available to you, unfortunately."

"Can you get through the fence? Without being caught?"

Val put a hand over his heart and huffed. "You offend me."

"We need a distraction," I said, ignoring his theatrics. "You got a holocaust cloak on you?"

"A what?"

"Never mind. Something big-go-boom would be good. Something to draw the guards' attention away from the fence long enough for me to get inside."

"There's a propane tank next to the rear building. See it?" Val gripped my shoulders and turned me in the direction he wanted me to look. Next to an outlying building, illuminated by the security light's yellow glow, sat a familiar white tank.

"Yeah, I see it," I said.

Val turned toward the warehouses and studied the patrol's movements. "You can handle the flame part. Once that thing blows, I'll slip around and try to help Thorin and Baldur."

I heaved a groan. "I don't know, Val. I'm pretty pooped. I haven't eaten, and I've slept like crap." Actually, I trusted my fire, but I wanted to save it for a dire situation, not use it up on a special effects show. Besides, Val had deserted Thorin and Baldur once already. I didn't want to give him the chance to do it again.

Val huffed. "What other ideas do you have?"

"I don't know. If we had a lighter at least." An idea struck me. "Will a flare do it?"

Val shrugged. "Possibly."

"There were roadside flares in the kit in the truck."

Val squared his shoulders and looked off in the direction of the Yukon, parked almost a mile's hike away. "Give me the keys and stay here. I'll be back."

I handed them over. "Even if you distract the guards, how am I going to get over the fence?"

Val rubbed his chin as he pondered the question. His brows rose, and he smiled. "Gotcha covered."

"Val, what are you—"

He stepped forward into the darkness, and *poof*, he vanished. I shone my flashlight in his direction, but the beam illuminated nothing. A moment later, Val reappeared in my light. He jogged forward and presented his treasures: a roadside flare and a rolled-up floor mat that must have come from the Yukon's rear cargo section.

"How do you *do* that?" I asked, aghast.

Val waggled his eyebrows. "I'm a god, Solina. You keep forgetting. There have to be some perks to this job."

I pointed at the flare. "Do you think you can do something with that thing?"

"Your doubt is insulting."

"Sorry."

Val waved off my apology. "When that thing blows, I don't know how long I can keep their attention. Be quick, Solina." He passed the floor mat to me. "Can you get this mat over the top of that fence? It's heavy."

"Your doubt is insulting."

Val rolled his eyes. "Don't take any stupid risks."

"Too late."

Val muttered something and squeezed my shoulder. "Cross your fingers," he said and disappeared again.

I edged closer to the fence, toting the rolled-up mat under my arm, and hunkered low in the shadows.

Two guards strolled past, both apparently oblivious to my presence. One of them was saying, "...taking a chopper, I heard."

"She won't believe us about the capture," the other guard said. "That crazy bitch has to come rushing out in the middle of the night to confirm it."

"Don't let her hear you call her that. She's brutal. No sense of humor."

"I hear she's..."

The two moved out of earshot before the second guard revealed what he had heard about Helen. *What other "she" could he be talking about?*

"Come on, Val," I muttered. "What's the problem?"

As if in reply, the sky tore apart. Val had said, "Let there be light," and there was. The explosion lit the night in a temporary, false day—a miniature sun that lasted an instant. Someone let out a whoop, and footfalls scurried, en masse, to the scene of the explosion. I edged closer to the fence and waited several moments to allow for stragglers and latecomers.

Like a heavy steam engine, my heart chugged in my chest. My lungs worked double overtime, a pair of concertinas playing the world's fastest polka. *It's now or never, girlfriend.*

I scurried to the fence, shoved my foot in, laced my fingers around the links and climbed, one handed, trying not to drop the mat. Near the top, I said a little prayer and leaned back, unfurled the mat, and slung it over the barbed wire. It landed off-center and slid to the ground at my feet.

"Damn," I whispered and jumped down to collect the fallen mat. How long would I have before the guards returned? Not long if they realized the explosion was something other than an equipment malfunction.

I climbed a second time and chucked the rug again. Val had been right: the rubber-backed carpeting weighed a lot, especially for attempting a one-armed toss. I heaved, and the mat sailed upward, reached the apex of its trajectory, and came down to straddle the barbed wire almost equally on both sides. *What are the chances of doing that again?*

The carpeting must have knotted around the barbs because the mat stayed in place as I climbed higher. I readjusted my balance and swung a leg up and over the mat, careful to keep my skin away from the threatening barbs. *Thank you, Tre, for the cardio and strength training. I owe you the biggest banana pudding ever.*

Barbs pressed into the rug, threatening to puncture my delicate flesh. Someone yelled again, and I froze. Then I drew in a deep breath and forced myself to move. Either the guards had seen me and I was doomed, or they hadn't and luck was momentarily on my side. Either way, I had to get moving. I twisted and lowered myself until I hung, arms fully extended, hands bearing the brunt of my full weight. I drew in one deep breath and another, and I let go.

My feet hit the ground, and I stumbled, recovered, and took off running deeper into the compound and away from Val's explosion. The doors of the first warehouse I came to were locked. The next ones weren't, so I ducked inside and paused, listening for footsteps, moaning, conversation, or dismayed shouts, but only silence greeted my entry.

The floor plan laid out the interior rooms in a four-square style: four doors leading off one main hallway—two to the right, two to the left. I opened my mouth to call for Thorin but paused midbreath. What if a guard had stayed behind to watch the prisoners? *If they're even in this building in the first place. You could just be playing a giant shell game.* What if they'd been taken away in a sleight-of-hand move, and *all* the buildings were empty?

Eenie, meenie, miney, mo. After utilizing my sophisticated analytical technique, I chose the first door on the right. If my life had been a movie, that was the point where the cellos would have started playing one ominous note, over and over, low and slow at first but mounting in pitch and tempo as the probability of danger increased.

Fear diluted my bravery, and the urge to run away, with or without the others, surged through me. Someone coughed in another room. *Another guard?* My bladder spasmed.

The same had happened to me as a kid whenever Mani and I played hide-and-seek. He won so many times on my forfeit because I thought for sure I would pee my pants before he found me.

I closed my eyes, said a quick prayer, and turned the handle. The door flew open, and I rushed forward, prepared to fight, but I stopped short when my gaze fell on the room's sole occupant. My mouth dropped open and I stuttered, "Wha... What the hell are *you* doing here?"

CHAPTER NINE

Skyla Ramirez sat in an old and very heavy-looking metal chair—*a medieval office chair?*—that appeared to be bolted to the floor. One handcuff circled her wrist, and another spanned her ankle. Both were linked by a long chain latched around the chair's leg.

She grinned at me as if Publisher's Clearing House had just showed up at her door offering a million-dollar prize. "I've been waiting for your dumb ass to get here and rescue me. Took you long enough."

I stood and stared at her, mouth agape, unblinking, breath stalled in my lungs. A wave of elation and disbelief broke over me and tugged like a rip current, drawing me into a swirl of disorderly emotions. She had consumed so many of my thoughts and worries for the past month, and there she sat, like a golden goose egg I'd thought I would never find.

Skyla snorted and rolled her eyes, and the gesture woke me from my daze. I rushed over, threw my arms around her, and squeezed until her ribs creaked.

"Oh, thank God," I said, struggling against my tears and the lump welling in my throat.

Hysterics would have to wait for better timing, though. I pulled away so I could look Skyla in the face and reassure myself she was real. I brushed my fingertips over her cheek, and she closed her eyes and smiled. "I've been looking for you forever."

Skyla's voice hitched a little when she said, "And you've found me. Good job, Mundy."

"But what about Nina? We actually came here looking for her."

Skyla shrugged. "Helen's been telling everybody *I'm* Nina. I haven't seen that chick anywhere. I'm starting to think Baldur made her up."

"Do you know where Thorin and Baldur are?"

"Haven't seen 'em."

"So, what are *you* doing here?"

Skyla smiled sheepishly. "Playing bait."

"For Baldur," I said as I realized the truth of Helen's plot—tell everyone Skyla was Nina and let the gossip mill spread the word.

"*And* for you," said Skyla.

"For me? I've been careful to stay off her radar." *But Rolf Lockhart had put me right back on it, and even an idiot could guess to whom I had run for help after I left San Diego.*

"You underestimate her radar. She set this whole thing up for you. Well, for you and Baldur."

"Helen told you all of this?"

I looked Skyla over again. Her dark, curly hair had grown a few inches, but otherwise, she looked the same. She appeared rested, healthy, well-fed.

"Life with the queen of the damned has been treating you pretty good."

Skyla's smile fell. "You think I've turned to the dark side or something?"

"There are a lot of questions about what went down at the lake." I had never doubted Skyla, not once, until that moment. My distrust felt dirty, and I hated humoring it long enough to question her. But there she was in Helen's possession and looking none the worse for it.

"Inyoni all but confessed," Skyla said.

"Doesn't mean she was working alone."

"Ask me." Skyla held up her wrist and rattled her chains. "I'll tell you everything you want to know. But we have to get out of here. Fast. I hope you brought something to cut me out of this."

I held up my hands to show they were empty.

Skyla glanced at the door. "Look, whatever stunt you pulled out there, it's worked for now. But they'll be back soon."

"What can we do?" I crouched and studied her bindings. "I don't keep bolt cutters in my pocket."

"Can you melt it or something?" Skyla rattled her cuffs again. "It's not very thick."

I wrapped a length of her chain around my fist and focused on my internal wellspring, to send fire streaking down my arms and into my palms. "I missed shop class in high school. I don't really know what I'm doing."

"You can turn into a freaking star, Mundy. I think you can handle a chain."

"I don't think you want to be in here with me if I go nuclear again." I grimaced. "I bet Thorin could break it with his pinkie finger."

"Thorin isn't here, so do your best."

I gritted my teeth. "What do you think I've *been* doing?" I closed my eyes and poured fire and willpower into my hands. Something must have worked because Skyla hissed.

"That's it," she said. "It's glowing. Brace yourself. I'm going to pull."

I spread my feet. Skyla tugged, but nothing happened... at first. Then Skyla cursed, and I stumbled back. She held up a much shorter length of chain. The last link had broken open, its ends now twisted and deformed.

"I can't believe that worked," I said and tucked away my fire. "Now, let's get—"

The door blew open behind me with such force that it banged against the wall like a gunshot. I spun around to face our intruders and reached for my fire, but Helen's guards had come prepared. One aimed a big red fire extinguisher at me. A second guard leveled his gun at Skyla. "Don't move," he barked.

"You think that thing's going to work on me?" I pointed at the fire extinguisher and raised my flames until they rolled over my hands and arms in a spectacular display of heat and light.

"Don't know." The guard blinked at me, wide eyed and wary. "But we're about to find out."

A third man stepped into the room and pointed another weapon at me, one I couldn't identify, and he pulled the trigger as his partner doused me in fire-extinguisher foam. Only after the barbs lodged into the skin of my chest and electricity coursed through my body did I realize he had shot me with a Taser.

My teeth clenched, all my muscles cramped in rigid knots, and a field of electric white burned across my vision. Skyla screamed my name.

Then the world went dark.

———◆———

I woke up to darkness. A nuclear bomb had exploded in my head, and my stomach contents were trying to make an emergency evacuation.

This was not my life, was it? Was this really who I was born to be? A girl who raided private compounds littered with armed security guards, attempted to rescue Norse gods from their own foolishness, and wound up knocked out and bound in.... *What* have *they done to me?* I was upright, standing on my own two feet, but something unyielding and heavy spanned my chest, shoulder to hip, around my ribs, sparing no room for movement and barely enough space for me to suck in a few desperate breaths that smelled of motor oil and mildew.

What the hell was I thinking? A couple of krav maga classes had not turned me into Chuck Norris.

"At night the boogeyman checks under his bed for Chuck Norris."

There is no theory of evolution, just a list of creatures Chuck Norris allows to live.

Chuck Norris has a grizzly-bear rug. It isn't dead. It's just afraid to move.

The guard's assault had knocked me loopy. I shook my head, clearing my thoughts, but regretted it when my brain screamed and banged a hot, burning beat against my skull. Thus, I closed my eyes and practiced my being-very-still skills.

If I tried, maybe I could convert into that *other* state again, but that meant abandoning Skyla and my allies and losing myself for who knew how long. I had no guarantee that, this time, I would come back again.

What would a Valkyrie do?

As I contemplated the answer to that question, the overhead lights flickered on and revealed the nature of my captivity. The guards had stowed me in a massive storeroom housing an innumerable number of huge metal containers, the industrial kind that came off of cargo ships before a crane loaded them onto trains and long-haul trucks. A cul-de-sac of boxes surrounded me, one on my right, one on my left, and one at my back. The bands around my chest consisted of some strange stone material, and they strongly resembled a pair of... *arms?*

The clack of approaching footsteps echoed in the expansive space, and a cold queasiness burbled up from my gut. *Is this it? Have Helen and her wolf come to devour me?* But Helen wasn't the one who rounded the corner of the nearest container. Nate McNary stopped several feet before me, and he smiled a wicked smile.

Nate appeared urbane as usual, dressed in an impeccably tailored suit. He looked nothing like a henchman but more like the sort who stood around at crossroads, waiting to give you anything you wanted in exchange for your soul. The only thing Nate had that I wanted to take was his life, and at that moment I might have sold my soul to get it.

I scowled at him and said, "We've got to stop meeting like this."

"I agree," Nate said. "Under different circumstances, maybe we could have had a rapport."

"Why do you help her? Is it family loyalty? You know what she wants to do. What guarantee do you have that you'll survive?"

Nate ignored my questions. He went to a nearby container, pried open a door, and spoke a few words I didn't understand. He waited several moments until something responded—something that sounded like stones rubbing together, like sandpaper and the gritty crunch of gravel underfoot.

Nate stepped away. More grinding noises echoed in the container, and heavy, clomping footsteps thundered on the warehouse floor. Initially, I couldn't comprehend what I saw. My mind blanked at the improbability of it. I had converted into a star, seen men shapeshift into wolves, watched other men transport themselves through thin air, but that... That defied explanation.

"Solina"—Nate shook his head piteously—"you've never seen a golem before, have you?"

I opened my mouth, but my voice had fled. Before me stood a man, one slightly taller and thicker than Nate, but he was formed entirely of stone and clay and rock. If I had seen him raised on a pedestal in a museum or fastened to a plinth in a fancy garden, he might have made sense. The figure defied all that because he moved. Like flesh and bone and blood, he stepped from the container and walked toward me. Another followed after him, and another. Blank faced, emotionless, the color of sand and mud, they marched forward and circled around me.

I glanced down and studied the bindings crossing my chest again. *Arms, indeed.* Another of the bizarre creatures was holding me in its stony, inert embrace. A strange sound—part disbelief, part horror and disgust—escaped my throat. Comprehensible words were beyond me.

"The entire warehouse is filled with them," Nate said. He did not try to hide the pride in his voice as he waved a hand at the boxes surrounding us. "Fifty in each container."

Still speechless, I gaped at him.

Nate tapped his temple. "Blowing your mind a little, isn't it? An ideal army. Faithful and loyal without fault, and they require no food, no pay, no rights." Nate chuckled. "Amazing, no?"

I swallowed and said, "What's Helen doing with them?"

"The details need not bother you. You won't be around to see them put to use, anyway. What a pity." Nate turned to the nearest stone man, golem, whatever. "Keep her here, and do not let go of her. Don't let her out of your sight. And, whatever you do, do *not* kill her."

A cell phone trilled, its tinny song reverberating through the empty space. Nate removed the phone from his pocket, thumbed the screen, and listened to the voice on the other end. "Yes, I have her, and she is secure." He listened again for a moment, grunted something affirmative, and ended the call. He raised his green-eyed gaze to mine. "We have visitors."

"Helen?" I asked.

A slight twitch of Nate's eyebrow and a devious smile provided all the confirmation I needed. *Well, damn.* Where there was a Helen, there was also a Skoll. If I was going to do anything to save myself, the time had come.

I gritted my teeth and glared at the stone horrors. I knew what I looked like: about as menacing as a wet cat. The three guards maintained their chiseled, stoic expressions. Maybe they had no other option. I snarled, an ineffable sound encompassing all my emotions. Heat and light leaked from my pores, from my hair, maybe from my mouth and eyes too. Everything went bright and hot.

"We've done this before," Nate said. "You forsook those who would die on your behalf. It seems that, if given the chance, you would do it again. Your friends *will* die, Solina. All of them. If you abandon them again, Helen will certainly kill them. Are you prepared to live with those consequences? I think a woman who gave up her life to find her brother's killer would not be so callous."

A cold laugh resounded through my thoughts. *Stupid man. How has he lived for eons without learning the danger of premature conclusions? He thinks he knows me. He thinks he can predict my decisions.*

"Oh," Nate said, chuckling. "The look on your face—such obstinacy! You think you'll fight your way out of this? You think there's a way you can still win? I hate to tell you..." Nate paused and pointed at the ceiling.

I looked up and recognized star-shaped sprinkler nozzles overhead. "How can I keep my fire in check when you put my life in the hands of a bunch of creatures who have stones for brains and expect them to know how hard they can squeeze before they kill me?"

As if proving my point, my stone captor tightened his hold, restricting my air supply. I let out a pitiful yelp. Maybe, just maybe, with enough time and effort, I could burn away his stony body. But I would probably run out of air and energy long before that happened. *Fight smarter, not harder.* "How are you going to explain it to Helen when one of these things squeezes me to pulp?"

Nate gritted his teeth. A muscle flexed in his jaw as he considered the possibility. Finally, he exhaled an irritable grunt and said, "Give the girl some breathing room."

The cage of my captor's arms relaxed, but I struggled and wheezed and gave Nate a pleading look, silently begging for more of his pity. He ignored me, which was fine. I had gained some precious wiggle room. It would have to be enough.

All my training with the Valkyries and Tre was preparation for a moment like this. Against a more formidable opponent, I would have never stood a chance, but a mindless block of rock was all brute and no cunning. Those odds favored me.

To conserve my energy, I drew my heat and light inside and put it away. The golem probably felt no pain, so classic techniques like smashing insteps and ball busting served no purpose. Regardless of the golem's magic, if the laws of physics governed his movements, then I stood a chance of defeating him. The creature held me from behind, his arms crossed over my chest like a seatbelt, one arm reaching from left hip to my right shoulder, the other wrapped under my arms and around my ribs. And oh, dear Lord, how his grip hurt, but adrenaline was pumping through my bloodstream and numbing the worst of it.

Like an Olympic gymnast preparing for her gold-medal routine, I put the steps of my counter attack—one Tre had taught me—through an imaginary dry run. Then I dropped into a crouch and pulled the golem forward onto the balls of his stone feet. Before he recovered, I reversed my trajectory, pushing hard through my thigh muscles, using my legs like posts. I shoved against the golem, twisting my upper body until I faced him. His grip slackened again, and his arms fell around my waist. *We must look like a couple of middle-schoolers in an awkward slow dance.*

Nate laughed, a hard sound like shattering ice. "She won't go down without a fight. How admirable."

I shoved Nate and the other stone figures out of my thoughts and concentrated on the problem before me. *Get free from this trap, and then you can work on getting free from the next one.*

After pushing my shoulder up and out, I pounded a fist into his jaw, to the regret of my poor knuckles. *Less punching, more squirming.* I braced my forearm against the creature's neck and used my arm as a lever, creating enough space to finally wriggle free. He lunged for me, but I danced aside, refusing that beckoning, stony embrace.

"Sorry, buddy," I said. "I like my men warm-blooded."

"Stop her," Nate ordered in a bored tone. He must have been so confident in the certainty of my capture. *I'll teach you not to underestimate me.* The other stone guards shuffled closer, but their movements were indecisive and slow. Nate's directive not to kill me must have confounded their thought processes, or whatever passed for thought in their stony heads.

I willed the remains of my fire into a burst of flames, and heat left my body in a momentary but massive energy discharge. I turned myself into the equivalent of a temporary, industrial blast furnace. I released all my inhibitions and gave myself over to the fire. Flames engulfed me, burning away not just my clothes, but the rage and the pain and the fear. The effect lasted a fraction of a second and left me empty, bankrupt, and impotent, and I'd probably stay that way until I got a full night of sleep and a few thousand calories inside me. But the fire bomb had done its job.

The sprinklers kicked on as promised, but Nate lay senseless and crumpled on the floor, his face red and blistered, the edges of his suit

71

charred. The closest two golems also showed blackened and well-cooked exteriors, but they remained on their feet, animate and threatening. They held their place, their expressions stoic, and their posture suggested uncertainty. Without their master's directions, they posed no more threat than statuary in a museum. Was Nate dead or just temporarily out of commission? I placed my bet on the latter. *No time to waste, then.*

My small victory was tempered when a sudden and unmistakable howl pierced the air. The wolf had arrived, and probably Helen, too. *Oh good, because this wouldn't be any fun if it were* easy.

I looked behind me, desperate for an escape route. On one side of my cul-de-sac, the industrial containers were wedged in a perpendicular configuration that formed an impenetrable wall. On the other side, the gap between the corners of two containers offered a tiny sliver of space, maybe just enough for an exit. I sucked in everything, making myself as skinny as possible, and thrust my hip and shoulder into the gap. With another desperate shove, I squeaked through, scoring and scraping the skin over my ribs in the process. *A small price. I would have paid more.*

The narrowness of the crack between the containers meant my brawny babysitters would never fit if they tried to follow me. Perhaps, just that once, luck had taken some pity on me after all. The wolf howled again, and his eerie song chilled my blood. *Go, go, go.*

The sprinklers cut off the same moment I reached the warehouse's rear wall. *Dead end.* I stumbled to a stop and held my breath, and for a single heartbeat, the world went utterly silent. But then the wolf barked, and I whirled around. Skoll, the ruddy beast of my nightmares, crouched at the far end of an alley between containers. He spotted me and lunged forward, throwing an extra dash of speed into his step. I ran and turned into another impassable cul-de-sac.

If I climbed, the wolf couldn't follow, right? Operating under that belief, I leaped toward one of the container's front doors. Using the hinges and the locking mechanism for footholds, I worked my way up high enough to scramble onto the box's flat top. I rolled to my feet, stumbled, cursed, and tried again to stand, but fatigue weighed against me. I panted like Darth Vader suffering a two-pack-a-day habit.

From the higher vantage point, I could see the exit, half a room away. Hopping from box to box, I skipped across the warehouse, aiming for escape, but I pulled up short when I saw two guards standing before the warehouse doors.

A thump behind me turned my attention away from the guards. Skoll, naked and in human form, had climbed to the top of a nearby container. He leapt to the box beside him, leaving two containers between us.

I threw up my hands and fell to my knees. "Okay, I surrender."

Skoll stopped and cocked his head like a dog hearing a funny noise.

"I can't believe you fell for that." I dropped to my belly, rolled over the side, caught the edge, and hung there long enough to heave a breath before I dropped to the floor. The instant my feet hit the ground, I took off running again, heading toward the exit.

My lungs burned, my legs screamed, and fear sat on my shoulders like a crazy monkey riding piggyback. *How long can I keep this up?* Not much longer, and the wolf's endurance surely eclipsed my own. I dodged around another container and another as desperate tears burned in my eyes. *Dear God*, I prayed, *don't let it end like this.*

Gunshots rang out, deafening as sound waves rebounded against walls and containers. Not knowing what that meant, I slid to a halt and listened.

"Mundy!" Skyla's voice echoed through the room.

Relief brought hot tears to my eyes.

"I don't know about you, but I've had enough. Whaddaya say we blow this popsicle stand?"

CHAPTER TEN

I RAN TOWARD SKYLA'S VOICE AND rounded the corner of a big blue box. If only it were the TARDIS instead of a mundane shipping crate... The exit loomed before me, and Skyla stood in the doorway, gun in hand, two human guards at her feet, blood pooling around their bodies. I had almost closed the remaining distance when a golem leaped from a nearby crate and landed on the floor between Skyla and me, blocking my way. Skyla didn't hesitate. She leveled her gun and pulled the trigger twice. The stone man's head exploded, providing the opportunity I needed to scoot by.

Skyla threw a hand out, urging me forward. She kept the gun aimed somewhere behind me, and when she fired again, the bullet whizzed past my head close enough to stir my hair.

When I stumbled, Skyla lurched forward, grabbed me, and said, "Let's go, girlfriend."

We staggered through the big doors, turned, and ran down an alley between two buildings.

"The hell was that thing?" Skyla asked. "Looked like a skinny version of Thing from the *Fantastic Four*. And where are your clothes?"

"Tell you later." I huffed as we ran. "Where are you taking us?"

"We've got to get the guys. I found them before I found you." She paused quickly for breath. "Baldur's tied up in mistletoe. Thorin's knocked out on something."

"Wh-what about Val? We split up right before I found you."

"Haven't seen him."

Skyla hugged a sharp turn and wheeled us around the back of a warehouse parallel to the one we had escaped. As soon as I cleared the corner, she leaned around me and fired a few shots. Someone barked

74

a sound of pain, but I didn't turn around to look. *Skyla is so freaking awesome.* I vowed to worship her at an appropriate opportunity.

"Where'd you get the gun?" I leaned over, braced my hands on my knees, and wheezed. "How did you get free?"

"You know I'm part ninja, right? Also I'm a chick, and men so frequently underestimate me. Now, come on." Skyla grabbed my hand and pulled me behind her as she took off again. "We're almost there."

Skyla and I turned another corner and threw our weight against a metal door. She yanked me through the opening and shoved the doors closed behind us.

"Help me," she said, going to a big metal cabinet sitting nearby. "Turn it over against the door."

We heaved, and the big box teetered on one edge. We pushed again, and the cabinet fell over, barring the door. Skyla turned and studied me, taking in my naked, bedraggled appearance. She tugged off her T-shirt, revealing her cascade of colorful tattoos, sports bra, and black leggings.

She threw the shirt at me and said, "Come on. The guys are just down this hallway. That cabinet won't hold anyone out for long."

While I shrugged on her shirt, Skyla led us to another heavy door, halfway down the passage. She pushed the door open, and I followed her into another large storage space. Row after row of plastic-wrapped, pallet-stacked boxes filled the room's interior. Skyla turned to the nearest heap, braced her sneaker against it, and shoved. The bundle shifted and fell against the door, raising a deafening clatter.

"What are you—" I began, but a guard rounded the corner.

Skyla fired her gun, and he fell to the floor. I turned away from the horrible blood spurt. My stomach rolled over, and bile climbed up my throat. Another sentry came fast behind his partner, but Skyla swung the grip of her gun and whacked him in the temple. Stunned, he stumbled forward, and Skyla struck him again. She jabbed her knee into the delicate area between his legs. The guard hunched over, fell to his knees, and moaned.

"Thorin and Baldur are at the front of this room," Skyla said as she disarmed the dazed guard. "I think Thorin's out cold, but Baldur's up. See if you can get them out of here while I deal with this guy."

I sucked a deep breath, pushed down my qualms about blood and violence, and ran for the front of the warehouse, expecting the bite of a bullet to tear through my chest any moment.

Baldur heard me coming and looked up. His blue eyes widened, and his mouth parted. "Solina? What are you doing here?"

"Trying to save your dumb asses." I knelt beside Thorin, who lay on the floor, unconscious and still as death. "How long has he been out?"

"He burns through the drugs quickly, so they keep remedicating him." Baldur sat on the floor, wearing shackles composed of a strange wooden substance woven into thick, ropy braids.

A mistletoe arrow had caused Baldur's original death, eons before. Now, apparently, it acted as kryptonite or an Achilles's heel, weakening him to less than mortal standards. Helen's guards had bound Thorin in more traditional metal handcuffs, which seemed pointless, considering his strength.

Baldur's next statement reiterated my own conclusions. "Those restraints would never hold him otherwise."

"It would be handy if those drugs would burn off again right now."

In sleep, Thorin looked no less menacing, as if somewhere under the surface he was waiting for the opportune moment to strike.

A shot was fired in the rear of the warehouse. Baldur and I jumped and looked over our shoulders. More gunfire. Voices shouted, several more besides Skyla and the other guard. Either our pursuers had found us, or Skyla had found more guards. The crack of gunfire was echoed by a grunt, another shot, and a horrible screech.

I jumped to my feet. "Skyla!" I yelled. "Skyla!"

She didn't answer. I started forward, meaning to go after her, but caught myself and stopped. I shoved her out of my thoughts and returned to the task before me. If Skyla was hurt, I would need Baldur's help getting her out of there. If she was dead... *No. Don't think about it.* I hadn't gone all that way to lose her again so soon.

Once I untied Baldur's bindings and unwrapped the mistletoe twine from his hands and legs, the Allfather stood, but he swayed on his feet. "Let's get you out of here, Solina." His voice was weak and unsteady.

"What about Thorin?" I motioned to the sleeping man at my feet.

"He can take care of himself."

"But he's vulnerable."

Baldur shook his head. "Not for long. We both know he'd want me to protect you first and foremost."

Skyla stumbled around the corner of a nearby crate and sank to one knee. She clutched her shoulder, and blood seeped between her fingers. "Helen's here," she said through gritted teeth. "Nate and the wolf too."

I went to her and grabbed her good shoulder. She sagged against me.

"Are you shot?" I asked. "I mean, I know you are, but are you gonna be okay?"

"Bastard clipped my shoulder." Skyla's pupils were huge, her eyes glassy, and her brown skin had gone frighteningly pale.

Baldur held out a hand toward me and hissed in a low voice. "We've got to get going, Solina."

Before I could reply, a new voice echoed through the room. "Where are they, damn it? Where the *hell* are they?"

Helen Locke. Her voice was unmistakable, and her tone sent ice prickles down my spine. Baldur, Skyla, and I ducked and wedged between a stack of crates. "Could any of you people *be* more incompetent?"

"Skoll says the girl is here," said Nate, who had obviously recovered from my attack. But his voice sounded rough and pained. "Her scent is very fresh."

I pointed at Skyla and hissed at Baldur, trying to keep my voice low. "Take her. Hurry. She's bleeding."

Skyla opened her mouth, presumably to argue, but I shot her a steely look, urging her not to argue. I loved her, and she was the best friend I'd ever had, other than my brother. No matter the cost, I had to choose her life over my own. *One of these days, that's probably going to get me killed.*

Baldur reached for Skyla but paused. He put his hand to his chest in a strange gesture. A shiver rolled across his shoulders, and paleness washed over his face. He shook it off and presented his clenched fist to me, like a child offering some secret, wriggling gift to his friend.

"Do you trust me?" he asked.

As if we have time for doubt. "Yes. I do."

Baldur leaned forward, pressed his fist against my chest, and spoke a strange word. The place where he touched me, over my sternum, burned as though he had struck me with a brand. I gasped and clenched my teeth to keep from crying out. When he moved his hand away, a pattern, pink and raw like a fresh burn, appeared on my skin.

"A rune?" I asked.

It resembled the marks I had seen on Thorin's iron cuffs and on the Valkyries' weapons.

"I don't have the time or energy for better," Baldur said. "This will be enough to make Helen and the others tend to overlook you. They won't be fooled for long, but it's the best I can do."

Baldur's superpowers were his godly mojo and general charm and charisma. I hadn't known he possessed runic powers too. *That could come in handy.*

Baldur squeezed my shoulder and whispered something that sounded like *"dagaz."* Then he pulled Skyla into his arms, and they both disappeared.

A couple of sharp barks exploded across the room, announcing Skoll had returned to wolf form and was on the hunt for me. Could Baldur hear my prayers? *Oh please, Baldur. Please, please hurry.*

The wolf yapped again and sneezed once, twice, a third time.

"Can you find their trail?" Helen asked from somewhere in the back of the room.

The tip-tap of canine claws approached my hiding place behind a stack of pallets. I clamped my lips together and held my breath, as if that would help. Skoll didn't need to hear me when he could simply snuffle me out. I probably smelled like fear and adrenaline and a bunch of other tasty things wolves loved to eat. Had Baldur's rune disguised my smell, too?

"There's something over here," Nate said, much closer to my hiding spot than he'd been moments before. "The girl, the other one—her blood is all over the place."

"She's been wounded," said Helen. "Good."

Snap, crackle, pop, and Baldur was back, somewhere close by, but not in my sight line. Behind me, a wolf howled.

Nate translated. "She's here. Now."

Helen screeched. "Then *find* her."

We played a second game of cat-and-mouse through the pallets, me searching for Baldur while Skoll, Nate, and Helen hunted for me.

Baldur found me first and grabbed my arm, ready to pull me through his magical portal, but Helen came instantaneously after him and latched onto my free arm. I tugged against her, but she had inhuman strength. *I'm like the baby King Solomon threatened to cut in half.*

"Nice try, Allfather," Helen said. She was as immaculate as the last time I'd seen her, in fitted skirt and elegant silk blouse. Malice glinted in her eyes, the ice-blue one *and* the black one. "But your rune work is weak." A triumphant smile spread across her lips as Nate and Skoll arrived—Helen's horrific reinforcements. "The girl is mine."

Baldur tightened his hold, his arms twined around my waist. My joints and muscles strained from the tension. "You've taken everything from me. You won't get her, too."

"I'll rip her in half. Skoll can finish her before she bleeds out."

Helen had demonstrated uncanny strength. I believed her capable of fulfilling her threat.

Baldur let out a war cry and tugged me with a tremendous heave. Helen held on like an overzealous leech. Skoll lunged for me.

In the freeze-frame moment in which I was certain I was about to die, I noticed the most ridiculous details: the color of Skoll's eyes, citrine flecked by peridot; the delicate weave of Helen's ivory blouse; the familiar gold charm, nestled in the cleft of her breasts. Rather than defend myself from the wolf or fight to push Helen away, I lunged for her necklace and wrapped my fingers around the heavy gold charm.

That might have been the move that saved me.

Out of reflex, Helen's grasp relaxed, and she reached for the necklace. My ears popped once, twice, like the pressure shift from a change of altitude. After an instant of dizzying blackness, Baldur lowered me to my feet in a dark, dusty field beyond the compound's fence line.

"This is as far as I can go," Baldur said, panting. "It should be far enough to avoid Helen's immediate detection, but we should get moving."

"Why doesn't she pop through space like you and come after us?"

"She is Jötunn," Baldur said as if that were a sufficient answer. When I gave him a questioning look, he said, "They don't have the runes for it. I only gave that ability to the Aesir who survived Ragnarok."

"If you could always move around like that, why bother with cars and airplanes? We've been wasting a lot of time."

Baldur patted his chest. "I'm the only one strong enough to take on a passenger."

Before I could ask for a better explanation, my ears popped again. A shadow lunged toward me, and someone dragged me off my feet. I fought my captor, certain Helen had managed to follow us despite Baldur's assurances, but I caught a familiar scent of rain and musk and a glint of blond hair in the ambient light. Thorin pinned me in his arms and buried his face in my neck. He said nothing but held me so ferociously tight that my ribs creaked.

"Almighty gods," he said in his rumbling baritone. "Tell me you're all right. Then tell me what the hell you're doing here."

For a moment, I sagged against him, relishing the relief of having most of my team back together—except for Val. In all that had happened, I'd had no time to worry about him. Nothing had given me reason to believe he'd been caught, and I was operating under the assumption he'd made it out. Thinking of Val sobered me. I stiffened and pushed Thorin away. His nearness did funny things to my thought processes.

"I'm fine," I said. "And I totally rescued you, by the way. You're welcome."

Thorin peered into my face and shook his head. "Swear to me you'll never do anything that stupid again."

"I won't swear any such thing. If I want to save you, then I will."

Skyla lay on the ground, nearly unconscious. Baldur squatted beside her, pressing his hands against her wound. A faint glow radiated from his fingers, and he was muttering a steady litany under his breath, but his eyes followed my every move.

I flung my hand around, gesturing at the others. "All of you," I clarified. "I can't do this on my own. If I ran away and left you all, how long do you think I would last? It's take a risk and maybe die now, or run and certainly die later." I inhaled and let my breath out in a gust. "It was a good choice, Thorin. Don't be a jerk about it, okay? I'm sorry for the cheap shot, but it's not like you've been king of wise decision-making lately. I told you going after Nina on that crappy lead was a trap."

Baldur interrupted my rant. "And it's all my fault. My shortsightedness and impulsivity put us all in danger. It's been so long since I've had to think about the consequences of my actions that I've lost my good

80

judgment." He raised a bloody hand toward Thorin. "I release you from your vows, cousin. You are no longer obligated to risk yourself or anyone else to uphold your loyalty to me."

"But—" Thorin said.

Baldur interrupted. "No buts. You must do what is best for us all. I am afraid I can no longer be trusted."

"I have none of your knowledge or wisdom."

"None of you have shown a lot of wisdom," I said, sticking my nose in the middle of ancient business, "but I think I can help you with your power, at least."

Thorin's brow wrinkled. "What do you mean?"

"Open your hand."

The look that shot across Thorin's face indicated he wanted to balk at my order, but he swallowed his retort and did as I said. I covered his hand with mine and dropped what I had been holding with a fierce grip all that time. The warm gold shimmered to life in his palm when I pulled away. Thorin went still as golden light flickered like a firefly on his face. He glanced up at me, eyes wide, lips parted as if uttering a silent cry of surprise. The intensity of his attention pressed against me, and I fidgeted, resisting the urge to flee. Or kiss him. Anything to wipe the unsettling awe and adoration from his face.

"Does it take any magic words?" I asked.

"Magic words?" Thorin asked, his voice dry and gruff, his eyes never leaving mine.

"*Presto chango*, or something like that."

"No." Thorin shook his head. Then he closed his palm over the gold and twisted his wrist. In a shift too fast to comprehend, the charm disappeared, and instead he clutched a hammer, Mjölnir, in all its majesty. The chain transformed into a leather lanyard, looped around his forearm, drawing attention to the iron cuff he wore. Baldur had fashioned a set of bracelets from Thor's legendary gauntlets, and Thorin wore them without fail, as if he'd always believed the hammer would return to him some day. And it had. The significance of that moment gave me chills.

"How did you—" he started.

I put my finger to his lips, stopping him midsentence. "Get us away from this place. Get Skyla some medical attention, and get me something to eat. Let me sleep at least twelve hours, and I swear I'll tell you the whole story."

Beneath my finger, Thorin's lips spread into a genuine smile so full of sincere happiness, I almost fainted at the beauty of it—the dazzle in his eyes, the way his face brightened, the shadow of a dimple in his right cheek. *Has that always been there?* He was a god in all his wonder at that moment, and if my knees quaked and wanted to give way, much blame could be placed on exhaustion and hunger but also on pure amazement.

CHAPTER ELEVEN

O UR RAGTAG GROUP HIKED ACROSS the field until we reached the shoulder of the highway. Baldur had stopped Skyla's bleeding, but she was weak and listless, so he carried her. I recognized she needed the help, but exhaustion robbed me of the last of my gallantry. I wanted a little coddling, too. Thorin carried bucketloads of compassion for Baldur—even to his own detriment—but when I jeopardized myself to rescue them, I apparently got nothing in return.

"Thank you," Thorin said, pulling me away from Baldur and Skyla. "I wish you wouldn't have taken the risk—I wish you hadn't *had* to—but thank you."

"Are you a mind reader, too?" I asked.

Thorin chuckled. "Hardly. You wear your thoughts on your face." He flipped his hand, and Mjölnir shrank into its golden-charm form. He took my shoulders, spun me around, pushed aside my hair, and latched the chain around my neck. "Do me a favor? Keep Mjölnir for now. Baldur knows we have it, but say nothing to anyone else, not even Skyla."

I turned around to face him and tucked the necklace under the collar of my T-shirt. "Why? Why don't you keep it, and why don't you want the others to know?"

"I want you to carry it—take it as a symbol of my trust, and also because if you wear it, it's less obvious what it is. No one expects you to have it, and it's like hiding it in plain sight. Let it serve as a reminder that I'll never leave you unprotected."

While jewelry was a common token of vows and promises, nothing was common or token about Thorin giving me Mjölnir. After all that had happened in the hours since reconnecting with him in Sacramento,

I was too exhausted and emotionally raw to absorb the full immensity of his gesture. Maybe later, after food, shower, and sleep, I'd be equipped for dealing with how I felt about it.

Thorin ducked his head. "It goes against my nature to be indebted, Sunshine. Tell me how I can repay you for what you've done."

"You already know what I want."

Thorin grinned. "A cheeseburger?"

"That would be a good start, but bring me Skoll's head on a platter, and everything I've gone through will have been worth it."

Thorin took my hand. He brushed his lips over my knuckles and rested our entwined hands over his heart. "For you, I swear it will be done."

A crackling, tingling tendril of heat crawled up my arm, starting from the place where Thorin's lips had touched me. His unexpected intimacy unsettled me, like a little earthquake straining barriers I had built to protect my vulnerabilities. I wasn't ready to dismantle my walls yet, so I yanked my hand free, and my reaction seemed to startle him. Thorin drew himself up straight, settled back on his heels, and put on a guarded expression.

"Quit being so damned charming and reasonable," I grumbled. "It just gets me confused."

Thorin threw his head back and laughed, which sounded like thunder and rain, a beautiful summer storm. Another tremor shivered through me, another small crack splintering my defenses. If he kept that up, being amiable and likeable, my heart was going to be in so much trouble.

I turned away from Thorin, intending to step toward the road, but my bare foot caught something sharp and jagged, and I stumbled. Before I could cry out or try to catch myself, Thorin caught me and held me steady.

"I'm almost afraid to ask," he said, "but where are your shoes? And the rest of your clothes?"

Thorin had saved my modesty too many times to count, and he had firsthand knowledge of the circumstances that cost me my clothes.

"Don't tell me I'm making you blush," I said.

Thorin chuckled and shook his head. "I want the full story from you, Sunshine. But later. When the timing is better for it."

Headlights appeared on the road behind Thorin. I gasped, certain Helen's men had found us.

Thorin tightened his grip on me when I moved to run. "I think this is our ride."

The vague shape of a Yukon materialized around the headlights. "No way," I said.

"Yes way," Baldur said.

The vehicle veered onto the shoulder and braked to a stop beside us. The passenger window lowered, and Val's grinning face greeted us. "Anyone going my way?"

Skyla raised her head from Baldur's shoulder. Her voice came out thin and scratchy. "For the first time in my life, Wotan, I'm actually happy to see you."

"You're not Nina, but I'm happy to see you too, Ramirez."

Baldur slid Skyla into the rear seat, and Thorin settled me in beside her before taking a seat next to me. Baldur joined Val in the front.

"Where to?" Val asked, his hand resting on the gearshift.

Thorin inclined his head toward me. "What is it, Sunshine? Food or sleep?"

"What about Skyla?" I asked. "We need to take her to a hospital."

"No hospitals," Val said. "Everyone knows gunshot wounds are reported to the police. We don't need the attention."

"And what kind of attention do you think it would draw if she died?" That sounded callous, but I would say anything if it saved my friend. "I don't care about police reports, Val. You're welcome to drop us off at the hospital and go if you prefer."

"She is not going to die," Baldur said. "I have experience in treating battle wounds as well as some healing skills. Do not worry for her, Solina. I will make certain she receives good care."

The darkness shaded Baldur's face, hiding his expression, but his godly essence swelled to fill the SUV's interior. When he worked his mojo, my willpower flickered like a flame before a drafty window. The power within me, my own *otherness*, withstood his influence, but mundane humans probably caved under his persuasion.

"Fine," I said at last. "No hospitals, but if anything happens to her, I'll hold you all responsible."

Val snorted, dismissing my threat. Baldur at least had the decency to nod solemnly.

"So, back to Thorin's question," Baldur said. "Food, bed, or bath?"

"Can't I have them all at the same time?" I asked. The Taser assault, the dousing from the fire extinguisher and sprinklers, and our retreat into a dusty field had left me resembling something pried from the bottom of a shoe. "I want to eat a four-course meal while I sit in a bathtub full of the hottest water I can stand until I pass out."

Val turned to look at me and cracked a sympathetic grin. "I think your food will get soggy, and sleeping in a bathtub greatly increases your chances of drowning."

"I don't care."

"Laughlin's close," Baldur said. "There will be plenty of hotels there. If these fearless ladies are still awake after we find a room, I'll get them something to eat even if I have to hunt it down and cook it myself."

"Val, how did you know where to find us?" I asked.

Val tapped a finger to his temple. "We have our ways."

"GPS," Skyla piped up from the back seat. "They've all got trackers on them. I'd bet my life on it."

"You could call it GPS if you like," Baldur said.

I suspected it had something to do with runes. Runes tended to explain everything magical concerning the Aesir.

"Go to Laughlin," Baldur said. "Let's find these women a hot tub and some room service."

Baldur put in a call on the way and reserved a suite. The city of Laughlin, he explained, was a miniature Las Vegas. When we finally stumbled into our rooms, we found a food-service cart awaiting us, and the smells wafting from it made my stomach growl.

"It's four o'clock in the morning," I said. "What hotel offers room service at this hour?"

"It's a casino," Val said. "The kitchens are open twenty-four hours a day. Gamblers have to have something to keep up their energy."

Skyla was out cold. Baldur set her on the living-room couch, draped a blanket over her, and tended to her shoulder. Concern showed in the lines around his eyes and in the firm set of his mouth, but he poked and prodded with the clinical, detached touches of a surgeon examining a patient.

When she groaned once, Baldur clucked his tongue. "The worst will be over shortly. Until then, I'm afraid you'll just have to grit your teeth and bear it."

With Skyla's care and healing entrusted to Baldur, I allowed myself a deep breath—the cleansing kind that gathered the worst of my anxiety and swept it out in a voiding exhalation. I glanced at the empty bed awaiting me in the nearest bedroom. Then my gaze slid to the piles of cold cuts and cheese on the room-service cart. Then I studied the luxurious tub peeking from the doorway of the massive bathroom down the hall.

"Don't know where to start?" Val asked, lifting the covers off the plates of food to sniff underneath.

One plate offered strawberries and something that looked like chocolate cake if chocolate cake were made of sin. I snatched the dessert and cold cuts from the cart and scurried to the bathroom.

"Need me to wash your back?" he asked.

I answered by slamming the bathroom door shut. The compulsion to flirt must have been coded in Val's DNA. Too bad the impulse to keep his mouth shut wasn't. During our past few hours together, my animosity for Val had faded, but my fonder feelings for him had not returned. *Can't we just be friends, free from awkward expectations?*

While waiting for the tub to fill, I devoured the cake, shoveling chocolate sponge and fudge cream into my mouth barehanded. After licking the plate clean, I started on the cold cuts. Once the tub had filled, I turned off the water, grabbed the strawberries, and eased into the water. If only some hunky dudes had stood over me, fanning me with palm fronds, I might have called it paradise. *Maybe I can talk Thorin into accepting the job.*

I relaxed against a water jet that pounded against the muscles knotted between my shoulders. The hot water soaked away my aches and pains. Between my breasts hung Mjölnir on its gold chain, heavy and comforting, and I tried not to think too hard about the impossibility of my surrogate ownership of one of the oldest and most powerful weapons of all myths and legends. *Maybe next, Zeus will ask me to hold his lightning bolts for him.*

I must have just dozed off when someone knocked on the door.

"Sunshine. Are you sleeping in the bathroom tonight?" Thorin's voice jolted me awake.

My heart stuttered into a heavy pitter-patter. "N-no," I said. "I'll be out in a sec."

Using my toes like a monkey, I popped the drain open. Fatigue and overexposure to the hot water had rubberized the bones in my legs. I stumbled out of the tub and leaned against the bathroom counter as I tucked a massive bath towel around my chest. My hands trembled. Something burned in the back of my throat, and my eyes watered.

I had put my feelings aside so I could function long enough to survive. The energy required to form the fire blast that defeated Nate had drained me, destabilized my self-control, and laid bare my weaknesses. But I was finally safe, warm, and unharmed. My fire was diminished but not gone—it glowed like the coals of a banked fire inside me. Everyone had escaped Helen's snare, and I had reunited with Skyla. She was at my side again, alive and on her way to recovery. That realization was my undoing. All my earlier fear, pain, and exhaustion tumbled loose in a tidal wave. My legs gave out, and I plopped to the floor and burst into tears.

"Solina?" Thorin so rarely used my name that hearing him say it was sobering. "Are you sure you're okay?"

I sniffed and wiped my face. A dismissal formed on my tongue, but I swallowed the urge to send Thorin away. He wanted to help. *Why not let him? Why not trust him just this little bit?* We could be... *friends.*

I cleared my throat and said, "I could use some help."

The door cracked open, and Thorin peeked in, worry showing in his expression. He almost never revealed his softer emotions—outrage, yes, anger aplenty, but not tenderness.

"My legs are rebelling against the rest of my body," I said and chuckled a hiccuppy laugh.

Thorin eased into the bathroom, knelt, and gathered me in his arms. My tears threatened to return, but I fought them. I could admit needing his help, but I refused to blubber. He pushed up from the floor, rising to his full height, and carried me to my room.

"You press yourself too hard," Thorin said, though his censure lacked its usual harshness. "You have many uncanny strengths, but you are not omnipotent."

"If I gave up when I was tired, I'd be dead."

Thorin made a noise in his throat that might have been agreement. "Still, you should take better care of yourself."

Thorin settled me onto a soft, flat surface—a bed, the most wonderful bed ever made.

I yawned and stretched. "I plan to, starting right now."

Thorin stroked the gold chain around my neck, running his fingers down its length but stopping where it disappeared beneath my towel. My emotions felt like exposed nerve endings, and Thorin's compassion was a soothing balm. I could have asked him to stay. Given another minute, I probably would have.

"Can you get me something dry to put on?" I asked instead—anything to get him away, to put some space between us. *Don't let vulnerability confuse you*, I told myself. *The regret isn't worth it.*

Thorin pulled away and rose to his feet. "What do you want?"

"T-shirt." I rolled onto my side, drawing my knees up to my chest.

Thorin dug through my tote bags and pulled out an old black T-shirt bearing a faded yellow Appalachian State logo. It had belonged to Mani once, but I had stolen it from his closet at home and managed to hang onto it despite everything. "Will this do?" he asked.

I motioned for him to toss it over. Thorin left me alone to change, turning out the light before he pulled the door closed. I yanked the towel off, threw it into a corner, and shrugged the soft cotton T-shirt over my head. I passed out before my head hit the pillows.

<hr />

A vision of flames danced through my head, burning through rows and rows of apple trees. The heat intensified, and flames devoured the oxygen, making breathing difficult. Fire converged on the edge of the orchard and rose up in a wall before me, towering over my head. The leaves and branches closest to the flames curled into black, smoky embers. Wood smoke and the sickly scent of burning apples filled the air.

I stepped closer to the blaze—maybe I wanted to tame it—but it was too hot, even for me. The sour odor of burnt hair, *my* burnt hair, drifted in the air. Compelled by a nameless force, I tracked the inferno's path, intent on locating the source.

"Fight fire with fire, they say." A woman's distant voice carried above the roar of the blaze. "If only they knew how true that was."

"Who's there?" I asked. "How are you doing this?"

The woman laughed but did not answer.

I walked and walked, traveling hundreds of dream miles until, finally, the row of flames thinned and shortened. At last, they narrowed to a fine point, a torch, vomiting a conflagration across the whole of my dream world. The torch bearer noted my approach and recoiled as if preparing to run away.

"Wait." I reached toward her. "Who are you? Why are you doing this?"

She swung the weapon and revealed it was no mere stick coated in pitch. She grasped a sword constructed entirely from flames. The shadowed figure motioned for me to approach. Light flickered off the high places of her face, but darkness kept her features vague, indistinguishable. Despite the fire's threat, I stepped closer—an unknown impulse controlled me. The swordswoman reared back, holding her weapon high, ready to strike. Fear lurched up my throat and tasted of bile, but I continued my approach, helpless and intent.

"What are you going to do?" I asked.

The swordswoman laughed again. She lunged, and her blade sliced through me.

I woke screaming loudly enough to shred my throat. Before I took in a breath to scream again, my door burst open, filling the doorway with light and the concerned faces of Val, Thorin, and Baldur. Val rushed to my side and turned on my bedside lamp. He studied my face, probably looking for a clue about what had happened.

"What was it?" Val asked, taking my hand in his. "Another dream? What did you see?"

"Fire," I said stupidly. Part of me had remained in the dream, and the reality of my hotel room was slow to return.

"What fire? Your fire?"

I shook my head. "No."

"Is the hotel on fire?"

"No. Back off and let me think."

Val scowled but did as I asked, dropping his death grip on my hand. I drew in a deep breath and surveyed my visitors. Baldur stood in the doorway, frowning, deep lines etching his brow. Thorin had stopped at the foot of my bed and wore his usual stoic expression.

"It was a sword of fire, and she said she was fighting fire with fire."

Everyone spoke at once, their excited questions jumbling into confusion.

I stuck my fingers between my lips and blew a sharp whistle. "Jeez, y'all, it's like an Abbot and Costello routine in here. Next thing, somebody's going to ask, 'Who's on first?' I'll start from the beginning. It won't make a lick of sense, but I'll tell you what I saw, and don't interrupt, or I'll kick you all out and go back to sleep."

The three men all managed to look properly chastised, even Thorin. I told them of the dream, beginning to end.

Then I inhaled another deep breath, exhaled, and let my shoulders sag. "Anyone have any ideas?"

Baldur, Val, and Thorin looked at each other, silently deciding who should tell me the bad news. Thorin scraped his fingers through his hair and stepped closer to my bed. "Surtalogi," he said.

"Gesundheit," I said, deadpan.

Thorin turned his eyes heavenward as if praying for patience. "Surtalogi is the name for the sword that belonged to Surtr, the fire giant who brought the final destruction on the world at the end of Ragnarok. It was his sword of fire that burned out the world."

"How did that work, exactly? You all keep saying the world burned, but how did you survive it?"

"Asgard was not the only plane of existence," Baldur said. "There was Niflheim, where Hela rules the spirits of the dead. It was untouched. And there was Gimle, a heaven of sorts. That's where most of the surviving Aesir went."

"You had a heaven to live in, but you gave it up for earth because…?"

Val snorted. "There's only so many millennia I could bear to be in the presence of the same handful of Aesir. And humans were starting to get interesting."

A pang of foreboding shivered through me. "So why am I dreaming about the sword now?"

Baldur moved away from the doorway and stepped closer. "No one saw the sword again after Ragnarok," he said. "But many have searched for it."

"Maybe Helen found it and is bringing it into play," Baldur said.

"If she has Surtr's sword, then the battle is won," Val said.

"Solina's dreams are often premonitions of what is to come. She prevented my death at the Aerie." Thorin deliberately avoided meeting my eyes, probably because that would have been too much like admitting my deceit had benefitted him after all. "*If* her dream was about Surtalogi, then it may be possible for us to find it first."

"But we probably don't have much time," I said. "My foresight tends to be rather… *shortsighted*."

"It's first on our list," Val said, rising to his feet. "We'll start hunting for it right now."

"No," Thorin said. "The wolves come first. Helen won't dare use the sword until Solina is dead. She's reenacting the old events in the same order as before. Using the sword at this point goes against the rules."

Val scoffed. "Helen plays by rules? Since when?"

"She wants a predictable result. She's a cold, calculating bitch."

A growl rumbled in Baldur's throat. "I concur with Thorin's assessment."

"You're a prejudiced old fool," Val said.

Thorin lunged, but Baldur shot out an arm and held him back. From my seat in the bed, I watched the three ageless beings spit and snarl at each other like wet cats until I could take it no more. I rolled my eyes, slid under the blankets, and let out a noisy sigh.

Thorin heard it. "Save this for later," he said. "Let her sleep—she's been through hell enough for one day. The least we can do is give her a chance to recover."

Val huffed. "She wouldn't be in this condition if you hadn't gotten caught up in Helen's obvious trap."

"Enough!" I yelled from underneath the covers. "Walking into that trap got us Skyla back. That alone was worth the risk. So, let this argument go, okay? Let's all go back to bed or whatever it is you guys do while the rest of us sleep."

When no one said anything in reply, I peeked over the blankets and glared at them. Thorin responded first. He squared his shoulders, spun on his heel, and strode from the room. Baldur followed, offering an apologetic smile on his way out.

Val turned and gave me a pleading look. "That sword is no joke. If you know where it is, you have to tell us."

"I don't know where it is, Val." I pointed toward the open doorway. "Let me go back to sleep—*please*."

A twinge of something piteous passed over his face. He nodded and left my room, closing my door behind him. I fell back on the pillows. The woman in my dreams wasn't Helen Locke, I was sure, but further speculation was impractical and a waste of energy. I curled into a ball and pulled the covers under my chin, and the rest of the night passed, devoid of any more interruptions from the Nordic three stooges.

After all that, maybe I should have had trouble going back to sleep. But I didn't.

CHAPTER TWELVE

"I KNOW YOU CAN HEAR ME." Skyla batted my head with a pillow. "Quit playing opossum."

"Stop it," I whined.

"You've been shifting around for the past twenty minutes. Go on and get up already."

"Is there a major crisis requiring my immediate attention?" I asked, refusing to open my eyes.

"No."

"Is anyone dead or dying?"

"Not anymore."

Skyla might have been making an offhand comment, but it reminded me of her dire situation the night before. I sat up, rubbed my eyes, and focused on her face, which showed more color and energy than it had last I'd seen her.

"You look better," I said.

Skyla bobbed her head. "I am better. The hocus-pocus Baldur worked on me was powerful stuff." She poked her shoulder, demonstrating her lack of injury. "Like it never happened."

"Good. I'm delighted you're back to full ninja strength. Now let me sleep."

Skyla muttered something not nice about my character and shifted around on my bed. A whiff of coffee tickled my nose, and I forced an eye open.

"Ah." She waved a coffee mug before me. "Val said that might do the trick."

I reached for the cup. "Gimme gimme."

"Nuh-uh-uuuh," she sang. "This is mine. You have to get out of bed and get your own. You've been asleep for over half a day. Enough beauty rest. I'm tired of keeping the guys company."

Someone cleared his throat in the doorway. I looked around Skyla to find Val holding two huge mugs.

"One of these is for you, if you'll come out and get it," he said.

"Sure thing… if I could get a little privacy first?"

Val ducked out of my room, and Skyla followed him. I shut the door and shuffled through the mess of clothes in my bags. I settled on a pair of leggings that looked relatively clean and a long knit shirt showing only a few wrinkles. Besides a case of major bedhead, I didn't mind what the dresser mirror reflected. For the first time in days, I looked rested, less pasty and pale, and more like my old self.

"Good morning, beautiful," Val said when I stepped out of my room.

He swiped a mug from the counter and presented it to me. He was showered and still damp around the edges. His T-shirt clung to his skin, and he smelled like bath soap. Beautiful as always but easy to resist, Val was a Da Vinci sculpture left in the elements to tarnish. Thorin, also looking fresh as a daisy, sat on the living-room sofa, staring intently at his phone.

"Um, thanks." I took the coffee cup from Val. "Why all the sweet talk?"

Val slipped an arm around my hips and held me in a loose embrace. "I'm just happy to see you alive and well. I take it you had a rather close call."

"Skyla's the one who got shot."

"But Skyla isn't the one who almost got eaten by Skoll."

"A little birdie's been clacking its beak."

"A big birdie," Baldur said, coming from the bathroom freshly shaved, his hair damp from a shower. "It was such a miraculous story—I couldn't hold back from singing your praises."

I ducked away from Val's hold and said, "I hope you sang Skyla's, too. Without her, we would have all been lost."

"Of course," Baldur agreed. "But it was your persistence that saved the day. And we still don't have the entire story. Skyla told me that when she found you, you already had your own escape quite under control."

"Not under control." My stomach swirled as I remembered just how close I had come to being a Skoll snack. "Not at all. I didn't tell you all the worst of it."

I summarized what had happened after Val and I separated at the warehouses. I told them about finding Skyla and about Nate splitting us up. Then told them about the improbable and incredible existence of Helen's stone warriors and my nearly fatal hide-and-go-seek game through the containers housing them. As they listened, my audience's faces showed varying expressions of amazement, disbelief, and anger.

Val had the decency to stare at his toes when I looked his way at the end of my story. If the decision had been left up to him, we would have run away, and the others would be badly suffering... or worse.

"What is she planning to do with an army of rock robots?" asked Skyla.

Baldur, Val, and Thorin looked at each other and shook their heads.

"We can only make assumptions," Baldur said. "But we don't know her plans for sure. We can guess, however, that those stone soldiers aren't merely robots as you say. Most likely, they are vessels for her undead hordes."

"Undead hordes?" Skyla asked. When Baldur opened his mouth to answer, she held up a hand. "No. Don't tell me. We've got gods, wolves, and swords, and that's all I can deal with right now."

"Baldur," I said, "you said Helen's reenacting events in the same order as before. Where do the golems come in?"

"At the end." He smiled sadly. "After Hati and Skoll swallowed the sun and the moon, there was a great war between good and evil—Aesir versus the agents of Chaos. Helen brought her undead army to fight on her behalf."

"This was when Odin and Thor were killed, right?" I asked.

Baldur swallowed and nodded.

"So the agents of Chaos won."

"That time. They won that time because it was how it was meant to be. This time..." Baldur shook his head and looked away.

"If it's true that she's doing things the same way as in the past, then that is her weakness. The thing we have to exploit."

"In what way?" Skyla asked. She sat on a bar stool, her legs tucked up underneath her, wearing a man's undershirt and large blue-striped boxers. *Baldur's?* A white bandage covered her gunshot wound, and its location suggested the bullet had done more than graze her.

"Maybe we can predict what she's going to do next and stop it," I said. "We were really, really lucky last night. Stupid lucky. Helen underestimated us." When Thorin flinched, I remembered the tranquilizers they used on him and the poisonous mistletoe for Baldur. "Well, she underestimated Skyla and me, anyway. Next time, she'll be more careful, more prepared."

"There won't be a next time," Thorin said. "We're done chasing shadows. I agree with Solina."

Wait, am I hearing things? Thorin just admitted to a room full of people that he agreed with me? I swallowed another sip of coffee—caffeine withdrawal might have been making me hallucinate.

Thorin stood and crossed the room to stand at Baldur's side. "I'm sorry, but Nina is the least of our worries. Helen uses her to distract us, but we have to let her go for now. We have to reprioritize, and first on the list is removing the threat of Skoll. With the certainty of Solina's life restored, we can focus on other goals."

Baldur looked stricken by Thorin's pronouncement. He dropped his shoulders but bobbed his head. "You're right. I'm afraid I've been compromised as an effective leader. I default to your judgment in these matters from now on."

"Wait a minute." Val waved his hand as if clearing the room of a disagreeable odor. "It doesn't work like that. Baldur, you were tasked by Odin, the Oracle, and by fate itself to take the role of the new Allfather. That's not something you can give away on a whim."

"I'm not giving it away," Baldur said. "I'm delegating. Throughout this ordeal, Magni has remained objective and detached from his emotions, an important skill for a leader in war, and make no mistake, Vali Odinson, this *is* war."

"Detached from his emotions?" Val said. "If that were true, then we would have never come on this wild-goose chase in the first place. Thorin is loyal to you to a fault. Why should your authority default to him? Are you saying I'm compromised? That I cannot do what needs to be done?"

"You know I am Odin's grandson by his firstborn," Thorin said, "if you want to compare family lineage. And yes, Val, you have proven repeatedly how you frequently think with your"—Thorin's eyes swiped over Val's figure—"libido. You are capricious, and your loyalty is questionable."

"Just because I'm not a blind follower doesn't mean I can't—"

"Boys!" I said, playing referee again. "Can we do this King of the Jungle fight later? Let's work on devising a cohesive plan. Let's end this thing while I'm still young enough to have a normal life."

"A normal life?" Skyla said. "You think you can go back to some mundane existence after all this?"

"White picket fences, two-point-five kids, and the American dream?" Val asked and took my hand. He rubbed a thumb over my knuckles and squeezed.

I shrugged one shoulder. "Sure, why not?"

"Your attachment to your humanity is a liability," Thorin said. His eyes narrowed at my hand clasped in Val's.

I pulled away and scowled at Val while Thorin continued.

"Helen will use it against you. As Baldur said, this is war, and there is no room for sentimentality." Thorin raised his chin, peered down his nose at me, and held himself rigid like a military commander. All the softness he'd shown me the night before receded.

Baldur was entrusting his authority to Thorin, who had Mjölnir to back it up. Where did I fit into that hierarchy?

I met Thorin's cold stare with my own bold gaze. I turned up my coffee cup, drained it dry, and set the mug on the counter without even a clink to give away my irritation. "It's business as usual, isn't it? You, Thorin, overbearing tightwad." I ignored the choking noise Val made. "Me, Miss Mundy, messy obligation. Just don't forget I'm not as helpless as I used to be, and you made me a promise."

Thorin nodded. "Skoll's head on a silver platter. I haven't forgotten."

"Good." I went to the kitchenette for a coffee refill, turning my back on Val and Thorin before I said or did something regrettable.

Skyla came scooting after me as the low rumble of male conversation filled the room. "He didn't mean it as harsh as it sounded."

"He's right, though," I said. "As much as I hate admitting it. My humanity *is* a liability, as well as my sentimentality. Regardless of our differences, I do have a great deal of sentimentality for my parents. Helen could easily use that against me. I've got to do something more proactive to protect them. I just don't know what."

Skyla tapped a finger against her bottom lip and furrowed her brow. "Maybe you could tell them the truth, or..." She inhaled a sudden sharp breath, and her face brightened. "Baldur."

"What about him?"

"This network of his—why can't he use it to watch out for your parents? They have unlimited resources, Solina. Ask Baldur to put guards on your parents or something like that."

"You think that would work? You think he would go for it?"

Skyla raised a shoulder and dropped it. "All you can do is ask."

Taking her advice, I pulled Baldur aside and pleaded my case—my parents' case, to be precise.

Baldur flushed and dropped his gaze. He worried his thumbnail as if picking a rough cuticle. "It shames me that you had to ask. I should have thought to do such a thing myself." He raised his blue eyes and peered at me through cinnamon lashes. "Forgive me, Solina. And of course. I'll make the call now and have someone stationed at your parents' house within the hour."

"Discreetly, though, okay?"

He nodded. "Of course. The less attention we attract, mortal or supernatural, the better."

I reached around his massive shoulders and squeezed him in a tight hug. "Thank you, thank you, thank you."

Baldur chuckled and patted my back. "You don't have to thank me. As I said, I should have thought of this myself. Thorin would say it's a smart tactical move that benefits us all."

I harrumphed and pulled away. "Thorin says a lot of things. Doesn't mean he's always right. But in this case, I won't argue."

Baldur brushed his knuckles over my chin, a fatherly rebuff. "Thorin has always been a singular sort. We haven't been required to access our humanity in a long time, and it's like shrugging on a dusty, stiff old cloak. But the longer we wear it, the more comfortable and natural it feels. Perhaps Thorin's humanity needs a little more time to break in, but it will. Just be patient with him."

"Hmm. If you say so."

Baldur's grin widened, and he winked. "Trust me."

<hr />

Later in the evening, Skyla came into my room, plopped on the bed beside me, and tugged at a few strands of my hair, separating it into thirds as if she meant to braid it. I had hidden away from the guys, pretending to watch a pay-per-view movie when, really, I was spending that time replaying the contrasting scenes of the gentle man from last night against the harsh but familiar Thorin who had basically told me again how my life meant nothing beyond the guarantee of his own survival. He had gotten into my head—maybe into my heart a little, too—and I hadn't quite figured out how to get him out.

"What is it?" I turned my attention to Skyla.

Skyla reached the end of the thin plait she had woven into my hair and started another row. "I wanted to talk to you."

"'Bout what?"

"The Valkyries. They would be an amazing weapon to have on our side. We know Helen has infiltrated at least some of them. I want to find out how far the corruption goes."

"And then what?"

Skyla grinned and sliced a hand through the air. "Then I'm going to cut it out. Get them back on our side—loyal and dedicated."

I sat up and folded my legs beneath me. "How are you going to do that?"

"I'm going back to the Aerie."

I grabbed her arm. "You can't leave me. I just got you back."

"I have to, girlfriend." Skyla pried my death grip from her arm. "I can't let Helen corrupt our best allies."

"You can't leave me alone with them."

Skyla gave me a knowing look. "You mean you don't want me to leave you alone with *him*, with Thorin."

"Him too."

Skyla took my hands and held them in hers. Her big, earnest eyes were pleading with me. "This is my purpose, Solina. Save the Valkyries from the poison within. It's my part to play in this. Once they're whole again, the Valkyries can assume their rightful place at the side of the Aesir. Helen will never be able to defeat you."

"Why does it have to be your responsibility?"

"Because even though I don't have the proof, I know I'm one of them. It's me who has to do this. An outsider. An objective third party."

"And why should they believe you?"

Skyla shook her head. "They shouldn't. That's why I have to go and convince them."

I pulled her into a tight hug and tried not to cry. "Other than Mani, you're the best friend I've ever had. I don't know what I'm going to do without you."

"Trust Thorin."

I pulled away and wrinkled my nose. "He's proven he's as fallible as the rest of us."

"Loyalty is not a fault, Solina. You were willing to take the same risks for me and for Mani. If you wanted to stay safe, you wouldn't be here right now. And if Thorin didn't respect you, he'd have already locked you away somewhere."

"I'm not as scared when you're around," I said. "I can't talk to them like I talk to you."

Skyla dipped her head and showed uncharacteristic humility. "It's not forever, babe. I'll be back, hopefully with a battalion of Odin's finest battle divas."

"And you've got to leave today?"

Skyla looked at the clock on the bedside table. "I've got to leave *now*. I'm catching a flight out in a couple hours. But don't worry. I won't leave you completely empty-handed. There's something else I need to tell you."

"What?"

Skyla grinned and waggled an eyebrow. "I think I know where Helen is keeping the wolf."

CHAPTER THIRTEEN

AFTER SKYLA BORROWED A SET of clothes from me and got dressed, I bit my lip and fought the urge to beg her to stay. "Be safe," I said. "And keep in touch."

She hugged me. "I promise."

Thorin was waiting for us outside my room when Skyla and I opened the door. "What's going on?" he asked. "What have you two been scheming?"

Skyla cut her eyes to me and bit back a smile. "He acts like he knows us or something."

Thorin frowned at me. "What are you up to, Sunshine?"

"You don't have to look at me that way. I was going to tell you."

"Sure you were."

"No, really. I'm going to need your help."

Thorin's head tilted, his eyebrow arched. He was interested. "Oh, yeah?"

"Skyla's time with Helen might have been useful after all. She's got some leads on where Skoll hides out when he's not chasing after me." I turned to Skyla and gestured to Thorin. "Tell him."

"Hati and Skoll were wolves, first and foremost." Skyla looked at Thorin for confirmation. When he nodded, she continued. "Their human exterior is more mask than man. It goes against their nature to live in big cities around lots of people. Hati couldn't hold down a day job because he didn't do well with socially appropriate human behavior. Only Loki and Helen have managed to control them. Otherwise, they're a public nuisance and a danger to Helen's inconspicuousness.

"So, Helen makes Skoll go into hiding when she doesn't need him because it keeps him out of trouble, but she keeps him close enough to call back at her whim."

"While I agree with all you're saying," Thorin said, "it's still a lot of speculation. If we are going to hunt Skoll, we need something more solid than that."

Skyla nodded. "I overheard one of the guards talking about Helen last night, before Solina came and rescued us all." She flashed me a smile, at which Thorin grimaced but said nothing. "One guy said he'd seen a lone wolf hanging around outside the warehouses. Then they argued about whether it was really just a coyote or not. The one guy was pretty damned insistent it was a wolf, though."

Thorin rearranged his posture, standing taller and surer. "Presuming that the guard did see a wolf, and not a coyote, and presuming that wolf was Skoll, how do we know he's still there? What if Helen's moved him to another location after our escape?"

I put a hand on Thorin's arm to turn his attention to me. "And what if she hasn't? It's as good of a place to look for him as any."

Thorin's brows drew together. "I couldn't convince you to stay here, could I? Let me hunt him alone?"

I pointed to myself. "Bait, remember? Skoll wouldn't let you get anywhere near him unless you have something he wants. And I think he wants me rather badly."

Skyla bobbed her head. "Helen's orders."

I shook my head. "No. I mean, I'm sure Helen's orders are encouragement enough, but don't forget I killed Skoll's brother. I know something about what's motivating him. Skoll wants revenge. If he's desperate enough, he'll do anything to get it. It could make him rash and clumsy. It could make him vulnerable."

Thorin gazed at me, his expression tinged with wariness. "I don't know whether to be impressed or to be afraid of you."

I snorted. "Did you expect that I would always be that naive and meek-mannered girl you picked up at the airport all those months ago?"

Thorin chuckled. "You were never meek, Sunshine."

"When I get to the Aerie, I'm going to put a bug in the Valkyries' ears," Skyla said, steering the conversation back on path. "I'll mention that you and Thorin are on your way to the desert to hunt Skoll."

The plot sank in. "If Helen has a double agent in the Valkyries, she'll pass the news to Helen, who'll send Skoll out to meet us," Thorin said.

"I'll have the proof I need to show the Valkyries that they've been compromised. Then we can work together to flush out the mole."

"And either way, we'll have Skoll's head."

"I have to get a move on," Skyla said. She swept me aside and went to the foyer. As she opened the door, she turned to Thorin. "I'll call and leave you a message with an update." Pointing a finger at both of us, she put on a stern face and said, "Play nice, you two."

Skyla walked out and didn't look back. I missed her the moment the door closed behind her. I turned to Thorin, who had shoved his hands into his jeans pockets and stared at the door, a reluctant look on his face as if, maybe, he shouldn't have let her go.

"When should we leave?" I asked.

"Sunrise," he said. "But we need to go out now and get supplies."

I went into my room to grab my shoes but raised my voice so Thorin could hear me. "Hati worked for you for a while, didn't he?"

"Skyla tell you that?"

"No, I read it in the police file on Mani's murder. Hati worked for you, but not Skoll. But did you ever see him? Were they ever together?"

Thorin appeared in my doorway and rested a shoulder against the doorjamb. "I knew who Hati was but not what he was up to." He looked down and scuffed the carpet with the toe of his boot. "And no, I never saw Skoll. Not in human form. It's not the first time I've run into them since Ragnarok, but I never suspected Hati was going to do what he did. I thought all that was over with a long time ago. It's no excuse. I shouldn't have let down my guard." Thorin took a deep breath, but whatever he was going to say next, he decided against.

I had no reply for Thorin except to say I thought he should have been more careful with Hati, but that would have been the equivalent of poking a beehive with a stick.

"This won't be luxury, Solina. It's a desert, and we're going in with the barest of what we need to get by."

I bit my lip and bobbed my chin in a curt nod. "I'm sure I'll be totally unprepared and be a complete wuss. I apologize in advance."

Thorin cracked a smile. "Thanks for the warning."

I followed him to the front door, expecting Val and Baldur to fall in behind us, but Thorin and I stepped into the hallway alone. "Where are the others?"

"I had already sent Val and Baldur back to Vegas before Skyla told us her news. It's Helen's headquarters. The only other place Skoll would be is at Helen's side. Val and Baldur are going to try to catch Skoll's trail there. If Skyla is wrong, and if Helen doesn't have a mole in the Aerie, I still want to get my hands on that wolf."

"Maybe we should switch places." I winked at Thorin. "Let Baldur and Val rough it in the desert."

When Thorin and I stopped before a bay of elevators, he pressed the call button. "No, I want you far away from Helen. Skoll poses much less threat and is more vulnerable on his own. Divide and conquer."

The elevator bell chimed, and the door slid apart to an empty car. Thorin and I stepped inside, and he pushed the button for the lobby.

"Couldn't the same be said for us?" I asked. "We're divided. Easier to conquer."

Thorin huffed a breath through his nose. "I've already raised all your doubts for myself. At some point, we have to stop questioning and start acting. You said so yourself."

"Using my own words against me? Good strategy."

The elevator opened, and Thorin and I strolled across the elegant lobby. People turned to watch him—he had that kind of presence. He'd been a god for eons, while I'd only played at it for a few months. My humanity still shrouded me while Thorin's fit like a sheer veil, barely hiding the divinity beneath.

"People notice you," I said in a low voice only he could hear. "Everywhere we go, you turn heads. It's like they can tell something's different about you."

Thorin's mouth curved into a crooked smile. "They're looking at you, too."

"No..." My protest started and stopped on that single word.

The gazes that first settled on him had turned to me, studying, evaluating.

"They're probably all wondering what a guy like you is doing with a girl like me."

Thorin snorted. "The only person you're fooling is yourself, Sunshine."

A valet had brought the Yukon from the parking lot and left it idling under the portico for us. Thorin tipped him and slid behind the wheel while I climbed into the passenger seat. Thorin pulled out from the hotel's driveway and eased into traffic. The sun had set, and the city lights limned his face—he looked like a two-dimensional illustration.

Thorin drove the whole way in silence, but as we pulled into the parking lot of a camping supply store, he took a deep breath and said, "I'll admit I've had conflicting interests before, but now I have Mjölnir, and I've been released from my vows to Baldur." He turned to me, and conviction blazed in his dark eyes. "There's nothing but you to hold me back."

"Me? How am I going to hold you back? I've never had the least bit of influence on you."

The muscle in Thorin's jaw clenched as he fought some internal battle. "That's not entirely true. But I'm asking you to trust me, no matter what. No matter if I say or do something that you don't agree with, or that pisses you off. I'm doing what's best for me, and that happens to be what's best for you, too."

I raised a sardonic eyebrow. "You see the world through your own Thorin-colored lenses, don't you?"

Thorin smirked. "You should give it a try sometime. It's an exceptional view. But you're deflecting. Do you trust me or not?"

"I—" My voice broke. I cleared my throat and tried again. "I don't follow blindly."

"I'm not asking you to do that."

I studied Thorin's face, although the darkness hid most of it. Somehow, he managed to exude an air of surety, confidence, and capability, offering a reassurance I hadn't realized I wanted until that moment. I bit my bottom lip as the tension built between us. He wouldn't let the issue go until I gave him an answer.

"Okay." I let out a heavy breath. "I trust you."

Thorin exhaled and seemed to relax. "Good answer, Sunshine."

After our shopping spree, we loaded the SUV with every camping necessity Thorin could think of—packs, a tent, water bottles, food—and returned to the hotel for one last night of luxury. Back in our room,

Thorin unloaded his laptop from its carry case while I dug through our purchases, packing things into an honest-to-god long-distance trekking backpack complete with a hip belt, internal frame, and a money-back guarantee if carrying it didn't result in blisters and a back ache.

"I've got to catch up on a couple of things," Thorin said. "Can you keep yourself busy and out of trouble for a while?"

I narrowed my eyes at him. "Really? Did you just say that? Because, as I recall, the last person to have their butt in a jam was not me."

"There's no Skyla around to back you up this time."

"You said *you* were going to be all I needed from now on."

Thorin cracked a slow grin and arched an eyebrow. I immediately regretted my choice of words. "And anytime you want me to prove it to you"—he glanced toward the bedroom he had claimed for himself—"I'm right down the hall."

I set my hands on my hips and jutted my chin. "You also said you have plenty of self-restraint."

"I can't help it if you throw yourself at me."

"In your dreams." I picked up the closest thing at hand, a pillow from the sofa, and chucked it at him.

Thorin laughed and ducked around the corner, disappearing into his bedroom. I went back to shoving things into my pack so I wouldn't meditate on how exasperating I found my roommate. After finishing that chore, I dug out the room-service menu and ordered dinner.

Some time later, Thorin shuffled into the living room, his pale hair hanging loose and unkempt around his face. My fingers flinched in an unconscious urge to smooth the unruly strands.

"Do I smell pizza?" he asked.

I motioned toward the box next to me on the coffee table. "Room service just left."

"Coffee?" he asked on his way to the kitchenette.

"No caffeine for me this late, but thanks."

After he finished preparing the coffee pot, Thorin returned to the living room and plopped down next to me on the sofa. "Baldur and Val said they've had no luck yet, but they're going to keep looking."

"You talked to them?"

"E-mail."

"You take chances with Wi-fi?"

"Encrypted satellite modem."

"You're awfully tech savvy for such an old dude."

A martyred expression crossed his face, and he pressed his hand over his heart. "I'm timeless, not old."

"Do you prefer the modern era, or do you wish things were like they used to be?"

Thorin rubbed his chin and adopted a thinking pose. "Modern conveniences are valuable, but sometimes I miss the old days. Things were simpler then. My place in that world was more certain, and relationships were a hell of a lot easier to figure out."

I cleared my throat and said, "What do you mean by that?"

"It used to be men and women formed symbiotic partnerships that were necessary for survival. It brought them together in a way modern people seem to have trouble achieving although I think they still crave it."

"Wow. Relationship perspectives from an immortal. How insightful."

Thorin leaned back and raised his eyebrows. "You don't agree?"

"I think you're probably right," I said. "Any good partnership, romantic or otherwise, is more successful when strengths and weaknesses complement each other. My parents are like that, in their marriage *and* business. They've been successful so far, so there must be something to it."

"They're fortunate, and so are you to have that example."

"I guess so. I always took it for granted."

Thorin exhaled. "That's the way of humans."

"What do you mean?"

"Such short-lived creatures. You'd think they would value every opportunity, every experience. But they throw so much away."

I wanted to defend my race, but my status as human was in limbo, and Thorin's argument had merit. "I can't disagree with you, not if I'm being honest with myself." I had never given the issue serious thought before. "Immortality is pretty incompatible with this realm. You and your kind weren't really intended for this world, and we certainly weren't made to sustain you for the long haul."

Thorin shifted and leaned an elbow on the armrest. He settled his chin in his palm, looking intrigued.

I tried to make the best of it and not sound like an idiot. "Short-lived creatures have short memories. From generation to generation, it's like we're playing that kid's telephone game. Do you know the one I mean?"

Thorin shook his head.

I explained. "A group of kids line up next to each other. The first one comes up with a random phrase. He whispers it into the next kid's ear. That kid repeats it to the next kid, and so on until it goes down the line to the last kid, who repeats the phrase out loud. Usually, what the last kid says has little in common with what the first one said."

Thorin smiled knowingly.

I thought he understood my analogy, but I clarified anyway. "Human history has been a lot like that. The things that happened hundreds of years ago got passed down and corrupted over time. The faction in power at the time tells the story the way that suits them best and makes their enemy look worse. The truth of what actually happened is probably a lot different from what we believe. I think that's how a lot of traditions and cultures died out."

"Humans have more reliable methods of making records, now," Thorin said. "Maybe things won't be so easily forgotten."

I shrugged. "Information and record keeping have become longer lived, but humans have not. Not really. Maybe we've gained a few more decades of life expectancy, but what's an eighty-year life span compared to eternity? We must seem like fruit flies to you."

Thorin chuckled. "Fruit flies couldn't have philosophical discussions, the last time I checked."

"You know what I mean. When you live forever, what possible influence can a single mortal being have on you?"

Thorin stared into me as if he was seeing more than my exterior. I leaned backward, realizing I had unintentionally drifted toward him. Our relationship was frequently like that—him antagonizing me one minute, drawing me in the next. Was his manipulation deliberate or simply an inherent element of his personality?

Thorin lowered his chin and looked at me through his thick lashes. "More than you could possibly imagine." He shifted so that a few insubstantial inches separated us, and a current buzzed through all of them. "But if humans have ephemeral emotions, then I assure you that my kind does not. The Aesir's memories are long and abiding."

The coffeemaker chimed, signaling it had finished brewing. *Talk about saved by the bell.* I jumped up and scurried to the kitchenette. When I came back to the living room, carrying a mug for Thorin and a water bottle for me, he had moved into one of the club chairs. I wasn't the only one who needed some space, apparently.

"How does one go about hunting wolves?" I asked, changing the subject to something less provocative. I passed Thorin his coffee and sat across from him on the sofa. "Especially in such a wide-open space?"

Thorin sipped from his mug and said, "Normally, you would track their signs, search for dens, feeding and kill sites, carcasses, scat, trails, and prints. I don't want to waste a lot of time, so we might have to set some traps, put out some bait."

"Maybe you could tie me to a cactus, let me hang out until Skoll catches my scent."

Thorin cocked his head as if contemplating my suggestion. "It's not a bad idea."

I chucked another pillow at him.

After demolishing the rest of my dinner, I went to bed and left Thorin alone with the TV and a late-night talk-show host. I showered, slipped into my pajamas, burrowed under the quilts, and fell fast asleep. The dream that woke me that night wasn't violent but was still plenty disturbing. My heart thumped and my breath heaved, but not from panic or fear. I left the bed, went to the window, and pressed my forehead against the chilly pane, seeking a draft of cool air to chase away the cloying remnants of the dream, to escape the images of bare skin, hands caressing, lips sampling, teeth nibbling.

Premonition or Freudian expression of latent desires? Either way, I spent most of the night trying to expel Thorin from my thoughts and relax enough to go back to sleep.

CHAPTER FOURTEEN

EARLY THE NEXT MORNING, AS the sun crested the horizon, Thorin and I stood beside the SUV, gazing over a desert that stretched for miles in every direction.

"We'll plan on a two-day hike to start," Thorin said as we strapped on our packs. "We'll make a circle and come back to the truck at the end. If we don't find anything, we'll restock supplies and go out again, making our path in increasingly wider concentric circles but keeping the truck as the axis."

"That sounds like a lot of walking," I said. "Good thing I've been working out."

I considered myself a fit person, but Thorin set a pace that discouraged talking. He kept a handheld GPS in his pack's side pocket and referred to it every so often to keep us on track.

"How did you do this before?" I asked when we stopped for a water break. "How did you hunt without GPS?"

"Landmarks, stars, intuition. We knew Asgard like an extension of our bodies."

"So what are you doing in Alaska? Why there, of all places?" I had wanted to ask that question for a long time.

"Alaska is a lot like Asgard: secluded, unpopulated, wild. It reminds me of home."

"Val said something about not liking large crowds and urban settings."

"Besides the fact that we are more comfortable when we're closer to the natural world, it's easier to avoid complicated questions. People notice, after a while, when we don't age or get sick or have the life span of the average person."

Thorin didn't wait for me to ask more questions. He stowed the

GPS in his pack and started off again. The new hiking boots had taken a toll on my toes. I apologized to my aching feet and fell into place behind Thorin. For the first couple of hours, the scenery astounded me: prickly Joshua trees, dry brush, sand dunes, and the Clark Mountains in the distance. My footsteps crunching in sand and loose rock created a numinous rhythm, leading me into a meditative state. I perceived nothing more than my heartbeat, my breathing, and the rocky earth crunching beneath my boots. Like some exercise in transcendentalism, I achieved an altered state of consciousness where grief, fear, and doubt didn't exist. *Okay, so maybe I understand why people like to do this sort of thing, after all.*

I lingered in that introspective trance until Thorin froze in midstep, as still as one of the boulders beside our path. "Look," he whispered.

I followed the direction of his pointing finger and saw a pack of deer, nibbling dry brush without a care for the humans invading their terrain. I gasped. "Deer in the desert?"

"Mule deer. They thrive here."

We stood and watched as the herd moved away, blending into the environment until I could no longer distinguish them from the rocks.

———◆———

Late in the afternoon, Thorin and I set up camp in a canyon that produced a view worthy of a "Visit the Mojave!" postcard. To prove I wasn't completely helpless, I pitched my tent by myself, cranked up the butane stove, and set about reconstituting my dinner.

"You don't eat much, do you?" I poured boiling water into a bag of freeze-dried tofurkey and rice I had picked up at the camping-supplies store. It weighed next to nothing in my pack and required no refrigeration, which made it perfect for camping. The meal also smelled like old shoes, but I was hungry enough to eat my boots, so the point was moot.

Thorin shrugged. "Can but usually don't."

"Why?"

He lounged against a boulder like a model in an advertisement for outdoor wear. *L.L. Bean* wishes *they had a model like him on their cover.*

He looks good in everything. Probably looks best in nothing at all, if my dream last night was a true indication.

"Don't have to," Thorin said. "I eat when I need to appear human or for pleasure. Food tastes good, but it's rarely necessary for survival."

"Cold and warmth? Does the chilly air bother you?"

Thorin huffed, and vapor spurted from his nose.

I shrugged deeper into my insulated jacket and tried not to shiver.

"I'm not your science experiment, Sunshine. Didn't your mother tell you it was rude to pry?"

I rolled my eyes and turned my attention on my dinner. "'Scuse me, Mister Sensitive."

"There may come a time when you need to know everything about me…" He sounded vaguely apologetic.

"But this isn't it," I finished for him. "So, if you're not up for a game of Twenty Personal Questions, what do we do to kill time? Did you bring a pack of cards or anything?"

"As a matter of fact…" Thorin riffled through his pack and brought out a familiar red-and-white box. "Gin?"

"Mani taught me how to play. He won that first hand but never another one after that."

"Oh yeah?" Thorin shuffled the cards with the skill of a Vegas dealer. He grinned and said, "Put your money where your mouth is."

I held out my hands, palms open and empty. "I'm broke."

Thorin dealt the cards with imperceptible speed, letting his human façade slip for a moment. "Then we'll use another currency."

"Like what?"

"Truth."

"I don't follow."

"Lowest deadwood points in each hand gets to ask any question he or she wants, and the loser has to answer with complete honesty. We'll play to five hundred."

I rubbed my hands together and anticipated victory. "I'll take that bet."

In the first round, Thorin knocked with a two of spades and an ace of hearts. I discarded some of my deadwood but still held over ten points in my hand. I sucked my teeth, making a sound of disappointment, and said, "Okay, hit me with your best shot."

Thorin stroked his jaw, and intrigue sparkled in his eyes. "Tell me about your dream. The one you had about me."

My thoughts went to the vision I'd had the previous night, and a betraying blush erupted on my cheeks. Thorin's eyes widened, and he blinked, obviously surprised by my response. He reached his knuckles toward my cheek, but I pulled away before he could touch me.

"What's all this about?" he asked.

I took a breath to deny but realized his original question had referred to the premonition I'd had about his death back at the Aerie. "Th-there isn't much to tell," I sputtered. "Tori probably told you everything I know."

"I want to hear it from you."

I set down my cards, hugged my ankles, and rested my chin on my knees. "There was a spear, but I couldn't see details. It was deeply buried and covered in blood. I saw it like a freeze-frame image, but I knew it was the beach at the Aerie. You were lying in the sand in a pool of blood, the spear piercing your chest. You were dead."

Thorin pressed his lips together and arched a circumspect eyebrow. "You didn't see who threw it?"

"It was too foggy, but I assumed it was Helen or one of her minions."

He shook his head. "A regular human cannot wield it. They could possibly carry it, but in battle, it would render them impotent. They wouldn't be able to lift it to use it against one of us."

"Maybe it was Helen, then."

"It was made for Odin. Only descendants of his bloodline can use his weapons. It's why only I can use Mjölnir, because I am Thor's son."

While we were in Vegas together, Thorin had mentioned how he and Val had possessed objects of great power but had lost them. Thorin had since recovered Thor's hammer, but Gungir, the spear, remained elusive—unless Val did have it but was keeping it hidden for some reason. I had often questioned Val's motives, but keeping the spear a secret after everything that had happened would be a new low, even for him.

"You have any siblings who survived Ragnarok?" I remembered a conversation with Tori, back at the Aerie. She'd said there were more Aesir than the ones I knew.

Thorin pointed at the playing cards. "You win the next hand, and I'll answer that question."

I didn't win the next hand, either, damn it.

Thorin grinned like a cat that had cornered a mouse. "Tell me what made you blush when I asked you the last question."

No way would I tell him the full truth: that I'd had... *inappropriate* dreams about him. Thinking fast, I said, "I was embarrassed."

"For what?"

"Being reminded of my deception and how it led to such a terrible ending."

"You're lying."

"Yes, that's what I was just saying. I mean, it was necessary to keep you alive at all costs, but to lose Inyoni and Kalani—"

Thorin grabbed my arm. "No, I mean you're lying about the blush."

I squared my shoulders. "No, I'm not."

"You got over on me once because I underestimated you, but now I know what your lies look like. Tell me the truth."

Since denial had failed me, I tried outright refusal. "No."

"Oh, it must be good if you're fighting this hard." Thorin tugged me until I was virtually in his lap. He locked his arms around me and grinned like a fiendish imp. "Tell me. I've had millennia to develop my torture techniques."

"You wouldn't."

"Try me."

I squinched my eyes shut, waiting for whatever torment he was planning. "Do your worst." I held my breath and anticipated his attack, but it never came.

When I opened an eye to peek at him, Thorin was staring at a distant spot and wearing a funny expression.

"What is it?"

"Shush," he whispered. "Listen."

I stilled my breath and imagined opening my ears. A distant *yip yip yeoooowl* echoed through the quiet desert night. The fine hairs on my arm and neck rose, and my heart skittered, playing a staccato rhythm against my sternum. Another, lower-pitched howl answered the first one. Deep shadows fell over the land as the late sun neared the horizon, painting the desert in pinks and golds and taking away the day's heat as it went. According to Thorin, wolves preferred to hunt at night, and those sounded eager for the darkness.

In the cooling desert air, my breath came out in frosty smoke signals of dread. "Please tell me it was a coyote."

Thorin shook his head. "Wolf. More than one."

"But Hati's dead. I'm sure of it."

"Maybe Skoll called in for reinforcements."

"What do we do?"

Thorin held his hand out to me, palm open. "Mjölnir. Now."

I tugged the gold chain and charm from my collar and yanked it over my head. Thorin snatched the hammer and pushed me from his lap. He stood, flipped his wrist, and gripped the weapon, ready for attack. In an instant, he had changed from twenty-first-century man to Viking warrior god. He lacked only a helmet and a bear-skin cape.

"This was too easy." I rose to my feet. "Finding Skoll this soon. It's uncanny."

"I agree."

The wolves howled again, closer that time. I counted four different voices but couldn't be certain. I stepped beside Thorin and scanned the landscape, though seeing anything farther than a couple of yards in the low light was impossible.

"It's like they were already here, waiting for us."

"Yes," Thorin said. "Exactly like."

"But how?"

"I don't know. Maybe Skyla didn't wait until she got to the Aerie to send out word of our plans. Maybe she didn't want to share credit with the Valkyries and went straight to Helen."

I coughed as shock and indignation stole my breath. "How can you say that? She saved us all at those warehouses. We wouldn't have made it out without her."

"I'm just considering all the possibilities."

"Okay, let's consider that it was your beloved Baldur who barreled headfirst into that trap. He knew Helen wouldn't hurt him—maybe he wanted you to get caught. Maybe he knew I would come trailing after."

Thorin sneered. "Baldur *hates* Helen. He would never cooperate with her."

"You ever hear of Stockholm Syndrome? Sympathizing with one's captor—it's not out of the question."

Thorin lurched forward and raised a hand toward me, fingers curled as if wanting to grasp my neck. "The last person to question Baldur's loyalties didn't live long enough to question him twice."

I set my hands on my hips and glared at him. "Get your priorities straight, Thorin. Save your threats for the wolves." I stomped a foot and threw my hands out. "You talk about humans wasting time with our short lives, but you're so ancient your thought processes have started to petrify. You've gotten complacent, and Helen took advantage of it."

Perhaps I shouldn't have aggravated his temper, but I was scared, and not just of the wolves. I was also mad at him for doubting Skyla. And, fair or unfair, I may have resented him for failing to see what was happening in time to save Mani's life.

The way Thorin affected me frightened me, too.

"Get outside yourself for one second and try opening your mind to the possibility that you and your beloved Aesir are more fallible than you think," I said. "I'll accept that Skyla has betrayed us *if* and *when* you show me the proof. But for God's sake, Thorin, *I* am not your enemy. I'm trying my damnedest to keep us both alive."

Something like lightning flashed in Thorin's dark eyes. Thunder rumbled in the distance. I sank inside myself and opened my vessel of fire.

"Put away your flames." Thorin's voice was low and raspy. He stepped close again. "I am not your enemy, either."

I backed away. "The hell you say. You threatened me."

A muscle in Thorin's jaw flexed as his teeth ground together. "You provoked me."

"Your self-control is slipping, and that's not like you."

Thorin's nostrils flared. "That's because you are singularly skilled at getting under my skin."

"You were being unreasonable, and you're mad because I called you on it. You're so used to having no one challenge you that you've gotten apathetic. *Someone* needs to wake you up."

Thorin stalked me again. I backed away, but the threat of the wolves kept me from leaving and running pell-mell for the truck.

"And that someone is you?" he asked.

Why didn't I find myself a red cape and an angry bull to wave it at? Fighting a wild beast was probably safer than provoking Thorin, but I had saddled my high horse. Might as well ride it. "Who else? You said yourself you live an isolated life. You're out of touch. You're like old technology—obsolete, archaic. You're prehistoric and nearly extinct, but unlike the dinosaurs, you refuse to accept it."

Thorin clenched his fists at his side and gritted his teeth again. I never knew what move he would have made next because the wolves cried out, nearer than before. Their howls raised the hairs along my arms and on the back of my neck. The hostility blooming between Thorin and me scattered like smoke in a stiff breeze.

"They're close." Thorin turned and slid in front of me, holding Mjölnir in a ready position. He called into the night. "Come for us, you worthless mutts. No more skulking out there in the dark. She's here. You want her. You can smell her. Why don't you come and taste her?"

I understood Thorin meant to bait them, but a cold spurt of nausea stirred in my stomach. I tightened my mental grip on my fire and stepped closer to Thorin. He reached back and rested his hand on my hip, more to keep aware of my proximity than to comfort me, but it did anyway, conveying a current of strength and assurance, and I channeled it into my own power source.

Harck! Harck! Ahhwoooo! The wolves threw back their own threats.

"I can't see them," I whispered. "Where are they?"

"Why don't you give us a light?"

"Now? Are you sure?"

Thorin looked at me over his shoulder. His breath rushed past my temple. "Trust me?"

I hesitated. "Just a minute ago, you were threatening me."

"*Solina.*"

"Okay, okay."

"Do it. Light up the night." My period of recuperation at the hotel had restored my powers—not to full capacity, but close enough. My fire show in the warehouse was nothing compared to the energy required to convert to that *other* state, and I had bounced back a lot faster. I stepped away from Thorin and let the flames out in two blazing fireballs that filled my palms. Oh, and it felt so good, like scratching a hard-to-reach itch.

"Keep it low," Thorin said. "Don't burn out all at once."

I clenched my jaw. "I know what I'm doing."

Thorin knelt beside me, and my light flickered over him like a campfire. He raised his weapon high, the Hammer of Thor, and brought it crashing down to the earth. Starting from the impact point, a crack shot out across the ground, growing and widening as it went—total special effects moment, but it was real. Thorin and I fell back as the crack turned into a fissure that bloomed into a crevasse six or eight feet deep and about the same width.

The wolves came to the edge, baring their teeth and growling.

"A male and two females," Thorin said as he drew back his hammer, preparing for a throw. "They're all wild. Skoll's not here, but he's got to be close."

After a flash of movement, one wolf went rolling, screeching, head over heels like a tumbleweed. It slumped into a furry pile and did not rise again. The other two wolves skittered away.

"Oh my God," I wheezed.

Thorin grinned at me and leapt over the crevasse, graceful as a lion. He called his hammer back into his fist, and he searched the darkness for signs of the other wolves.

"We can't keep this up all night," I said. "I won't last long at this rate."

"Just one mistake on their part is all it takes."

Rocks clattered behind me, and I spun around in time to duck a flying ball of gray fur. The wolves Thorin had sent into retreat had recovered and gone the long way around for a rear attack. One wolf, the gray one, rolled midair and landed at the fissure's edge. The other wolf, a brownish one, came toward me in a crouch. Thorin threw his hammer as I lunged at the gray wolf, meaning to shove him into the crevasse. The victim of Thorin's hammer, the brown wolf, barked a painful cry and fell silent. My prey yelped and darted around, moving more like a fish than a wolf. My fingers brushed his coat, singeing him, but he flitted aside before I could really hurt him.

"God, they're fast," I said.

The astringent stink of singed fur wafted to my nose. The gray wolf hunkered several yards away and growled at me. He wasn't Skoll—he was too small and dark.

I bared my teeth and laughed at him, doing my best Skyla impression. "What are you waiting for?"

His muzzle crinkled into a mask of rage, and his teeth glistened in my light. He snarled and leapt toward me. I braced for his impact and called out more flames, but he twisted midleap, landed several feet away, and dashed around the edge of the crevasse, heading for Thorin.

"Thorin!" I shrieked.

He spun, bringing Mjölnir around in an arc that connected with the gray wolf. At the same time, a fourth wolf sprinted forward, appearing like a ghost from the darkness. He leapt for me, teeth bared, snarl ripping apart the night.

Skoll.

I gathered the remains of my fire, imagining nuclear bombs and sunbursts, and lunged to meet him. Skoll shrieked, a howl of mortal pain, and everything went as bright as a million flash bulbs. I was going, crossing over that line, the transition and loss of self. That conversion was happening again, and I couldn't stop it.

"No, no, not now. Not now," I said, as if protesting could help.

Nothing could help, though. Nothing could stop me.

But then, a boom of thunder... and another.

A torrent of rain gushed down as though God had gathered all the oceans and poured them over me, and all the lights went out.

CHAPTER FIFTEEN

I CAME BACK TO MYSELF, AWARE of cold wetness but not much else. "Sunshine?"

I pried open my eyes but wrenched them shut again when a blinding light stabbed into my field of vision. "Ow!"

"Sorry." Thorin clicked off his flashlight, and darkness enveloped me again.

I was zipped up in my sleeping bag, snug as a bug in a rug—a bare-naked bug. After freeing an arm from my mummy bag, I raked damp tendrils of hair from my face and asked, "Why am I wet?"

"I put out your fire. Is that how it happened at the lake in New York?"

"Yes." I heaved a sigh. "I gotta work on it. I can control it up to a certain point, but after that..." I puffed out my cheeks, made an explosion noise, and spread apart my fingers, miming the disbursement of smoke and flames. "It's all or nothing."

The fire had burned away my clothing, and yet again, Thorin had seen to the defense of my modesty—what little of it was left.

"Oh God," I groaned.

"What?"

"I was just realizing..." *Realizing I've lost count of the number of times you've seen my bare behind.*

Thorin crouched beside me and watched a pot of water bubbling on my butane stove. He kept his face turned, showing only his profile. *Good.* Talking was easier without the discomfort of his direct stare.

"Would you mind getting a shirt from my bag for me?" I asked.

Thorin's lips curled, and even from the side, I could tell he was smirking.

"Already ahead of you." He pointed at a stack of clothes lying on the ground between us.

I snatched the pile and slithered farther into the sleeping bag. "What do you mean you put me out?" I asked as I wriggled into the leggings and a long-sleeved thermal. "This is a desert. Where did you find—" I remembered the storm. "You went all God of Thunder, didn't you? Wish I had been aware of it. I bet it was awesome."

"You weren't so bad yourself." Thorin lifted the pot, poured steaming water into a mug, gave it a stir with a spoon from my mess kit, and presented it to me.

I scooted out of the sleeping bag, took the mug, and sniffed—hot chocolate.

"I've never seen anything like what you did, not since the days of the original Sol."

Fresh from the pan like that, the hot chocolate should have scalded me, but I drained it in a couple of giant gulps and held it out for a refill, doing my best Oliver Twist impression: "Please, sir, I want some more."

Thorin filled my mug again, dumped in two Swiss Miss packets, and stirred it into a thick, sugary mess.

"You knew the real Sol?" I asked.

Thorin looked up at the stars. "I knew her."

"What was she like?"

His Adam's apple bobbed a few times before he answered. "Lovely. Radiant, I guess you could say. She wasn't around much. Things were more literal where I come from. When the legends say Sol rode in a chariot around the world, it was truth in Asgard. Her husband, Glenr, was her driver. Maybe the humans perceived her as the sun, but to us she was real. She was always a little frantic and tired, but she had a fiery personality." He chuckled. "A lot like you."

I ran my finger around the bottom of the mug to dig up the fudgy bits that hadn't quite dissolved. "You liked her?"

"Yes. I liked her a lot."

If I pried further, he would probably shut down as he usually did, so I changed the subject. "Where are the wolves?"

In reply, Thorin clicked on his flashlight. The beam landed on a lumpy, bloody pile of fur. I sucked in a breath and almost choked. "Are any of them Skoll?"

"No. It's the group he was with. I think they were sick. Rabies or something. It might explain their behavior."

"And Skoll?"

"Your fire chased him away. He was burnt pretty badly. He looked like a blistered lab rat."

"You didn't go after him?"

"And let you go shooting star and risk losing you again for another month? I don't think so. Don't worry, Sunshine. He's going to be licking his wounds for a while. We'll find him again soon enough."

Going after Skoll and killing him would have guaranteed the failure of Helen's plans and removed the threat to Thorin and his kind, but Thorin had chosen to let the wolf go and take care of me, instead. My heart twitched, and another crack shot through my walls. *If he keeps this up, I'll have nothing left to resist him with.*

I studied the dead wolves again and pitied them, regretting their deaths. "You really think they were sick? Or are you just saying that to make me feel better?"

"Look at them. They're skin and bones, missing patches of hair. They smell *terrible*, and not just wolf musk but something rotten. They weren't far from death, anyway."

"And Skoll could control them?"

Thorin shrugged. "I suppose."

I gnawed my bottom lip and replayed the fight in my mind. Skoll's escape embittered me and stoked my ire. If not for the loss of my self-control, we might have succeeded in killing him. My failure tasted as bitter as old coffee grounds. I resisted the urge to spit.

"Sunshine?" Thorin asked, as if sensing my distress.

I waved him off, rolled out of my sleeping bag, and shuffled into the tent. After rifling through my pack, I found a pair of warm socks and slipped them on. *How am I supposed to hike out of here in sock feet?* I set that problem aside and set about repacking my things, anything to keep me distracted from dwelling on my mistakes and shortcomings.

Thorin moved around outside, clinking dishes and rattling gear, but that fell away, and silence settled over the desert. Rather, all the people fell silent. Wind whispered, and desert owls screeched and sang their other strange noises. Distant coyotes—*not the wolves this time*—howled and barked. Their haunting voices provided the perfect accompaniment for my grief.

Maybe Thorin had thought my despair deserved some alone time, because he was absent from camp when I eventually crawled through the tent flaps and shuffled into the moonlight. All traces of Thorin's deluge had sunk into the dry earth, but the new crevasse remained. I walked over to it, sat down, and dangled my feet over the edge.

Thorin naturally moved as silently as a ghost, but the skitter of rocks and crunch of grit announced his approach, as though he meant for me to hear him coming.

"What do we do next?" I asked.

Thorin crouched beside me and tossed a rock into the chasm, and it *tick-tack*ed all the way to the bottom, bouncing off the walls as it went. "We should go to Vegas. I think Skoll would go back to Helen to give her a report, to hide out until he recovers. We also need to start looking for signs of Surtr's sword."

"You want to kick Skoll while he's down?"

"That would be ideal," he said, staring into the shadows of his ravine. "What do you want to do?"

"I want to go back to Alaska."

Thorin's head jerked up. His eyes cut to me, and the moonlight glowed in their dark depths. "Really?"

"I felt close to Mani there. I'm missing him very badly right now."

Thorin nodded. "Of course."

"I don't have anywhere else to go. I can't go home—it would bring trouble to my connections there. I'm half surprised Helen hasn't already used them to get to me."

"She's always been single-minded. Now, she has a lot of variables to juggle. She might not risk going after your family for fear of spreading herself too thin. I think we shouldn't underestimate her, though." Thorin paused and exhaled. He looked down, found another pebble, and threw it into the ravine. "I would be wrong to dismiss your concerns about your family. They are a weakness for you, and the best way of dealing with that is to end this matter as quickly as possible."

"Las Vegas is the reasonable choice," I said. "If you think that's where we should go, then I won't argue."

"We'll leave in the morning. It's about six hours until sunrise. You should try to get some sleep." Thorin stood and held out a hand for me. When I took it, he pulled me to my feet. "When this is over, I'll take you back to Alaska. We'll go on one of Mani's favorite hikes." Again, that unexpected empathy—Thorin kept me guessing. Always guessing.

"I thought Mani and I would be together forever, that I'd always know everything about him. He wasn't supposed to be a stranger to me."

Thorin had the sense to keep quiet rather than offer clichéd prattle to try to comfort me. We walked back to the tent, and I gathered my sleeping bag and laid it out inside. Thorin zipped the flap behind me as I snuggled down into my cocoon of insulation.

"Thank you," I said through the thin nylon walls.

"For what?"

"Fighting Skoll… saving me from losing myself again." After pausing to let out a big yawn, I said, "And thanks for letting me sleep. The fire always wipes me out."

His footstep scraped over the ground. "You don't have to thank me. Just get some rest. Who knows what tomorrow will bring?"

"Okay," I said, yawning again. "Good night, Thorin."

"Goodnight, Sunshine."

At dawn, Thorin woke me. We put away the entire campsite without a word. Not until we had our packs in place on our backs did he breach the silence.

"I brought the truck close. You won't make it far in those sock feet."

"That was nice of you. I appreciate it."

Thorin shrugged. "Don't give me too much credit. I was partly being nice and partly not wanting to waste any more time."

He stepped close to me and pulled something from his pocket. It was Mjölnir, the chain-and-pendant version. He swept my hair aside and fastened it back in place around my neck. It hung down low, the charm falling into the neck of my jacket and settling against my skin as though it belonged there. As though I had always worn it.

"We're not hunting the desert anymore," he said. "There's no need to hike. I'm in a hurry to move on."

"What did you do with the bodies?" I had noticed when we finished packing up that the wolves were gone.

"Buried them. Seemed the decent thing to do."

Unshed tears burned in my throat. I said nothing but nodded. The wolves were wild beasts, creatures of the natural world—not my brother, not a friend or a person—but I mourned them anyway. Theirs were three more lives lost to Helen's scheming. Their deaths weren't fair, even if they were sick and suffering. At least Thorin had given them quick mercy.

Once we stowed our packs in the back of the Yukon and climbed inside, I jacked up the heater. Thorin maneuvered, slowly and carefully, over the bumpy terrain until we reached pavement. The moment our wheels touched asphalt, he stomped on the accelerator and put the Mojave in our rearview mirror.

Later, when Thorin's cell phone picked up a signal, it beeped, letting him know it had messages.

"Check those, will you?" He dug the phone from his hip pocket. "It's probably Skyla wanting you to call her." He was wrong.

Val's voice played over the speakerphone: "Baldur's gone. There is a handbasket on its way to hell, or maybe I should say on its way to Hela, and I'm pretty sure he's in it."

"Get to the point," Thorin grumbled.

"Baldur said something about having found Nina, and he was going to get her. I've been calling him ever since. His phone rings straight to voice mail, and he's refusing to respond to any of my other attempts to contact him. Call me."

The message ended, and a monotone phone voice announced that Thorin had no new messages.

"Not now..." Thorin groaned and rubbed a hand over his face. "Call Val. Find out what he knows."

Val picked up on the first ring. "Thorin, thank the gods."

"It's me," I said. "We got your message. Thorin's driving. I'm putting you on speaker."

"What happened?" Thorin's voice carried a hint of exasperation.

"Baldur got a call a couple of hours ago—right after we got back to Vegas. He started acting all secretive, going outside so I couldn't hear his conversation. A few minutes later, he came into the room and said, 'I found Nina. I'm going to get her,' and then he left."

"You didn't stop him?" Thorin asked.

"How am I supposed to stop the Allfather when he wants to go somewhere? One minute he was there, and the next"—Val made a snapping noise—"he was gone."

"He didn't say where he was going? When he would be back?"

"No. He just went. He looked half crazed."

"We're on our way back. We'll go after him as soon as I get there. Keep your phone at your side. Call me if anything changes. We should be there in another hour or so." With that, Thorin ended the call and dropped his phone into the console between us.

"You know," I said. "From the moment I first met him, Baldur seemed a little... *unstable*. It's gotten worse."

"I've not seen him like this in a long time. His experience with Helen was..." Thorin scratched his jaw while he thought of what to say. "It was torturous. It broke him. He's not the person he was before."

"You're going after him again?"

"I have to. If Helen gets her hands on him, I'm not sure he'll survive it."

"He's immortal."

Thorin looked at me from the corner of his eye. "That's even more reason to keep her from him. She can't kill him, but she can make him wish he was dead."

———— ◆ ————

When we reached the outskirts of Las Vegas, Thorin's phone rang again, and Skyla's name flashed on the caller ID. Thorin held out the phone to me. "You should probably answer."

I swiped the Answer icon and uttered the beginning of a greeting, but Skyla cut me off. "Stop talking and listen to me."

"Okay, okay. What's going on?"

Skyla's voice shook as she said, "You have to get out here, now. The Aerie's been attacked."

"Attacked? What are you talking about?"

"Put her on speaker," Thorin said, and I did as he instructed.

"Someone set fire to the place, and it's burning right now, as we speak. More like a bomb than a fire. It trapped some of the Valkyries in the dormitory wing. They couldn't get out. They... they..." Skyla muffled a moan, but her grief carried across the airwaves, regardless. "There've been women on guard duty since your dream, Solina, but they didn't know what was going on until it was too late. It all happened so fast."

"What about you?" I demanded. "Are you all right?"

"I couldn't sleep, so I was out in the training barn. The dormitories, though... By the time we broke through the fire, she... she..." Skyla fell into weeping again and couldn't finish her story.

"She who? Who did this?"

Skyla took a deep, wobbly breath, trying to regain her composure. "Tori. One of the sisters here fought her, tried to stop her, but she got away."

"How many?" asked Thorin, his tone flat and lifeless. "How many were lost?"

"M-maybe half. We managed to save some of the women. Some are still on the fence. They've already been taken to the hospital. Maybe fifteen of us are left, but they're spooked."

Thorin gripped the steering wheel tightly enough for his knuckles to go white, and the leather creaked in protest. "Skyla, something's come up. We can't come to the Aerie right away. I want you to try to hold the survivors together. Don't let anyone leave. Solina and I will be there as soon as possible, but it may be a day or two."

"Wait." Skyla's tone changed from pained to confused. "What are you talking about? What's happened that could be more important than this?"

"Yes, Thorin," I said. "This is no coincidence. Not after my dream about the fire sword. This might be our chance to track down Surtalogi. We have to go before the trail goes cold."

"I have other obligations," he growled.

"What the hell is he talking about, Solina? And what dream are you talking about? What sword?"

"He's talking about Baldur," I said. "He's gone again. The dream is a long story. I'll tell you about it when I see you."

"Baldur's insane." Skyla had moved past confusion and was steaming toward fury. "He's put everything in jeopardy with his bullheaded pursuit of a ghost. Let him go. This is more important."

"I agree," I said.

"Look, Skyla," Thorin said. "Do what you can. See what you can find out. We'll be there as soon as we can."

"The hell with that," Skyla said. "You listen to me, Aleksander Thorin, I don't care—"

Thorin cut her off. "End of discussion, Skyla. Solina will call you back to update you soon. Bye-bye, now." He swiped his thumb over the screen and dropped the phone into the console between us.

I stared at him, mouth agape, not quite believing what had happened.

"Have you lost your mind, too?" I said. "I will *not* risk my life on *another* wild-goose chase for Baldur. We're done with that. You said so yourself. Baldur released you from your vow. He's a god. He has to bear the consequences of his actions. He can take care of himself."

"No, he can't," Thorin said. "He's out of his mind. He has to be protected from himself."

The mercury of my internal rage thermometer crept higher. By the way he kept a death grip on the steering wheel, I gathered Thorin was feeling something similar. In another minute, one of us would probably explode. I hoped it wouldn't be me as my flare-ups tended to be messy.

"To what end?" I asked. "What does going after him do for us in the grand scheme of things? It puts everything in danger. You curse me for taking stupid risks, but when the shoe is on the other foot, it's perfectly justifiable."

Thorin pounded his fist on the dashboard. "You don't understand."

I crossed my arms over my chest and leaned in. "Then explain it to me."

Thorin turned toward me, and where I expected to see rage, I found panic and desperation. "There are thousands of years between us, Baldur and me. That doesn't get wiped away with a few words. It has always been my duty, the God of Thunder's duty, to protect the Allfather. It's hardwired in us and not something easily overcome.

"When Baldur came out of Helen's underworld after Ragnarok, he was shattered. He was wasted and mostly out of his mind. He was supposed to be the next Allfather, but he was a raving, mad ghost of what he used to be. He was—" Thorin choked, coughed to clear his throat, and continued. "He was covered in scars and half-healed wounds from the hundreds of times he tried to kill himself. It didn't matter that he couldn't do it, that Helen could keep him alive no matter what he did to himself or what tortures she exacted on him. He kept trying anyway."

I covered my mouth after it fell open. "Oh my God," I said through my fingers. "I didn't know."

"How would you? But maybe now you understand why I have to help him. I have to find him before Helen takes him again. He won't survive it this time. She'll keep him alive, but he'll be dead inside."

The intensity of Thorin's feelings ignited the air between us. I wanted to reach out and touch him, reassure him, but I refrained. Touching him might have brought forth a vision, and I didn't want to invade the sanctity of Thorin's thoughts or share in the horror of his memories.

"Of course, you have to go. I'll go to Skyla by myself. Like you said, Skoll's off somewhere licking his wounds. I'll be safe for a little while. I'll go to the Aerie and learn what I can about what happened, then I'll come back to Vegas and—"

"*No.*" Despite my efforts to avoid him, Thorin reached across and grabbed my wrist. I braced myself against the avalanche of images his touch evoked: a scarred and broken Baldur, recently emerged from Helen's domain as Thorin had seen him so many years before. He was pale and so weak that Thorin had to carry him. Knots and snarls tangled his hair and beard, and he was muttering a litany of senseless words, every one in three being "Nanna," as Nina was known back then.

I swallowed the sob forming in my throat and jerked away. Thorin scowled and opened his mouth, probably to say something harsh, but he stopped, having noticed my distress. He studied my face. His gaze fell first to his hand and then to mine, and the sternness in his face eased. "You saw it? You saw Baldur, how he was?"

I nodded and bit my lip, afraid to say anything because I was pretty sure the only thing that would come out was a sob.

"So you see? You understand why I have to protect him."

I nodded again and blinked back tears.

"But I told you I wasn't going to let you out of my sight again."

"I can't leave Skyla." My voice was low, raspy, broken. "What if this is our chance to track down Surtalogi? We can't waste this opportunity."

Thorin turned and stared at the road and ground his teeth together. "Dammit." He pounded the steering wheel. Three more times he brought down his fist, accentuating his words: "Damn, damn, *dammit.*" I marveled that the steering wheel hadn't crumpled under his assault.

I reached to pat his shoulder but drew back. No touching him for a while if I could help it. I didn't need to see any more of his horrible memories. "I couldn't have said it better myself."

CHAPTER SIXTEEN

THE MOMENT THORIN AND I walked through the door of Baldur's Bellestrella villa, Val swept me up in a bone-crunching hug. Though it obviously pained him to do so, Thorin agreed to our separation, and he all but ordered Val to go to the Aerie with me. Usually, Val would have balked at Thorin's officiousness, but Thorin's edict probably mirrored what Val would have done anyway.

"Don't you need Val to help you?" I asked.

Val scowled at me, but I ignored him. Having Val at my back, a second pair of eyes watching for treachery among the Valkyries, was probably a good idea. If he could do that without expecting anything from me in return, I would have had fewer reservations about pairing up with him.

Thorin shook his head. "By keeping you safe, Val will be helping us all. I don't like it, but sending him with you is the lesser of two evils."

Val huffed. "Thanks for the vote of confidence."

"I'm confident you'll serve your purpose if you can keep your focus on the job at hand, rather than trying to get in Solina's pants."

Val threw back his shoulders and smirked at Thorin. "How does it feel, going to bed every night with nothing but your self-righteousness?"

"Oh, good God almighty," I said. "You two are worse than a couple of tomcats whenever you get together."

Val turned his smirk to me. "Meow, baby."

I threw out a hand, like a cop trying to stop traffic. "Save it, Val. We've got to hit the road. I want to get to the Aerie before the trail gets cold. Skyla's about to flip out."

"How's that different from any other day?"

"Call me as soon as you get there." Thorin pointed, not quite shaking his finger at me. "I want a play-by-play report. You call me and tell me what you had for breakfast if there's a chance it has a bearing on the fire sword or Helen."

Thorin pressed his pointer finger against my sternum. "So help me, if you withhold anything or downright lie, no matter your good intentions, I'll come for you with chains and an armored truck."

Thorin likely expected a sharp retort from me, and I really wanted to give him one, but for Skyla's sake, I sucked down my pride and flashed Thorin a toothy smile. "Sure thing, sugar."

Val snorted. Thorin frowned.

I rolled my eyes and tugged at Val's arm. "C'mon, tomcat. Let's hit the road."

Val hurried to open the door for me, but I backtracked when I remembered another issue requiring resolution before we all went our separate ways.

"I forgot something," I said. "I'll meet you out front, okay?"

Val gave me a sour look but did as I asked.

I turned to Thorin, who watched me, brows drawn down, a frown tugging at his mouth. I reached behind my neck and unfastened the chain supporting Mjölnir. "I think you'll be needing this."

Without taking his eyes from mine, Thorin held out his hand. I pooled the necklace into his palm, and he closed his fist around the warm gold. He stepped closer and put his free hand to my jaw. His fingertips rested like a breath on the pulse point in my neck. Surprise and uncertainty rooted my feet to the floor.

"Solina." Thorin could undo me so easily, saying my name like that—like a prayer. He was possibly nothing more than a manipulator like his cousin, except he had a subtlety Val lacked.

No, I don't believe that. He's not devious. Just driven and resolute.

"Please," Thorin said.

Hearing him implore me, his tone soft and needful rather than demanding and harsh—I might have given him my soul when he talked to me that way. Instead, I steeled myself against his allure.

"What is it?" I asked. "What do you want?"

"Above all else, you must keep yourself alive."

"I know." I lost my patience and threw my hands out at my sides.

"Your life is so important to you, but is it possible for you to realize mine is at least as important to me? Unlike you, I get a finite number of years. I'm not anxious to give them up any earlier than I have to. So stop reminding me how important it is that I stay alive. I know. I know it like I know the sky is blue."

Thorin's lips quirked up in a half smile. "So, you're still trying to convince me it isn't always about me?"

"I don't know why I bother. It's an impossible task."

"Mostly, yes. You're right. But sometimes…" His voice drifted away, and his ghost of a smile went with it. The brown in his eyes deepened to black.

I met his gaze, though it took a great deal of self-confidence to do so. "Sometimes what?"

"Sometimes, there's something… *else*."

The air between us filled with potential, the kind of energy waiting for one spark to set it loose. I couldn't do it, though. I wouldn't be the one to strike the flint.

Thorin drew a deep breath, and his hand fell away. "One last thing before you leave." He raised a hand, and Mjölnir dangled from his fingers, swaying on its gold chain. He undid the clasp, slipped the pendant from the necklace, and stuffed the hammer into his pocket. "Wear the chain. When the hammer is separated from its lanyard, they can be used to track each other. As long as you are wearing this and as long as I have Mjölnir, I will be able to find you, no matter where you go."

I let him put the necklace around my neck, substantially lighter without the golden nugget of Thor's Hammer weighing it down. Thorin let me go without another word. My heart thudded as I trudged through the hotel.

Mani used to listen to my problems, giving advice when I asked or lending a sympathetic ear when I needed that more. Having a guy's perspective had kept me out of more than one bad relationship. Actually, it kept me out of pretty much any relationship. Maybe that explained my problem. Enduring emotional conflict with Thorin—and Val—on my own totally sucked.

"You smell like him," Val grumbled when I climbed into the Yukon's passenger seat.

I turned to face him. "I accept I clean up pretty good sometimes. I've come into some nifty special powers. But, really, it's not every day an otherwise ordinary, small-town girl has two immortal men chomping at her heels. What is it? If it's my deodorant, I can switch brands."

"So you admit he's trying to seduce you. That pretentious, two-faced—"

"Stuff it, Val. Neither of you are paradigms of virtue."

"At least I don't put on a show, trying to make you think I am."

"He's *not* trying to seduce me." *Thank God for small favors.* And *big ones.*

Val cut his blue eyes to me with a beleaguered expression before turning his attention back to the road. "We had this discussion before, Solina. You need your ego stroked or something?"

"Just the opposite. I need a reality check."

"Your loyalty, courage, dedication to something you believe in... it's a rare thing."

"It's not so rare," I said and scoffed. "And you knock Thorin for it all the time."

"Because it's misplaced. His attachment to Baldur is going to wind up getting everyone in trouble."

"I agree, but I also see Thorin's point. Everyone needs a friend when they're standing on the edge of the abyss."

"Hmm," Val said in an evasive way. "But back to your original question. I'm more than happy to tell you all the reasons I find you irresistible."

"No. Forget I brought it up."

"You need someone in your life to remind you of these things so you never have to doubt."

I rolled my eyes at him. "I might get an overinflated sense of myself."

"Having healthy self-esteem is a good thing." Val grinned, and a mischievous sparkle lit in his eyes. "Besides, your ego will never be bigger than mine."

"Too bad you can't just pop us through space like Baldur," I said when Val and I arrived at the outskirts of Mendocino, "teleport or apparate or whatever you want to call it."

135

"It's always been that way," Val said. "Not sure why. Maybe it's one way Baldur can limit us and exert some of his own superiority. If I try to, uh, *transport* you, we would mostly stand around with a lot of popping and ringing in your ears. If I had one of the ancient weapons, Gungir or Surtalogi, they might amp up my battery enough to make a jump with someone in tow, but it doesn't matter since both items are missing."

"Gungir isn't missing," I said.

Val snorted. "Seeing Odin's spear in your dream is not the same as knowing who actually possesses it. I think if someone did have it, they wouldn't keep it a secret for long."

Thorin had, of course, decided to keep his possession of Mjölnir quiet, but how long would that last if he continued to use it as he had in the desert? Mjölnir's gold chain suddenly hung a little heavier around my neck. Val sensed the downturn in my mood, and we spoke no more about ancient weapons.

<hr />

Hours later, when we turned onto the long driveway leading up to the Aerie, I caught the acrid scent of a spent fire. We passed a couple of sheriff's cars leaving the scene, covered in grime and smoke residue.

"This is going to be ugly," Val said as we bumped along the gravel path.

"I've tried to prepare myself for the worst." And I did, but my theorizing and imagination wasn't enough.

The early-morning sun lent enough light to expose the tormented old home, charred and still smoking in spots.

Skyla came running the moment we turned into the parking lot next to the house's dormitory wing. "Thank the gods you're here." She flung her arms around me. She smelled of smoke, and soot had settled on her like a sticky shadow. "It's been so awful."

I hugged her back, trying to give some of the comfort she so obviously needed. "I can see that."

Val stood behind us, arms crossed over his chest, and surveyed the destruction. His face wore a neutral expression, but it looked more like a mask covering something not so amiable beneath. Fiery destruction, smoke and flames... Maybe it all reminded him of Ragnarok and the home he'd lost so many years before. How long did memories like that stay with beings like him? *If I was immortal, a million years wouldn't soften the ache of losing Mani.*

"What can we do to help?" I asked.

"I don't even know where to start," Skyla said. "One fire truck is still dousing the dormitory wing. Most of it will have to be demolished. We've got to go through and see what can be saved, what can be cleaned, what has to be trashed."

"What about the kitchen?"

Skyla gave me a funny look. "I guess it's fine. Most of the main house escaped the worst of the fire. There's no power, though."

"If the equipment is gas, then we should be okay."

"What are you going to do?"

"I'm a Southern girl. That means I deal with tragedy and grief by stuffing it full of food."

In less than an hour, I had turned out pans of hot biscuits and honey-nut muffins. I sent Val into town for extra ingredients, and he came back, packing enough groceries to feed an army. My return to the kitchen, to my routine and my comfort zone, settled my haywire emotions. Seeing the Valkyries finding consolation in my food, when they hadn't found it anywhere else, reminded me why I liked baking in the first place. Maybe some of the Valkyries were Helen's agents, but surely most of them weren't. Right then, they were merely a bunch of women suffering a horrible tragedy, and I knew something about how they felt. The food was my gesture, my attempt, to bring them comfort. And I thought the emergency responders might appreciate having a decent meal, too.

After breakfast, I cleaned the kitchen and started on pans of peanut-butter cookies, oatmeal bread for sandwiches, and sweet-potato biscuits waiting to be stuffed with ham and spicy mustard. Skyla and Val occasionally came in to check on me, but mostly they stayed occupied with cleaning and moving furniture. Keeping busy turned out to be a crucial coping mechanism for everyone.

Near sundown, Skyla joined me in the kitchen to talk while I prepared for dinner. Sweat and soot matted her hair, and dirt smudged her face. Her shoulders sagged. "I don't think Tori went to Helen after she burned the Aerie," she said, prefaced by nothing.

Crouched before the oven door, I turned and peered over my shoulder at Skyla. A shadow moved in the doorway, and Val stepped into the room. He was also dirty and disheveled, but he bore it gracefully. He took a seat across from Skyla and turned his chair to watch me. Clad in elbow-length mitts, I reached into the oven, towed out a huge, hot pan of lasagna, and plopped it onto the counter.

"Then where do you think Tori went?" I asked and leaned over to peel back the lasagna's foil cover. Garlic-and-basil-infused steam rose up and enveloped my face. I inhaled and let the breath out in a satisfied sigh.

"She's doing this on her own," Skyla said. "I just have to prove it."

Val's brow furrowed as he studied Skyla. His gaze shifted to me, and he shrugged as if to say he didn't know what Skyla meant.

"How are you going to do that?" I asked.

"I have an idea, but it's a little crazy." Skyla toyed with her placemat and gave me an uneasy look.

Her discomfort worried me. She never hesitated, never second-guessed herself.

"Crazier than everything else that's happened?" I asked.

Skyla shrugged. *You be the judge*, her expression said. "You remember how I told you that the Valkyries chose which soldiers died in battle so they could bring them to join Odin's army?"

"Yes?" I glanced at Val, but he shook his head.

"Right." She nodded. "So, the Valkyries have the ability to commune with the spirits of the dead."

I held up my hand. "Skyla, if you're going to tell me you see dead people, I think my head might explode."

Skyla bit her bottom lip and held it between her teeth, saying nothing.

"*Do* you see dead people?"

"One," she said. "I saw one."

"Who?" Val asked, accepting Skyla's claim with alacrity.

"It was one of the women who had died in the fire. Her name was Ariel." Skyla stopped. Her gaze dropped to the floor, and her chin wobbled under the effort of restraining her tears. "I found her body after we hacked our way into the dorm. Smoke inhalation, I guess, because she looked untouched."

Val and I held ourselves rigid, waiting for her to finish her story. I wanted to put my arms around her and offer consolation, but the stiffness of her shoulders seemed to rebuff sympathy.

Skyla cleared her throat and continued. "Anyway, I had carried her outside and was on my way back in when this... this *glow*... this *apparition* appeared in front of me. It freaked me out at first, but it took form and spoke my name. Then she disappeared. I knew it was her, but how could it be?"

Skyla raised her eyes and looked into mine, pleading for me to believe her. I offered what I hoped looked like an encouraging smile.

She let out a breath and squared her shoulders. "I'm going to try to speak to her again. Ask her if she knows anything."

"Why would she know anything the living don't?" Val asked. "If Tori was behind this attack, then those who died must have been ignorant of her intentions, or else they would have been better prepared to defend themselves."

"Maybe she saw who started the fire," Skyla said. "Maybe she saw someone else or overheard something in her final moments. She would have been a lot closer to the action than the women who survived. Besides, I've talked to every sister here, and either they don't know what happened, or they are refusing to talk to me because they think I'm an outsider."

"Okay," I said. "It's no crazier than anything else that has happened lately. How does contacting the dead work?"

"I'm not sure," Skyla said. "I want you to help me search the library. I'm hoping one of those books has something helpful."

Val shook his head and shrugged. "Sorry, but why don't you just ask one of the sisters?"

Skyla snorted. "I already told you they won't talk to me, especially not about proprietary things like communing with the dead."

A door slammed somewhere in the house, and the mutterings of distant voices carried into the kitchen. Moments later, the Valkyries filed in through the kitchen, filling the room with chatter and their plates with lasagna. Their sudden arrival interrupted our conversation, so Skyla, Val, and I used the distraction to slip away to the library, located in the basement of the main house. The stone foundation and ceiling had protected it from the fire, and a heavy wooden door with an old-fashioned lock protected it from intruders—like us.

"Damn." Skyla worked the handle as if it might give in if she antagonized it enough.

"Val," I said. "Can't you blip in there and open it from the other side?"

"I've never seen inside the library before. I have to have seen a place, be able to hold a vision of it in my mind, or I have to follow someone else's path. Why don't you just go ask for the key?"

"Who even has it?" said Skyla.

"The librarian would be my guess," I said.

"Well, duh. But who is the librarian?"

"Tori?" Val asked.

The mention of her name inspired a memory from my previous visit, when Tori had told me my lack of knowledge about my ancestry was appalling. "No. Tori mentioned her to me once. Her name is..." The weight of the name pressed on my tongue, but my brain didn't want to cough it up. "Elaine... Emily... Emma?"

"Embla?" Skyla asked. "There's a woman here named Embla."

"Yes. I think that's it."

"How do we get the key from her?"

Val's face screwed into a sardonic expression. "Uh, what if you just *asked* her for it?"

"What if she wants to know why?" Skyla asked.

"I could tell her I want to research Sol's lineage," I said. "Tori suggested I should do that last time I was here."

"What if Embla insists on coming with us?" Skyla asked. "What if she wants to supervise your research and help you find things? We can't have her looking over our shoulder. We can't risk letting anyone find out what we're up to until we know who we can trust."

"I still don't understand why you changed your mind about Tori being Helen's agent," Val said.

"First," Skyla said, "we asked Inyoni, as she was dying, if Tori was the one she had been talking to. It was hard to tell, but it seemed she was trying to tell us it was someone else. Also, Tori could have easily had

Solina killed here at the Aerie rather than having Skoll follow her out to some remote location on the other side of the country, but she didn't. I think Tori ran for other reasons. Maybe she's running from Helen's spies inside the Aerie." Skyla narrowed her eyes. "I'm trying to stay open to all possibilities."

"So, we're back to figuring out how we get the key," I said. "If Embla even has it in the first place."

"We need to search her room," Skyla said.

"If you were the librarian, wouldn't you keep the key with you most of the time?"

"So we're going to mug her?" Val asked.

"You got any better ideas?"

"She usually trains in the barn in the mornings," Skyla said. "If she keeps the key on her, she probably doesn't wear it then. I can go ask her to fence with me in the morning—my sword work needs the practice anyway."

"So we find the key while she's training. I'll unlock the door, let Val get a good look at the inside. We'll get the key back to her before she notices it's missing."

"Then," Skyla said, "we can come back later, when no one will notice. Val can jump into the room and let us in."

With our plan in place, Skyla left to go find Embla and make a date for a morning workout. I went upstairs to seek out what remained of my lasagna dinner and found a few noodles and cheese crumbs left in the pan. I sighed and started cleaning the kitchen mess.

"Sit down," said Val, who tugged me to the kitchen table and pulled out a chair. He pushed me into it, and I didn't resist. "I'll get the dishes. I don't know what it is with you and your fondness for pulling all-nighters, but you're going to make yourself sick." Val turned to the sink and filled it with water. He crumpled the aluminum pan that had once held my lasagna and tossed it into the trash can. "In fact, you should go to bed. There's nothing more that can be done tonight."

I rubbed my eyes and rested my hand in my chin. "Sleeping's not all it's cracked up to be. Lately, it's all bad dreams. I wake up more tired than I was when I started."

Val squirted a healthy dose of dish soap in the sink before making neat piles of pots and pans for hand washing. He bent and loaded plates and glasses into the dishwasher.

"How very domesticated of you," I said. "A god doing the humble chores of a housekeeper. Can't you wave your magic wand or something?"

Val turned and smirked at me. "I'm not sure it wouldn't end up going the way of *The Sorcerer's Apprentice.* Besides, there's comfort in manual labor. Your hands are busy, leaving your mind free to wander."

"And where does your mind wander, Val?"

Val rolled up his shirt sleeves and plunged his hands into the sink to scrub a greasy saucepan. "When you've been around as long as I have, there are lots of things to think about. I think about the old days, the friends I've had and lost." He winked at me over his shoulder. "The new ones I've made."

"Is it hard being ancient?" I meant the question half as a joke.

However, Val took it seriously. "It's lonely."

"You've got friends."

"Not many who know the truth. When you have to keep things from people, it makes it hard to get close to them—and human relationships are so temporary." He turned and looked at me again. "And the ones who do know the truth, they either want to use me for something, or they push me away out of fear for what I am."

"Not all of us," I said.

Val shook his head. "You've pushed me away, Solina. You fear me whether you admit it or not."

I nodded. "I fear being hurt. I'm afraid of being used."

"So you see, we're not all that different."

"Except for the fact that you're immortal, and I am very *not*. I don't get as much time as you do to recover from mistakes. You must understand my need to be careful."

Val narrowed his eyes. "There's careful, and there's wasting time."

"It's a thin line," I said.

"One that you are treading oh so carefully."

I chewed on that thought for a moment but could formulate no response. I stretched, yawned, and rubbed my face again. "I'm beat. I wonder where I'm supposed to sleep."

"I put your stuff in the room you stayed in last time you were here," Val said.

"Oh? It survived?"

"A little smoky, but it'll do."

I shuffled out of the kitchen and up the stairs to my room. Val had dismissed me without uttering a single lascivious crack about my solitary sleeping arrangements. His uncharacteristic grimness would have worried me, but then I found my room, the big four-poster bed, and my pajamas. I didn't worry about Val anymore after that, and the moment my head hit the pillow, I didn't worry about anything else, either, not even my promise to keep Thorin updated. *Tomorrow*, I vowed as I drifted into the warm, fuzzy fog of sleep. *I'll call Thorin... tomorrow.*

CHAPTER SEVENTEEN

"SOLINA. GET UP."

I rolled over and pulled the bedcovers over my head. Skyla ripped the sheets and comforter away and smacked my hip. I cracked open an eyelid and focused on Skyla, who stood over me, grinning. Excitement shone in her face. Behind her, the pale-purple sky of a predawn morning peered through my room's window.

"*Whaaat*?" I whined.

"I'm going out to the barn. Are you going to look through Embla's things, or what?"

I yawned and rubbed my eyes. "It goes against my religion to get up earlier than God does. Where's Val?"

"He's waiting out in the hall. Get dressed and get a move on."

I groused some more but did as she said, sliding out of bed half awake and drunk with early-morning drowsiness. Skyla slipped into the dark hallway, and Val came in to take her place.

"What are you doing?" I grumbled, poking through my bags for something to wear. "I gotta get dressed."

"Don't let me stop you."

I frowned at him and pulled out a long-sleeved shirt, underwear, and a pair of jeans. Grabbing up my toiletry bag, I shuffled down the hall to the bathroom to brush my teeth and dress in privacy. When I returned, Val was standing at the window, looking out at the scenery.

"What is it?" I hopped on one leg while pulling a sock into place.

Val turned to me and smiled. "It's beautiful out there, isn't it?"

I nodded. "It is. I wish I took more time to enjoy it. Mendocino is really a stunning place, out here on the edge of the world."

"So, why don't we enjoy it?"

"What do you mean?"

"Let's do something fun," Val said. "Everything is run or fight all the time. Let's go down to the beach and look for shells or go into town and find somewhere good to eat for dinner tonight."

"That sounds like a date." I slid my feet into my boots, wrapped a cotton scarf around my neck, and went to join Val at the window.

"You do still owe me one."

I arched an eyebrow at him. "I do?"

"We were supposed to have dinner together in Vegas, remember?"

"That was before, Val. The last time we were here, things didn't end so well between us. We've never talked about that."

"We can talk about it tonight."

"That doesn't sound like fun."

"Dinner, Solina. That's all I'm asking. As friends."

"Friends?"

Val shrugged. "It's up to you. I've learned the hard way not to push you."

Giving in to Val would end badly, I suspected. But I missed his familiarity. I missed the part of him that had been a good friend. He hadn't been acting like himself lately, and I wanted to know why.

"I don't want to leave the Aerie," I said. "But I'll meet you at the beach after dinner."

Val exhaled and smiled. He motioned toward the door. We left the house in silence, taking care to muffle our steps and let sleeping Valkyries lie. We encountered no one as we crossed the yard to the outbuilding, where the clash of metal announced Skyla and Embla were already at work in the gym. Val waited outside while I slipped into the shower room at the front of the building. The bright white room smelled of soap and harsh cleaners. Embla had bundled her bath things and a change of clothes on a bench near the community showers, but a quick check uncovered no sign of the library key.

Outside, I collected Val from his hiding place in the shadows and headed for the main house. "The key's not in there," I said. "Unless she's got it on her right now."

"We need to look in her room."

"I don't know where her room is. If she was in the dormitory wing that burned, then we might be in trouble." My breath hitched, and I paused midstep. "What if the key burned, too?"

"I'll bash in the freaking door, Solina, or I'll pin down one of the sisters and sit on her until she talks. All this sneaky bullshit is getting on my nerves anyway."

"Yes, we know subtlety has never been your forte, but I'm not eager to announce our activities to the whole Aerie just yet." My gaze unfocused as I considered what to do. My brain hurt from all these unusual planning and scheming exercises. "I'll go back inside, find someone awake, tell them I'm looking to talk to Embla, and which one is her room? Simple, right?"

Val didn't argue, so I told him to hang out in my room until I had need for him. My ears popped, and he blipped out of sight. I choked on a breath of surprise, wondering if I would ever get used to that. I skipped up the house's front porch steps, pushed open the front door, and stepped into the foyer. At the sound of voices coming down the hallway, I turned.

Two women, Amala and Naomi, if I remembered correctly, greeted me with warm smiles. I pursed my lips and put on an expression I hoped looked like genuine confusion and stopped in their path. "Sorry to bother y'all, but I really need to talk to Embla. You know where her room is?"

The tall woman, who I thought was named Amala, pointed at the ceiling. "She's upstairs in the left wing, across from the bathroom, but I don't think she's there. She usually goes out to the gym in the mornings."

"Oh yeah?" I turned and glanced at the front door. "Well, maybe I'll check out there."

"We're going to breakfast," said Naomi, a compact, dark-skinned woman who wore her hair in a soft poof haloing her head. She looked angelic, but I had seen her training in the gym. She was fierce and lethal with fists or blade. "Why don't you come with us? Embla will probably be back soon. Maybe you'll see her in the kitchen."

I bit my lip and tried to look apologetic. "I'm not much of an early eater. I might come grab some coffee in a few minutes, though." I stepped aside and let the two women pass before I turned and headed to the stairway leading to the second floor. The left wing had survived the fire, but the end of the hallway connected to the dormitory wing, so the structure had suffered a lot of damage. Smoke had marked everything, tinting the walls a sad, greasy gray, and the floor had buckled in places. I eased down the hall, looking for the bathroom and the room across from it.

The fact that Embla occupied a room in the main house spoke to her seniority in the Aerie. The youngest women lived in the dorm and shared a large communal bathroom. Embla probably shared her bathroom only with Tori and—before the fire had claimed her life—Aoi, another of the older women at the Aerie.

Someone had cleaned soot from the surface of Embla's door, and its warm wood gleamed in comparison to the dirty walls around it. I turned the knob, and the door creaked open. Entering someone else's room without permission or knowledge felt like a violation. My stomach rolled over in protest, but I discarded my misgivings and stepped farther inside. Embla had obviously cleaned. Her room showed no sign of the fire other than a faint smoky odor that would probably linger in the walls for years to come. She had furnished her apartment with simple charm: an antique, wrought-iron bed, an oak dresser, and a small bedside table with a brass lamp. I went to the little table first and fished through the bric-a-brac on top—hair pins, silver hoop earrings, reading glasses, but no key.

I fell to my knees and peered under her bed. Embla stored several pairs of shoes and an old metal box under the dust ruffle. I slid the box from under the bed, unhooked the latch, raised the lid, and found a bundle of photos. The box contained no keys, and I should have put the pictures away, but something about the subject of the first photo aroused my curiosity.

The initial image showed two young women hugging each other as they posed for the camera with huge smiles. They resembled each other—Embla and another dark-skinned woman who could have been her sister.

The women in the pictures aged, and the photos showed the woman who wasn't Embla standing beside a handsome young man in uniform. In the next photograph, the woman held a baby. The baby turned into a toddler, a little boy, then a preteen. Then the pictures showed another baby, a little girl. Eventually, the images focused solely on the girl. All the next photos had either been taken from a long distance or had the grainy texture of a telephoto lens. I studied the woman and her two children, wondering why they held such interest for Embla. Maybe she simply cherished her family, and her connection with the Valkyries had impeded their relationship.

I thumbed through a few more photos in the stack and stopped cold.

In the latter part of adolescence, the girl in the photos was unmistakable. She stood in a grassy yard in front of a building that looked like a high school. Other teenagers milled about, but Skyla stood alone, her arms folded over her chest, a blank, unassuming look on her face. Dark hair hung in long ringlets to the middle of her back, but the bright eyes, strong chin, and sharp cheekbones formed her unmistakable face.

Skyla's pose and stance suggested she was unaware of the photographer. What did it mean that this picture was here, in Embla's room? My brain whirred like a set of old gears. It hiccupped and sputtered but produced no answers. I shoved the picture into my back pocket. The rest I set back in the box, which I returned to its place under the bed.

I had spent a lot of time studying those photos and didn't know how much longer I had until Embla returned to her room. Panic tingled through my nerves. My pulse thrummed, and my hands shook as adrenaline drizzled into my bloodstream. *Faster. Move faster.* I pawed through Embla's dresser, the only other piece of furniture in the room, and in the top drawer I found a jewelry box. The lid creaked when I opened it, which sounded like a scream to my raw nerves. Inside the box lay a strand of freshwater pearls, an old princess-style diamond ring, and a thin silver chain threaded through an old skeleton key. I rubbed my thumb over its tarnished surface. *That's got to be it.*

I closed the jewelry box, slid the dresser drawer back into place, and eased out of the room, careful to check for sounds of approaching footsteps. When I judged the way clear of witnesses, I dashed down the hallway and burst through the door into my room. Val was reclined on my bed, feet crossed, head pillowed on his hands, twined behind his head.

I pursed my lips and narrowed my eyes at him. "Comfortable?"

Val ignored my question and rolled off the bed. "You found it, didn't you?"

I dangled the key on its chain before his face. "Take it. Get down to the library, get your mental image, and get back up here so I can put it back."

Val took the key but paused to brush a hand over my temple. "Calm down, Solina. I could hear your heart beating from across the room."

"I'm no good at this cloak-and-dagger stuff."

"We don't have to worry about the CIA recruiting you, huh?"

I swallowed—anxiety had dried my throat. "Go, Val. I'm ready to be done with this."

Val smiled, winked, and—*pop*—disappeared. I held my breath until he returned. He passed me the key, and I snatched it, scurried down the hall again, and dumped it into Embla's jewelry box. As soon as I put my hand on the door to leave, I heard two voices in the hallway. One belonged Skyla, so the other was presumably Embla.

"I think you're going to be surprised," Embla said. "Just give me a second to grab it."

Floorboards creaked outside the bedroom door. My insides turned to ice. Following a desperate impulse, I dropped and rolled under the bed. Through the crack beneath the dust ruffle, I watched the door open, and Embla's feet stepped into the room.

She went to a closet, moved things around, and said, "Ah ha!"

I held my breath, paranoid Embla would hear air shushing through my nose. Whatever she found had captured her attention. She stood at the closet, fidgeting with something. I inhaled a shallow breath and held it again, mentally urging her to leave. With my nerves already strung to their max, I nearly screeched when someone knocked on the door.

"Embla?" Skyla asked.

I breathed out a silent sigh.

"Oh, Skyla, I found it."

Skyla stepped into the room. She sucked in a breath that sounded like awe. "That's it? It's really lovely."

"Isn't it?" Embla said.

"And you don't mind if I use it?"

"You've got quite a way with a blade, and I think you'll find this one fits you perfectly."

"I can't wait to try it."

Both of them turned and stepped back into the hallway, and Embla pulled her door shut behind her. I exhaled and lay in place, relishing the relief that flooded through me. With my composure restored, I rolled out from under the bed, pressed my ear to Embla's door, and then slipped out into the hallway, closing her door behind me. Val met me at the landing to the stairway.

"What the hell happened?" he whispered when I drew up to his side.

"They came back too soon."

"I know." Val brushed my shoulders and back, shooing away dirt and dust bunnies. "Skyla came into the room and freaked when I told her you were still putting the key back in place."

"I heard them coming and hid under the bed—classic espionage technique. Maybe I should work for the CIA after all." I told him about the conversation I had overheard and gave him the picture of teenaged Skyla.

Val looked at it, and his brows drew together. "What's this?"

"I found it in a box in Embla's room. There were stacks of them, mostly of Skyla growing up, but there were pictures of a woman who must be Skyla's mother and a boy who must be her brother."

Val's blue eyes flicked up to mine and held my gaze with a hard look. "Are you going to tell her?"

"Of course. She's been dying to know the truth of who she is. This might be the proof she needs."

"If she tells Embla, she'll know someone's been in her room."

"I trust Skyla knows how to be discreet. But even if Embla knows our scheme, I think it'll be worth it."

Val and I went to the kitchen in search of coffee. A headache was already worrying my temples, punishing me for engaging in early-morning, clandestine activities without sufficient doses of caffeine. Amala and Naomi were there, finishing their bowls of oatmeal. I poured a big mug of coffee and doctored it with cream and sugar. Val settled into a chair at the kitchen table, clutching his own cup, filled to the brim. For the gods, coffee must have been one of those things of pleasure rather than necessity, and Val never denied an opportunity to indulge in the things he liked.

Amala frowned at me. "I had hoped you might make more goodies for us like you did yesterday, but I only found oatmeal and cereal."

"Maybe I can make up for it by lunchtime. How about brownies?"

Amala sighed, but a smile tugged at the corner of her mouth. "I guess… if that's the best you can do."

I laughed and went to the Aerie's massive pantry to sort out the necessary ingredients while Val went in search of other occupations. Brownie baking started my second day of keeping busy in the kitchen while the household buzzed around me. Just before noon, Skyla strolled into the kitchen and sniffed at my plate of double-fudge brownies.

When she reached for one, I smacked her hand. "Save them for lunch."

"But I missed breakfast."

"Have a banana." I pointed toward a bowl of fruit on the kitchen table.

Skyla set her jaw and went for the brownies again, snagging one away before I caught her. "Ha!" She shoved it into her mouth, making her cheeks bulge. "God," she mumbled, "these are like chocolate orgasms."

"Do you think I should put those on the order form for the bakery? Chocolate orgasms, eight ninety-nine a dozen?"

"I'd buy them," she said with a sigh. "I'd buy any kind of orgasm I could get."

"I don't know why you and Val hate each other so much. You're both so much alike on this subject."

Skyla shrugged, swallowed, and stuffed another brownie in her mouth. I shook my head and went back to stirring a giant pot of vegetable soup. Although a baker by trade, I was a monkey with more than one trick when it came to the kitchen. "How did your workout go?"

"Embla gave me a new blade to try."

"I heard."

"Right. I wondered where you were hiding."

"Under the bed."

"I almost died when Val said you were in Embla's room when we came back. What were you doing in there?"

I gave her a rundown of our morning's activities and finished by pulling the photo from my pocket. "I found something else you're going to be interested in."

Skyla took the photo and looked at the image. She gasped and slapped her hand over her mouth. While she struggled for composure, I told her about Embla's box and the other photos I found in it.

"My mother and my brother?" Skyla said, breathless. "What does she know about my family?"

"I guess you'll have to ask her, but you can't tell her how you know. If she knows we were in her room, it puts everything at risk. You're right not to trust anyone here." I motioned to the photo. "You have proof you've been lied to, but don't let your indignation interfere with our plans."

Skyla's face reddened, and she gritted her teeth. "Are you insinuating I don't know how to handle myself?"

I raised my hands in a defensive pose. "I didn't say that to offend you. I can only imagine your outrage. But above all else, we've got to find out what happened to Tori and that sword."

"I *know* that." Skyla slapped the tabletop. "I know my mission, and I won't jeopardize it for personal issues. I mean, if you of all people can keep your head on straight, don't you think I can do the same?"

"Me of all people? What's that supposed to mean?"

Skyla's shoulders slumped. "I meant it as a compliment. I meant a relatively naive small-town girl got thrown into this big, steaming pile of crap, and she's handled it with decorum. You've had every right to have a meltdown and fly off the handle, but you've held it together."

"I don't know if you were paying attention, but I *have* had a meltdown. And it lasted for a month."

"Oh, I was paying attention," she said. "That wasn't a meltdown."

"What was it then?"

"A flare-up."

I snorted and grinned. "Are you calling me a hemorrhoid?"

Skyla barked a sharp laugh that dissolved into a fit of quivering giggles. "Sh-should I start carrying around some of that cream?"

"Sure," I said, hiccupping with laughter. "But only if you think it would help."

I rubbed my hands over my face, clearing away the last of my mirth.

Then I sighed and leaned against the kitchen counter. "I need to call Thorin and give him an update. I promised to stay in touch, but I haven't had a chance. Things around here have been... *distracting*, to say the least."

"You two seem to be getting along better than before," Skyla said. "There's still tension between you, but it's a different kind."

I pressed my lips together and avoided her gaze. "Maybe we understand each other a little better than we used to."

Skyla made a sound in the back of her throat. "Don't lie. You think he's hot."

I rolled my eyes at her. "Even I wouldn't lie about that."

"Go call him." Skyla grinned. "Tell him I was a Valkyrie after all."

I pushed away from the counter and slipped my arm around Skyla's shoulder for a brief hug. "Somehow, I don't think he'll be surprised."

But I didn't find out whether Thorin was surprised by Skyla's lineage. When I ducked up to my room to give him a call, his phone rang and went to voice mail. After several failed attempts to reach him, I left a message assuring him no further emergencies had arisen, and I urged him to call me as soon as he could. I fingered the chain around my neck, and the gold radiated heat from where it had lain close to my skin. Despite its warmth, a cold shiver snaked over my skin.

Thorin said he could use the chain to locate me if something happened to me. But if something had happened to him, how would I know? How would I ever find him?

CHAPTER EIGHTEEN

OLD PAPER AND BEESWAX CANDLES scented the air in the Valkyries' library—a welcome respite from the smoke. The room's antique furnishings and tapestries sent me back in time to another century, one with suits of armor. Except for books and scrolls and some musty old furniture, the library was empty. All the Valkyries had gone to bed except a few who patrolled the grounds outside. *Hope nobody gets a sudden late-night craving for historical records.*

"So, we're looking for some kind of book that tells you how to commune with the dead?" Val asked.

Skyla's brow furrowed. "I guess so. Unless you got a better idea."

No one did.

We pawed through the stacks of books and scrolls. Some things were obviously unrelated to our search, and I passed over them after a quick glance. I paused here and there to read pages in journals and diaries that referenced the Valkyries' interactions with battles and wars throughout history. I found one that mentioned World War II. The journalist had served as a Night Witch, a member of the 588th Night Bomber Regiment of the Soviet Air Forces. Without the need to fulfill the Aesir's ancient charge, the Valkyries found other ways to meet the call of the battlefield. What a history lesson those diaries would have made. *But I'm not here for a history lesson.*

Eventually, I worked my way to a scroll-stuffed cubby hole. The first parchment roll revealed a genealogy record. Tori said the Valkyries kept track of their bloodlines, and there lay the evidence. I dug through a few more, looking for a trace of Skyla's past. Before I could find her, though, I found a scroll detailing the lineage of Mani and Sol. I wheezed. My knees turned to water, and I plopped to the floor.

"What?" Skyla rushed to my side. "Did you find something?"

"Look at this." I handed her the scroll, which she stretched across an empty desk.

Val pulled me up to my feet, and we stood behind Skyla, reading over her shoulder.

Skyla ran her finger down line after line until she found an entry for Mani and me. "Look," she whispered. "It's you."

In bright, illuminated inscriptions, a record keeper for the Valkyries had marked every generation in the Mundy family line where a pair of twins had appeared. Sometimes, they were a hundred years or more apart, but they happened frequently enough to show the trait persisted in our family. Our very distant blood connection to the original Sol and Mani came through my father. Seeing it laid out in print, for thousands of years, gave my history gravity and a tangible reality.

"How did they know?" I asked.

Skyla shrugged. "Birth records are easy to find. Maybe it's the librarian's job to watch out for these kinds of things."

Those scrolls confirmed that, in some subtle way, Mani and I had always been together.

"He isn't really gone, then, is he? This is proof that someday, some part of his spirit and mine will be together again."

Skyla blinked, and her face went slack. She swept a finger over Mani's name, scribed in shimmering, silver ink. The names blurred together when tears gathered in my eyes. I blinked and backed away, taking several deep breaths to recover my composure.

"It's like a pedigree," Val said. "We can breed you and get top dollar."

I grunted and smacked his shoulder. "Too bad there aren't any suitable studs."

Skyla opened her mouth to form a retort but stopped. Her face softened. "Do you think there might be a chart for me?"

"That's what I was looking for in the first place," I said.

Val huffed. "I thought we were looking for instructions on contacting the dead."

"I was, but when I stumbled on these scrolls, I thought about Embla having those pictures of Skyla, and I thought there might be more proof in here."

Skyla peered up at me, her eyes shining and earnest. "Would it bother you to keep looking?"

"Not at all," I said.

We worked late into the night, stopping a few times to retrieve drinks and snacks to fuel our research. I finished the pile of scrolls without finding specific mention of Skyla's family, and none of us knew what that meant, but sometime in the early morning, Skyla discovered what we originally had come for.

"Look," she said, "a grimoire."

"Oh, oh," I said, "I know what that means. A book of spells."

Val's mouth twisted into a quirky frown. "How'd you know that?"

"I read."

"The old Valkyries weren't witches who chanted spells," Val said. "They lived in our realm and traveled to Midgard, *Earth*, whenever Odin asked them."

"Things have changed, haven't they?" Skyla asked. "You don't live in Asgard anymore, and there is no Valhalla. The Valkyries had to come up with another way."

"So what do you need?" I asked. "Eye of newt, wing of bat?"

Skyla briefly smiled as her eyes grazed back and forth over the spellbook's text. "Looks something like a séance. Draw some runes, meditate, set a conducive atmosphere. The most important thing is the person attempting to make contact be sensitive to the spirit world, which the Valkyries inherently are." Skyla looked up. "Give me some peace and quiet. I'm going to give this a go."

"You don't need us to sit in a circle and hold hands?" I tried not to laugh.

"Do you need a crystal ball?" asked Val, who wasn't holding back his laughter at all.

Skyla ignored him. "Shoo. Both of you, *out*."

I trudged up the basement stairs with Val, my body heavy with exhaustion. He reached over, put a hand on my shoulder, and squeezed. I imagined those strong fingers digging into the tense muscles in my neck and craved the relief it would bring, but inviting Val to my room for a massage session meant inviting the worst kind of trouble. I sighed, letting out my exhaustion and frustrations in a long breath.

"Tired?" Val asked.

I started to assure him I was fine, but my step fell short and I stumbled on a stair. Val caught me and swept me up in his arms.

I squealed. "What are you doing?"

"You promised we could have some fun today." Val carried me to the top of the stairs before setting me on my feet.

"I walked with you on the beach after dinner," I said as we crossed the open foyer leading to the staircase.

"You stayed a pace ahead of me the whole time, and the wind blew so hard I couldn't hear myself think."

Val was right. I had walked quickly on purpose, keeping a safe distance from his smooth tongue.

"You said we could talk," he said.

I did say that. Doesn't mean I don't regret it.

We ascended to the second floor in silence. When we reached my room, I went to the bed and slouched on the foot of the mattress. "You want to go first?"

Val frowned. "I don't know what to say. 'I'm sorry' seems hardly sufficient."

I raised an eyebrow and sniffed. "It's a start. At least it means you take some responsibility for your actions."

Val stepped closer and leaned a hip against the bed near the headboard. A pensive look stole across his face, masking his usual good cheer. "Our kind have always been passionate, Solina: jealous, possessive, ferocious. We do nothing by halves. Hating. Fighting... Loving. It's all or nothing for us. For a human, I could see where that would be overwhelming."

"So you're saying you can't help it when you act like an overbearing control freak?"

Val's eyebrows arched, and he leaned back, his mouth popping open in a soft *O*. "Is that really how you see me?"

"Not always. But when that side of you comes out, that all-or-nothing side, it's scary."

"It wouldn't be if you trusted me."

I folded my hands in my lap and studied the ridges of my knuckles. "Trust is a gift not easily given."

"And laboriously earned. Is there anyone you *do* trust, Solina?"

I shrugged. "Skyla. My parents, maybe. They love me in their own weird way. They used me a lot, too, but some of that was my own fault."

"Do you trust Thorin?"

I shrugged again. "He's not the one trying to seduce me. I am a means to his ends. You're the one who insists on having more. You're the one trying to put me in a position where I could get hurt."

"You've already been hurt," Val said. "And lived to tell the tale."

"Doesn't mean I'm eager to do it again."

Val nodded. "I am immortal, Solina. I have an eternity. If time is what you need, then time is what you'll get. I'm not going anywhere."

His answer resolved nothing, but maybe it meant a truce between us, and I welcomed it.

I rubbed my tired eyes and slumped back on the bed. "What time is it?"

Val checked the display on his phone. "Three."

"It's obscenely late." I looked back and studied Val. In the darkness of the room, he appeared as little more than a shadow. My memory filled in the details: shaggy auburn hair and a day-old beard. Devilishly handsome, as usual. Our relationship might have been simpler, easier, if he were a human man, but he wasn't, so I wouldn't my waste time on "what-ifs".

Val held still, letting me study him. "What are you thinking, Solina? Even in the dark, I can tell you're thinking."

I took a breath to say something, but before I voiced my thoughts, the bedroom door creaked open, and a thread of light spilled into the room.

"Solina?" Skyla hissed, tiptoeing closer. "Are you awake?"

I sat up. "Yes, I'm awake."

"I found her. Ariel. She's here, and she'll talk to us, but we have to do it fast. She won't last much longer."

"Us?"

"Well, you and me. She's a little wary of Val."

I rose to my feet. "I don't blame her."

"Hey," Val objected.

"Val?" Skyla asked. "You're in here too?"

"You have a problem with that?"

I interrupted before they could start something. "I don't know for sure, but it's probably rude to keep a ghost waiting."

"I'm coming with you." Val took a step toward the door.

"No," Skyla said. "She only wanted to talk to me and Solina. We can't risk you scaring her off, and we can't waste time appeasing your ego."

"You promised to respect my autonomy," I said. "Remember?"

Val crossed his arms over his chest, glowering, but agreed. "Okay, but I expect a full report."

"Thanks for understanding." I turned to follow Skyla.

In the hallway, Skyla whirled around on me and narrowed her eyes. She looked pointedly toward the dark room where Val had stayed behind. Then she looked back at me. Without further comment about finding me sharing intimate space with her mortal enemy, she spun on her heel and led me down to the library.

Candles lit the interior in a warm glow. Nothing unusual jumped out of the shadows, and I wondered about the validity of Skyla's scheme.

"This is Solina," Skyla said and motioned in my direction.

I scanned the room. Nothing. No one. "Who are you talking to?"

"Ariel."

"There's no one here."

"You don't see her?"

I pursed my lips and shook my head, wondering if sleep deprivation had made Skyla hallucinate.

"That doesn't matter. She can see you."

"Where is she?"

Skyla motioned toward a tapestry hanging on the stone wall. The fabric swayed, and I squeaked.

"Don't hurt her feelings," Skyla said.

"I'm sorry. I haven't been trained in proper ghost etiquette."

"Well, get over it. She won't be able keep it together much longer." Skyla turned toward the tapestry where Ariel's ghost supposedly stood. "What can you tell us about the fire, Ariel?"

"Surtalogi," said a disembodied voice.

I was glad to hear my suspicions confirmed, even if it was by a disembodied spirit. "That's what we thought," I said.

Skyla turned to me with an eyebrow arched in question.

"I dreamed of it."

"And you didn't tell me?"

"When has there been time? Besides, it's not something I wanted to talk about around any of *them*," I said, meaning the Valkyries. I gave Skyla a quick summary of my vision and explained how the three gods and I agreed Surtalogi had mostly likely furnished the fire. "I had no idea who was wielding it, though. I didn't think it was Helen."

"Not Helen, not Tori," said the voice... Ariel... whoever.

"What do you mean not Tori?"

"Tori is not your traitor."

"Then who is?" Skyla asked.

"The Valkyries... rotten to the core. We were collecting artifacts of the gods, under the direction of our patron, but we were secretly seeking to empower the Valkyries and end our dependence on the gods. We found many things... Surtr's sword." Her voice weakened as she spoke, and her last words ended in a ghostly murmur.

"No way," Skyla said. "They are handmaidens of the Aesir. They've maintained their customs to religious dedication. They're not going to pervert that after all this time."

"We are hostesses of war," Ariel whispered. "We ache for battle. We long to return to Valhalla and Folkvangr and see our halls renewed. To do that, we need independence."

"You too, Ariel?" Skyla's voice rose.

I put an arm to her shoulder to remind her where we were and that someone might hear her.

"Did you forsake the Aesir?"

Ariel took so long to respond that I wondered if she had left. When she finally spoke, her words were barely audible. "Blinded by delusions of glory... Confession for atonement. Tori denied the plan. Still loyal to Aesir. Tori was to be killed. Tori fought." Ariel's voice faltered again, and I barely made out her last words. "Aerie burned... Tori ran."

"Tori took the sword with her?" I said.

"Yes," Ariel said.

"Where is she now?" Skyla asked.

"*Grim... Thorin... Corvallis...*"

The candles flickered as a gust of cool air blew through the room. Several candles went out, dimming the room further.

"Ariel?" Skyla asked. "Are you here?"

We held our breath and waited, but she had gone.

"Did she say *grim*?" I asked. "What does that mean?"

"I'm not sure."

"And Thorin and Corvallis? Does she mean Corvallis as in Oregon?" I'd never heard Thorin mention a connection to Oregon, but there were probably lots of things Thorin had refrained from mentioning, especially if any of them were of a personal nature.

Skyla shrugged. "Your guess is as good as mine."

"Looks like I need to get ahold of Thorin, ASAP. In the meantime, I could ask Val—"

"No." Skyla latched onto my arm and squeezed. "Don't breathe a word of this to Val."

"I'm not always his biggest fan, either, Skyla. But he's a good source of information. Why shouldn't I ask him?"

"If Tori wasn't Helen's spy, then who told Helen where we were at Oneida Lake?"

"Why Val?"

"He had opportunity. So many times, he's had opportunity. He knew where you were when you were kayaking with me. He knew you were in the desert."

"He didn't know we were at Oneida Lake… unless you're saying the Valkyries were feeding him information. And if that's true, why would he kill them?"

"It's classic James Bond, Solina. Kill your own spy to throw the enemy off the trail. With Inyoni and Kalani dead, we would never know who to suspect other than Tori. Inyoni as good as said she was leaking word to someone. Maybe it was Val. Maybe she didn't know he would pass it on to Helen."

"Val had plenty of opportunities to kidnap me and take me to Helen himself, but he hasn't. Why not?"

"He's keeping your confidence so you'll feed him inside information. He can't kill you himself, but so long as you trust him and let him close, he'll always know where you are, and when the time is right, he'll call for Skoll."

"No," I said, shaking my head. "It's too convoluted. The truth is usually simpler than that. I won't believe it. Not Val. You were wrong about Tori, and you're wrong about him."

"Maybe." Skyla shrugged. "I hope you're right."

"What about you?" I asked. "You've had all the same opportunities as Val to give me away. More."

"We're going to do this again? Haven't I proven myself to you enough by now?"

I dropped my head and shook it. My heart wrenched at the idea that Skyla might be anything other than what I believed. "I don't know what to think. But, yes, I do trust you." I raised my head and met her gaze. "And I do know we need to find Tori before Helen does. We need to find out what *grim* means, and what Thorin and Corvallis have to do with it. I'm going to track Tori down. Maybe she can help us bring down Helen."

"You're going to recruit her?" Skyla asked with a sparkle in her eye.

"Or we can go back to Vegas and sit on our thumbs."

Skyla laughed. "Girl, you've been hanging around with me for far too long. I'm obviously starting to rub off on you."

I grimaced. "Don't take this the wrong way, but I hope it comes off with a little soap and water. I liked myself fine when this all started, and I hope to keep some of that girl with me when this all comes to an end."

"So what are we going to tell Val?" Skyla asked.

"Tell him the ghost didn't know anything useful. We can tell him that she saw Tori using the sword, but she didn't know where she went with it."

Skyla agreed to my suggestion, and after I helped her remove all traces of her séance, we parted ways outside the library. My thoughts centered on my bed, and my body craved a few hours' sleep to make up for all we'd lost during the night. Val had left by the time I came back to my room, and I was relieved. I peeled off my clothes and fell into bed, too tired to find pajamas.

CHAPTER NINETEEN

U NABLE TO IGNORE THE PERSISTENT sunlight beaming in my face, I gave up and got out of bed. The lacy draperies over the windows did little to shield the light, and since most of the Valkyries rose at dawn, the possibility that a guest might like to sleep in likely never crossed their minds.

I showered, dressed, and went to find Skyla. She wasn't in her room, and her bed looked as though she had never lain in it. Maybe military types made their beds every morning, but something told me Skyla had never gone to bed after we left the library, even though she had looked exhausted. I found her in the kitchen, drinking coffee with Val, of all people.

Dark circles shadowed her eyes, the result of a night without sleep. I sank into a chair next to her and gathered her hands into mine. "Skyla, what's going on?"

"What do you mean?"

"You've been up all night."

"Yes."

"Why?"

"I couldn't sleep. I've been thinking about Embla and my mother and what it all means."

I shifted my attention to Val, who had shaved and changed his clothes. "You look rested."

"Don't let it fool you," he said. "I spent the rest of the night searching the grounds for any sign of a lead in case things didn't pan out with Skyla's séance."

"Did you find anything useful?"

"I followed a trail of burnt ground for a while. It led away from the house, north, but it faded out and disappeared where the highway cut through."

"Tori hitched a ride?"

"Or had someone waiting for her."

Since Skyla wanted to keep our conversation with Ariel mum, I had little else to say on the matter of Tori's disappearance. I changed the subject by going to the refrigerator and digging out a carton of eggs. "Anyone want something to eat?"

"I'll take something," Skyla said through a yawn. She laid her head on her arms.

"Why not go to bed if you're so tired?" Val asked.

The coffee pot had enough left to pour another few cups, so I made one for Val and another for Skyla. She grabbed it from me and sucked down a huge gulp before answering. "No time to sleep."

"So," Val said, "did you learn something last night after all?"

Skyla frowned into her coffee. "I talked to a ghost, all right. But she mostly mumbled unintelligible things."

"Maybe you need more practice," he said.

"Practice doing what?" asked one of the Valkyries, who shuffled into the kitchen, frowning, her gaze locked on the empty coffee pot. It was Embla, and Skyla and I both froze. "Sword fighting? I expected to see you in the gym this morning, Skyla, but you didn't show."

"I-I had a late night," Skyla said. "I didn't feel like it today."

"You've got to take better care of yourself. If you want to be at your best, to be the kind of warrior we need you to be, you can't stay up all night talking to ghosts."

Skyla gurgled something nonsensical before stuttering, "How-how did you know?"

"It's *my* library," Embla said. "I know everything that happens inside its walls."

"Why didn't you say anything?"

"At first I wasn't sure what you were up to, but I decided if it was something important enough for you to steal into my room, hide under my bed, root through my things, and take my spare key, then it was something that didn't require my interference."

Blood drained from my face. "Do you have hidden cameras?"

Embla smiled and shook her head. "No. Just a good sense of when things go amiss in the room I've lived in for twenty years. You smell like a summer day, Solina. After all that smoke and soot, you were like an air freshener. Also, I haven't cleaned under my bed since the fire, but there was a large patch absent of dust and soot in the vague size and shape of a young woman."

I blushed with mortification. "Well there goes my CIA application after all." All that sneaking around for nothing. Why couldn't I just sink into the floor and disappear?

Embla turned to Skyla again. "I suppose Ariel wasn't the only ghost you were thinking about last night either, was it?"

"What do you mean?"

"Your mother."

Skyla's face slackened, and her mouth fell open. "What are you saying?"

"Solina found the evidence, didn't she? A picture of you as a sweet, young girl. I know each of those photographs as a mother knows her children's names, and I know when one goes missing. It seems you've learned more than you bargained for in your search for that key."

"Why do you have those pictures?" Skyla asked.

Embla shrugged. "Because. Your mother was my sister, and I am your aunt."

The room went silent and airless as a vacuum.

"M-my mother was an only child," Skyla said after overcoming her shock.

"It would seem that way, but no, she was my little sister. We had an older sister, too, but she died as a baby. Your mother never knew her."

I saw a similarity in their looks—matching eye shape and bone structure. They shared the same distinct chin and jaw lines. Embla's skin tone was darker and cooler, and her black curls were tighter and a little coarser. Skyla's Puerto Rican genes added amber tones to her skin and lightened her hair color several shades, but their genetic relationship was obvious once it was pointed out.

"My mother never mentioned you," Skyla said.

"She wouldn't. It's the side effect of leaving the Aerie."

"My mother was a stay-at-home mom. She was on the PTA and baked cookies for fundraisers. What do you mean she left the Aerie?"

"Kara was Valkyrie," Embla said, "just like me. She was my sister, my closest friend. Our mother died not long after Kara's birth. The Valkyries showed up a few days after her death and told Kara and me what we were. They took us to the Aerie to raise us and train us. We never saw Father after that—I barely remember him. Your mother and I were inseparable... until your dad came along. That girl fell hard and fast. A man in uniform has a way of doing that."

"So," I said, "no coincidence you followed in your father's footsteps."

Skyla pulled a face. "He wasn't going to raise any princesses."

"That explains a lot."

Skyla ignored me and turned back to Embla. "She sure didn't seem like any of the Valkyries I've met so far."

"The sword I gave you yesterday belonged to her," Embla said. "I wanted to tell you, but I didn't know how. The Valkyries' existence is supposed to be a close-guarded secret. If a sister chooses to leave the order, she has to take a vow of silence."

"Who would believe her anyway?" Skyla asked. "To anyone but us, it would sound crazy."

"Still, the sisterhood takes no chances. If a woman chooses to leave, she has that freedom, but she must keep our secret. It's more than a simple promise that binds her tongue. She'll be physically unable to speak of it, and eventually her memories of us will fade." Embla gave Skyla a meaningful look. "By the time you came along, the Valkyries were a distant memory to her—more like a dream. She wouldn't have spoken of us. She *couldn't* have."

Skyla frowned at Embla. "What could have made her want to leave this?"

Embla shrugged. "Love."

"Oh, gag me. My mom and dad fought like cats and dogs."

"That doesn't mean they didn't love each other."

"Bullshit," Skyla said. "He spent as much time as possible away from us."

"What about when she got sick? He was there for her."

"How would you know?"

Skyla had never offered much information about her past, and I had never had the guts to ask. Truthfully, I had let my problems overwhelm me, and I hadn't spent much time worrying about Skyla's background. That was self-centered of me, perhaps, but there in the Valkyries' kitchen, I found Skyla's lineage intensely interesting. Val looked equally intrigued.

"You never saw me," Embla said, "but I was there. I watched her. I watched you."

Skyla's cheeks flushed a deep, angry crimson. "Why wouldn't you tell me? You knew, but you kept it from me. Do you know what it would have meant for me to know who I was?"

"I wasn't sure it was a good idea in the beginning," said Embla. "I debated whether this was the life for you or whether you should be allowed to live as a normal woman. But I see now that your heritage will not be denied."

"Did Tori know about me?"

"She knew your mother."

"Why did she lie?"

"At the time, I thought she was protecting us. Now, I think she was protecting her own self-interests. I'm sorry I didn't come to you with this sooner. I could have helped you so you wouldn't feel the need to sneak around."

Val sighed and rolled his eyes. "I told them to just ask in the first place. But, *no*, they wanted to be a couple of Charlie's Angels."

Skyla pouted. "No one would talk to me, Embla. If I brought it up, people changed the subject or flat out told me to mind my own business. Besides, we didn't know who to trust. Some members of the Aerie have shown questionable loyalties."

Embla chuckled. "We are an elite bunch of snobs, aren't we?"

Skyla dropped her gaze and shrugged.

How diplomatic of her, I thought.

"You were right not to trust anyone. With Tori gone, there's a vacuum of power. Who or what will fill it has yet to be seen. Some of the sisters may be willing to look for the Aerie's next leader outside the Valkyries as easily as they would look inside."

"Outside the Valkyries?" Skyla asked. "Like Helen?"

Embla's mouth twisted as if she'd swallowed something distasteful. "Yes. Like Helen."

"What about you?" Val asked. "Where do your loyalties lie?"

Embla blanked her face and said, "With the order of the Valkyries, of course. Always and forever, my sisters come first."

While I made brunch for us all—omelets and toast—Embla told us about the memorial service the sisters had planned for after sundown to remember the women lost in the fire. Embla asked if I would arrange a reception with snacks and hot drinks for when the service ended, and I agreed.

After they cleaned their plates, Skyla and Embla went to look through the collection of photographs Embla kept under her bed. I stayed in the kitchen to wash dishes and start on the list of items Embla had requested. Val left to find his own entertainment, giving me the time I needed to give Thorin a private call.

I dashed upstairs to dig my phone from my bag. When I dialed Thorin's number, it rang and rang, but he never answered, and the call never switched to voice mail. I gave up and called Thorin's store.

Val's roommate answered. "Thorin Adventure Outfitters, Hugh speaking."

"Hugh, it's Solina."

"Solina. We have to stop meeting like this... over the phone. I'm much sexier in person."

I rolled my eyes. "Right. So sexy. It's the reason I have to stay away from you all the time. Couldn't keep my hands off you otherwise."

"You say that like it's a bad thing."

"So, besides wanting to hear your stimulating voice, the reason I'm calling is that I've sort of lost contact with Thorin. Have you heard from him lately?"

"The last I knew, he was with you."

"Something came up, and I had to take a side trip without him. Skyla and Val are with me, though. Thorin's not answering his cell, so if you hear from him, tell him I called and that I'm okay."

"Um, sure. Anything else?"

"I guess that's all... No, wait a minute. Does the term *grim* mean anything to you? You ever hear anyone mention it in relation to Thorin and Corvallis?" Bringing up Ariel's words was impulsive, but Hugh was far enough removed from the whole ordeal to be a safe contact. I hoped.

"Sure. It's the Boss Man's brother."

"It is?" My voice went high with surprise. "He has a brother named Grim?"

"Yes. Modi Grimr Thorin."

"Why have I never heard of him?"

"They're not close."

"So, how did you know about him?"

"Me and Boss Man go way back."

That made me pause. "How far back? Like... ancient?"

"Is that what you're really calling about?"

I huffed. "Do you know where this brother lives?"

"Corvallis, I think. Why are you asking?"

Bingo! I had a new lead on Tori, but I wasn't about to share that news with a guy I barely knew. *Think fast, Solina.* "I overhead Thorin mention it, but didn't think anything of it at the time. Maybe that's where Thorin was going when we lost touch. If I could call Grim, I could find out if Thorin is with him. It's pretty important."

"His contact info is probably in the store's database."

"Could you check?"

"I don't want to piss Thorin off, handing out information about his family."

"Hugh," I said. "This is important. Give me the number. I'll take all the heat, I swear."

"Have you ever seen Thorin when he's pissed?"

I almost choked on laughter. "I've seen it, been the cause of it, and lived to tell the tale. Now, Hugh, *please.*"

"Okay, but don't tell him I told you."

"I owe you one."

"How 'bout a beer next time you're in town?"

"Hugh, if I make it back to Siqiniq, I will buy you a whole damn keg."

I dialed the number Hugh gave me, reeling at the possibility of the existence of yet another Aesir. In the desert, I had asked Thorin if he had siblings, but he changed the subject. Hugh had said they weren't on good terms, which might have explained Thorin's reticence.

I expected to get a voice mail and was not surprised when an automated voice told me to leave a message. I stated my name and reason for calling but doubted anyone would really call me back. I was wrong, though. Moments after I left the message, my phone trilled to life. Caller ID displayed the number I had just dialed, and I stared, eyes bugging wide, as if witnessing a miracle.

The phone rang again. I shook off my stupor and answered. "Hello?"

"Solina?" asked the caller.

"Wha—*Tori*? Is that you? Where are you?"

"I will ask the questions. I am no longer free to trust anyone."

"You don't trust me?" I said. "Um, daughter of Sol here, next step on Helen's road to eternal damnation. Or did you forget?"

"I haven't forgotten. If you're the second step, then the third step is the sword, which I have."

"So I've heard."

"You're still alive because Helen wants the sword and she knows you're tracking it."

"I have drawn a similar conclusion, but what does that have to do with whether or not you trust me?"

"She could be using you to get to me. So could the Valkyries. They want it just as much as Helen."

I waved in a dismissive gesture even though Tori couldn't see it. "No one knows I'm talking to you."

"You're calling me from the Aerie. You do realize the Valkyries are compromised? They have ears and eyes everywhere."

"How do you know I'm at the Aerie?"

"They're not the only ones with surreptitious allies."

"What does that mean?"

"It means be careful in all you do and say in that place."

"I'll keep that in mind."

"Why isn't Alek with you?"

"Now that's just creepy." I looked around the room as if I might find a camera spying on me somewhere. "Thorin is out looking for Baldur while I came here to look for Surtalogi. Skyla spoke with Ariel's ghost—seems Skyla's really Valkyrie after all, which you knew and lied about. Ariel said you fought with the sisters over the future direction of the Valkyries."

"They wanted us to forsake the Aesir and serve ourselves. The foundations of the Valkyries are crumbling. I blame myself."

"You can discuss that with your shrink," I said. "I'm only interested in that sword and keeping it out of Helen's hands. I have more support and more resources than you. What makes you think you're the best one to protect it?"

"I'm not alone. I am quite safe and capable of defending myself."

"You're with Grim. How do you know he can be trusted?"

"He is Aesir, and he was... *is* the Valkyries' patron. He is sworn to protect us and provide for us."

"Mm-hmm, and I see how much promises mean in your world."

"He is also my lover."

Eww. I wrinkled my nose. *Too much information.*

"The sword is safe," Tori said. "I will keep it from Helen's hands. You can focus on keeping yourself alive."

"Oh, well... Okay, then."

"So, you're going to let it go?"

"Hell no. You've lost your mind if you think I'm going to let you keep that sword to yourself and cross my fingers and hope you or your boyfriend won't betray me when Helen names the right price."

"There's no guarantee we would survive a second Ragnarok. It's in our best interest to prevent Helen from fulfilling her scheme."

"Uh huh, and I should take your word for it." I exhaled an irritated grunt. "Thorin won't be satisfied with your guarantees, either."

"But you don't know where he is."

"I'm not worried about that at this moment."

Tori's voice turned harsh. "Your bravado is false, Solina. I hear the fear in your voice."

"I am terrified." I hardened my tone to match hers. "Every day I have to fight against letting the fear paralyze me. But I'm not going to let others hold my fate in their hands. Not anymore."

"You are not safe among the sisters. You should leave the Aerie as soon as possible."

"And go where? I will always be running until Helen is stopped. That sword could go a long way toward accomplishing that goal."

"And you will be the one to wield it? Ha!"

"Will Grim kill Helen? Will you?"

Tori did not answer, and her silence indicated reluctance.

"You're content to sit on it, aren't you?" I said.

"There's no need for unnecessary risks. My vow is to the Aesir. It is to them that I must remain loyal."

"What if the Aesir want you to keep me alive?"

"I'm sorry, Solina, but if you were their most important concern, Thorin wouldn't have left you on your own."

I stopped and swallowed back the sudden bitterness in my throat. "He didn't leave me on my own. I have Skyla and Val with me, and I'm not helpless or defenseless, not like I was when you first met me. And what about everything you said before? You kidnapped me to keep me safe. Now you're turning your back on me?"

"I'm sorry, Solina. But that was before... before everything went to hell at the Aerie, before I lost all my sisters. I have the sword. Keeping that safe is my primary concern."

"You suck," I said, which was lame and puerile, but I had depleted my supply of witty rejoinders.

"Get out of the Aerie," Tori said. "Sooner than later."

"Where do I go? Who do I trust?"

Tori sighed. Her breath carried over the phone. "Trust only yourself."

CHAPTER TWENTY

T RUST WAS A SMALL WORD bearing the weight of substantial significance. In a way, Tori was right: I could really only trust myself, but I wouldn't last long on my own that way. I needed alliances. I needed friends. I needed Skoll dead and Helen returned to her underworld lair. My chances of realizing that goal increased in proportion to the number of people who signed on to help me achieve it.

I had Skyla and Thorin on my side, and in my count, Skyla equaled the force of at least three or four average people. Thorin, with his hammer, counted for ten or twenty or possibly more. But Skyla and Thorin had ties that bound them to other obligations: preserving the Valkyries' integrity and protecting the Allfather.

Val, however, had once said he had totally dedicated himself to me. He had proved himself loyal, and whatever I asked of him, I suspected he would give. But at what price?

Shortly after I ended the conversation with Tori, Skyla found me packing my bags. She came into the room, clutching several photographs to her chest. "What are you doing?" she asked.

"Packing."

"I see that. And where do you think you're going?"

"Away. The Aerie is compromised. I'm not safe here."

Skyla scowled. "These women may question the Aesir's rule, but that doesn't mean they've turned on you."

I stopped packing and stood up straight, hip jutted, arms crossed over my chest. "You think they're going to stand between me and Skoll? Or do you think they'll put the knife in my back first and cover their own asses? If I'm dead, Skoll can't kill me, right? And if Skoll can't kill me, Helen loses. End of story."

Skyla opened her mouth to answer but stopped.

She knows I'm right. "I've got to stay off Helen's radar until I can get in touch with Thorin again," I said. "I think Tori has Surtr's sword and she's with Thorin's brother. His last known whereabouts are in Corvallis, as Ariel said. I thought I'd head that way."

"What did Tori say about the sword?"

"She isn't going to give it up." I rehashed the phone call for her.

At the end, Skyla's shoulders drooped, and she sagged onto the bed. She looked exhausted.

I sat down beside her. "I won't ask you to go with me, Skyla. A life on the run is no life at all."

Skyla sucked her lip between her teeth and gnawed on it. "You can't go on your own. It would be completely irresponsible of me to let you do it."

"But you want to stay here," I said.

"It's a crucial time. The Valkyries are a balloon cut from its string. They have no direction. The right person could come along and lead them astray, or—"

"Or the right person could put them back on task, remind them of their purpose, rally them to help us on our way to victory, and there will be puppies, unicorns, and rainbows for all."

Skyla huffed. "Let's let *me* be the cynic. I like you better as an optimist."

"Being a pragmatist is more likely to keep me alive. Which is why I'm not going to Oregon alone."

"You're not? But who…" A pained look passed over her face. "Val?"

"Better the devil you do know than one you don't. I *know* Val. I don't know Grim, and I don't want to risk facing him alone."

When I'd first gone to Alaska, I was a naive twit. I thought I'd pop across the country, ask some questions, look around a little, and go home. I was more scared of leaving my comfort zone than finding and facing a murderous psychopath. Maybe I had believed I would find nothing except some closure and convince myself to accept Mani's death once and for all. But I knew the truth now: men were beasts, and gods were monsters. They were not windmills, yet I still tilted at them. *I must be crazy. Utterly out of my mind.*

Skyla pursed her lips. "I don't like it, but I'm not going to be the one to tell you what to do. Just promise me you'll keep your eyes open at all times. Be skeptical of everyone. Even Val."

"I promise. I'll wear eyes in the back of my head."

Skyla told me she wanted to take a nap before the Valkyries' memorial service and to recover from her sleepless night of exhuming ghosts, so I left her and went to the kitchen to finish cookies, cheese straws, and some other snacks for the reception afterward. Baking kept me so busy that I failed to notice the sky darkening outside the kitchen window. Sunset fell over the Aerie, and women's voices rose and fell in hushed conversation as the Valkyries passed by the kitchen entrance. In a long line, they trickled outside, resembling wraiths and ghosts in the dying light. Many of them wore white ceremonial dresses and gauzy shawls like the one Tori had worn the first time I met her. Skyla was among the last in line, but she had opted to remain in her street clothes. I tried and failed to imagine her in one of the gauzy gowns.

As she passed by, she popped into the kitchen and asked, "Are you coming?"

"I hadn't quite made up my mind."

"Come on." Skyla motioned toward the front of the house, where the others had exited. "It might do you some good. And if not, then come for me. For moral support."

I nodded. "Okay. But I have to finish up in here first."

I arranged my last pan of chocolate-chunk cookies on a silver serving tray and set it among the other munchies I had displayed on the Aerie's formal dining-room table. A big coffee urn perked on the kitchen counter, and water simmered in a huge pot for anyone who wanted to make a cup of tea or hot chocolate.

"What are you doing still hanging around the kitchen?"

Startled, I spun around and found Val leaning in the doorway, his brows drawn down, his lips thinned and frowning.

"Just dragging my feet. I'm never anxious to go to these kinds of things."

"Because of Mani?"

I nodded. "It's still pretty raw."

Val's expression softened, and he opened his arms to me. I hesitated.

He gave me a look that said, *Really?* I sighed and went to him and sank into his big, warm hug.

"C'mon," he said after a moment of silence. "We'll do this together."

Val led me outside, and we met up with the Valkyries. They bunched together at one side of the house, a few feet from where the yard fell off into the Pacific Ocean. The wind blew ferociously, but the bonfire around which the women had gathered burned bright and hot.

"The bonfire is an ideal symbol." Embla's voice rose above the wind. "The blaze represents the light of all the lives that were lost. The heat represents the warmth of our memories of our sisters."

The fire and the chill in the air reminded me of home, movies in front of the fireplace in our den. Mani and I used to make pallets on the floor and have our own slumber parties, falling asleep to the crackling of the fire. Val pulled me close and slid an arm around my shoulder. Even though I could generate my own heat, I sank into his warmth, and all questions of fidelity drained away for the moment. Val often seemed to understand me in a way no one else did. Yet, I doubted him, and things between us remained complicated. Val had been Mani's best friend. Of all the people involved in my life now, Val had known me the longest. Our shared history was difficult to dismiss.

Skyla stood across the fire from us. She caught my eye and screwed her lips into a scowl, showing her aversion to my intimacy with Val. She might not understand why I let Val get close, but he represented a link to my past, a totem of better times. That night was the kind when leaning on sentimentality should be forgivable.

While Embla talked, one of the sisters weaved through the crowd, passing out individual stems of white calla lilies. Val accepted his flower, tucked his stem into the bend of my elbow, and slid his arm back around me. Embla read a brief biography on each of the fallen women. She recited Auden's poem, "Funeral Blues." By the time she read the line about packing away stars and dismantling the sun, barely a dry eye remained. I shoved my emotions down deep, refusing to give in to my sorrow. Grief can look like a shallow hole until you step in and find out it's really a bottomless pit.

Skyla also held in her heartache. As the Valkyries took turns telling anecdotes about their lost friends, her face hardened, stony and forbidding. She held her shoulders stiff, a physical dam to hold back a flood of emotions I could probably guess, knowing her as I did: sorrow for the lost lives, hurt for the denial of her sisterhood because of secrets and lies, and outrage at the Valkyries' factiousness.

I envisioned her as an angel of judgment, bringing retribution and righteousness upon the Valkyries. Skyla had confirmed her legacy, and her involvement would certainly influence the Valkyries' future. To the sisters of the Aerie, that influence might feel like a tornado tearing up, chewing to bits, and spitting out. Then Skyla would lead them in building anew.

Poor things—they have no idea what's in store for them.

After a final moment of silence, Embla tossed her lily into the fire, and everyone followed her example. When the last flower succumbed to the flames, the outer ring of women peeled away and turned toward the house. Before I could take a step in that direction, however, Val tightened his grip and dragged me farther down the cliff line, away from the house.

"What are you doing?" I asked, pulling against him.

"I want a few minutes alone with you. You've been avoiding me all day, and I want to know why."

"I have not. We've been busy—"

"No, Solina." The distant bonfire provided enough light for the high places on Val's face to stand out against the gloom of night. The shadows emphasized his scowl. "Something happened when you talked to that ghost, and I'm not going to let you deny it any longer. Tell me what she said." Hints of vanilla and chocolate sweetened Val's breath. I suspected he had stolen one of my cookies. "I see you making up excuses in your head."

"I suck at lying."

"Yes, my lovely, you do." Val leaned in closer. "Tell me."

I'd never meant to keep the news from him anyway, not after talking to Tori, but I had been waiting for the right time to tell him. Out there on the cliff, with the roaring wind to cover our conversation and no chance of being overheard, I spilled the proverbial beans. "Tori has the sword. She went to Grim."

"Ah, and where is Grim?"

"Corvallis."

"Hmm. Probably. Grim has been an anthropology professor off and on for a long time. Teaches at Oregon State."

An academic profession was so unassuming, but Indiana Jones had used it to his advantage, why not a Norse god? Especially one who had an interest in recovering powerful relics.

"You were going to go after him?"

"Yes," I said. "And I want you to come with me."

Val's eyes widened, and he gasped. I had never known him to admit a loss of words. He shook off his surprise and asked, "When do we leave?"

A slow grin unfurled across my lips. "I've already packed my bags. Come find me at midnight."

CHAPTER TWENTY-ONE

I HAD HEARD CORVALLIS PUT ON a dazzling display of natural beauty in the fall, but December was quickly approaching, and the trees had shed their leaves. Thick clouds and a gloomy drizzle had settled in, turning the landscape into a green-gray soup. Despite those things, the city radiated an innate charm—most college towns did, in my limited experience.

Perched on the west bank of the Willamette, downtown Corvallis beckoned visitors into its eclectic collection of shops and restaurants. In the distance, to the west, a set of hazy peaks watched over the sleepy town.

I took in the views through gritty, sleep-deprived eyes. I had intended to sleep during the nine-hour drive from Mendocino, but I couldn't relax and had dozed in short fits and starts.

"Look," Val asked, "why don't we get a room? You can sleep for a while. We'll get breakfast or brunch. Then we'll go see what we can find."

"Just stroll onto campus?" I asked, stifling a yawn. "Hello, Grim, we're here for the sword." I lowered my voice to imitate a man's deeper timbre. "Oh, why certainly. I have it right here. Let me just get it for you."

Val smirked. "Do you have a better idea?"

"Nope. That dramatization was the full extent of my plan."

"It's an optimistic plan. I like it." Val plucked his phone from its perch on the dashboard and asked the electronic personal assistant to find us a place to stay. She produced the names and addresses of several nearby hotel chains and a couple of bed and breakfasts. "No Bellestrellas in this town," Val said.

"If it has a bed and a hot shower, it's a winner."

"Who knew you had such low standards?"

I smiled and winked. "I'm hanging out with you, aren't I?"

Val chose one of the places on his artificial assistant's list and followed the GPS directions to a bed and breakfast on the edge of campus in an older part of town. He steered the Yukon to the curb and parked in front of a beautiful old Cape Cod. Two massive rhododendrons stood sentry on either side of the front-porch steps. The rhododendrons reminded me of home, of the Appalachian foothills, and a twinge of homesickness plucked at my heartstrings. I vowed to get an update on my parents' status from Baldur the next time I saw him. Until then, I put my parents and thoughts of going home again out of my mind.

Val carried my bags inside. We had arrived in time to sit down to a home-cooked breakfast: eggs, thick sliced bacon, whole-grain toast, fruit compote, and homemade jam. I shoveled in the food like the half-starved woman I was, and the more I ate, the sleepier I got.

When I finally set down my fork and admitted defeat, Tom, one of our hosts, cleared away my dirty dishes. His partner, Gene, led Val and me up to a cozy bedroom and set our bags on the floor by the bed. I minded sharing a room with Val a lot less since learning he didn't actually sleep, so long as he respected my boundaries.

After Gene left us alone, I told Val I wanted a shower and an hour of sleep. Exhaustion, pain, and hunger had taken a toll on my supernatural abilities in the past. Not knowing what to expect, if we would find Grim or not, I wanted my capabilities fully charged and ready to go if I needed them.

"Will an hour be enough?" Val asked.

"It has to be. Otherwise, I'll end up sleeping all day, and I want to find Grim as soon as possible. If he has someone inside the Aerie reporting to him or Tori, then he might already assume we're on his trail. He might run or go into hiding or something."

"You've never met Grim," Val said. "So trust me when I say he would never go into hiding. He and Thorin are chiseled from the same block of obstinate."

"Still, I don't think it's smart to wait too long. An hour, Val. Don't go to Grim without me. Don't harass any undergrads, either."

He pouted. "That's no fun."

"Go take a walk or something."

Val shook his head and turned for the door. "No, siree." He stepped into the hallway. "No fun at all."

When the alarm went off, I felt as though I had just closed my eyes. I patted around the nightstand until I found my phone and silenced the ringer. I rolled over, intending to go back to sleep, but my phone came to life again, buzzing and rattling on the nightstand.

"Grrr," I said and grabbed the phone. By then, I had awoken enough to realize the phone was ringing not because of the alarm, but because Thorin was calling me.

"What do you want?" I growled.

Thorin ignored my irritated greeting and said, "It's nearly noon. What are you still doing in bed?"

"Really? You called to harass me about my sleeping habits?"

"I called because I want a status update."

"After all those threats about keeping in touch, you haven't been particularly easy to contact."

"I've been in a hospital. Haven't been able to keep my phone on."

"Hospital?" I sat up and rubbed my eyes. "What's going on?"

"We might have found Nina. There's a Jane Doe here. She was in a car wreck. Baldur is checking her story."

"Really? Is she okay?"

Thorin exhaled. "Not really. But I think she will be."

"You think it's her?"

"For Baldur's sake, I certainly hope it is."

The bedroom door eased open, and Val stuck his head in. When he saw me, awake and on the phone, his eyebrows drew down.

I read the question in his expression. *Thorin,* I mouthed to him.

Val rolled his eyes and came fully into the room, carrying two Styrofoam cups. He went to a seating area in the corner, settled into an armchair, and set the cups on the coffee table beside a glossy book full of Oregon landscape photos.

"Any news on the sword?" Thorin asked.

"Funny you should ask." I filled him in on our discovery of Skyla's relationship to Embla and my phone call to Tori.

"So," Thorin said. "Grim."

"You might have mentioned him before."

"It was strictly need-to-know information."

"Well, guess what? I have developed a severe and chronic case of needing to know."

"The only thing you *need* to know is to stay far, far away from him."

"Too late for that."

"No," Thorin said, and I imagined him smearing a hand over his face. "Please, please tell me you didn't."

"I could, but you don't like it when I lie to you."

"Where are you right this minute?"

"I'll give you a hint. It starts with a *C* and rhymes with Horvallis." I held the phone away from my ear while Thorin cursed a blue streak. Val looked up from the photography book in his lap, grimaced, and shook his head.

"Solina," Thorin finally said in a more reasonable tone. I put the phone back to my ear. "He cannot be trusted. He's my brother. I know what I'm talking about."

"I don't have to listen to you at all. If it mattered so much, you would be here. But you're not." I had basically restated what Tori had said to me earlier, and I felt disloyal repeating her words, but my feelings made the sentiment no less true. Thorin *should* have been there with me, and maybe I was more jealous of his loyalty to Baldur than I wanted to admit. "I understand your need to be with Baldur. I'm not asking you to leave him, but by staying there with him, you forfeit your right to express an opinion on my activities.

"I am going to find your brother, Thorin. If you know anything about him, anything useful that might help us, please tell me. What I really need is leverage. Does he have any weaknesses, anything we can use against him? Is there anything he wants?"

"The only thing Grim has ever really wanted was Mjölnir," Thorin said. "What do you think is going to happen? You're just going to change his mind with a little reasoning?"

"Probably not. But I can't just sit around and do nothing."

"Please. Please don't do this." Thorin sounded defeated, and I almost changed my mind. His anger and his belligerence I could resist, but a vulnerable Thorin was difficult to defy—difficult but not impossible.

I started to say something consoling, but Val crossed the room and took the phone from me. "Thorin. I've already made an appointment to meet with Grim on campus. There's a flaming sword on the loose, and I intend to recover it. It was lovely hearing from you. Tell Baldur we said hello and call back soon. But not too soon." Val swiped his thumb over the screen and ended the call.

"Oh, that's really going to piss him off." I pantomimed listening for a distant sound, cupping my hand behind my ear. "I can hear his head exploding all the way from here."

Val chuckled. "Did you get enough sleep?"

"I guess. Why?"

"We have an appointment with Grim in"—Val glanced down at the screen of the phone—"thirty minutes."

"Thirty minutes?" I rolled out of bed and crouched over my bags. When I found my scruffy suede boots, I plopped to the floor and tugged them on. "You found him. He's here?"

Val nodded. "He's got an office in the anthropology building on campus. I called and talked to his secretary."

I grunted and heaved myself up from the floor. "Is one of those cups for me?" I pointed to the pair sitting on the coffee table.

Val swiped one and presented it to me. "Indeed."

I stuck my nose to the opening in the lid and inhaled. "God, I love you."

"You only love me for my coffee."

I shrugged. "Beggars can't be choosers."

Val had already located the anthropology building, so we wasted no time wandering around campus. He led me to the entrance of an elegant Victorian-style building constructed of tan bricks, maroon trim, and black slate shingles. A slab of gray stone, etched with "Waldo Hall, 1907", arched over the front doors.

"It looks like something from a fantasy novel," I said. "Do you think if we stand here long enough, British children in blazers and knee socks will come marching out?"

"I hope not," Val said. "I'm not particularly fond of wizards or witches or wardrobes of any sort."

"Just prehistoric gods, wolves, and weaponry."

Val tugged open the front door. "Of course."

He seemed to know which way to go, so I followed him through the winding hallways until he stopped us before a suite of faculty offices.

"*Doctor* Thorin?" I said, reading from a placard by the door.

"We all have credentials, Solina. It would be difficult to get by in life without them."

"I've never needed credentials to get by."

Val smirked. "You've also never lived for an eternity."

When Val and I entered the office suite, a secretary looked up from her computer and smiled at us. Well, she smiled at Val, anyway.

"We're here to see Dr. Thorin," Val said.

"Do you have an appointment?" She fluttered her lashes at my big, brawny companion.

I coughed and cleared my throat.

She looked at me and dropped her smile.

It's okay, I used to bat my lashes at him too. You'll get over it.

"I spoke to you on the phone just a few minutes ago," Val said. "I'm Val Wotan. This is my partner, Solina Mundy."

The girl's face brightened, and she smiled. "Oh, I remember. Okay, Dr. Thorin is finishing up another meeting. He should be here shortly." She motioned toward a sofa adjacent to her desk. "You can wait over there."

When Grim returned to his office and turned to note our presence, I saw his eyes were lighter than Thorin's, his smile a little colder and crueler. No one had indicated Modi and Magni were twins, but the brothers looked more alike than many twins I knew, including Mani and myself. Closer inspection revealed Modi Grimr Thorin wasn't an exact copy of his brother. Grim's hair was a shade darker and several inches shorter, and Thorin likely held the height and weight advantage between the two.

When Val and I rose to greet Grim, he beat us to it. "Wotan? Long time no see."

"Not long enough," Val grumbled.

"To what do I owe this honor?"

"I think you know why we're here," I said.

Grim's jaw clinched, and he glared at me. Despite his lighter irises, he possessed the same black-eyed hostility as his brother. "Why don't you come into my office? We can discuss your concerns in private."

Grim showed us into a cozy, cluttered office outfitted in an eclectic mix of miscellanea: maps of ancient Scandinavia, antique helmets, wooden shields, and one very ordinary sword. He motioned to two mission-style chairs positioned before his desk. "Have a seat, although you're welcome to stand. I can't see how this will take very long. You wasted your time coming here. The Valkyrie made it clear that I intend to keep Surtalogi in my possession."

"The Valkyrie?" I said. "You mean Tori?"

Grim shrugged and pulled out the leather chair behind his desk, but he hesitated to sit. Val and I had not taken the seats Grim offered us, either. We were playing the anti-musical chairs game—the first one to sit would lose.

"Did you honestly think you would come here and change my mind?" Grim asked.

"Maybe," I said. "Maybe I hoped you could be reasoned with. Maybe I thought to come and see what kind of person... being... *god* you are."

"And if you judge me lacking, then what?" Grim shook his head. He turned his chair, sat, and swiveled around to face his computer.

Grim's taking a seat felt less like submission and more like dismissal. He wouldn't see me as a serious threat unless I proved myself one. Thorin had once told me the gods disliked unnecessary and public attention. Nothing to draw undue notice. *Let's see just how public and unnecessary I can be.*

I raised an index finger, and a flame lit at the tip. Stepping forward, I placed my fingertip to the very old, very dry wooden shield hanging on the wall near Grim's desk. Probably an important artifact from some time long before. *Sorry, history. Sometimes a girl has to take drastic measures. Besides, you were never all that nice to my gender anyway.* Maybe I owed history a little payback for its many slights against womankind.

The old circle of wood smoldered. Val watched me and quirked an eyebrow. The flames caught, and the shield ignited. Val smirked. Grim leaped up from his seat, grabbed a coat from the rack at the other side of his desk, and used it to smother the flames. While Grim struggled to rescue his ancient artifacts, I went to work setting little fires all over his office.

Juvenile? Sure. Attention grabbing? Absolutely.

"What the *hell* are you doing?" Grim asked.

"Forcing you to stop ignoring me," I said as Grim scurried around the room, undoing my damage before the fire alarms kicked in, or so I hoped. An evacuation would negate the whole purpose of our meeting. "You can't intimidate me, Grim. I've fought and killed wolves in the desert with your brother, infiltrated privately guarded compounds, confronted stone soldiers, and rescued gods from their own stupidity. I've transmuted and traveled cross-country as a freaking shooting star.

"There is very little that scares me anymore, Modi Grimr Thorin, and if I have to piss you off to get your attention, I will. If I have to burn this whole damned building to the ground, I will."

Grim had put out the remaining fires, and he stood at the corner of his desk, breathing hard. Blackness filled his eyes, bleeding out into the whites until he looked alien. Demonic. I had never seen Thorin's darkness extend that far. I had seen his anger, yes, but I had always believed he would never really turn it on me. Grim had never made any such assurances.

I put away my fire and sank into one of Grim's visitor chairs. *Now who is dismissing whom?* "You are a single individual without allies, and you've turned the Valkyries against you. How long would you last on your own against Helen? She has an army, Grim. I've seen it. Give us the sword. We have more reasons and more resources to keep it from Helen than you do."

Grim crossed his arms over his chest and leaned a hip against his desk. "You're assuming Helen could find the sword in the first place. Do you think I keep it on me? Wear it as a trinket like my brother wears the hammer? And if the sword is so important, why isn't Magni here? He sent a little girl and an impotent god in his place."

"I know who I am." Val's voice was low and menacing. "I know what I am. I'm not in denial. I am not grasping at straws."

"That sword is no straw," Grim said.

Val shrugged. "You've lived a long time in Thor and Magni's shadows. You've never had a taste of real power. The sword is your chance. I get it. Doesn't mean I accept it."

Grim rose up to his full height and clenched his fists at his sides. "And does it gall you to live in Baldur's shadow? Solina, has Val told you that he grew to full adulthood within one day of his birth? He was birthed solely for the purpose of killing poor, blind Hodr as revenge for his part in killing Baldur.

"You served your purpose, Vali Odinson. You killed Hodr and fulfilled your father's need for revenge, but Baldur is resurrected, now. His restoration negates any reason for your continued existence, yet you are bound to serve him for eternity, knowing he's weak and addled and obsessed. How you must detest him, and yet you still call him Allfather."

"So you both have inferiority complexes," I said, ending Grim's tirade.

Val's face had turned a frightening shade of fuchsia, and he clenched his knuckles so fiercely that I wondered how the bones didn't break through his skin.

"Work it out at your next Aesir Anonymous meeting. In the meantime, we're getting nowhere." I rose to my feet. "Let's get out of here, Val. Like he said, he doesn't keep the sword here, and he's not going to tell us where it is. And I don't know what else to do unless you want to resort to torture tactics."

Val flashed a fiendish grin, and the cold menace in his voice made me shiver when he said, "I am not opposed to torture."

I took Val's hand and placed my palm on his face, forcing him to look at me. "Maybe some other time. It can be our last resort. But please, before there is blood, let's go."

Val stared into me, and I saw the gears turning inside him as he fought to reestablish his self-control.

Finally, he swallowed and nodded. He pulled away from my touch and turned his back to Grim. "Fine. Let's get out of here before I change my mind."

CHAPTER TWENTY-TWO

"WELL THAT WAS POINTLESS," VAL said as we left campus and headed toward the bed and breakfast. His hard, angry footsteps radiated his fury.

The things Grim had said were horrible, but I might have dismissed them if not for Val's visceral reaction and if I hadn't read something similar about Val when I had researched Aesir legends during my downtime in San Diego. I could distance myself from those ancient events when I saw them only as inanimate words on sterile paper or computer screens. The Aesir's experiences were fairy-tales of long ago, but Val's anger drew the past forward, made the legends real, and made me sympathize with him rather than dismissing him as a fictional character whose pain disappeared the moment I closed my book.

If Grim's words and the legends I had read were true, then they explained a lot about Val's loutish tendencies. A son born solely to be used as a weapon of revenge... that couldn't be good for anyone's emotional health. Val was accustomed to being used, so perhaps using others was what he understood best.

"But it's not surprising," Val said. "I never thought we'd get that sword from Grim with a please-and-thank-you attitude anyway."

"The point of that meeting was not necessarily to recover the sword," I said.

Val balked. "It wasn't?"

"No. It was politics and mind games—planting seeds of doubt that will encourage Grim to look over his shoulder, question his next move. If we keep the pressure on him, keep watching him, he'll eventually make a mistake. We can't give up yet. Besides, I've got a few more ideas up my sleeve."

Val arched an eyebrow and grinned. "Oh yeah?"

We stopped beside the Yukon, and I motioned to the passenger door. "Get in the truck."

"Where are we going?"

"I'll tell you on the way."

I slid behind the wheel, buckled in, and pulled away from the curb. Then I entered an address into the Yukon's GPS and followed the map it drew for me. After a few short twists and turns through town, I stopped us again on a residential street lined in old, turn-of-the-century homes. I pointed at a green two-story craftsman perched at the top of a steep driveway several houses down from where we had parked. "Grim's house."

"Totally college professor." Val studied the house. "How did you know where he lived?"

"Got the address from Hugh."

"Hugh? You told him what you were up to before you told me?"

I shrugged. "He had Grim's info in the store's contact list."

Val scowled. Then he blinked and shrugged. "You think the sword is hanging over Grim's mantle or something?"

"No. But maybe there's something. A hint. A clue."

"What are you going to do if Tori's there?" Val asked.

"If the idea is to force them into action of some sort, then confronting her could be a good thing. If she runs, we'll follow. She won't leave without the sword."

"And what if she stands her ground?"

"Then I guess we should be prepared to fight."

Val exhaled a noisy breath, put on his best Scooby Doo voice, and said, "Rokay, Raggy. Ret's go have a rook."

Val and I climbed the empty driveway and circled around behind the house. I jiggled the handle at the back door. "It's locked, and there's no car. I think no one's home."

Val leaned forward and peered through the door's windows. Then my ears popped, and he disappeared. He reappeared in an instant, grinning at me from the other side of the door. He swung it open and bowed for me as I stepped over the threshold into a designer kitchen decorated in the latest fashion. Too new, too clean, too showroom perfect—the only thing suggesting anyone lived there was a faint odor of stale coffee and a dirty mug in the sink. A worn pair of women's sneakers rested against the baseboard beside the kitchen door.

"Tori's?" I asked, pointing at the shoes.

Val's head bobbed in agreement. "Doubt those would fit Grim. Purple isn't really his color."

"What about an alarm?" I asked. "Should we hurry?"

Val pursed his lips and arched an eyebrow. "Do you think we call the cops? Do we want the law digging into our affairs?"

"Um, no?"

"I'll bet you Grim doesn't keep anything of value here, anyway. This is just for appearances. If anyone stole anything, he'd just buy a replacement."

"There's probably not much chance we'll find anything useful here, is there?"

"Leave no stone unturned." Val tugged me farther into the house.

A quick perusal of the downstairs revealed nothing, and only Grim's office looked regularly used. We searched desk drawers, a filing cabinet, and bookcases. When we found no map with an *X* marking the sword's location, no hastily scribbled note saying, "Don't forget to pick up Surtalogi from the dry-cleaner," no verbose ghosts or glowing arrows pointing us in likely locations, Val herded me up the stairs to investigate the second floor.

Hotels and model homes had a more lived-in appearance than Grim's house.

"It really is for show," I said, standing in the middle of the master bedroom. "And not a very good one. Who would believe he actually lived here?"

We found no laundry, no personal effects on the nightstand by his side of the bed, and the furnishings looked as though they had come fresh from a photo shoot for middle-class interior decorating.

I stopped and inhaled a deep breath. "It smells like carpet and paint."

"Maybe he has a really thorough housekeeper," Val said. "But if he does have guests, why would they wonder? Who would have a reason to question? People are mostly lazy about the truth. If lies are easy and convenient, people will usually accept them."

"You speak from experience?"

"You disagree?"

"I don't accept lies, even the easy ones. I think I've proved that."

"You are an exception, a very perplexing and often infuriating one." Val stepped closer and scrubbed a thumb over my lip, wiping away my pout. "I respect you for it, Solina. But it won't do you any favors. There's safety in believing lies."

"So Helen would have left me alone if I had just believed Mani died in some mundane manner? I don't think so."

"No." Val shook his head. "She still needs you dead, but she wouldn't have bothered taking up the fight against anyone else."

I thought of Kalani and Inyoni, who was not innocent but so young and naive. "Are you trying to say it's my fault other people have been hurt by Helen?"

Alarm flashed across Val's face. "No. I'm absolutely not saying that."

"What *are* you trying to say?"

Val exhaled a noisy breath and tossed his hands out at his sides. "Whatever it is, I've fouled it up. All I meant was that Grim keeps up the lie—we *all* keep up this lie about who we really are, and it keeps people safe, ourselves included. Our kind don't die, but it's not so hard to make us hurt. That's a very fearful thing when you know suffering can last an eternity."

What kinds of hurts had Val suffered that could last for an eternity? And do I really want to know? Probably not. Not today anyway.

"Well, I—" I started.

Val put a hand over my mouth, silencing me. Downstairs, a door slammed shut, and footsteps resounded off the kitchen's tile flooring. Val dragged me to Grim's walk-in closet, eased open the door, stepped in, and pulled the door closed behind us.

The footsteps, accompanied by a familiar voice, pounded up the stairs. "No," Tori said. *The bitch.* "I've just got to grab a few things, and I'll hit the road." After a moment of silence, she said, "I'll be there around sundown at the latest. Probably before then." She paused again, and I gathered she was on her phone, maybe with Grim. "Okay. Got it. I'll see you then."

Tori's footsteps clacked on the bathroom-floor tiles. The clinking sounds of something—*Toiletries? Cosmetics?*—carried to the closet. Val and I held our breaths, and my heart pounded frantically against my ribs. I didn't fear discovery, really. Even if Tori found us hiding in the closet, at most we would lose the advantage of secrecy. *It's not like she'd attack us. Or would she?* Maybe her arrival was providing the break we needed, though. She was going somewhere, meeting someone. If Grim wouldn't lead us to the sword, then Tori gave us our next best lead. Val must have thought the same thing. His grip on my arm tightened, and he pulled me closer.

Tori left the bathroom and went back downstairs. Val and I exhaled but stayed in the closet, still and silent, until a downstairs door opened and closed, signaling Tori's exit.

"Are you thinking what I'm thinking?" I asked.

Val nodded. "Follow that Valkyrie."

Careful not to give ourselves away, Val and I slunk away from the house and climbed into the Yukon. I let Tori's blue Subaru go a good distance down the road, but not out of sight, before I started our truck and pulled away from the curb.

"Where do you think she's going?" I asked. The question was mostly rhetorical as I assumed Val and I had drawn similar conclusions. "Grim?"

"That's my guess," Val said.

"But where? Where would he go?"

"When you've been around as long as we have, you tend to collect places—homes, hidey-holes, temporary and long term. He could be anywhere. Or nowhere."

Tori led us through town on a route that delivered us onto I-5, heading north. She merged onto the highway, and I dropped back, letting several cars fill the space between her Subaru and our Yukon.

"I'm going to check in with Skyla," I said, digging my phone from my pocket. "See if the Aerie has heard anything."

"You think that's a good idea? I thought the idea of sneaking away in the night was because we don't trust the Valkyries."

"I trust Skyla, and I think it would be a good idea if *someone* knows where we are. Just in case."

Val waved his hand as if saying, *Fine, do what you like.*

Skyla answered on the first ring. "Mundy, it's about time I heard from you. Any word on the sword?"

192

I filled Skyla in on our trip to Corvallis, my conversation with Thorin, my meeting with Grim, and the results of our investigation of Grim's house.

"So, you're following Tori out to who knows where to do who knows what?"

"Pretty much."

"Just you and Val?"

"Who else?"

"How about a couple Valkyries? For backup."

"What do you mean?"

Skyla's exhalation carried through the phone's speaker. "Just listen and keep an open mind."

She launched into a story about how Embla and Naomi, one of the other women jockeying for leadership of the Valkyries, had awoken for their regular early-morning training and discovered the Yukon missing. They had gone to Skyla and gotten her to admit what she knew about the disappearance of one sun goddess and her faithful Aesir sidekick.

"You told them?" I asked. "You know I don't trust them."

"Well, I *do*," she said, defensive and resolute.

"You've known Embla is your aunt for five hot minutes, and you think you can trust her? That's not your call to make."

"Well, who the hell else do I have if I don't trust her?"

"You have *me*. You have your loyalty to my brother's memory."

"I *am* loyal to you. Everything I've done is for your benefit. You think you're going to do what? Confront Grim and Tori, a god and one of the Valkyries' best fighters, and talk them out of the sword? You already told me how well diplomacy worked with Grim. Are you really ready to fight them for it?"

"Yes," I said. "If I have to."

"You're not a fighter, girlfriend. Not one equal to Grim and Tori."

"I have my fire."

"You can barely control it. You're a danger to yourself."

Skyla could have slapped me or punched me in the gut, and it would have hurt less. My breath left in a gasp. Tears burned in my eyes. There I was, like the hundreds of motorists around me, rolling down the highway, so unassuming, so normal. But inside that ordinary SUV,

I struggled to maintain my composure because otherwise I would blow Val, the Yukon, and possibly several innocent travelers into smithereens. Otherwise, I would prove Skyla right.

Val, being the strong, sensitive type—*ha ha!*—detected my distress. He reached out and grasped my free hand, a gesture of solidarity.

"Solina, I'm sorry." Skyla's tone softened. "That came out all wrong."

I said nothing. I could say nothing. She was sort of right. She had stated the truth, and I had no right to criticize her for it. Still, I felt betrayed.

"Look," Skyla continued. "None of that matters. What I really need to tell you is that Embla, Naomi and I are already on our way. We hit the road first thing this morning. We're nearly to Corvallis, but we're rerouting to come after you."

"You're what?" I said, nearly speechless again. My mind reeled.

"We're not leaving this to you and Val alone," Skyla said.

I sighed and dragged my fingers through my hair, and the scrape of my nails against my scalp soothed me.

"Solina, tell me what you're thinking."

"I don't know what I'm thinking," I said. "I'm pissed, and I feel a little betrayed, but at the same time, I'm relieved. I was freaking out. The possibility of confronting Grim with that sword and Tori... She's kicked my ass so many times, and she wasn't even trying hard." I heaved a breath. "And you're right about my fire, although I want to bust you in your face for saying it."

Skyla laughed, and something about her humor relieved the heartache she had given me moments before. "You've got guts, girlfriend."

"'And girls with guts survive.' I know, I know. Doesn't feel like I have guts. Feels like I have a ball of quivering nerves."

"But you're going through with this anyway?"

"Going through with what? I have no idea what's going to happen. I still might chicken out. Or Grim might feel diplomatic and sign a treaty or something."

"You won't chicken out. Not when you know you've got three kickass Valkyries at your back."

"And Val." I turned my gaze to my companion. He squeezed my hand but rolled his eyes.

"Yes," said Skyla, her tone flat as a Nevada highway. "We got Wotan, too. Hooray." She cleared her throat and regained some of her previous spark. "We're probably less than two hours behind you. We'll put some pep in our step and try to catch up to you. Keep us in the loop with Tori's twenty. And don't do anything until we catch up to you."

"Tori's twenty?"

Skyla huffed. "Her location. *Twenty* is radio code for location."

"But we're on the phone," I said, purposely obtuse.

"*Girlfriend.*"

"Okay, okay." I read her our nearest mile marker and promised to call her the moment Tori changed her route.

◆

We drove and drove, and the afternoon wore on, and the sun fell lower in the sky. I had dropped back until Tori's car appeared as a light-blue dot in the distance. Val reassured me that his supernatural—and therefore superior—vision had not lost sight of her, but the distance virtually guaranteed Tori wouldn't notice us following. Highway signs indicated points of interest along the way, and I made an educated guess about her destination.

"Portland?" I asked. "You think she's going to Portland?"

Val bit his lip and shook his head. "No. She said she'd be there, wherever *there* is, around sundown. We've got another two hours before then."

"What's after Portland?"

"If she stays on this highway, then it's possible she's heading to Seattle. We'll just have to wait and see."

Tori didn't drive to Seattle, though. After nearly three hours on the road and crossing the border into Washington, she exited onto Highway 12, heading east. The nearby billboards advertised local tourist attractions and a ski resort called Crystal Mountain.

"Crystal Mountain?" I said as Val texted Skyla the exit number. "They're going skiing, and Grim had her stop by the house to pick up their skis?"

"It's near Mount Rainier," Val said. "Back country. It's starting to make some sense."

"It is? How?"

"I told you we collect places. I have the place in Siqiniq with my roommates, right?"

"Hugh and Joe, yes?"

"Right. But that isn't the place I call home. Not really. It's a façade, just like Grim's house in Corvallis is a pretense. It's an accessory for whatever persona we're currently wearing. Asgard was our true home, but we've made replacements, here, in Midgard. When we're not playing a role, when we can shed our masks and be who we really are, we all have that one place we like to go, the place where our hearts live. It's a sacred place."

Val's confession—for in a way, that's what it was—sank to the bottom of my heart, like a heavy secret. He had confided in me, sharing something I sensed was deeply personal for him and maybe for all the Aesir. I wanted to ask him what landmark he had chosen for his sacred place but thought better of it. Thorin had used the term "need-to-know," and the location of Val's true home likely fell under that category. If Val wanted me to know, he would tell me.

"Do you think that's where Tori is going? To Grim's sacred place."

"It would mean he holds her in very high esteem."

"I got the impression from talking to her that they have that kind of relationship."

"Or he wants her to think they do." Val's voice lacked any emotion.

"Why do you say it like that?"

"Grim is a manipulative bastard."

"Aren't you all? When it suits you."

Val turned and gave me a harsh look but didn't try to defend himself. "Mount Rainier, Alaska, Baldur's home at New Breidablik, they all resemble one another, geographically speaking. It's not a coincidence. The mountains, the snow—they were integral features of Asgard. We prefer these places because they remind us of a home we can only visit in our memories."

"Thorin has one of these places, too?"

Val pursed his lips. "He does."

"And Grim's might be near Rainier somewhere."

"It's my working theory. Whether it proves true or not depends on where Tori leads us and what we find when we get there."

"Why don't you know where Grim lives? Don't you all send each other Christmas cards or anything?"

Val snorted. "After Ragnarok, after all those years of being stuck together in Gimle, we were more than happy to allow each other some well-deserved privacy."

The roads wound and curved as we drove deeper into the mountains. Dusk's dark hues settled around us, heightening our tension and foreboding. Val, still watching with preternatural vision, warned me that Tori had slowed as we approached an area that the road signs called Mineral Valley. I eased back on the accelerator as she veered right onto a smaller road. I asked Val to text Skyla again and hoped the message went through despite the patchy reception.

"Fall back a little further," Val said.

"Are you sure? It's hard to believe you won't lose sight of her."

"Trust me," Val said. "Hawks can see from about a mile away, right? Hawks have nothing on me. It works sort of the same way that we move through space like we do."

I gaped at him. "You can blip your eyesight through space?"

"Not exactly, but that's the best way I can explain it."

"It's magic," I said. "Or whatever it is that makes you guys tick."

"It's what makes you tick, too, Solina. It's the same force that gives you fire."

"Sol gives me my fire."

"You *are* Sol," Val said. "The more you embrace your powers, the more indistinguishable you become."

I had nothing to say to that because I had formed a similar conclusion for myself.

At places where the tree line opened, glimpses of a silvery lake shone through, reflecting the purples of the twilight sky. And in the distance, a massive snow-capped peak, glorious and imposing, loomed over the landscape. I sucked in a breath of awe.

"Rainier?" I asked in a whisper as if speaking of a holy thing.

Maybe it was holy. All the grand cathedrals mankind had built over the centuries attempted to mimic that kind of wonder, that sacred place

Nature created to pay homage to God. Sorry, mankind, but Nature's craftsmanship was clearly superior.

"Amazing, isn't it?" Val said.

"Unbelievable. There's nothing like that in the mountains where I come from."

"There's nothing quite like it anywhere. I told you, we choose sacred places."

Tori turned again and disappeared from sight. I swerved the Yukon onto the shoulder and let the truck roll to a stop. "That's a private drive she turned onto," Val said "The lake is just on the other side of these trees. There's nowhere else for her to go unless she plans to get in a boat. Wherever she was going, that's where it is." Val pointed toward the place where Tori's taillights had vanished. "And that's where you and I have to go, too."

I shivered and rubbed my hands over my arms. All the bravado I'd gathered in Grim's office earlier in the day drained away, and a cold lump had formed in my gut. "What if she knows we followed her? What if Grim sent her up here, suspecting we would watch them and follow their path?"

"What if he did?" Val asked. "What if this is all a great big trap?"

"It wouldn't be the first time for us, would it?"

"The last time we were in this situation, you called Baldur and Thorin idiots for falling into it. Say the word, Solina, and we'll turn around and go back."

"Go back to what?"

Val shrugged. "You tell me. This is your adventure."

I leaned away from him and furrowed my brow. "Like you don't want that sword as badly as I do."

A single eyebrow arched, and he shrugged. *Maybe I do, maybe I don't,* his expression said.

I turned my gaze out onto the darkening road again. "You think there are apples anywhere down at the end of the drive?"

"Apples?" Val asked.

"They were in my dream. I encountered Tori and the sword in an apple orchard in my dream."

"This *is* Washington. And the Cascades are apple-growing territory, so I guess it's possible."

"So, there's a pretty good chance that by following Tori, I'm going to fulfill the events of my dream. Question is whether we survive it or not."

"Did we drive all the way out here for nothing? When have you shied from a fight?"

I sucked in a big breath, blew it out through my nose, and threw open my car door. "It's like cold water. We can stand here and look at it forever, and it won't get any warmer, or we can just grit our teeth and dive in."

In the fading light, Val and I found the driveway onto which Tori had turned.

"I should have brought a flashlight." I closed my eyes to better focus on my internal power source. Over the past few months, I had learned my biggest conflagrations required the opposite of restraint—I had to abandon self-control. A subtle glow required focus, more application of self-discipline. I was good at subtle glows.

Val gasped. I opened my eyes to see what had startled him and realized I could see him because my candle-glow trick had worked.

"Holy shit," he whispered.

I shrugged. "What? This? This is nothing."

"But I've never seen it, not like this." Val's eyes narrowed, and a hurt look crossed his face. "I've heard you and Thorin describe it, but I've only seen your flames, a small presentation of them anyway, when you were mad." Val was talking about the time I had slapped him at the Aerie.

I stiffened my shoulders. "You earned it."

Val stepped closer and put a hand to my face. "You're right. I needed that lesson. You deserved better from me."

I swallowed back a sudden welling of emotion and clenched my jaw. How was he so damned good at getting under my skin?

Val framed my face in both hands and leaned closer, our breaths intermingling. He still smelled vaguely of chocolate-chip cookies. "I don't know what's going to happen next," he said. "If it's like your dream, it could be bad."

I swallowed again and nodded.

Val pressed his lips to my temple—a sweet touch, not possessive and demanding but indicative of affection.

Maybe an old dog can *learn new tricks.*

Instead of desire or serenity, Val's touch elicited a thundering rumble inside my head. The sounds of a distant, snarling beast filled my ears. And the cries of a man in horrible pain rose above it all. The accompanying images appeared smudged and blurry as if trapped behind a dirty windowpane. The vision showed me a man, bare chested and bound to a stone plinth. A wolf crouched over him, teeth buried in the pale, soft flesh of the man's stomach. And blood. Everywhere blood.

As the vision faded, the man screamed again—a horrifying torrent of begging and pleading. I pulled away from Val and put my hands over my ears. Always, with Val, those intimate moments triggered dreadful sensations.

"What is it?" Val asked, struggling to keep me in his arms although I fought to get away, to escape the angry beast and a dying man screaming in my ears.

"These visions." I fell to my knees, closed my eyes, and shook my head. "I never wanted to be an oracle. Never wanted to know other people's horrors."

"What did you see?" Val asked.

"A beast, snarling, snapping his teeth. And there was a man, screaming, dying. H-he..." I stopped, took a breath, and tried it again. "He was being eaten alive."

Val choked and sank to his knees before me. His voice came out dry and raspy when he asked, "Was it... Was it Mani?"

"No." I shook my head. "I know what Mani's screams sound like. This wasn't him. I've never seen this before. He said something, but he spoke in a language I didn't understand."

"What did he say?" Val put his hands to my shoulders and squeezed. "*What did he say?*"

"I-I don't know. It sounded like, like, '*Nine brrotheer. Nine.*' Over and over."

Val dropped his hands from my shoulders. He rolled back on his feet, stood, and moved away, turning toward the trees at the roadside.

"Val?" I rose to my feet and reached for him, but he answered in a ragged and broken voice. "He was saying, 'No, brother... No, brother, no.'"

"Brother? What was that? What did I see?"

Val inhaled, and the breath expanded his ribs and shoulders. He stiffened his spine and stood taller. Then he turned to face me, his expression inscrutable. "Something that happened a long, long time ago. It's not essential to the here and now. I'll tell you some other time, when there isn't something more important to focus on."

I nodded, accepting his explanation. In my research, I had focused on Idun's apples and what they could mean about my dreams and premonitions. I hadn't delved deeply into the more obscure legends, and my knowledge of Val's purpose as Odin's instrument of revenge against Hodr was rudimentary at best. Did the memory I just witnessed have anything to do with Hodr's death? When I had thought, just a little while before, about what pains Val had suffered that would stay with him for an eternity, I had decided I didn't want to know. Whatever I had just heard from the past, it was horrible, anguished, terrifying. If Val wanted to keep the details to himself, I might consider that a blessing.

CHAPTER TWENTY-THREE

V AL AND I SKULKED DOWN a long pathway that ended before a large log cabin. *Log manor? Log estate?* Warm yellow lights shone from several first-floor windows, putting off enough glow to illuminate a deep wraparound porch. Beyond the rear of the house, the lake mirrored the cloudless night sky. A dark disruption in the reflective surface suggested the shape of a long, jutting dock. The darkness covered the details of the house and grounds, but its sheer dimensions suggested something grand and impressive.

"Jackpot?" I whispered.

"Turn off your glow," Val said, his voice low. "I don't want them to know we're here yet. Let's wait and watch for a while." He took my arm and led me to the treeline bordering the yard, where we eased behind its cover. "How long before Skyla and the others get here?"

"The last text said they figured they were about half an hour out."

"We'll reconnoiter until they get here."

"You think Tori and Grim will come outside and do some sword practice if we wait long enough? We're going to have to be more proactive."

"I just want to know if there are any surprises waiting for us."

"I think Grim's trap will be subtler than that."

"Don't be so sure."

While we waited for Skyla and the others to arrive, Val and I crept around the property, hanging close to the treeline. No other cars accompanied Tori's in the driveway, but we couldn't check the garage without making a lot of noise—not that Grim needed a car to travel if he was anything like his kin. The exterior of the house and grounds remained quiet and dark, and blinds were drawn over the windows in the house, preventing us from looking inside. As the night deepened, so did the cold. My teeth chattered, and shivers trilled over me. We couldn't risk my fire, or even my softest glow, but unless something happened soon, I thought I might march up to the house and start the hottest open-house party to ever descend on Mineral Lake.

"Last time I tromped around a lake in the dark, it didn't go so well for me," I said. "But I can't wait much longer. The tension is killing me, and I really, really have to pee."

Val snorted. "You want to go and ask Tori if you can use her bathroom?"

"If Skyla doesn't get here soon, I might."

I did end up squatting in a thicket of brush, and while I tugged my leggings back in place, Skyla finally texted, *We're here*. I tiptoed back to Val and showed him my phone screen. He nodded, and we retreated down the driveway, heading to our Yukon. At the road, I lighted my internal candle again, and three gloomy figures emerged from the shadows to meet us.

"I take it nothing's happened yet," Embla said.

"Quiet as a graveyard," I said. "We've watched the house. The lights are on, but no sign of activity. Haven't seen Tori, Grim, or the sword."

"Well." Embla jutted her chin. "Let's go knock on some doors. That bitch burned my Aerie. It's time for a little payback. Solina, are you with us?"

"With you?" I asked. "I've been here, freezing my ass off in the woods, waiting for you to get here. Question is, are you with *me*? If we get that sword, what guarantee do I have that you won't turn around and use it on me?"

Embla knitted her brows. "Skyla told us about your concerns. They aren't unwarranted, and you're smart to be wary, but we don't intend to kill you. We want to protect you. You'll just have to believe us, or you're free to leave and go about your business on your own."

Val stepped forward and put a hand on my shoulder. "She's not on her own, and we've already made up our minds. We'll stay, and we'll fight."

Embla processed for a moment. She bobbed her chin. "Good. Lead the way."

We walked, without preamble or hesitation, down the driveway, through the yard, and onto the porch. Embla and Naomi peeled off from our group and scurried to the rear of the house. *What now?*

Before I could put my question to words, Skyla pounded her fist against the door, a thunderous knock. "Tori Ito, we know you're here," she yelled. "Come out and face us. Don't hide behind your pitiful little god."

Skyla pounded on the door a few more times, but either Tori had decided to hide from us, or she wasn't home. Skyla rattled the doorknob. "Locked."

I looked at Val. "This is where you come in."

Val huffed but complied with my request. He peered through a crack in the window blinds near the front door. The air popped in my ears, and he disappeared. The front door opened an instant later, and Val smiled and motioned for us to come in.

Skyla and Val fanned out through the house. I let Embla and Naomi in through the back-porch entrance. They took the upstairs while Skyla, Val, and I searched the downstairs.

"Clear!" Skyla called from her corner of the house.

I found Skyla in the living room and motioned to the kitchen. "It's clear in here, too."

Val returned from searching the other downstairs rooms. He shook his head. "Nothing."

Embla and Naomi tromped down the stairs and rejoined us.

"Nothing," said Naomi.

"What game are they playing?" Embla asked.

Through the kitchen window, beyond the yard, somewhere on the dock, the sudden glimmer of a flame arced through the sky.

"Look." I pointed. "I guess they're playing capture the flag, er, sword."

The flame waved, leaving a contrail of bright, burning plasma, like the color guard in a demonic high-school marching band. *Come and get me*, it said.

"If they want a fight, they'll get a fight," Naomi said, growling.

Skyla grabbed Naomi's arm and stopped the Valkyrie from charging forward. "That's what they want. They want us to go rushing out there, rash and unprepared."

Naomi was the smallest of us all, but she wore the most vicious expression: teeth bared, eyes sparking with fury. She drew a long blade from a sheath at her hip. I had learned in my previous training at the Aerie that the Valkyries' weapons carried an extra bit of power in the form of runes, gifted to them from Odin years ago. The Valkyries imbued their blades with the power of those runes, and it gave them the necessary edge to defeat mythological creatures. Perhaps even the gods.

"I'm not unprepared," Naomi said.

"You're talking about fighting a son of Thor," Val said. "Grim might not have Mjölnir or Thorin's other enhancements, but he won't go down easily. There's a reason the Viking berserkers worshipped Grim before going into battle. He got his battle rage from his father. You don't stand a chance against him when he makes up his mind to fight. He's a brawler, and he's lethal with just his bare hands. He's had to be because he has nothing else to fall back on."

"But say we got lucky anyway," I said. "You can't kill Grim and expect there won't be repercussions from the other Aesir."

"Solina's right." Val squeezed my shoulder. "Thorin won't take kindly to you poking lethal holes in his only brother."

Naomi huffed and rolled her eyes. "Okay, I won't try to kill Grim. Not unless he forces my hand."

"Embla," Skyla said, "if you, Naomi, and Solina focus on the fire sword, then Val and I will keep an eye out for Grim. He has to be here. He obviously lured us here."

I pursed my lips at Skyla and huffed. "I thought you said I didn't stand a chance against Tori and that I was a danger to myself."

Skyla lowered her gaze and looked away. "I have a feeling your fire might be our best chance against that sword."

"Glad we can agree on that."

It wasn't much of a plan, but we were armed and somewhat prepared. As long as Grim and Tori had the sword, and as long as we wanted to take it from them, they would have the advantage. I didn't mean to let them keep it for long.

An arc of fire blazed in the distance again, tempting us like cheese enticing rats to the trap.

"Sometimes, you just have to take the bait," I mumbled to myself.

Through the back door and out into the yard, Embla, Naomi and

I moved toward the lake, tentative and wary but focused on the sword and its wielder. Val and Skyla hung back, anticipating Grim's approach. We reached the dock, and I stopped to look back, to verify that Val had taken his place behind me as promised, but a cry of alarm and the sick *thwack* of battered flesh announced that something had gone terribly wrong.

Val cursed. Another, deeper voice barked out a harsh word. A crack was followed by another shriek that sounded like Skyla in pain. Someone cried out again, and a limp body flew through the darkness before splashing into the lake, beyond the end of the dock.

What the hell?

Skyla grunted, and I raised my fire. She and Grim were knotted together like Olympic wrestlers. He twisted and slammed her to the ground. Skyla's head rocked back and cracked against the ground, and she fell still and silent at his feet. *Oh, God, no...* Val had tried to caution us, but his warning failed to adequately prepare us for the truth. If Val, a full-blooded Aesir, couldn't stand up to Grim longer than he had, the rest of us had even less hope. We'd never really stood a chance against Grim, against a son of Thor whose ultimate weapon was his own two hands and an insane lust for battle.

My ears popped, and an instant later, a set of powerful arms wrapped around me and squeezed. I called out my fire and cranked my internal torch full throttle. Grim yelped and dropped me, and I turned to face him. In the circle of my light stood a large man who I might have mistaken for Thorin if not for the brutality in his face. Skyla had crumpled, lifeless, at his feet, and Val was gone.

Grim's lips split into a sneer. Cruelty shone in the gleam of his teeth. Grim watched me with focused attention, possibly searching out my weak spots. I had them, for sure, but he wouldn't find them without a fight.

"What do you want, Grim?" I asked, crouched in a defensive stance.

"Your death by Skoll is a great threat to my well-being," he said.

Where had I heard that *before?*

"I survived Ragnarok once. I will not take my chances again."

"There's no mistaking whose brother you are." Besides looking a great deal like Thorin, Grim also sounded just like him.

"Magni is soft. He has failed in his duty to his race."

"But not you. You're going to kill me and assure your perpetuity. That's how your brother put it."

Grim smiled, and his iciness brought goose bumps to my arms. "I am most certainly going to kill you. Just not right this minute."

"You won't touch her. Not now, not ever." Naomi appeared from the darkness and moved into my circle of light. She had drawn her sword and pointed it at Grim.

"Put away your toy, Valkyrie," Grim said, condescension thick in his tone. "You are my servant. You will do no harm to me."

Embla stepped up beside Naomi. She raised her weapon, a long, dark blade the perfect length for throwing. "For too long we've been your servants. We have fulfilled your desires and demands at your whim—at the whims of all Aesir. In return, we have been used and discarded—shoved in a corner and forgotten. For centuries, we have trained and prepared. We held ourselves ready, but for nothing. The days when we were your servants, your *whores*, are over."

I expected Embla's words to outrage Grim. Instead, he threw back his head and laughed. Embla's grip tightened. Naomi leaned in closer. Animosity and the promise of violence sparked through the air like static electricity.

"I have cared for you," Grim said, "provided for your every need. I have celebrated your success, and in your despair, I gave you support. I have always been faithful to you. In return, you betray me." Grim pulled himself up tall and straight. He threw his gaze into the distant darkness. "All have forsaken me, except one. Only she has remained true."

A streak of light blinded us. The Valkyries cried out, and Embla threw her knife as a wall of fire erupted through the night, cutting between the Valkyries and me. Naomi shouted my name. I called to her, trying to reach for her, but the flames were too hot.

"Fight fire with fire, they say." It was the voice from my dream—and it belonged to Tori.

No big surprise, but the fact she would turn on me like that stung my pride.

"Tori!" Naomi screamed over the roar of the fire. "Why are you doing this?"

Naomi lunged closer, ready to strike, but Tori swiped her weapon, Surtr's sword, and sent a literal rain of fire falling over the Valkyries. They shrieked and fell back.

Tori's attack on the others had absorbed her attention. Taking advantage of her distraction, I prepared to strike.

Grim understood my intent and called out, "Tori, watch it!"

Tori spun, and the sword vomited flames over me. I had yet to develop my ability into much of an offensive weapon unless someone stood still long enough for me to give them a bear hug made of fire, but my abilities provided for a pretty terrific defensive shield. I raised my fire and created a barricade, a protective wall that resisted the scorch of Surtalogi's flames.

Voices yelled and cried out around me, but my own fight required all my concentration, and I had no attention to spare for the others. I let down all my walls and engaged Surtalogi fully, pouring out my flames. The sword took everything I gave and more. I pushed harder, fearing that I was treading close to the threshold between corporality and supernova star power, when I would convert to that *other* state of being. But that moment never came. The sword sucked away my heat and light until my well ran dry.

"Tori, that's enough," Grim said.

Tori turned the sword aside, throwing a fiery wall up between me and the Valkyries who might have helped me. I fell to my knees and slumped to the ground. A dark and bitter chill filled the place where my fire had lived. A void opened in me and drew me toward a frigid, bottomless abyss. I had nothing left with which to resist. Naomi cried out my name once and fell silent.

Strangely, the face I saw in the dimness of my fading consciousness wasn't hers. No, in those last moments, my gaze fell on a shadowy figure standing in the gloom behind Grim, watching my defeat with a cold, detached expression.

I reached out and pointed, willing someone to turn around and see him—to verify he was real. But the darkness came, and I passed out, not knowing if I had really seen Rolf Lockhart or if my imagination had made him up.

CHAPTER TWENTY-FOUR

A BLACKENED AND ANCIENT CITY LOOMED over me—a skeleton left out in the elements to age and decay. In the distance rose a monstrous mountain range, crowned by snow. The sourness of old smoke lay heavy on my tongue and stung my eyes. I walked the dead city's streets, dodging broken stones and bricks, fallen pillars, and shattered glass. A frozen wind tore through the torched and ruined landscape, carrying the shrill cries of ghosts.

One voice rose above the others, mournful and wrecked. I searched for it, stepping over and through piles of rubble and ash. The voice called higher and louder. Like a siren, it screamed and wailed until I could no longer bear it. I crouched, covered my ears, and squeezed shut my eyes.

I stayed like that for an eternity before the sound faded. When I finally pulled my hands away, an echo rang in my ears, but the horrible noise had faded away. The place where I'd stopped was the courtyard of what had probably once been a fine home. A few beams and doorframes remained, teetering on a foundation of besmirched stone. In the yard beside me stood the burned-out remnants of a tree, little more than a twisted, blackened stump.

Compelled to touch the charred remains, I went to the tree and flattened my palm against its cold, dead bark. At the instant of my touch, new shoots sprang from the blackened body. I gasped and pulled my hand away, and the new growth withered. I touched the stump again, and the shoots recovered and grew. The roots beneath me stretched and wriggled in the ground like a child waking from a long sleep.

Branches unfurled, and tiny green buds sprouted on their tips. The buds grew into leaves and sweet white blossoms. I held my hand to the tree and watched it shed its black skin, revealing warm brown bark underneath. The flowers fell off, and in their place formed little green bulbs. The bulbs grew into apples that turned bright yellow before deepening into burnished gold.

Finally, the tree stopped and rested. I took my hand away to test what would happen. The new growth remained, the fruit sparkling in the sunlight. I grasped an apple and plucked it free. The air around me went still. The breeze died. Every leaf on the tree froze in place. The whole world held its breath, waiting for me to take a bite.

I rubbed the apple's skin over my lips, teased it with my tongue, and sank my teeth into its flesh. Its juices dribbled down my chin, and I knew I was eating the apple from my dream—the sweetest, brightest flavor I had ever tasted. The breeze returned, but with a freshness that hadn't existed before. I heaved in a deep lungful, and the coldness of it stung and cramped in my chest. I gasped and coughed and fought for air, but it was frozen, and I could not breathe.

Darkness surrounded me. I rubbed my eyes, but none of my visions returned. No tree, no burnt city, no imposing mountains. Nothing. I tried sitting up, but dizziness washed over me.

Haven't I been in this situation before?

But no stony arms were binding me in place. My own weakness was keeping me immobile. Grim had done me the courtesy of providing a thin blanket to cover my bare flesh, but it left my extremities cold and numb. I envisioned my toes turning black and falling off. The one comfort in that horrible situation hung heavy around my neck: the gold chain, Mjölnir's lanyard. It had survived the firefight.

"Does Sleeping Beauty finally awake?"

"Grim?" My words came out in a rasp from my dry and frozen throat.

A match struck, and a lantern flared to life. Light bounced off Grim's face, but the shadows drew harsh lines that turned him into a haggard and haunted creature. He grinned, the lecherous beast, and leaned closer. Heat from the lantern supplied the only relief from the frigid air, and I wanted to hug it, but raising my hand would've required strength I didn't have.

"Where am I?" I asked.

"Somewhere safe."

"Safe from what?"

"Meddlers."

"What happened?"

"Surtalogi feeds on fire. It sucked yours away until you were empty."

"Why is it so cold?"

"Ice." Grim patted the walls. "A whole cave made from it."

He wore a fur-lined parka. The hood hid his hair and made his resemblance to his fairer brother more pronounced. It creeped me out, big time.

"I-I'm going to freeze to death," I said, my teeth chattering.

Grim clicked his tongue and shook his head. "No, you won't. Not yet." He passed me a cup of something hot and steaming. "Drink this. The cold should keep you too weak to use your fire, but you'll be able to generate just enough heat to keep yourself alive."

"Why? If you kill me now, Skoll will be out of luck, Helen's plan will... Oh, I see. Helen is the whole point of this. Right? I'm Helen bait."

Grim nodded. "Surtalogi is one of the few things that can defeat her, and her death is long overdue."

"What happened to Val?"

"Last I saw, he was broken in two, lying at the bottom of Mineral Lake."

"Dead?"

"Probably not, but he'll be useless for a while."

"Skyla?"

"That new Valkyrie bitch? She's out of luck. Brave, fierce, but still ultimately no help to you." Grim shifted and moved away, taking the tiny bit of lantern heat with him. "Drink that syrup and go back to sleep." He moved farther away. "It's the only escape that will offer you any comfort."

"Wait," I said.

Grim paused. He didn't turn around, but his stillness indicated he was listening.

"Are you working with Rolf Lockhart?"

"Lockhart?" Grim asked, his back still to me. "Never heard of him." With that, he disappeared into the darkness. I tried getting to my feet, but my legs refused to cooperate, and the shivering took over so that I could barely move at all. After sucking down the contents of the cup—sweet, warm, and thick—I reached into my wellspring of fire and found a sorry dribble of energy. I brought it to the surface, and the faintest light glowed from my skin, like foxfire generated by the honey fungus on dying trees.

Mani had taught me those kinds of things when we went camping as kids. He was such a Boy Scout. I closed my eyes and revisited the camping trip with Mani when he'd first showed me the foxfire, little mushroom bundles growing on decaying trees. From a distance, their glow looked like the eyes of enchanted creatures watching us from the forest shadows. I wanted to pick them and take them home. Mani wouldn't let me.

"They won't glow if you pick them," he said. "They'll die, and their lights will go out."

I snagged an apple from a low-hanging branch and ate it as I toured the remains of the house. Ash, charcoal, and a pile of heavy rocks littered the floor and surrounding yard, but little else remained. No knickknacks or personal items, no crockery or furnishings. When I finished my apple, I tossed the core out the window frame and thought no more of it. But when I returned to the yard minutes later, a ring of fine, green grass had sprung up around the apple core. *Hmm?*

Curiosity piqued, I crouched over the apple core and poked it, pushing it beyond the perimeter of the grass circle. The grass remained, not drying and curling into brown straw or disappearing as magically as it had appeared. Although I doubted my idea's effectiveness, I collected the apple core, picked out the seeds, pawed a hole at the center of the grass patch, and buried the seeds.

Nothing happened. I held my hand against the mound. Still nothing. I sighed, sank down on the ground, and waited for whatever would come next.

"The wolf, Hati, he's dead?" Grim asked. "You killed him?"

I nodded. Talking depleted my energy, and I needed every drop to stave off the cold. Grim had woken me to feed me another cup of syrupy energy goop and had started his inquisition, testing my knowledge of Helen and Thorin. That cave, all darkness and numbing cold, sucked away all concept of time and place. Had I been there for hours, or days? It felt like years.

"B-burned him to ash," I said through chattering teeth.

"And what of Skoll?"

"B-burned, too." I summarized our fight with Skoll in the desert but avoided mentioning Thorin's use of the hammer.

"But he survived."

I nodded.

"You haven't seen either of them, Helen or Skoll, since?"

I shook my head. "Came straight to the Aerie."

"Looking for the sword?"

Nod.

"Where is my brother?"

Shrug.

"Why did he leave you unprotected?"

"V-Val—" I started.

Grim barked a sharp laugh. "He's sunk so far into humanity he's forgotten himself. He's no threat to me, and he's a poor guardian for a daughter of Sol."

"Solina."

"What?"

"My n-name is Solina."

Grim laughed again. "Soon, your name will be forgotten. It doesn't matter to me. When did you last see my brother?"

Shrug. "Went to help Baldur find Nina."

Grim snorted. "Baldur the Allfather, lovesick halfwit. But you don't know where they went?"

Head shake.

"I've sent Helen word about my capture of you. As soon as I'm sure she's taken the bait, I will end this suffering. It shouldn't last much longer."

I didn't have the energy to cry. I shrugged and closed my eyes.

213

The apple seeds had sprouted. Two little green shoots reached toward the sky. I brushed my fingers over the tender green stalks, hoping to encourage their growth. My touch had no influence, though—not as it had on the mother tree—but that didn't matter. Those two little signs of life in this long-dead place eased my heartache and emptiness. I ate as many apples from the mother tree as I could stuff in my stomach, and I buried seeds all about the burned-out building.

For what felt like hours, I planted, moving out from the house in concentric circles. I couldn't rebuild the city, but I could build an orchard. By the time I had planted the seeds from all the apples I could eat, I had created a perimeter around the house, two rows deep. The sun was setting as I buried the last seed. My stomach groaned from overeating, and dried juice coated my fingers and wrists in a sticky film.

I returned to the yard outside my burnt house and eased down against the base of the mother tree. The grass beneath it had grown into a thick green carpet. In fact, anywhere I had planted a seed already showed signs of life. Little green patches dotted the yard, and only a few burned, dry places remained. Soon those would be gone, too.

I leaned back against the tree and stretched. I turned my face up to the sky and greeted the rising moon. "Hello, Mani. Long time, no see."

The floor shuddered, and the cavern groaned and squealed. Ice splinters broke free and rained over me. The cave had come to life. During my last round of oblivion—I wouldn't quite call it sleep—my fire had gone out. Normally, my heat melted the ice enough to keep me lying in a shallow, lukewarm puddle, but it had since frozen hard.

I sought my internal power source and found a small, burning ember. Not enough for a full flame, but much more than I'd expected, enough to combat the cold. *But how...?*

The apples.

The apples were the figment of a dream. Imagination. Hopeful thinking.

Is that all they are?

I didn't know how they could be anything else. But the proof lay in the fire. Not the pitiful trickle borne of Grimm's strange energy drink—the force inside me was stronger than that, but it wasn't enough.

Not yet. But soon.

I sat in the grass at the base of my tree and stared at the big silver moon filling the sky. So close and huge, it pressed against the roof of the world as if reaching down for my touch. A breeze ruffled my hair. I lifted my face toward it, inhaling the scent of apples. Some of the fruit had fallen and sat bruised on the ground around me, skins split and heading fast toward rot, and the air smelled of cider. Time, in that place, moved in funny ways.

"Mani, what did we get ourselves into?"

The moon did not respond.

"You suspected you were something more than a simple man, didn't you? And you were always so much more than just a brother to me. I guess that's the curse of twins. When you died, I should have suspected something was up. Losing you shouldn't have hurt that badly. It wasn't normal. Even Mom and Dad could move on. They made you, gave birth to you, and they could let you go. Why not me? Why couldn't I let go, Mani?"

In the solitude of that place, the slightest rustle equaled the explosion of thunder. The tree leaves brushing together and the percussion of approaching footsteps created an orchestra of noise. I sucked in a breath and held it. Had the wolf found me, even in this place? But the intruder wasn't Skoll or Helen or Grim.

It wasn't Mani either.

"When it comes to letting go, you haven't been given much choice, unfortunately." Aleksander Thorin stepped out from the orchard's shadows, and the moonlight crowned his pale hair and molded him in quicksilver. "It was you who decided to track down the truth of your brother's murder, but even if you hadn't, this ordeal would have been foisted on you eventually.

"Also, you have yet to show you are the sort to run away from a challenge. That is not fate's fault so much as an admirable and yet equally annoying facet of your character."

215

I snorted. "Maybe Skoll could have done me the favor of killing me in my blissful ignorance rather than letting me die well informed but in much greater pain."

"Die? You're giving up already?"

"And let you off the hook? No, I don't think so."

Thorin grinned. "That's good to know, because I was wondering whether I should waste my time coming to rescue you or not."

I grimaced, rolled to my feet, and stood. "Maybe if you had come with me in the first place, I wouldn't need rescuing. What are you doing here? I thought this was some happy place I made up in my head, but if that were true, then there's no way I would have dreamed about you."

Thorin's eyes sparkled, and his grin widened. "Your subconscious disagrees with your ego. I think you want me rather badly."

"I want to not die rather badly. If you can help me with that, then yes, I could see how it would appear I might desire your company."

Stepping closer, Thorin peered into my face. His expression revealed genuine concern. "How are you doing, Sunshine? No bravado. Be honest with me."

I shrugged. "I think I should be doing a lot worse than I am, actually."

Thorin's brow furrowed. "What do you mean?"

"I mean that it was Grim's intention to keep me on the edge of death. But this place and these apples..." I motioned to the mother tree overhead. "I think if I had enough time, they might bring my fire back. But then what?"

"Knowing Grim, I suspect you don't have much time. He intends to see you dead, Sunshine."

"I intend to see him fail. I'm just not sure how, yet."

Thorin stepped closer and took my hand in his. He brushed his thumb over my knuckles before bringing my fingers to his lips. "You won't have to fight him alone. I'm coming for you."

"How will you find me?"

Thorin reached out and fingered the gold chain around my neck. "I told you I could track you."

"Well, bring some warm clothes when you come. I think my toes are getting frostbite."

Thorin's grin fell away. He grimaced and asked, "Anything else I should bring?"

"Holy retribution for your brother. That should do it."

"Happy to oblige." Thorin dropped my hand. He turned and started toward the trees.

I called to him before he faded into the shadows. "Is any of this real? Or did I just make up this place in my imagination?"

"You don't know?" Thorin, nothing more than a flickering shadow, looked back at me. Disbelief wrinkled his brow, and he quirked his lips into a peculiar smile. "How did you come to the house of Idun if you did not come on purpose?"

"Idun? What is that supposed to mean?" I yelled to his fading figure. I knew of Idun's apples of immortality from my research, and I had seen an old and mature orchard in my visions. I was not in that place, though. "Where am I *really*?"

Before he disappeared, Thorin uttered a final word.

Maybe I didn't believe him, but I was certain he said, "Asgard."

CHAPTER TWENTY-FIVE

"SUNSHINE, *WAKE UP*." HANDS GRIPPED my shoulders and shook me until my teeth clacked. "Wake the hell up, Solina. *Please*."

I peeled my eyelids apart, possibly ripping out a few eyelashes that had frozen together. Warm light from a lantern pushed back the darkness and revealed Thorin's face hovering over mine. Gabriel, Raphael, Michael... none of the archangels surpassed his beauty at that moment. I tried to smile, but my chapped lips protested.

"Hey, gorgeous." Thorin pressed his lips to my forehead. He had put nothing romantic into his greeting, just relief—not that I was in a state to appreciate his affections, anyway. "So glad you decided to join the land of the living."

Thorin helped me slip into insulated pants and a long-sleeved fleece shirt. He bundled me into wool socks and snow boots and tugged me to my feet. He wrapped me in his own parka, which retained his body heat and smelled of rain and storms. I would have wept at the relief of it, the sublime pleasure, but I was too dried out.

For the first time, I got a good look at my prison. Blue-white walls, dim in the lantern light, stretched several feet over my head, curving into an arched ceiling. If I fully extended both arms, my middle fingers might have brushed the walls on either side of me, but the length of the cave extended into a long, dark throat the lantern light failed to reach. The cave groaned and popped, and ice flakes sparkled in the air, whispering threats of my doom. I shivered.

"Let's get you out of here." Thorin wrapped an arm around my shoulder, supporting me.

"What about Grim?"

"Let me worry about him, okay?"

"The sword?"

"Solina"—Thorin tightened his hold on me—"all you need to worry about is keeping yourself together and in the present until we get out of here."

One more concern, and then I would let Thorin take over for me. "Helen?"

Thorin chuckled. "Frozen to death, and you're still stubborn as hell. Grim didn't set this up for Helen."

"That's right. I set it for *you*, dear brother." Grim appeared in the gloom, illuminated by the flame of the sword held casually at his side.

I gasped and reached for my own fire—a measly supply but not completely bankrupt. I held the heat beneath my skin, not giving away my status to Grim, but prepared to defend myself if necessary.

"As if I would risk letting Helen and her filthy mutt get anywhere near the daughter of Sol."

"Why?" I croaked, meaning, *Why this complicated kidnapping? Why Thorin? Why* not *Helen?*

Grim understood my question. "Once I'm finished with you, who gives a damn about Helen's plans? The only reason you're still alive is because I needed you to wear that necklace."

"He wants Mjölnir," Thorin said.

"He knows?" I asked.

"I'm guessing it was the storm in the desert that gave it away."

Grim nodded. "That storm lit up my senses. I hadn't felt that energy in centuries, but there was no mistaking what caused it. You had to know I would sense it."

"How did you know I had it?" I asked. The words stung my raw throat.

"I didn't," Grim said. "I intended to kill you, but I saw you had Mjölnir's lanyard. It's the thing that kept you alive. I would have finished you the night you came for the sword, otherwise."

"You could have just killed me and taken it. Tracked the hammer yourself."

"No," Thorin said. "The moment he took possession of it, I would have known it was him who had it. I would never have come to him."

"Blood calls to blood." Grim's rancor showed how much he loathed their familial ties. "It worked more in my favor if lover called to lover."

"I'm here now," Thorin said. "Mjölnir is with me. Leave Solina out of it."

Grim's eyebrows arched high. "And let Helen have her? Oh, no, nothing has changed. The girl still has to die. It's the only way to ensure Helen fails."

An explosion of sound burst through the cavern. Grim blipped out of sight and appeared a few feet away from Thorin and me, but his attention was not on us. He focused on Skyla, who stood beside us, legs braced wide, frame held rigid, gun poised to take another shot.

Oh, thank God! Should have known it would take more than a bump on the head to keep her down.

Grim laughed at her. "Faster than a speeding bullet. Superman got all of his tricks from me."

"You sure do like the sound of your own voice." Skyla pulled the trigger a second time.

Grim moved so fast I couldn't keep up with him. He finally came to a halt, however, when he materialized with a massive hand gripping around his neck, a hand that belonged to Baldur.

"Allfather," Grim gasped. "What are you—" His question ended in a wheeze.

"Baldur," Thorin said. "Get Solina out of here. Grim is *my* problem." Thorin's black eyes sparked. "I promised to keep Solina from harm, and you've made me break that vow, brother."

"It was nothing personal." Grim tried to chuckle, but Baldur squeezed, and Grim choked on his laugh, literally.

"Baldur, take Solina away from here. Please." Thorin's voice sounded as if it had issued from a grizzly bear, and rage oozed from his pores until all humanity left him. "We both know it will take something as strong as Mjölnir to bring him down."

Baldur met Thorin's eyes, held his gaze for a moment, and nodded. He dropped Grim, flickered to Thorin's side, and took hold of me. My ears popped, and blackness whirled before my eyes. We stopped outside the cavern. Low-hanging clouds and a stiff breeze stirred snow into icy whirlwinds.

"I'm going to get Skyla," Baldur said. "Once she's safely out, I'll take you away from the mountain."

"Mountain?"

"Mount Rainier. Grim has kept you in a glacial cave for almost two days. It's a miracle you've survived." Baldur popped out of sight. I counted several heartbeats, expecting his immediate return, but the minutes of his absence ticked by without his reappearance. My impatience urged me to do something, to take action... to fight. I needed Baldur. Thorin, too. Without the gods to help me off this mountain, I had nowhere to go. I stepped toward the cave but lost my balance when the ground shuddered. The ice shook and heaved as if the glacier meant to break apart.

Skyla's voice rose above the din, panting and cursing like a sailor. "We're on the same side, you crazy bitch!"

"It's too late for that," said Skyla's opponent, Tori.

Where did she come from?

Tori heaved a breath and said, "Grim wants Solina dead."

"You're his slave? Can't think for yourself?"

The two women tumbled out of the cavern into the open ice field a few yards away from me. Neither noticed my presence as they were too wrapped up in their fight.

"It's for the greater good!" Tori screamed. Their feet scuffled over the ice, and they panted like dogs. They darted toward each other, pivoting in circles, occasionally falling to wrestle each other in the snow.

"Screw the greater good!" Skyla gasped for a breath. "The greater good never did me one single favor."

"You... You want to throw it all away for *her*?" Condensation puffed from Tori's mouth and nose like a steaming locomotive. "You risk the world for one woman?"

"For a brother and sister who were more family to me than my own blood." Skyla backed away and huffed out her own steady stream of frozen breath. "Mani was ripped from me too soon. I'll be damned if anyone takes his sister, too."

The two fell against each other again. Skyla struck out with the heel of her hand, and Tori spouted a brutal shriek as something crunched—a joint or possibly a bone.

"The world will be destroyed." Tori panted, obviously speaking through a great amount of pain. "You'll have no one to blame but yourself."

Baldur blipped to my side, clutching his ribs. Blood seeped between his fingers, and his breath came in rough spurts. "Tori's appearance was unexpected. She got the jump on us."

"What happened to you?"

"Tori had a blade, something infused with mistletoe is my guess."

"Will you be okay?"

"I'll manage."

"What about Skyla's gun?"

"Dropped in the tussle, I presume." Baldur bent to scoop me up. He moved as if preparing to leave.

"No," I said. "We can't leave Skyla."

Baldur frowned but turned us to face the fight.

"You could have helped us, Tori," Skyla said in a raw and ragged voice.

Back on their feet again, the Valkyries were locked in a desperate embrace.

"You could have stopped Helen," Skyla said. "You could have told me the truth about myself and let me help you lead the Valkyries on the path they were intended to take."

"It's no good. The Valkyries are lost. Forget them."

"You're a spineless bitch, Tori. The Valkyries are better off without you."

Tori spat out a shriek that sheared through the crisp air and raised the hairs on the back of my neck. She pivoted, jerked Skyla off balance and jabbed a knee into her side. Skyla wheezed and fell to the ground as Tori turned and came for me.

My flames erupted in a cloak and cowl of blazing glory. Another set of clothing burned and gone, but Skyla was worth the risk of frostbite. I widened my stance and lowered my center of gravity. Tori could kick my butt in a fistfight, but let her see how she did against my fire.

"Solina," Skyla called my name, warning me. She struggled to her feet.

Baldur moved, lightning fast, and knocked Tori aside. Before she regained her balance, I pounced.

Tori screamed. She shifted her weight, rolled, and threw me off. I scuttled back and regained my feet.

"Solina." She breathed heavily, gritting her teeth. Her winter clothes had protected her, mostly, but a red welt rose on her cheek. Her gloves and winter coat hung in tatters. "It has to go this way. We can't risk the wolf killing you."

I bared my teeth at her and growled. "If you had my back, if you fought on my side, Skoll would never stand a chance. But instead, you chose to sacrifice me because why? Because it's easier? Because Grim told you to?"

While I talked and held Tori's attention, Baldur teleported himself behind her. Ice cracked under his feet, giving his position away. Tori spun, faced Baldur, and raised her knife, presumably the one laced with mistletoe. Baldur had already tasted that poison—no need for a second helping. I leapt forward, aiming to tackle Tori, but she danced aside, and I skidded on the ice, missing her by a breath. My flames sputtered. I had used most of the energy the apples had given me, and I had nearly reached the bottom of my fuel tank.

Skyla stumbled to her feet and clutched her side. She lunged, throwing a fist into Tori's jaw. Tori wheeled back, and Skyla kicked her feet out from beneath her. Tori fell to her back and cried out. Skyla straddled Tori, sitting on her, and wrapped her hands around Tori's neck.

"Solina," Baldur said. "Kill your fire."

"What? Why?"

"Just do it!" he ordered.

The command in his voice required compliance, and I couldn't resist, especially in my weakened state. My flames guttered and died. Baldur threw his arms around me, and in the moment before he carried us away, someone screamed. The cry ended in a horrible gargle.

"No," I said as my ears popped. "We can't leave them."

"My job is to protect you, Solina. I can't take any more chances. We must go."

***

Baldur dumped me in a room heated to sauna proportions and ordered me to sleep. I didn't know where he had brought me, but I asked no questions and offered no protests. My mind sank into a white haze, and I embraced the reprieve it granted. The sandman carried me into unconsciousness, and all the gods together couldn't have stopped him.

I woke later, shivers wracking my body with horrible spasms. My muscles cramped in such terrific pain I thought they might tear away from the bone. I might have screamed. Someone came and held me, feeding me warm medicinal drinks that burned my throat but eased the cramping. The trembling subsided, and I sank back into a blessed oblivion.

CHAPTER TWENTY-SIX

FOR THE FIRST TIME IN what felt like ages, I woke up warm and cozy, but thirst had turned my throat and eyes into sandpaper. Skyla appeared at my bedside, waiting with a mug of hot chicken broth and a glass of water.

"Sip this slow." She passed me the mug.

I sucked down the broth and gave it back to her for a refill.

She chuckled and shook her head. "I said *slow*."

"Try telling that to my stomach," I said.

Skyla obliged my request for seconds and returned a few moments later with another cup of soup.

"Where are we?" I asked after scanning my surroundings—log walls, chintz curtains, hand-stitched quilts.

"A rental cabin near Rainier. We set this up as sort of a base camp, but we didn't intend to stay here this long. Baldur was too weak to make the jump all the way back to New Breidablik with passengers."

I took her hand and squeezed it. "Baldur made me leave you. I'm sorry. I didn't want to."

"We're all together now. He came back for me."

"Are you okay? The fighting was so horrible."

"I've got a bruised rib, some sore knuckles, but otherwise, I'm fine."

"What happened? Is Tori...?" My mouth went dry, and I couldn't finish the question.

Lines of strain appeared around Skyla's mouth and eyes. "Tori wasn't going to stop. She was intent on killing you and on getting me out of her way so I couldn't interfere. She was a fanatic—dedicated to her beliefs."

"You were a soldier. And a Valkyrie." Sensing Skyla's discomfort, I changed the subject to something less disturbing.

"Tell me everything." I fell back against the pillows. Getting out of bed felt like a Sisyphean task. "Where is Thorin?"

Skyla sighed and slumped beside me. "You've been out of commission for a day. We woke you to force you to drink a few times. You stumbled to the bathroom once."

"Ah. I thought it was just part of some weird dream."

Skyla chuckled. "You did talk about apples a lot."

My apple orchard had grown exponentially. I'd spent a lot of time in that dreamy place while my body recovered from hypothermia and dehydration. Not once in that place did a wolf try to eat me or a maniacal god try to kill me. My subconscious was being decent enough to let me dream of good things for a change.

Skyla's gaze dropped, and her chin dipped. "Don't know about Thorin, though. He hasn't shown up yet."

I sat back up, and my mouth fell open. "Hasn't Baldur been back to look for him?"

"No, he's wounded as well. Plus, he's been nursing the two of us, and he has Nina to worry about. They found her in a pretty bad situation. She's kind of a mess."

I sat up straighter, energized by curiosity. "Nina? So he did find her. How?"

"Long story."

"Like we have anything else to do."

"Maybe you should come into the living room. Baldur probably would want to tell his part. It's not like I was there for it."

"What about Val? Has he not made contact either?"

Skyla patted my shoulder and shook her head. "I'm sorry, Solina. The last I saw, Grim had broken him almost literally in half and thrown him in the lake. I don't know if they're able to recover from those kinds of things."

My heart swelled into my throat. I turned away and covered my eyes. A big, cold fist squeezed my heart, and the air in my lungs turned to ice.

Skyla rubbed my back while I struggled against tears and fought back the urge to scream and maybe throw something, tear apart a pillow or punch a wall—impotent gestures that might momentarily ease my internal pain but would otherwise solve nothing. I needed a plan, an action, something more productive. *But what?*

"Maybe Val survived it," Skyla said, "but we saw no signs of him after Grim disappeared with you and Tori. Just as it is with Thorin, it's a case of wait and see. It sucks, but that's the way it is."

Skyla scooted off the bed and stretched. She hadn't cut her hair in a while, so the halo of curls around her face had grown into something wilder and unruly. A huge T-shirt and sweats—probably something belonging to Baldur—swallowed her compact frame. I wore similar attire.

She noticed me giving her the once-over and made a sour face. "This living like a vagabond is getting old."

"Tell me about it." I scooted to the edge of the bed, wondering when I had traded my body for that of a ninety-year-old suffering arthritis in every joint. Skyla heaved me up onto my feet, groaning at her own injuries as she did. We supported each other as we wibble-wobbled into the living room.

An unfamiliar woman looked up from her book as we entered. She wore her hair in a wild mane of tight black ringlets that trailed over her broad shoulders. She sat in an overstuffed chair across from a crackling fireplace and stared at me with big brown eyes. I sank into another overstuffed chair, and Skyla plopped down on a huge ottoman next to me, folding her legs criss-cross applesauce.

"Nina," Skyla said, "I don't think you and Solina have been formally introduced. Solina Mundy, meet Nina Norgaard."

Nina nodded at me but kept her face impassive. Closer inspection revealed she was older than me—maybe by as many as ten or fifteen years. She also had a few weeks-old bruises and abrasions. From a distance, her dark skin camouflaged the damage, and she looked as ageless and pristine as the subject of a hallowed painting. "Everyone's talked about you a lot," Nina said. She looked me over before turning back to her book. "Not sure what all the fuss is about."

I ignored her cutting remark and smiled and tried to sound friendly. "Everyone's talked about you, too. I can't wait to hear your story."

Baldur, maybe having heard the chatter of multiple females, entered the room and greeted me with an enthusiastic hug. "So glad to see you on the mend."

"Feels good to *be* on the mend," I said. "I can't thank you enough for what you've done for me."

"No thanks are necessary. Just doing what I should have been doing all along."

"What about Thorin? Skyla says you've had no word from him?"

Baldur lowered his eyes and frowned. "I can't say for sure what happened to him."

"Can't you go look for him?"

Baldur's gaze shifted to Nina. His face showed all his feelings, love but also apprehension. "I don't want to leave her," he whispered. "She's not stable."

"So we sit here and wait for Thorin to show up?"

Mjölnir's chain still hung around my neck, and it would draw him to me... if he was capable of tracking it. The "if" was what worried me.

"Yes. We will rest and continue to heal. You'll have to trust Magni to take care of himself."

"But Grim had the sword. It's a horrible weapon."

"Magni has Mjölnir—it should not be underestimated." Baldur's assertions didn't mollify me, but he couldn't have cared less about my concerns. His attention shifted to Nina again, his eyes soft and unfocused.

Intent on her book, Nina behaved as though no one else existed in the room.

"Tell me about it." I motioned in her direction. "How did you find her?"

Baldur huffed, almost a laugh, but an ironic one. "The doctors had put her in a medically induced coma, and it was like she was dead all over again." She had survived an inexplicable single-car wreck on a stretch of rural desert highway outside Farmington, New Mexico, and the hospital staff had registered her as a Jane Doe. The car was a rental registered under an alias. She had no identifying papers with her, no driver's license, and no cell phone. Her prints matched nothing in the national registry.

When the local police put out an APB about her on state and federal circuits, however, she showed up on Baldur's radar, which he had built by meticulously begging, bribing, and threatening anyone who had the means to keep him and his private detectives appraised of any developments. Baldur had created a massive web that almost guaranteed Nina's eventual discovery.

"I personally followed or paid someone to follow any lead," Baldur said.

"How did you know she would show up in the US?"

Baldur snorted. "I didn't."

My mouth fell open. "You've been watching for her internationally?"

"Globally."

"And you're sure it's her?"

Baldur nodded, and his face showed no uncertainty. "She's been hurt, though. More than just the car wreck. I think Helen must have broken her before she put her in that hospital."

"Why would Helen try to kill her?"

"I don't think Helen wanted her dead. She set it up so I would find her. One of Helen's shell companies was paying Nina's medical bills."

"How long had she been like that?"

"A few weeks. The doctors were bringing her out of the coma when Magni and I arrived. She didn't know anyone or anything about what had happened to her, but I had already made arrangements to bring her home with me."

"Why would Helen do that to her?"

"Helen never relinquishes her grasp on anyone without putting them through hell first. I should know."

"Why would she let her go after all this time?"

"To distract me. To hurt me. To keep me busy with Nina's rehabilitation instead of focused on guarding you. There are many reasons."

"But you have her back. That's got to be a great relief."

Baldur smiled and ran a hand over his face, rubbing away the bleary look in his eyes. I'd never seen a god look tired before, but the white lines around his eyes and mouth showed the effects of his strains and injuries. "I have her, and I won't let her go."

Baldur made a simple supper of eggs, bacon, and toast. Nina ate without speaking unless spoken to and without meeting anyone's eye. She tried her best to ignore Baldur altogether. I understood what Skyla meant about Nina being "not quite right." After I cleaned my plate twice, Skyla helped me hobble back to bed.

"I'm going back to the Aerie in the morning." Skyla leaned in my doorway and watched me settle into bed. "I'm not doing anyone any good sitting around here. I'm about to go stir crazy."

"You're doing me tons of good," I said through a yawn. "Every time you leave me, bad stuff happens."

Skyla sighed. "I know. Believe me, I *know*. I feel torn in two all the time."

"Take it as a compliment. To be needed so badly, it means you're doing something right."

"If you want me to stay, I will."

She meant it, and for that reason, I knew I had to let her go. "Go to the Aerie. Fix the Valkyries. Bring them over to our side. Make up a theme song and a costume while you're at it. You're my own personal hero, straight out of the comics."

"Don't give me all the credit." Skyla smiled. "I was wrong to say the things I said about you. You are a fighter, Solina. I expected to find you half dead when we got there, but there you were at the end, fighting Tori in a blaze of glory."

I nodded. "You were wrong, but it's okay. We all have our moments of weakness. I've questioned your loyalty once. Now we're even."

"I won't doubt you again."

"Thank you for coming for me."

Skyla shrugged and looked away. "I couldn't have done it without Thorin. He was like this raging beast, flattening mountains, laying down forests. When I called him after you disappeared, he had already gone to Corvallis to look for you. He knew something bad was going to happen with his brother. He left Baldur and came for you. He would have gone to the ninth gate of hell to get you, Solina."

"He feels responsible for me."

"If Grim had killed you instead of Skoll, it would have ended all the Aesir's problems very neatly. Thorin didn't have to rescue you."

"You talked him into it."

"I didn't have to say anything to him, Solina. I called him and had him meet us at Grim's house at the lake. One look at my face, and Thorin was ready to go up the mountain that very moment. I had to convince him to hang out long enough to make a reasonable plan." Skyla gave me a doleful look. "When we met up outside that cave, he barely spoke a word—just ground his teeth until Baldur and I were in place. I've known Thorin for three years. He's always been so cool and collected."

"Pssshaw," I said. "As if."

"You get under his skin, Mundy. I've never seen him so furious and so... so *scared* in all the time I've known him. I've climbed ice floes with him. We once outran an avalanche by the skin of our teeth. We faced down an angry bull moose on a hunting trip, and Thorin didn't even flinch. In fact, he laughed at the moose and killed it with a freaking longbow while he was still chuckling. But this time, he was scared. He was afraid of losing you."

I shook my head and yawned again. "It's hard to see him as the sort who cares for anything other than his own hide." *Or maybe that's just how you want to see him. Because it's safer and easier.*

Skyla reached for my light switch and flicked it off. The room went dark, and before she left me, she said, "I think it's safe to say he cares for your hide, too."

CHAPTER TWENTY-SEVEN

I SEEMED TO RETURN TO THE apple orchard only moments after I closed my eyes. Thorin had called it the house of Idun, but I had spent so much time there restoring the grounds and renewing the trees that I felt the right to claim some sort of ownership. The moment I stepped foot into the grassy yard, however, I saw I wouldn't have it to myself.

"I wondered if you would show up," Thorin said. His wore his hair tied back in a long tail, and he was soot smudged, sweaty, and... *shirtless*. The torc that Baldur had made from Thor's belt circled his neck, a braided iron ring that contrasted with Thorin's supple skin. My mouth went dry at so much beauty on such grand display. He remained intent on his work, stacking stones from a large pile at his feet onto a wall on one side of the crumbled house. Elegant muscles flexed beneath golden skin, and my fingers itched to touch him. He was a god, the strongest among them, and his frame and form epitomized extreme might and power.

I swallowed and, with a mostly steady voice, asked, "What are you doing here?"

"What does it look like?" Thorin heaved a boulder into place beside the remnants of a door frame.

"You're rebuilding. But why?"

"Needed a place to hang out for a while. Things have gone bad."

"In what way? What are you talking about?"

Thorin brushed his hands over the thighs of his old-fashioned work pants—something I

had never seen him wear before. I had never noticed what I wore when I came here, but I looked down and found myself dressed in

232

something like the Valkyries' ceremonial garb: a white gown flowing in elegant panels, draping down to my toes. *Okay, that's weird.*

"I told you my brother was trouble," Thorin said.

"You just couldn't wait to say, 'I told you so'?"

"I was right, wasn't I?"

"I told you not to go looking for Nina out at those warehouses in Arizona, and you didn't listen to me about that, either."

"We're both too stubborn for our own good, I guess," he said. "The difference is in the level of risks we take. The consequences are not as dire for me as they are for you."

I narrowed my eyes. "You think I don't regret it? You think I haven't learned my lesson? Paid my price?"

"This all could have been avoided."

"If I let you keep me in a cage," I said. "Or you could borrow your brother's idea and just kill me rather than wasting all your energy trying to keep me alive. It's the sure thing, you know. Grim was right about that."

Thorin growled and stalked closer.

"I'm more trouble than I'm worth," I said in a defiant tone. Without self-pity, I meant my words as a challenge. "Don't you think?"

Thorin sounded like a bear when he spoke again, all low and guttural. "What are you playing at? Why are you always intent on antagonizing me?"

My shoulders slumped, and I exhaled. *To push you away, of course.* "I couldn't fight your brother, so maybe I'm taking my frustrations out on you." I dragged my eyes up over his body, making my appraisal obvious. "You can take it, though, can't you?"

I crossed the distance between us and stepped behind Thorin. "Look at you." I traced a finger across his bare back, from shoulder to shoulder. His skin was warm and alive under my fingertip. "You're a real-life Atlas, shoulders that can bear the weight of the world. You'll save us all, won't you?"

"Morbid, Solina." Thorin turned to intercept my orbit. He took my hand, the one tracing over his back, and clasped it between both of his. "It's not your nature."

"How do you know my nature?" I asked.

However, Thorin was right. That forwardness was unlike me, but I didn't exactly feel like myself in that place. Asgard.

"I know you better than you think I do," he said. "You forget I knew you in another life."

My eyebrows arched high. "How is that possible?"

"In your soul, you are Sol. You always have been, and you always will be."

I tugged my hand, and Thorin released it. I stepped away, relieving some of the tension between us. Thorin's words disconcerted me, and I needed to process.

"Why are you here?" I asked. "Why are you rebuilding Idun's house?"

"I came here a day ago, and I haven't been able to leave," Thorin said. "That's never happened before."

"So you're setting up house and planning to stay for a while?"

"It rained last night, and it was miserable. I've got to make shelter until I can figure out how to get away."

"Come with me. I'll take you back."

He shook his head as a sad smile tugged at his lips. "It doesn't work that way, Sunshine."

"If you don't want to be here, I'll help you go," I said, confident in my ability to lead him away. I waved my hand around the lush yard and growing trees. "Though why you want to leave this place, I don't really know. It's so peaceful. No wolves. No fire. No monsters."

Thorin's sad smile brightened. "It is lovely, isn't it? You should have seen it before, when it was all fresh and alive." He collected his shirt from the ground, wiped his face, and cleared the soot from his arms. He stepped toward me again, close enough to reveal the copper flecks sparkling in his eyes. "Something has gone wrong."

"You said that before. I'm not sure what you mean."

"I shouldn't be stuck here."

"I'll figure out how to get you unstuck."

"No. No matter what happens to me, you must keep yourself safe. Do *not* attempt to find me."

"Don't find you? But you're right here." I laughed a nervous titter, and my heart beat in a cadence of alarm, fast and fluttery.

"That's right. I'm here. And this is where you'll leave me."

"I'll leave when I good and well feel like it."

Thorin's breath tickled my face as he chuckled. "I meant that you won't attempt to do anything to make *me* leave."

"Like I'd think for a minute I could make you do anything you didn't want to."

Thorin's eyes darkened, but not in anger. "You make me do all kinds of things I never intended to do."

Although Thorin and I stood inches apart, it felt as though we were staring at each other across a wide valley filled with unspoken sentiments. Thorin's allure pulled at me, urging me to act, to do something decisive for once. I resisted that impulse, and as if sensing my reticence, Thorin stepped back and shook his head. "You don't have to leave, but I wish you would. I've got to get back to work."

His dismissal stung, but it cleared my head. I latched onto it and used the hurt to temper my urges. *It's not right to want someone so much. He's a god, and I am not. How can it go any way but badly between us?* "Don't do anything to hurt my apples."

"I wouldn't dream of it." He turned and walked back to his rock pile and crouched among the stones. "They've kept me going. They've attracted small game, squirrels and birds. This place is coming back to life." He turned to look up at me. "I don't know how you did it, but it's a miracle."

"It has to be a miracle. I don't know quite how it happened either." I told him about how the first tree had come back to life under my touch and how I'd planted the seeds from the first apple harvest.

Thorin smirked and shook his head. "I never thought I would see the day."

"You think it means something?"

"I don't know what it means, but I'm thankful for the little bit of life you've brought with you."

"Is it really Asgard?"

Thorin selected a rock and rose from his crouch. He hauled it to the newly erected section of Idun's house and heaved the stone into place. "It's really Asgard. It exists on a plane that is contrary to human existence."

"It's like a dream. It's hard to believe any of it might be real. I don't think I'm fully myself when I come here. Part of me is somewhere else."

"The part of you that comes here is the spirit of Sol that gives you your ability with fire." Thorin stopped working again and gave me a solemn look. "So long as you live, you remain tethered to her. She is you, and you are her. That which defines you as Sol is not tangible. Your spirit can exist in Asgard, but not your humanity."

I motioned toward the burnt-out skyline behind us. "Do you think it could be rebuilt?"

"I would have said no before, but I'm beginning to wonder."

"I could stay and help you," I said. "I like it here."

"When you are separated like this, you are putting yourself in danger. If Helen found you in the earthly realm right now, you would be easy prey. This is only a half life for you. You must go back."

"And leave you here, alone?"

"I've been alone for centuries, Sunshine."

I crossed the yard and stopped at a spot that kept the rock pile between us. "What happened to you?"

Thorin, moving like a snake, slithered around the meager barricade of stones and towered over me, his eyes blackened by the ferocity of his imperative. "Forget about me. Baldur will take you to his home and protect you. Forget about going after Helen. Forget about Skoll. Keep yourself alive. Forgive me for the comic-book dialogue, but the fate of your world rests on your life, and you cannot jeopardize that on my behalf. Not for me, not for Val, not for Skyla, the Valkyries, your parents, or your brother. If Helen wins, if Skoll takes you, then all of that is gone. My life doesn't even begin to weigh on that scale."

Thorin's hand shot out and latched onto my upper arm, squeezing. "Tell me you understand."

"I understand." I returned his bold gaze and didn't shrug off his grip, although my arm throbbed in protest.

"Tell me you'll do as I say."

"You want me to forget about you?"

Thorin snarled. "Yes."

I spread my lips into a thin, defiant smile. "I've never done a damn thing you told me to do before, Thorin, and I don't plan to start doing it now."

I awoke with a gasp. The sudden shift from Idun's garden to the real world upset my sense of balance, and the room swirled around me. The howl of Thorin's outrage echoed in my ears, but the man himself remained in Asgard, trapped. The cabin breathed as a squall of wind passed by. I inhaled several deep breaths and sent them out in one therapeutic whoosh. When my heartbeat settled into a normal rhythm again, I eased against the headboard and let my mind drift back, replaying my encounter with Thorin.

Thorin's argument presented solid reasoning. His life for the fate of the world? Logically, I would have said no, he wasn't worth that much. Something inside me wanted to disagree. I shifted in the big, empty bed and sat up, intending to go to the kitchen for a drink of water. I considered finding something mind-numbing to watch on TV and shutting out my thoughts for a bit. Going back to sleep was a hopeless goal.

As I reached across the bed to snap on the lamp, I noticed something on the pillow beside me, something heavy enough to sink into its downy filling. When my fingers curled around the item, I recognized the shape, but it radiated none of its usual warmth. All my aches and pains drained away as panic sent me racing from the bed, calling for Skyla.

Skyla threw open her bedroom door and rushed to meet me in the living room. Whatever she saw on my face sent the blood draining from her own. "What is it?" she demanded. "Helen? Skoll?"

"No." I presented my discovery. Skyla looked down at my open hand and gasped.

By then Baldur had joined us. He saw my prize and swore. "Mjölnir? Is Magni back?"

"No. I found it lying on the pillow next to me."

"What does it mean?" Skyla asked.

Baldur shook his head. "Nothing good. Mjölnir would never leave Magni unless it was taken from him unwittingly or if he lost the will to possess it."

"Lost his will?" Skyla asked. "Like..." She swallowed and started again. "Like, if he died?"

"It only means he's lost the force of will required to possess Mjölnir. Something terrible has happened, but I cannot presume to know what."

"He's not dead," I said. I told Baldur and Skyla about Asgard and what Thorin had said in Idun's garden about not being able to leave. "You can go there and get him, Baldur. You can make him leave."

Baldur shook his head. "I'm afraid not. Not without knowing where Magni's corporeal body is. His godhood cannot exist in this plane without his body."

"Are you saying Asgard is, like, an afterlife or something? You have to be a spirit to go there?"

"Not an afterlife. Just an alternate plane of existence with different physical laws."

"We have to go back to the glacier," I said. "When I lose things, I always look in the last place I saw them."

"He's not a set of keys. You're in no condition to go traipsing around Mount Rainier. You nearly froze to death, Solina."

"If Thorin hadn't come for me, I probably would have. He came for you when you needed him, too, Baldur. You're going to abandon him when he needs the favor returned?"

Baldur's face crumpled. "No, but I've got Nina to think about, and keeping you safe is above everything else."

I squawked and pounded a fist on my thigh. "Why can't you just blip over there and take a look?"

Baldur sucked in a deep breath and blew it out in a rush. "Yes. I can do that much, at least."

"Skyla," I asked, "are you still planning to go back to the Aerie?"

Skyla shrugged. "Well, I was—"

"Good. Just promise me you'll make time to look for Val."

"Solina, you know how I—"

"I don't want to hear it," I said. "We're not going to abandon people every time a little bit of trouble comes along. If you find Val, tell him everything he's missed." I turned and pointed at Baldur. "You get your ass back up that mountain and find out what happened to Thorin and Grim."

Baldur shook his head and gave me a defeated smile. "Are you sure you're not fully Aesir? You command like a full-blooded goddess."

I braced my hands on my hips and managed to peer down my nose at him despite his height advantage. "I'm a fast learner."

CHAPTER TWENTY-EIGHT

FTER SKYLA LEFT FOR THE Aerie, Baldur made me demonstrate the extent of my recuperation before he agreed to leave me alone with Nina as my only companion. I managed to create a palm-sized fireball but had to stop when dizziness overwhelmed me.

"This goes against my better judgment," Baldur said.

"Your better judgment sucks," I said.

Baldur winced, and his face reddened. "You have a fiery tongue, girl. My advice is to use honey rather than acid when you're asking for favors."

I bit off a retort, realizing he had a point and I had no right to disrespect him, especially after he had helped rescue me and set up shelter for the women who had found themselves suddenly under his protection. Besides, he had readily agreed to carry out my request.

"You are completely right. That was harsh, and I'm sorry." I pecked a quick kiss on his cheek. My gesture flustered him, flushing his fair completion. "Thank you for checking on him."

Baldur's gaze flicked to Nina's closed door. She had stayed hidden in her room all morning despite all the noise and excitement. "I'll be back as soon as possible. If something happens and I don't come back, take Nina and leave. Stay on the move until you can meet up again with your Valkyrie friend. She is fierce and brave. I think she is your best bet. Maybe she will find Val."

"I hope so. Losing both of them would be a hit I'm not sure I could take."

"We are a tough breed. Don't discount him, and don't discount Magni."

Baldur moved, about to turn and leave, but a sudden memory struck me, and I reached out to stop him. "Keep your eyes open, Baldur. It

239

could have been a hallucination, but it's better to be safe than sorry, no?" And I told him about seeing Rolf Lockhart in my last moments of consciousness after my fight with Grim and Tori.

"Maybe you were having another vision."

I nodded. "Maybe, but I wouldn't take it for granted. We don't know who he is or what he's capable of. Just… be careful."

Baldur squeezed my shoulder. "It was good that you told me what you saw. Even if it was a premonition, we can't know when it might come true. I will be watchful."

Baldur left after that. I went to the living room and turned on the TV. It did nothing to distract me, so I paced the living room. Eventually, my nervous energy sent me out to the front porch to check for signs of Baldur's return.

The rental cabin sat at the base of Mount Rainier, just outside the national-park boundaries. Tall aspen and pine trees surrounded the house, and the sharp bite of winter flavored the air. Under better conditions, I would have enjoyed the refuge of such a magnificent setting. I huddled deeper into the blanket I'd taken from my closet and lost myself in thought. Maybe that's why I failed to notice Nina had joined me until she spoke.

"It's cold out here. How can you stand it?"

I flinched and twisted around to find her peering up at the blue sky, peeking through the breaks in the tree tops. "I've got an extra layer on," I said. "Maybe you should grab a coat or something."

"I don't have a coat. Baldur hasn't stopped in one place long enough to get me a decent set of clothes."

"He's juggling a lot of things. I don't think it will be like this much longer."

"No, it won't. The wolf will eat you soon."

I recoiled, hoping I had misunderstood. "What did you say?"

Nina shrugged and strolled to the railing at the front of the porch. "The wolf will eat you. I'm sure of it."

"What a horrible thing to say."

Nina turned around and leaned against a post. She crossed her arms over her chest, hugging herself for warmth. "Doesn't make it a lie."

"What do you know about it, anyway?"

"Only what Helen told me."

My eyebrows arched. Aghast, I said, "You and Helen are buddies?"

"Of course not. You can't really call your foster mom a buddy, you know?"

I wheezed. *Bombshell much?* "Helen's your *foster mom?*"

"She never adopted me, but she raised me after my mother went missing on the streets when I was a baby. Never knew my dad."

A cold sweat broke out at the nape of my neck, and my stomach burbled unhappily. "Does Baldur know this?"

"He hasn't asked," Nina said. She widened her dark eyes into a kooky stare and tapped her temple. "Not too bright, that one."

"You're on good terms with Helen, still?"

Nina shrugged. "Haven't talked to her in a while. I left her when I turned eighteen, went out on my own. She's a little... *intense*, let's say. We bashed heads a lot."

"But you keep in touch?"

"Up until the wreck, yeah, we talked every couple of weeks."

"And since the wreck?"

"I've been debating whether I should contact her. If I gave you to Helen, she might welcome me with open arms, but this Baldur thing might work out pretty good for me, too."

"You two are soul mates. He's loved you for eternity."

Nina rasped a dry laugh. "That's what he keeps telling me—reincarnation or some such nonsense. Past lives." She stuck her tongue between her lips and blew a raspberry. "That's what I think about that."

I scrunched my nose at her. "I see Helen's had a lot of influence on you."

"Maybe." Nina shoved herself off the porch rail and strolled back to the front door. "It pleases me to keep your secret, Solina. I can't be sure Helen's plans include a place for me. I know she used me to get to Baldur, and that makes me more than a little resentful. But you can be sure if the scales tip in her favor, I'll sell you out in a hot minute."

"Why would you tell me this? Most predators don't give their prey a heads-up."

An innocent, childlike look came over her face. "I honestly don't know why I would tell you except I think I feel sorry for you. I think you deserve fair warning."

This chick is one tinfoil hat away from being the mayor of Crazy Town. "Do you know how insane you sound?"

"Yes, I do. Crazy has been my game for a long time. I totally hate myself for it, too." Nina stepped closer and pulled up her sweater sleeve, revealing a thick, puckered scar snaking from her wrist to the inside of her elbow. "Tried to cure myself when I was sixteen. Didn't take, though. Helen found me soaking in a bathtub full of red water and got me to the hospital in time."

I wiped my hands over face, trying to clean away the vision stirred up by Nina's words. She told her story as if she had suffered a case of appendicitis instead of an attempted suicide. Horror and pity waged war within me. Nina didn't behave as though she wanted my sympathy, though.

"You know I'll have to tell Baldur," I said.

Nina's jaw clenched. Her eyes glittered like hard black stones. "Of course you will. I hope you tell him and cut his heart open with it." She turned on her heel and went back inside after that—thank God—and left me to digest her disturbing revelations on my own.

She was right that sharing the information with Baldur would hurt him, and when it came to Nina, he had already suffered too much. Still, he had to know. The decision of what to do with her after that would be his. For my part, I planned a quick separation as soon as Baldur brought news of Thorin down from the mountain.

On the run again—it barely bothered me anymore.

The clear day eventually gave over to clouds and stiff winds. I ceded my outdoor vigil and went inside. Nina had secluded herself in her room—*good riddance*—and I went into my bedroom and tried to relax. I must have dozed off because I awoke to darkness, the front door banging open, feet stomping, and Baldur calling my name.

I rolled out of bed and scurried into the living room, where Baldur stood, his face grim, worry etching lines around his eyes and mouth. His shoulders bowed under the burden of keeping a swaying and nearly unconscious God of Thunder upright. I gasped as he stepped forward and deposited Thorin onto the sofa in front of the fireplace.

Drawn and haggard, with a rough beard and circles of trauma and pain ringing his eyes, Thorin had obviously survived a horrible ordeal. But he was there and alive, and nothing mattered more than that. A wild and uncharacteristic frenzy haunted Thorin's eyes. My gut clenched, and I knotted my fingers together and waited for Thorin to look my way and recognize me.

"Thorin?" I asked. "Are you okay?" Though he obviously wasn't, I didn't know what else to say.

Thorin looked at me because I spoke to him, but no light of recognition brightened his face. His brow creased, and in a dry and raspy voice, he mumbled something vaguely Germanic sounding before falling silent again.

My insides caved in, and my heart sank to my feet. I looked at Baldur, pleading for reassurance. "Can you help him?"

Baldur shrugged. "He was half buried in a crevasse when I found him. Time and rest are the best medicine. He'll heal quickly, I promise." Baldur knelt before Thorin and examined his compatriot. "Mild hypothermia. A strained ACL in his knee, but not torn. A few bruised ribs and a wicked concussion. He should be mostly fine in a day or so. Sore and tender in spots for a while, but back to his old self in no time. Surprisingly good condition, considering."

Throughout Baldur's inspection, Thorin remained silent. He stared at the ceiling, his eyes dull and listless.

"Aleksander?" said Baldur. Thorin did not respond. "Magni?"

At that, Thorin looked up, and Baldur spoke to him in the old language. Thorin blinked a few times and stuttered an answer.

"What did he say?" I asked.

"He remembers me, but it wasn't in this place. He doesn't know where he is. I get the impression he doesn't know *when* he is, either."

Baldur and Thorin conversed again in their ancient tongue. Finally, Thorin nodded and closed his eyes. I almost sobbed but shoved my fist against my lips and turned back to Baldur. The sight of Thorin, defeated and confused, hurt my heart.

"I told him to rest," Baldur said. "He said he felt there was something he was supposed to be doing, guarding, watching out for. I told him he had been a valiant soldier, but it was time to rest and let us take over for a while."

Baldur rose to his full height and ran his hands through his hair so the cinnamon strands spiked like a porcupine. "We need to think about going to New Breidablik. It's a fortress and the safest place to keep you. Helen would hesitate to attack us there."

"I'm not safe anywhere."

"That's somewhat true, but my home is your best bet."

I sighed and rubbed my eyes. "How much do you really know about Nina?"

"What do you mean?"

I told Baldur everything, trying my best to repeat, verbatim, my strange conversation with Nina. I kept my eyes covered, too much of a coward to face him as I talked. I didn't want to see his pain. His heavy steps crossed the room, and the upholstered chair in the corner creaked as it accepted his weight. I finally braved a look and found him slumped over, holding his head in his hands.

"I knew some of it," Baldur said. "I had a private investigator look into her background as soon as I found her."

"She's Helen's foster daughter, and you thought it was a good idea to put us in the same house together?"

Ever since Rolf had showed up in San Diego, I had been waiting for someone to stab me in the back—if not him, then the Valkyries or Grim—and suddenly, Nina was there, who had all but told me she'd sell me out if it suited her. I'd be damned if I would sit around waiting for her to do just that.

Baldur jerked his head up from his hands and glared at me. "It's not like I had time to figure out an alternative plan. I can't leave her alone. I've been careful, Solina. I've watched her incessantly. She hates me for it, too."

"Does Thorin know about her?" I glanced at the subject of my query, who stared, empty eyed and vacant, at the fireplace. "I mean before, when you were all in the hospital."

"I doubt it."

I doubted it, too. Thorin's devotion to Baldur ran deep, but cracks had started to show. The surprise about Nina's provenance might prove the breaking point.

"She's a pitiful thing, Baldur. She needs lots of care and attention. I think if anyone could help her, it would be you. But you can't protect me and give her the level of attention she requires at the same time."

Baldur shrank back. "You can't ask me to abandon her."

Utterly frustrated by Baldur's opacity, I threw up my hands and screeched in frustration. "I don't want you to abandon her. I want you to take her back to your home and leave me here with Thorin."

"No, Solina, I can't—"

I waved my hand and cut him off. "You can't have it both ways." I lowered my voice, which had risen to a shout. "And I won't spend another night under the same roof as her. At this point, she needs you a lot more than I do."

Baldur's nostrils flared, and his neck and ears flushed. He sat rigid in the chair and fumed a few more minutes before he stood up and pointed a finger at me. "Fine. You said before that I had used bad judgment. I've even admitted it myself. Maybe it's time I defer to your *wisdom*." He sneered at the last word.

Baldur's pity party burst my self-righteous bubble. Something about seeing the Allfather, leader of an ancient race of superbeings, reduced to a temper tantrum brought me plenty of regret and no satisfaction.

"I don't want it to be like this," I said. "No bitterness between us. You helped Thorin save my life, and I am indebted. But you can't be effective torn in two like this. You said Helen gave Nina back to you because she wanted to see you distracted. If that's her plan, it's working. Don't let Helen win. Help Nina heal. Love her—I don't think she's had that."

"But you'll be on your own with him." Baldur motioned to Thorin. "I'm not sure he can be much help to you."

"It's my turn to be a help to him. I owe him this."

Baldur's chin dropped to his chest, and I knew I had won my argument. "Let me leave you with some cash, at least. You'll need supplies."

"Thank you, Allfather." I crossed the room and pulled Baldur into a hug. "We wouldn't have made it without you."

CHAPTER TWENTY-NINE

FRIGID GUSTS BATTERED THE OLD Jeep Baldur had found for me. It rocked like a ship in a sea squall. Dense clouds had gathered over Mount Rainier, and snow fell in ungainly clumps. I had a moment to appreciate the serenity before the storm took a deep breath and exhaled. Lacy flakes turned into frozen darts, whipped into whiteout frenzy by fierce winds. Cold air seeped between the seams in the Jeep's canvas top. I turned up the heater and clutched the steering wheel until my knuckle joints creaked.

By the time I returned to the drive leading to the rental cabin, the snow had covered the path until it appeared as nothing more than a faint indention in an otherwise indistinct landscape. The late-afternoon sun had started to set, casting everything in gloomy shadows. I braved the pathway in four-wheel drive, bumping and jostling until I dead-ended in front of the small log house roofed in tin sheeting. I imagined smoke curling from the stone chimney and decided to start a fire after carrying in the groceries and supplies I had bought in town, including a couple of pairs of jeans, T-shirts—for me and for Thorin—and necessities like toothbrushes and shampoo.

After stowing everything away, I went into the living room and knelt before the fireplace to clean away the old ashes, a chore to divert me from Thorin's unsettling presence. Before he left, Baldur had explained the situation to Thorin in their ancient language. Thorin assured Baldur he understood, and he promised to stay with me.

As I shoveled ashes into a metal bucket designated for that purpose, I threw a glance over my shoulder. Thorin still sat on the sofa, unmoving and staring at the floor. I blew out a breath, and ashes swirled into the air. I turned to the box of kindling beside the fireplace and stacked them into place.

"You saved my life," I said, "and I can't even properly thank you."

"What?" Thorin asked.

I flinched and turned to face him. "Wait. You understood that?"

His brow furrowed. "I'm a fast healer. I think."

"Does that mean you recognize me?"

Thorin's dark gaze slipped over me, but it remained cold and distant. "No. Not yet."

My heart sank. "At least I won't have to resort to sign language to communicate with you."

I rolled onto my feet and went to the door. A hoard of logs was stacked in a shelter on the side of the porch, and my indoor supply needed restocking. Thorin rose and followed me out. He held his arms outstretched before him. I translated his meaning and stacked him with firewood up to his nose.

After dumping his bundle into a crate near the fireplace, Thorin crouched at my side and helped arrange the cold logs on the grating. "Have a light?" he asked.

I pantomimed thumbing the striker on a pretend Bic lighter, and a small flame sprouted at my fingertip. The tinder caught and roared to life. I shivered, shaking away the lingering cold in my blood, and went to the kitchen to retrieve a bottle of wine and a corkscrew.

Thorin moved away from the fireplace and slumped in the corner of the couch, eyes closed, arms loose at his sides.

The cork slipped out with a satisfying *thock,* and I poured a glass for me and waved the bottle toward Thorin. "Want some?"

One eyelid peeled open, followed slowly by another. He struggled to focus on me.

"Wine?"

"Coffee?" he asked.

"Sure." I turned to the coffee machine and babbled as I measured grounds and filled the carafe. "How about food? I know you don't usually eat, but you look a little malnourished. I have soup, or I can make you a sandwich, or if you rather—"

"It's fine," Thorin said. "Coffee is fine."

I started a pot brewing and, when it finished, brought a tray of coffee, wine, and a plate of cut fruit and cheese for a picnic on the living-room floor. Crossing my legs first, I lowered to the rug, putting the fire to my back and Thorin at my front. He worked to maintain lucidity, and the strain showed around his eyes. He deserved to be left alone, but I was selfish. I needed to see him alive and physically present, not in Asgard but in my world. I needed to hear his voice and relish the relief of it.

"Do you remember who I am?" I asked.

"A daughter of Sol, evidently." Thorin shook his head. "But no. Nothing recent. Not yet."

"Do you remember why you were up on that mountain?"

"Baldur told me it was because I was rescuing you from my brother."

Guilt weighted my heart, and it thudded heavily. If I hadn't gone looking for that stupid sword... If I hadn't taken Val along with me... If I hadn't... If I hadn't...

"You remember Grim?"

"I don't remember fighting him recently, but we've rarely agreed. It doesn't surprise me."

"He wanted Mjölnir."

"That also doesn't surprise me. Baldur also told me Grim wanted to kill you."

"Did he tell you why?"

"Helen Locke is trying to reinvent Ragnarok. Grim thought your death would prevent that."

"And you have no idea what happened to Grim or Surtalogi?"

Thorin's chin dropped to his chest. "Nothing."

I put my hand on his knee. He raised his eyes to meet mine.

"I'm sorry," I said. "It must be a horrible feeling."

Thorin made no indication either way. He stared back at me, unblinking. I reached behind my neck and unfastened Mjölnir's chain. Thorin's eyes lit the moment I brought the weapon free from the collar of my sweater. "I've been keeping it for you."

"You?" he asked, markedly curious. "How did you come to have it?"

"You gave me the lanyard a while back, said you could use it to track

248

me." I smiled at the memory of him finding me in the cave, his beauty, his warmth. "It's how you found me, how you saved me from Grim."

"But you have the hammer, too."

"It showed up a few nights ago. I woke up to find it on the pillow beside me. Baldur said it returned to its lanyard when you lost your ability to command it."

I held the necklace out to Thorin. He set his coffee mug on an end table, took the chain from me, and cupped the gold Mjölnir charm in his palm. He flicked his wrist, a gesture older than his memory loss, and brought the full-sized hammer to rest on his knee. "You must be someone special to me."

Heat flooded my cheeks.

Thorin saw my reaction, and a smile spread across his face. How stunning, how dazzling was his joy. "I guessed right?"

I shook my head and turned away to bury my attention in the plate of food. "Not special. Important, maybe. You were dedicated to preventing my death. You gave me Mjölnir to hold for you after I recovered it from Helen. You said I was the only one you could trust with it, and it might be good for others to think it was still lost."

Thorin's brow creased as he thought about my words. "But my brother knew I had it?"

"You had to use it once, to protect us, and he said he could feel its power. I don't understand how that works."

"The hammer speaks to Thor's blood kin. We all hear its voice. But why did I use it if I wanted to keep it a secret?"

"You fought Skoll with it."

"I did?"

I told Thorin what had happened in the desert. He listened, enraptured, but nothing I said ignited his own memory of the event. His brow creased again. "If I was protecting you, how did my brother get you?"

"Long story. You sure you're up for it? You probably need to rest."

Thorin readjusted his position on the couch, sitting up straighter and hardening his face. "Tell me everything. From the beginning."

I poured another glass of wine and took a huge gulp. Then I turned to Thorin and said, "Once upon a time, there was a girl named Solina

Mundy. She had had a twin brother named Chapman Mundy. He used to work for you."

I talked late into the evening, stalled by a million interruptions—Thorin asking questions or requesting more details. I switched from wine to water once the alcohol and the warmth of the fire softened my focus. At some point, I pillowed my head on my hands and leaned against the sofa cushion next to Thorin's leg. At some point, his hand found its way to my hair, his fingers combing through the loose strands—so intimate and so unlike him. I said nothing, for fear he might take his hand away.

"I can hardly believe it," Thorin said after I finished recounting my story. "It all sounds too fantastic."

I didn't move an inch, not daring to break our connection. "You're a god. Everything about your existence is fantastic."

"We shouldn't stay here much longer," he said in non sequitur. "The location is compromised. Too many people know where to find you."

I waved toward the door. "Where should I go?"

"Where do I live, now?"

I raised my head up at that, and Thorin's hand slipped away. "You don't remember that either?"

Thorin's eyes rolled up to the ceiling as he struggled with his memory. "I remember a place on a mountaintop. Lots of snow. I'm not sure how old the memory is. Does it sound familiar to you?"

"I was told such things were sacred to your kind, and you don't give their locations away easily. I've never been to your home."

"Never?"

"For all we've been through together, we barely know each other. Well, I barely know *you*, anyway. Not the personal stuff. But I trust you. You've risked your life for me. You've killed my enemies."

"That's a lot." Thorin slid his fingertips under my chin and urged me to look up at him. "Trust is what's most important."

"I have trusted you with my life almost from the first day I met you, but I've never trusted you with much more than that."

"Oh?" His brows arched in question. "Nothing in your story suggested I've been cavalier with your feelings."

"You've never had a chance to."

Thorin chuckled at my petulance. "Despite everything you've told me, everything you've been through, you chose to stay here, alone, with me. That tells me all I need to know."

Thorin let me talk him into taking one of the bedrooms and moving from the confines of the sofa. He tested his weight on the mattress, and the springs groaned in protest.

"Maybe we should go to your store first." I leaned against the doorjamb. "Going somewhere familiar might jog your memories."

Thorin leaned over and unlaced his boots. "I have a store?"

I huffed. "What *do* you remember?"

Thorin kicked off one boot and went to work on the other. "When Baldur first found me up on the mountain, I couldn't even remember my name, but after he started talking, a lot of old memories came back." He kicked off the second boot, stood, and peeled off layers, starting with a bulky wool sweater.

"I regret that I don't remember your brother," he said, the words muffled by his thermal shirt as he pulled it over his head. "I especially regret not remembering you. But our kind heal quickly. In the morning, I would be surprised if I haven't mostly recovered."

Thorin shed layers down to a thin undershirt that hugged every line, every curve, plane and valley. That too came off, leaving him bare chested and me dry throated. It went against the laws of everything good and holy for a man to look that fine. I turned away.

"This place has some sort of bathing accommodations, correct?"

"Y-yup, um, down the hall." I pointed dumbly, still looking anywhere but at him. "There's, uh, there's a-an extra towel or two on the shelf in the bathroom. You can use my soap and stuff."

The floor creaked as Thorin stepped closer, pausing in the doorway beside me. His scent filled the space between us. I did not inhale and savor it. I swear I didn't.

"Thank you," he said, his words low and gruff.

I swallowed. "No problem. Least I could do since you saved my life and all."

Thorin didn't move or say anything. I sensed he wanted me to look at him, to see him rooted in place so close to my side... Too close, too warm. I swallowed again, steeled my nerves, and pried my eyes from the ceiling. Once he had my full attention, Thorin let a charming, devilish smile curl at the corner of his lips. "Good night, Miss Mundy."

"You call me Sunshine." The words came out raspy.

"Do I?"

I nodded.

Thorin smoothed a loose hair from my cheek and tucked it behind my ear. Every function in my body stuttered to a halt. "Well, good night then, *Sunshine*."

Thorin slid past me, and his touch warmed me from head to toe. It lit fires in my cheeks, and champagne bubbles fizzed in my veins. He padded down the hallway into the bathroom, and the moment the door shut behind him, I broke from my daze and fled down the hallway back to the safety of my room.

What's going on with him? I wondered as I slid under the quilts on my bed. *A little amnesia and all his personal constraints disappear?*

I turned off the lamp on my bedside table and stared up into the darkness. *No problem. I have more than enough inhibitions to cover us both.*

CHAPTER THIRTY

WHETHER I MEANT IT TO or not, my hearing tuned in to every creak and groan of the house, every noise Thorin made—the abrupt cessation of running water, the rattle of shower curtain rings sliding across the metal rod, something clattering in the sink. A moment later, the bathroom door creaked open, and heavy footsteps crept down the hallway. His bed squeaked as it accepted his weight. I imagined I could hear his breathing, but it was only the wind.

I lay awake long into the night, holding my breath, listening, picturing Thorin with his hands tucked behind his head as he stared up at the ceiling, trying to remember. When I had roomed with Val, he acted sleepy in the mornings, but he had also wanted to hide his godhood. Maybe, like eating, sleep was optional.

Before that day, I had never caught Thorin sleeping, or even tired for that matter, but the recent trauma must have tested even *his* stamina.

I had never allowed myself to think too long or too hard about my feelings for Thorin. Recent revelations proved my emotions had grown beyond superficial attraction. But even before my exposure to the dangerous world of immortal gods, I had trouble with relationships, particularly the romantically inclined ones.

Once, when Mani and I had gotten into some petty fight, he told me everyone called me an ice princess—ironic, considering my heritage. The reputation was justified when I looked back on it. I never felt superior to anyone as gossip suggested. Mostly, I was afraid—afraid of rejection, afraid of being hurt, afraid of losing. Until Mani died, my feelings had been unfounded. I never really knew loss or heartbreak, nothing to make me dread forming attachments.

Perhaps I'd been composed with the memories of a life-before.

Maybe they were ingrained in my DNA, and maybe those memories struggled to dictate my life. Over the centuries, Sol must have suffered a great number of hurts and lost many loves. Did her fears whisper in my atoms?

I knew one thing for certain: losing Mani was the single most horrible experience of my life. If I cared for Thorin a fraction of how much I had cared for my brother—and I suspected the amount was much more than a fraction—then letting Thorin get past my defenses was a huge risk. Failure was too great a threat, and success posed its own separate hazard.

Any relationship I built with Thorin had a limited shelf life from the start. One way or another I would die—by sickness, old age, or wolf. Thorin was immortal, I was not, and that created a formula for certain disaster.

I would do well to remember that.

I slid into sleep at some point and dreamed of Asgard for the first time since having left Thorin in Idun's garden. All subsequent attempts to initiate interdimensional travel or arouse precognitive visions had resulted in nothing more than a headache. My insight asserted its own will and ignored my demands for obedience.

I strolled through my orchard, grabbing at apples but never plucking them free. Like a ghost's, my fingers passed through the fruit, encountering nothing solid. I strolled up and down the rows, not quite lost but unable to find my way out.

I maintained my calm at first, but time passes in a peculiar way in dreams, and I realized I had wandered the orchard for hours without reaching Idun's house or the wrecked city of Asgard. A cold drop of panic trickled down my spine.

Up and down the rows, ducking through trees and looking for something familiar, I ran faster and faster until I tripped and sprawled face-first on the lush green grass. I rolled over and examined the scene, expecting to find a root to blame for my fall. Instead, I had stumbled over a scroll. To discover such a thing in the middle of an apple orchard seemed perfectly rational, as strange things often do in dreams. I picked up the scroll and unrolled the parchment.

On its aged and deteriorated surface, I recognized the outline of a genealogical chart, one similar to those I had studied at the Aerie's library when I helped Skyla search for the grimoire. The chart tracked Baldur's lineage and Nina's reincarnations and the births of their offspring. If the Valkyries possessed a match to that record in the physical world, then they had stored it somewhere other than the library because I had looked through every scroll in the Aerie's collection without ever finding one like that.

I traced my finger along notations until I arrived at one marking the birth of the most current children and grandchildren of Baldur and Nanna, aka Nina. Three daughters had been born over two decades. The first, Thea, died as an infant. The second, Embla, was still living. And a third, Kara, died after giving birth to two children: one boy, named Paul, and one girl, named…

Skyla Frigga Rodriguez.

———◆———

Thorin's voice ripped me from my dream. Frantic and hoarse, he roared in the language Baldur had used with him—Asgardian, perhaps. A cold sweat broke over me, and my heart climbed into my throat, fluttering like a bird trapped in a chimney. Someone had found us.

I eased out of bed, tiptoed through the darkness, and pressed my ear against my door. Something heavy crashed to the floor as Thorin railed against his attacker. But why go for Thorin instead of me? I eased my door open and peered into the dim living room, where the dying fire provided the only light. After finding nothing alarming there, I ventured out, stepping like a cat, listening hard enough to make my ears hurt.

Thorin went silent. I hurried forward, balancing on the balls of my feet, hoping to sneak to his room in silence. Thorin roared again, and something else crashed. *So much for stealth.* I dashed the last few feet and pounced into his doorway with my fire crackling, ready to burn, devastate, and consume whichever of my enemies dared breach the sanctity of my little cabin.

Instead, I found Thorin, feral, raging, and naked except for his iron bracelets and torc. I would have felt embarrassed for him if I thought it bothered him… or if he hadn't looked so completely magnificent. He appeared to have fixated his attention on fighting a ghost or maybe a whole legion of them, the way he swung his weapon. He had reduced his nightstand to kindling, and an old upholstered chair lay on its side, beaten to within an inch of its life.

"Thorin." I stepped farther into his room.

Thorin spun on me, Mjölnir raised high. He said something in his ancient tongue. I didn't understand it, but the way he forced his words through gritted teeth made me step back and reconsider.

"Thorin?" I said, speaking in a low and soothing tone. "You're dreaming, having a nightmare. I need you to wake up, okay?"

I reached behind me, feeling for the light switch. I kept talking, hoping to soothe him and ease his agitation. "You're with me now, and you're safe. You've fought bravely, but it's time to give it a rest."

Thorin stepped closer, baring his teeth. The light from my fire reflected in his eyes, and shadows daubed his face so he looked like a hellish fiend. I slid one foot back, preparing to retreat if he decided to attack, but it came up against the wall. I had run out of room.

"It's time to let that demon go," I said. "We've got plenty more to chase after, and I need you to be cool about it, okay?"

Thorin stepped closer yet, still clutching Mjölnir and panting, ribs heaving like bellows. His breath coursed over me, hot and humid.

"Thorin, please, you don't want to hurt me."

Apparently, he disagreed. His hand flashed to my throat and circled it, squeezing.

"Thorin!" I gasped and choked. With a ball of fire gathered around my fingers, I swung and slapped him across his cheek. "Wake up!"

Thorin fell away, blinking and shaking his head as if aggravated by a bothersome gnat. I found the switch and flipped on the overhead lights. He blinked again and rubbed a hand over his eyes. Still pressed against the wall, I waited for an indication that he had gathered his wits—what little of them remained, anyway.

Thorin looked around the room, taking in the damage, and turned his gaze back on me. "Solina?"

My lungs froze, and my muscles tensed. I couldn't have blinked if my life depended on it.

"What happened?" he asked, looking around the devastated room. "What...?"

Something inside me thawed, and my systems came back online. "Thorin?"

He looked back up at me, his eyebrows raised. His gaze focused on me in a way it hadn't before, sharp and full of familiarity. "Sunshine?"

Relief coursed through me, as swift and powerful as a tidal wave. "You remember?"

Thorin blinked again. "Why wouldn't I?" He glanced down and noted his nudity. His head shot up, and his eyes locked on mine. "What's going on, Solina?"

I breathed a huge and gusty sigh and wiped away my pending tears before Thorin noticed. *He'd hate to think I was crying over him.* I cleared my throat and put on a neutral face. "Bad dream, I guess."

Thorin noticed Mjölnir still clutched in his fist. He flipped his wrist and turned it back into the golden pendant. "I didn't hurt you, did I?"

I shook my head. "Not so much. I can dish out almost as well as I can take."

Thorin stepped closer, and I tensed. He noticed, and his brows drew together. His gaze dropped to my neck. He reached out and brushed his fingertips over the bruise forming beneath my jaw. "I did this?"

I mimicked his gesture and touched my fingers to his cheek, displaying an angry red welt in the shape of my hand. "And I did this."

Thorin caught my hand on his face and held it there. His eyes, dark and glittering, bore into mine. "I worried about being able to protect you, but I didn't think it would be from myself."

I swallowed, but my voice still came out gruff. "I've been ravaged by a wolf, converted to pure energy and back, and I've been nearly frozen to death. This is nothing."

"Still, I am sorry."

I stiffened my spine and moved away from him. "C'mon, put on some pants, and let's go to the kitchen. I'll make us some tea. It'll calm our nerves."

Without any hint of self-consciousness, Thorin crouched and dug his pants out from somewhere beneath the bed. Maybe he didn't care, but I turned away and gave him a moment of privacy. I started down the hall, and he fell into place behind me, still zipping zippers and fastening buttons.

In the kitchen, Thorin leaned against the counter and watched me rifle through the cabinets, looking for my box of chamomile. "Why are you here? Why aren't you with Baldur?"

I found the tea and set about filling a kettle with water. "Someone had to wait for you. I've lost too many people already. I don't want to lose any more. Besides, Baldur is only focused on Nina. They're both a little..." I swirled my finger around my temple to insinuate their current mental state. "What else should I have done?"

"You should have run. Kept moving. Staying in one place too long is dangerous. You shouldn't risk yourself."

"You've told me that before."

"I see you didn't take my advice."

"I told you that I don't automatically do everything you tell me."

Thorin's blond brows arched high. "Yes, I remember."

I set the full kettle on the stove, lit the burner, and motioned to the kitchen table. Thorin slid out a chair for me and settled into the one beside it. I sank into the seat and let out a heavy breath.

"So tell me what has happened since I saw you last," Thorin said.

"Since you gave me to Baldur in the cave and stayed behind to fight Grim?"

"I remember, up to the point where Baldur took you away. From then until you woke me just a moment ago, everything is a blur."

And so, for the second time that night, I told Thorin everything he had missed.

CHAPTER THIRTY-ONE

I DON'T KNOW WHEN I FELL asleep again, but I woke on the sofa tangled in an old crocheted afghan. Light from a cloudless morning sky illuminated the room. I sat up and rubbed sleep crust from my eyes. The afghan carried Thorin's familiar scent of rain and ozone, but the man himself was missing. I shrugged the blanket around my shoulders like a shawl and shuffled down the hall.

"Thorin?" I called into his room.

He wasn't there, but he had cleaned up the wreckage from the previous night. The evidence suggested he had risen early and not that my enemies had snatched him out from under me while I slept. I shifted my weight and turned on my heel, meaning to return to the front of the house, but a phone rang and stopped me in my place. The sound came from within Thorin's bedroom, muffled, but unmistakably his ring tone. I crossed the room, following the ringing, and crouched beside his bed. Beneath the dust ruffle I found Thorin's cell, lying just beyond my reach among the company of a few dust bunnies. *Must have been kicked under here by accident last night, when he was fighting ghosts or nightmares or whatever that was.*

On my knees already, I slunk onto my belly, extended my arm to full length, and stretched for the phone. *Maybe it's Skyla. Or Val. Whoever it is, he or she's gonna hang up before I get to this thing.* Stretching again, I managed to latch a couple fingertips around an edge on the phone case and dragged it out.

Afraid of losing the caller, I hurried to accept the call and put the phone to my ear. *Please let it be Val.* "Hello?" I said as I slid out from under the bed.

A moment of silence, a cold chuckle, and then, "Hello, Solina. Or should I call you *Sabrina?*"

It wasn't Val at all.

Shivers rolled over my shoulders and dribbled down the length of my spine. "Wh-who is this?" But I already knew.

"I'll give you three guesses."

I swallowed and took a deep breath, trying to overcome my shock. "Rolf."

"In the flesh, so to speak."

"Wha—How did you get Thorin's number?"

"I told you." He chuckled again. "I *know* everything."

As silent and graceful as usual, Thorin appeared in the doorway. He opened his mouth, as if to ask a question unrelated to the current situation, but his dark eyes skimmed over me, kneeling on the floor, phone to my ear, and he swallowed whatever he'd meant to say. Blood had drained from my face the moment Rolf verified his identity, so I probably looked pale and drawn. Thorin's nostrils flared, and he frowned. He stepped fully into the room, his posture wary and alert. "Who are you talking to?"

"Ah, is that the God of Thunder I hear?" Rolf asked. "Perfect. Put me on speaker phone. He needs to hear this."

I looked up at Thorin and met his gaze. His eyes were turning black, reacting to my distress. I stretched forward, passing him the phone, and said, "Put it on speaker."

Thorin scowled but did as I said. He swiped his thumb across the screen and held the phone out between us. "Who is this?"

"Hello, Magni," Rolf said. "I'm afraid you won't really know me. Not now—not as I am after all these years."

"It's Rolf Lockhart," I said when Thorin raised a questioning eyebrow at me. "Or, that's what he said his name was when I met him in San Diego."

"Who were you?" Thorin asked him. "Before?"

"Who I was then is not important. Not now."

"What do you want?"

"It's simple." Rolf's tone was calm, neutral, almost nonchalant. "I have the sword, Surtalogi, and I want you, Magni, Son of Thor, to come and take it from me."

The room spun. I closed my eyes and put a hand to my pounding temples. "I knew I saw you at Grim's house."

Rolf hacked a derisive sound. "You were the only one."

"You were there," Thorin said. "At the cave. During the fight with Grim. I remember."

"Do you remember fighting with Grim, being so single minded that you didn't notice me until I brought that ice cave down on you and took the sword while you were busy scrambling for escape? You nearly succumbed. You're a lucky bastard, aren't you? Always have been. Damned Aesir and their charmed lives."

"Where's my brother?" Thorin asked.

"Oh, he's your brother when you think someone else has done something to him. You were so ready to kill him yourself. What does it matter if I was the one to finish him off?"

Thorin grunted as though someone had punched him in his stomach. "He's dead?"

Although I was inclined to say *Good riddance*, then wasn't the right time.

"I can't show you his severed head or anything, but you were the only one that came out of that ice cave that day."

"So you want me to come. And we fight for the sword."

"Yes. You and only you. No tricks, no cheating. You can have the sword if you can take it from me."

"Easily done." Thorin glared at his phone as if issuing it a challenge.

"Not so fast," Rolf said. "You can't bring Mjölnir or Megingjörð or the Járngreipr, and you must come alone."

Thorin wore Thor's belt, Megingjörð, as a torc around his neck. Supposedly, it doubled his strength. Without the Járngreipr, the gauntlets he wore as retooled cuffs around his wrists, he wouldn't be able to lift his hammer. Thorin arched an eyebrow, obviously intrigued. "Trying to level the playing field? What if I refuse?"

After a dramatic pause, Rolf said, "If you refuse my terms or if you violate my conditions in any way, I'll give the sword to Helen."

"Why?" I asked, finding my voice. "Why are you doing this?"

"For revenge, of course." Quickly, before either of us could form a reply, Rolf spat out the rest. "I'll give you an hour to think it over. Call me at this number when you have your answer."

The call went dead.

I remained on my knees, head bowed, eyes squeezed shut, bottom lip pinned between my teeth, biting until I tasted blood.

"Solina," Thorin said, speaking my name in all seriousness.

My eyes flew open, and I looked up at him. He wore fresh clothes—jeans and a soft flannel shirt I had bought for him when I'd gone to town the day before. Everything seemed to fit, so I had done well, guessing at his sizes. The shower and a few hours of rest had restored his healthy coloring, and he looked a lot more like his old self, but with several days' growth of beard that he rarely sported. He had also tied his hair back in an uncharacteristic knot.

He crouched beside me, still holding his phone. "Are you all right?"

"Yes." I pushed up from the floor. "What revenge is he looking for?"

Thorin shook his head and shrugged.

"And you really have no idea who he was or what he wants with you now?"

"I'm sure I'll find out soon enough."

"That's what I said when he let me go in San Diego. I still don't know why he did that. It's almost as if he wanted me to go running back to you. But why?"

Thorin gritted his teeth and said, "I. Don't. Know."

I patted his shoulder. "It was mostly a rhetorical question, big guy. Don't get hung up on it. Like you said, I'm sure we'll figure it out soon enough. But in the meantime, what are we going to do?"

Thorin's brow furrowed. He rubbed a hand over his jaw and thought for a moment. "Baldur is here. He should know about this. We'll tell him, and then we'll decide."

I followed Thorin into the living room. Baldur was sitting on the sofa, sipping a cup of coffee. He smiled and waggled a couple of fingers at me. Seeing Baldur's face triggered a memory of my dream, of the scroll I had tripped over in the orchard. If I could believe it—*and how can I not?* —he wasn't merely the Allfather sitting there, grinning at me. He was also Skyla's grandfather. I shook away the thought. *Not important right now. Deal with it later.*

I turned away from the men and started toward the coffee pot.

"So," Baldur said, "I see you both survived the night?"

My gaze darted to Thorin, who tried his best to smother a smile.

Survived, indeed. I still had the bruises of Thorin's choke hold on my neck, and Thorin's cheek showed the pale pink imprint of my burn.

"Don't take this the wrong way," I said, "but what are you doing here, Baldur?"

"Checking up on my patient."

"He's doing a lot better, don't you think?" After pouring a cup of coffee, I went to the refrigerator to look for creamer. "Miraculous, almost."

Baldur rubbed his neck and flexed his shoulders as if he felt tension in those muscles. Immortal Norse gods didn't have to eat or sleep, but they apparently suffered stress pains. How did that make sense?

"I was telling Thorin about what I found when I went back to the glacier to look for him," Baldur said. "Whatever happened after I took Solina and Skyla away, it destroyed most of the evidence. It was obviously a big fight. Lots of fallen rocks—the cave is just a depression in the ground, now. Lots of melted ice refrozen into unnatural configurations."

"It was the sword," Thorin said. "There was a cave-in during the fight."

Baldur's auburn eyebrows arched. "Five minutes ago, you couldn't recall anything. Where did the sudden epiphany come from?"

"From Rolf Lockhart." Thorin told Baldur about the rest, about Rolf's demands, and about how neither of us knew Rolf's true identity or what wrong he sought to avenge by fighting Thorin.

"What do you think?" Baldur asked. "Will you do what he wants?"

"I don't think he left us any choice."

"Do you trust him to meet you alone? Fight fairly?"

"Hell no," Thorin said. "Rolf only said I had to come alone and unarmed. He never said anything about the same rules applying to him."

"Let us come with you," I said. "We'll stay far enough away that he never has to know we're there. If we're close by and you need us, Baldur can have us at your side in an instant."

"No." Thorin shook his head. "I can't risk giving Rolf reason to take the sword to Helen. Whatever his vendetta against me, it's not worth Helen getting her hands on Surtalogi."

"So, you'll fight him without Mjölnir?"

Thorin nodded. "If I have to."

"But you still have the lightning," I said. "The storms. That isn't dependent on weaponry or, um, accessories, right?"

"It's rune craft," Baldur said. "Originally created by Odin and passed through the blood of Thor's offspring. Magni's way with thunder and lightning is as inseparable from him as his blond hair and brown eyes. You could say it's in his DNA, I guess."

I imagined a scientist decoding Thorin's genes and finding tiny runic symbols engraved in his chromosomes. "And there's no removing it from him, right? No tricks that Rolf might have for stealing Thorin's power?"

Thorin shook his head. "Only the Allfather has that ability, right?"

Baldur pursed his lips. "After this many eons? I don't think even I could take away your thunder."

"How long since you've had a knock-down-drag-out with an immortal?" I asked.

Thorin arched a single eyebrow. "Are you implying I might be rusty?"

"I wouldn't dare. I was just... *curious.*"

"Don't worry about it, Sunshine. Fighting is ingrained in my DNA, too."

"So it's settled? You're going to accept Rolf's challenge."

Thorin glanced down at his phone. "I'll call him now and tell him."

Rolf answered Thorin's call right away, and Thorin grumbled answers and questions at him until they'd settled on the details. Negotiations concluded, Thorin ended the call and stuffed the phone in his pocket. "Tomorrow at dawn," he said, not meeting my gaze. Instead, he stared out the living-room window, his eyes distant and unfocused.

"Where?" Baldur asked.

"He gave me GPS coordinates. Said it was in an open area outside Portland."

"Portland?" I asked. "Why there?"

Rather than answer, Thorin turned his attention back to me and crossed the space between us. He grasped my arm, between shoulder and biceps, urgent but not intimidating. "I know you would tell me if you had seen anything. But I still have to ask."

"I'm sorry." I shook my head. "The fire, the apple orchard, that's all come to light. There aren't any more mysteries."

"What about…" Thorin stopped and cleared his throat. He lowered his voice. "What about when you touch me?"

"I don't think it works like that. The things I see when I touch people, they're memories and thoughts, not predictions."

"Maybe, if you were to try, you could see something in my past that I've forgotten."

"I don't know, Thorin," I said, reluctant to delve into the dark places deep inside him. Never mind that a being as old as him had accumulated several millennia of memories. Talk about a search for a needle in the most epic haystack. "Besides not knowing if I can even do anything like that, I might find things you'd rather I didn't see. It's not like you to willingly give away personal information."

Quietly, so only I could hear, Thorin said, "I trust you, Sunshine."

My breath caught and hung in my lungs like a kite string trapped in a tree limb. "Are you sure?"

As Thorin stared into me with the warmest look I had ever seen in his eyes, he nodded, took my hand, and held it between his own, close to his heart. The beat of that mighty and timeless muscle thumped under my hand—so human, and yet so *not*.

Baldur cleared his throat and stood up from the kitchen table. "I'm, uh, I'm going to get some air. I'll be back after a while." And, *pop*, he was gone.

"Okay." I returned my attention to Thorin. "I'll give it a try."

"It's all I ask."

I closed my eyes and inhaled a deep breath. "I guess… I mean, I don't know how to do this, but I guess it would be best if you can clear your thoughts. Don't concentrate on anything and just zone out if you can."

Thorin mumbled something affirmative, and his warm breath rushed over my face. He had kept his walls up so long, he had probably forgotten how to let them down, and I saw nothing, at first. But slowly, slowly, I sank through a gray fog and dropped into the light of a recent memory. I saw myself from his point of view, the day we'd first met, when he picked me up from the airport in Anchorage.

Maybe it's all coincidence, and I sincerely hope it is. This isn't the first time the past has reincarnated. Some players from the original game have

265

reappeared from time to time only to experience a violent death in a way that suggests history is prone to revisit some of its more... thrilling moments.

But this girl, coming here after the brutality committed on her brother— she's either stupid, brave, ill-fated, or some of everything. I should have sent her flight back home before it crossed the first time line, saved us all a mountain of trouble. Now Val and I are burdened with watching over her, surreptitiously keeping her safe until I find out if her brother's murder is happenstance or omen.

Thousands of years of peace have blessed me and my kind, but all existence is based on cycles. If the end of this current phase is near, I'll do whatever it takes to ensure I am a part of the rebirth, just like last time. Solina Mundy will not *get in my way.*

Ah, there she is, fighting through the crowds at baggage claim. She's a golden-skinned, blond-haired elf. Sol was the predecessor of their kind—the Ljósálfar—and this girl has definitely inherited the genes. Hmm, she sees Val now—recognition lights in her eyes... and attraction.

I feel sorry for her already.

Thorin's first perception of me was interesting, but unhelpful. I pressed forward, or backward, receding through Thorin's timeline. Flashes of things jumped out at me—history retreating in bursts of colors, thoughts, sounds, smells. So many smells. Rain, of course, gun smoke, wood smoke, spicy pine needles, roasting meat, salt water, forest floors and decaying leaves, decaying bodies, blood, blood, and more blood.

I stopped and slowed my breathing. Like a deep-sea diver halting her descent, I floated, weightless, in a vast ocean of memories, thoughts, words, conversations, emotions. They piled around me, eager like street beggars, demanding attention, crying for consideration. Shoving. Pushing. Suffocating.

All of his thoughts at once—it's too much pressure.

Which way is up? Which way is out?

Can't hear....

Can't think....

Can't breathe...

Buried beneath a pile of blankets, I hunkered in the corner of the sofa and clutched a steaming mug of coffee. Thorin had stoked the coals in the fireplace and added more wood. Flames roared and crackled across from me, but I still trembled.

Thorin sat a few inches away, a stolid sentinel, his gaze never wavering from my face for more than the few seconds it had taken to make a cup of coffee for me. "I'm guessing you've never experienced anything like that before."

"Huh-uh." I shook my head.

"I thought—" He paused, swallowed, and started again. "For a minute, you stopped breathing, and you went pale as a corpse, and you were cold. You've never been that cold." And he should know. I had lost count of how many times he had moved my limp and unresponsive body after one trauma or another. *It's too many times, that's how many.*

"I felt like I was drowning," I said. "I couldn't breathe, and I didn't know which way was up, which way to go to get to the surface. Everything went dark, but I heard you calling my name. It was a lifeline. I followed it back."

Thorin leaned forward, teeth grinding, jaw working. His hand balled into a fist on his knee, white knuckled, imperative. "I don't want you to do anything like that again. Ever."

I set my mug on the end table next to me and withheld the dramatic sigh trying to escape my throat. "It's another tool, like my fire. It may take some time and practice to master, but I need to learn to use it."

"No, Sunshine. I—"

I raised a hand, stopping him. "You wouldn't discard your hammer just because you smashed your thumb with it one time, right? I'll only get better if I practice, but I think I'll stick to working with people whose memories are a bit shallower. Don't ask me not to, because I'll refuse."

Thorin huffed. He leaned back and crossed his arms over his chest. "It's pointless to argue with you when you've made up your mind, isn't it? Your ability *is* a tool, possibly even a weapon, and maybe you should learn to control it." He raised a finger, stopping me before I voiced my agreement. "Wait, I'm not done."

Of course he isn't.

"But we'll do it carefully, and we'll do it together, even if you're practicing with someone else. Don't try this again on your own. Not without me."

I nodded. "Okay. I won't, unless you're there to watch. You'll be the lifeguard. You can pull me out when I get in over my head."

Thorin exhaled and relaxed his shoulders for the first time since I'd regained consciousness. "After all that, I still have to ask: Did you see anything useful? Any memories of Rolf?"

I sank into my blankets and momentarily put aside his question. The worst of my shivering had eased, but a half-frozen slurry still seeped through my veins. I reached for my fire and brought it up to a low, warm roast.

Thorin sucked in a startled breath. "What are you doing?"

"I'm tired of shivering."

He arched an eyebrow. "Well, don't burn down the cabin. Baldur won't get his deposit back."

Saying his name must have worked like an incantation because Baldur chose that moment to reappear in the middle of the living room. A cowlick of cinnamon hair stood up on the crown of his head like tail feathers. He looked at me, glanced at Thorin, and asked, "What did I miss?"

Thorin and I looked at each other and burst out laughing.

"Long story," Thorin said after recovering his composure.

"Did you learn anything useful?"

"Only that it's dangerous to journey through an eternity of memories," I said. "Otherwise, no." I gave Thorin an apologetic smile. "Nothing about Rolf."

"Maybe you have no memories of him," Baldur said. "Maybe he means to take his revenge against someone else by hurting you."

Thorin snorted. "There's no one left who would care if any hurt was done to me."

"*I* would be hurt," Baldur said.

I would be hurt, too, I didn't say although it was true.

Thorin gestured to Baldur. "Anyone who wanted to take revenge on you vicariously, through someone else, would just take it out on Nina. Not me."

"Then it looks like you'll have to wait to find out what this is about until tomorrow," I said. "Because we're not going to figure it out on our own."

"So, in the meantime, we sit and wait?" Baldur stuck out his bottom lip like a petulant child. "I hate that plan. I could put his name out to my network, see what comes up."

"That's a good idea," I said, "and we probably should have done that a while back. Now, it's probably too late. We don't have much time."

Baldur lowered his gaze and shoved his hands in the back pockets of his jeans. "It's my fault for not taking his potential threat more seriously."

"Then I'm equally as guilty," Thorin said. "I underestimated him."

"It's too late for playing the blame game." I shook off my blanket. "Let's find something better to do with our time than play the Shoulda Coulda game." After rising to my feet, I turned off my internal radiator, spread my stance wide, and bounced on the balls of my feet. "C'mon, Lord of the Rain Dance." I rolled my hand in a come-hither gesture. "Let's see what you got."

Thorin smirked. "What are you doing?"

"Asking you to dance. What does it look like?"

"It looks like you're asking for a butt kicking."

I rolled my head, stretching my neck until several vertebrae popped. "Let's see how you do without your hammer, Holy Thunder."

Baldur whooped.

Thorin narrowed his eyes at me, but a smile played on his lips. "Holy Thunder?"

"It'll be your professional wrestling name. Or how 'bout Wonder of Thunder?"

"I like that one," Baldur said. "It rhymes."

In a flash too fast to see, Thorin left the couch, tripped me, and dropped me to the floor.

I wheezed until my breathing found its pace again. No harm done. Thorin had been gentle in his assault, and I *had* sort of asked for it. "Rolf moves fast like you do." I rolled over to my knees and pushed myself onto my feet.

Thorin paced a circle around me, a stalking tiger. "You want me to slow down, Sunshine? Make myself a better match for you?"

269

"This isn't about fighting me." I sought my fire again. Subtle flames filled my palm, but I held them low, at my side. Thorin continued his orbit, seemingly unaware I had armed myself. "This is about you fighting another immortal—someone a lot more like you than I am."

"How do you know he's immortal?" Thorin asked.

"Call it an educated guess."

"You said you fought him before. How did you overcome him?"

"Smoke and mirrors."

Thorin came to a stop in front of me. "What does that mean?"

I lunged and threw a regular punch at Thorin's jaw. When he leaned away from it, I brought up my fireball and swung for his chin, but my handful of flames burned only the empty space where Thorin had stood an instant before. *Good thing that's not my only magic trick.* When Thorin reappeared behind me, I was already turning for him.

He struck out, an open-handed blow at my ribs. He pulled his punches for me, in consideration of my fragile, human body—I had learned that while fighting him at the Aerie. Instead of dodging or blocking the hit, I stepped into it. Softened or not, his strike drove the breath from my lungs and weakened my knees. But the maneuver had served its purpose, and the shock on Thorin's face temporarily dulled my discomfort.

Taking advantage of his stunned state, I rammed a fiery uppercut into his jaw. His head snapped back. I kicked his knee, and he crumpled into a kneeling position. *I am a generous god. I require only that you kneel. Mwa ha ha!*

Thorin recovered and stumbled back, rubbing his jaw and staring at me as if I had sprouted a second head.

"And that, good sir, is the fine art of misdirection," I said, still breathless from the effects of his punch. "That's how I fought Rolf."

"You took a punch?" he asked, incredulous.

"No. I surprise-attacked him with pepper spray. The point is, improvisation is key. If you can't win by skill or might, do the unexpected."

"Who taught you that?"

"A police officer in San Diego." When Thorin opened his mouth to ask about Tre, I cut him off and said, "Not relevant. Point is..." I stopped and grinned. "I got past your defenses."

"In more ways than one," Thorin grumbled. "But I get your point. You've seen that sword in action when Grim used it against you. I'll prepare for this fight as best I can. I won't let him take me by surprise again."

After I threw on some clothes and another layer of insulation—a parka and snow boots—Thorin, Baldur, and I moved outside. Thorin set aside his bracelets and torc before he jogged the porch steps leading down to the front yard, and the snow came to his knees. It didn't deter him. Without saying a thing, Baldur joined him, and the two men sparred.

Baldur and Thorin moved in a fluid style, like ocean waves battling wind. And the snow, kicking up in puffs and clouds as they skipped, lunged, kicked, and punched, created a mystical haze, insinuating magic and heightening their otherworldliness. Mostly, they moved too quickly to comprehend, but in the still moments, they epitomized the archetypes of balance, poise, and lethality. I had never seen anything quite so beautiful or so deadly.

No wonder mankind worshipped them, once upon a time.

CHAPTER THIRTY-TWO

THE AFTERNOON WORE ON, AND Baldur and Thorin tired of their fighting. After promising to come back before dawn, Baldur returned to New Breidablik to tend to Nina, leaving Thorin and me alone together for another night.

"Is it my fault?" I sat next to Thorin on the sofa and nibbled on a grilled-cheese sandwich and a pile of apple slices—late lunch or early supper, depending on interpretation.

The sunlight had dimmed in the living-room window, and in another hour or two, night would fall upon us again. *Only a few hours left before this cataclysmic event. Only a few more hours until Thorin fights for his life, not that we haven't all been fighting for our lives, one way or another, ever since Mani died.*

"Is what your fault?" Thorin asked and swiped an apple slice from my plate and popped it into his mouth.

Look, he does *eat. Will wonders never cease?* "This confrontation with Rolf. If I had listened to you in Corvallis and not confronted Grim on my own, chased him down at his house... Maybe none of this would be happening."

Thorin shrugged. "Maybe, if you had waited for me, Grim wouldn't have been able to abduct you. Maybe we could have taken the sword from him together. But speculation is pointless. It is what it is, and we'll deal with it. Besides, I get the feeling this was all rather inevitable. If you hadn't noticed, our kind are enthralled to fate. We might be gods, but even we must bow before the command of providence. There's no getting around it."

"So, you're saying this fight with Rolf is a consequence of fate?"

Thorin rose from the sofa and paced before the fireplace. "I've been thinking about it, over and over. Going back to the start, to when you first encountered Rolf in San Diego, you said you felt like he let you go on purpose, and you wondered why."

"Yes." *Where's he going with this?*

"It's like he wanted to scare you into coming out of hiding. Like he wanted you to come back to me."

"Why? It's not like he knew I would find the sword."

"Maybe he did know."

"How?"

Thorin gestured to me. "'How' asks the woman who dreams about the future."

I gaped at him. "You think he had a premonition?"

"Whatever the reason, I propose that this was the result he wanted all along."

"How could anyone orchestrate all that we've been through?"

Thorin shook his head. "Not orchestrate, Sunshine. Just push and nudge when necessary, wait and watch when it's not."

"All to get the sword and challenge you to a duel? Why wait all this time? Why not just stab you in the back?"

"There's no honor in that."

I arched an eyebrow at him. "Honor in revenge?"

"What is revenge but courage to call in our honor's debts?"

"Your words?"

"No, but only because I couldn't say it any better myself. Perhaps Rolf's been seeking an opportunity for a long time." Thorin turned and crouched before the fireplace. He picked up the poker and stirred the embers. The logs popped and crackled, and the fire revived. "Maybe Helen's plan provided an opportunity that never existed before. I have a feeling Rolf's secrets aren't the only ones that will be coming to light in the days ahead. Before all is said and done, many more skeletons will be coming out of many more closets."

"I don't have any skeletons in my closet."

Thorin bit his lip and turned away.

"Ah, but you do." I set my empty plate on the lamp table and tucked my sock feet up beneath me. "Of course you do. You're thousands of years old. You don't live that long without having some regrets, right?"

"More than you could imagine. And if it's my time to pay for them, maybe I'll have to."

The desire to ask about his skeletons swelled in my tongue until I thought I'd choke on it. I bit my lip instead and swallowed my questions. *I know him well enough. He'll tell me if I need to know. Trust in that and respect his privacy in the meantime.*

So, rather than questions, I offered reassurance. "It won't be your time. You'll beat Rolf. No question."

Only when I said it did I comprehend my absolute lack of doubt and total confidence in Thorin's success. I wanted Rolf and Thorin to finish the fight, sooner than later, to end the annoyance of waiting. I wanted the sword in our hands, under our control, and anticipation had generated butterflies in my stomach, but that feeling was nothing more than Christmas Eve jitters, the excitement of inevitable reward. No fear tainted the undercurrents of my anxiousness.

Thorin stopped pacing before me and canted his head in a curious way. "You're so confident?"

I eased off the couch, stood up before him, and met his stare. "You're the God of Thunder; the son of Thor, the strongest of the Aesir; immortal; impervious. When you're at my side, there is no doubt, no fear of failure. My belief in our enemies' defeat is certain. My faith in you is absolute."

Outside, the thunder rumbled, sudden and unexpected. The cabin shuddered, rocked by the percussion of sound waves. Thorin stepped closer. "Say it again."

"Say what?" I backed away from him. The thunder rumbled again, softer.

"Your faith in me. Say it again."

"Why?"

"Don't you know? Belief makes us stronger."

Fire burned in my cheeks, and I looked away. "Words mean nothing. Faith, if it hath no works, is dead." I had memorized that one in Sunday school as a child.

"Death and life are in the power of the tongue," Thorin quoted in reply—Proverbs, if I had to guess. "Say it, Solina. *Please.*"

No, not this. Anything but his big brown eyes, staring into mine, all but begging. "Please" really was a magic word—it conquered my resistance.

I squared my shoulders, raised my chin, took a deep breath, and said, "I, Solina Mundy, Daughter of Sol and sun goddess incarnate, have absolute faith in you, Magni Aleksander, Son of Thor and God of Thunder." I leaned forward and jabbed a finger in his chest. "But I'll choke if you make me say it again."

Thorin threw back his head and laughed, and the thunder laughed too, rattling windowpanes. He stood too close, and too much electricity hummed in the air—the literal kind and the metaphorical. If he touched me, I would be a goner. I moved away from him, putting the sofa between us.

"Where are you going, Sunshine?" Thorin asked, still grinning at me. A soft, ephemeral glow exuded from his skin, emphasizing his beauty.

Give a guy a compliment and it goes straight to his... um... divine essence.

"I can't stand this waiting around. I know I'm never going to be able to sleep. I saw some snowshoes in the closet in my room. How about we take a walk, or is that too mundane for a supernatural being who can blip through space?"

Thorin chuckled again. "No, not mundane. It'll make for a good distraction. Let's go."

I was wrong. On top of a night of inadequate sleep and a near-death experience, the two-hour trek in freezing temperatures through knee-deep snow was, in fact, enough to exhaust me. Warm and drowsy before the fireplace, a half-drunk glass of wine in hand, I passed out remarkably soon, but I awoke to Thorin lifting me, carrying me to my room.

"No," I protested. "You don't have to—"

"Quiet. You've had enough sleeping on that couch."

"What time is it?"

"Midnight."

"How much longer?"

"I'll leave soon. I'd like to get there before sunup so I have some time to study the terrain."

My heart sank. Even though I'd professed my faith in him a few hours before, the idea of letting Thorin go fight Rolf on his own did not sit well with me.

"When's Baldur coming back?" I asked.

Thorin eased me onto the bed and drew up the covers. "He said dawn."

"I don't like it."

Thorin grunted. "Neither do I."

Thorin leaned down, and his fingers swept around my neck. A familiar weight settled on my sternum.

"What are you doing?" I asked.

He took off his bracelets and torc and placed them on the nightstand next to my bed. "Can't bring it with me. You'll have to hold onto it for a while. But I'll be back before you know it."

I stroked a finger over Mjölnir's warm surface. "Promise me?"

"Promise you what?"

"Promise you'll come back."

"I'll swear to come back if you make a promise to me in return."

"What's that?"

"Don't try to come after me. Don't interfere with this fight. It's not just the sword at stake. It's for your own safety, too. Promise you'll stay away."

Could he see me roll my eyes in the dark? "Even if I wanted to, how could I? It's not like I can just blip through space like you and Baldur."

"If you want something badly enough, Sunshine, you'll find a way."

True, that. I had never been an outright liar, but I could be... *evasive* when necessary. "If you know me as well as you say you do, then you know that isn't a promise I want to make or keep."

"Sunshine," Thorin said, his voice low and foreboding.

"I promise to stay out of your way." Whether Thorin could see it or not, I put three fingers to my brow in a Boy Scout salute. "I promise that, when you leave, I won't go with you."

But nobody said anything about going later. Any attempt to subvert Thorin's orders depended on the vulnerability of Baldur's sympathy. Manipulative? Yes. Did I care if it meant ensuring Rolf's defeat and securing our possession of the sword? Not so much.

"There's a lot of wiggle room in that promise," Thorin said.

"Take it or leave it. It's the only one I'm going to give."

Thorin groaned. "I ought to tie you up and put you back in that ice cave."

"You could. But you won't because if you did something like that, then there is one promise I would make you, and I would keep it."

"What's that?"

"When I got free, and I *would* get free, you wouldn't find me again, and we'd spend the rest of my days playing the most epic game of hide-and-seek that ever existed."

Thorin huffed. "You've threatened me with that before."

"It isn't a threat." I jimmied my covers higher, snuggling them around my neck. Then I rolled over, giving Thorin my back—a dismissal, if he translated my body language correctly. "Like I said, it's a promise."

CHAPTER THIRTY-THREE

I WOKE AGAIN IN DARKNESS, AND the numbers glowing on the alarm clock beside my bed displayed the time: a few minutes after four o' clock. *Guess I'll have time to sleep when I'm dead... if I'm lucky.* The house creaked. Something thumped and rattled. I slid out of bed and opened my door. A light shone from across the living room. I followed the aroma of freshly brewed coffee and found Baldur leaning against a kitchen counter, mindlessly swirling a spoon around his mug.

"Where is he?" I asked and crossed my arms over my chest. Cool morning air seeped through my thin cotton T-shirt, and I shivered. Without taking my eyes from Baldur, I backed into the living room, snatched the afghan draped across the sofa, and wrapped it around my shoulders.

"Already gone. He left about half an hour ago."

"And we're just going to sit here, twiddle our thumbs, and wait for him to come back?"

Baldur set his mug on the counter. Shadows haunted his eyes, and deep lines scored his forehead and formed parentheses around his mouth. "What else are we supposed to do?"

"Go after him."

"That would violate Rolf's terms."

"Since when do we let Rolf dictate what we do?"

"He'll give the sword to Helen if we don't."

"And if we don't go, and if Rolf does something tricky—and you *know* he's going to do something tricky—then who's to blame when Thorin suffers the consequence?"

Baldur set down his coffee and stood up straighter. "And what if something happens to you? I'll be the one who has to live with the God of Thunder's wrath. Do you know what that's like?"

"Uh, yeah," I said wryly. "I've had some experience."

"For an eternity?"

Okay, got me there. I gave him a crooked smile and shrugged.

Baldur smiled in return. "I don't know why he calls you Sunshine. Your nickname should be Bulldog."

"I'd take it as a compliment."

Baldur snorted, and it turned into a chuckle. "You would. Okay, Solina. If you've got an idea, I'll hear it. Thorin going to Rolf alone and unarmed doesn't sit well with me either, if you want to know the truth."

I nodded. "I do have an idea. It's not much, but something is better than nothing, I guess."

Baldur made a beckoning gesture, urging me to get to the point.

"You remember what you told me when we were trying to escape from Helen's warehouse? You said you could create a rune that would make me totally invisible if you had your full strength and time to prepare. Well, you still don't have much time to prepare, but I figure you have more than you did back then."

Baldur cocked his head like a curious dog, and some of the worry lines faded around his eyes and mouth. He glanced at the window and the sky beyond it, as if judging the nearness of sunrise. "I have the time."

"You have enough strength?"

"Guess we're about to find out."

"Is it that easy?" I asked. "I wish for invisibility, and you snap your fingers and make it happen?"

"Easy? Have any of your abilities come easily for you, without cost?"

"Of course not."

Baldur nodded. "It drains your physical energy, and it's finite, right? Your powers aren't unlimited."

"Right. It also means I've spent a lot of time running around naked."

Baldur chuckled. "It's going to cost you a normal life, too. Even if this all ends, things will never be the way they were."

"It also cost me a brother. If I hadn't lost Mani, I have a feeling I would still be as mundane as ever."

Baldur set down his coffee mug and folded his arms over his chest.

279

He tilted his head and looked at me through his lashes. "Do you know how Odin got the runes in the first place?"

I nodded. I had read the story in my research, although the details were cloudy. "He hanged himself from the world tree and stared into the well at its base until the runes accepted his sacrifice and revealed their shape and power."

Baldur huffed and rolled his eyes. "Out of the mouths of babes..."

"I summarized," I said. "I know it was more complicated than that."

Baldur shrugged. "Not really, Solina. What you said was the important part. The sacrifice. The suffering. That is the cost of runes. I have paid the price, dearly. Over and over."

"But the Valkyries use the runes, too," I said. "They inscribe them on their swords. Thorin has them on his bracelets."

"Odin gifted those runes to the Valkyries, as was his right. But creating runes that can change a person's essence or give them powers they never had before or defy the forces of the natural world..." Baldur looked away and waved a hand as if dispersing the rest of his thought, but I picked up his meaning.

"Only you, right? Because you've paid the cost, in your faultless death, in your time with Helen, in the way you lose Nanna over and over again. That's the price of being Allfather and of having the abilities you have?"

Baldur swallowed and bobbed his head.

"Does it hurt you when you do something like this? When you make a rune that can defy the natural world?"

He smiled, but it didn't reach his eyes. "Only a little, Solina. I barely notice it anymore."

After a disturbing and gut-wrenching flight through the æther, Baldur and I crouched at the edge of a random field, in an indiscriminate rural area near Portland. For the first few minutes after my feet touched solid ground, my vision spun and my ears rang. My stomach swirled and heaved, and my heart skittered around my chest like a demented demon. The last time I had traveled via Aesir Express, I was mostly insensible. After that recent and more conscious experience, I decided I preferred oblivion.

A chill breeze stirred the grass, churning up odors of hay, old leaves, and soil. I tugged my parka's hood over my hair and huddled into the warmth of its fleece lining. Several hundred feet away, in the gloaming light and early-morning fog, stood Magni Aleksander Thorin, Son of Thor and God of Thunder. He had spread his feet wide, his shoulders were squared, and he kept his hands fisted at his side.

A passing stranger might have commented on Thorin's incongruous presence in the middle of an empty field, but he was otherwise unremarkable—as unremarkable as a six-foot-five man wearing his long hair in braids could be. His faded jeans fit him loosely, allowing room to maneuver, and he wore a dark wool sweater. I easily pictured him in leather, armor, and furs, and that mental image sprouted goosebumps across my arms.

Baldur and I had watched Thorin for a while, and he hadn't moved, hadn't uttered a sound. He made no indication he knew we were there, which was the point. It meant Baldur's rune was working as planned. As long as Baldur touched me, I could see him. The moment he let go, he faded into mist. Therefore, I planned to keep at least one hand on his shoulder at all times.

I brushed my fingers over the burn on my chest, the place marked by Baldur's magic. What he had done and how he'd done it remained a mystery, but he'd said the rune-maker's willpower and intent were crucial ingredients. Baldur's magic occupied a hollow place inside me, and where my fire felt like an eternal, smoldering ember, the invisibility rune felt like nothing. The sensation wasn't cold or numbness, just... a notable absence of feeling.

"What do you think he's doing?" I whispered.

Baldur and I had discussed the possibility of creating a rune that would keep others from hearing us, but we realized we might need to communicate our presence to Thorin in a hurry, possibly to shout a sudden warning. In the end, we agreed a rune of silence might be more trouble than it was worth. Whispering was easy and a lot more flexible.

"Meditating," Baldur said.

"What—" I started, but a shimmer of light and shadows played

281

across the field, several yards beyond Thorin. Its strangeness startled me and sent all questions out of my head.

The shimmer coalesced into the form of a man. From that distance, the early-morning gloom hid the details of his face, but the dark hair and striking stature gave him away. Seeing Rolf Lockhart again brought back memories of our fight in San Diego. An image of Tre's crumpled body flashed across my mind's eye, and my imagination replaced Tre with Thorin. I shook my head, blinked, and pushed aside the image. Tre was no immortal, no God of Thunder, and as if to prove my point, a lightning bolt seared across a sky filling with gunmetal rainclouds. Thunder rumbled an ominous warning, and the already dim light faded, plunging us into darkness.

Rolf brought out the sword, and the light from its flames repelled the shadows falling over the two men, standing face-to-face in the middle of the field. If they said anything to each other, their words didn't carry over the thunder and whipping winds. I stepped forward, but Baldur caught my arm and pulled me back.

"Where are you going?" he asked.

"To get a better look."

"It's bad enough I brought you here, but I'm not going to let you get any closer. Not so you or I can get struck down by some inadvertent lightning bolt. If Thorin needs our help, we'll reassess. Until then, let's stay out of his way."

I shot Baldur a dirty look but did what he said. Whether I liked it or not, he had a point. Thunder and lightning were weapons requiring a wide battlefield.

"Why do you think Rolf brought Thorin to this place that gives him such an advantage with his powers?" I asked. "Tell him he can't bring Mjölnir, but let him have an open area where he can easily access his thunder and lightning. If I was going to fight Thorin, I'd meet him in an underground bunker. No windows, no place for the lightning to get in."

As if to support my argument, a spear of electricity stabbed down from the atmosphere, crackling and popping and raising the hairs on my arms and neck.

"There are many things about this situation that make no sense," Baldur said. "We can only wait and see."

Maybe the two adversaries had said nothing up to that point because when Thorin finally spoke, his words rose above the storm's uproar. "That was a warning," he said. "The next one won't be. Hand over the sword, Rolf... or whoever you are."

Rolf smiled, baring his teeth in a distinctly wolfish way. Skoll and Hati were accounted for, and nothing in history or in all our encounters indicated either had a score to settle with Thorin, but countless other wolves peppered the ancient legends. Perhaps the forces that reincarnated *some* of the Norse pantheon had decided to reincarnate them *all*.

Rolf rolled his wrist, and Surtalogi spun in a pinwheel of flames, throwing sparks and fire like an erupting volcano. Thorin stepped back and made a gesture, and lightning exploded overhead in a complex web of veins, as if the sky had turned into a massive, pulsing heart, pumping electricity through the atmosphere.

You should run now, Rolf. Run now, if you can.

"There is no justice in letting you die in ignorance," Rolf said, raising his voice above the storm. "But it won't come easily for you. If you want to know who I am, you'll have to fight for it."

"It would be my pleasure."

Another motion from Thorin's hand brought the lightning down, a missile aimed at his enemy. Rolf swung, flames spewed, lightning struck, and an explosion of energy and sound rocked the space around us. It rattled my bones and battered the air from my lungs. I staggered and gasped. Baldur grabbed me and held me up.

Rolf attacked, drawing the sword up from his hip in an undercut. Surtalogi's fire reached for Thorin, but a gust of wind and a pillar of rain deflected the flames. Surtalogi guttered, its light flickering, but Rolf flashed away from Thorin and whipped the sword into a blazing frenzy again. Another swipe of flames, another streak of lightning, and the two supernatural beings fell into an incomprehensible battle that mimicked the style of Thorin and Baldur's earlier practice fight.

"I can't keep up," I said to Baldur. Wind tugged at my hood, and wayward rain gusts rattled against me like BB-gun pellets. "Who's winning?"

Baldur's gaze followed Thorin's and Rolf's movements, his eyes flickering as if experiencing a waking REM cycle. "Magni has the advantage in attack, but Rolf is quick in his defense. But he's tiring. If Magni maintains his strength, Rolf's defeat will be swift."

"Could you maybe pop in there and grab the sword?" I asked.

Baldur huffed. "One doesn't simply 'grab' a sword made of fire, Solina. Rolf isn't going to let go of it easily either. Trust Thorin. Let him do his job."

Another concussion of light and sound underscored Baldur's conclusion. Thorin and Rolf stopped several yards before us, both heaving for breath, both wearing matching expressions of viciousness and obstinacy. Thorin stood, shoulders thrown back, fists raised. With his head tilted back, he peered down at Rolf, who stooped on one knee before him, empty-handed. The sword lay several feet away, cold, inert, and as ordinary as an artifact in a history museum.

"Will you tell me now?" Thorin asked. "Have I not earned the right to know your name? Your *real* name?"

A cold smile formed on Rolf's lips. "Maybe I'll tell you when I see the light fading from your dying eyes, Magni, Son of Thor."

Thorin bared his teeth and growled. "That's not going to happen."

"I wouldn't be so sure."

Rolf threw back his head and roared something in their ancient Aesir language. The ground shook, and the earth roiled, heaving and splitting open in a scene from a horror movie. Instead of spitting out half-rotted, undead corpses, the ground spewed forth an army of darkness, a battalion of horrors I had hoped to never see again. Helen Locke's stone men rose to their feet, faster and more fluid than anything formed from mud and rock should have managed. They circled around us, twenty or thirty golems, all wearing their stolid, emotionless expressions and waiting for Rolf's command.

Guess that explains the need for the open field.

Baldur huffed a harsh breath beside me. He hadn't let go of me throughout the battle, and his hands tightened around my arm, either stopping me from moving forward to join Thorin's side or stopping himself.

"You said you wanted a fair fight," Thorin said.

Rolf snorted. "As if a fight against the Allfather's warlord could be fair in any situation. Even without your hammer, we both know you are the superior warrior. I am only trying to level the battlefield."

"I told you he was going to be tricky," I hissed in Baldur's ear. I yanked my arm, urging him to let me loose. "We can't stand here and watch. Thorin's going to need help."

Baldur glared at me, and blue flames burned in his eyes. I'd seen that same look in Val's eyes before, and the resemblance between the two half-brothers was uncanny.

"Not yet," he whispered. "Too soon."

I gritted my teeth. *He's right. We've still got the element of surprise on our side. Use it when it's going to make the biggest impact.*

"This isn't the first time I've battled Hela's legions," Thorin said.

Rolf laughed. "You haven't encountered her new and improved version, though. Twice the speed, twice the strength. Twice the fun."

He shouted another word, and the golems moved in. Thorin reached overhead, and the skies responded, a netting of electricity crackling across the heavens before falling apart into individual lances of light, heat, and energy. The hair on my arms and neck rose. A hum filled my ears, drowning out everything else. As the barrage of lightning bolts screamed toward the stone army, Baldur threw an arm around me. My ears popped, and a swirling blackness filled my vision.

My senses returned moments later, revealing that Baldur and I were standing in a grove of trees. No thunder, no lightning, no golems. No Thorin and Rolf, either. I whirled on Baldur and shoved a hand against his chest. "What the hell did you do?"

Baldur leaned forward, and his eyebrows drew together. He turned on his godly mojo and shook his finger at me. "You wouldn't have survived that attack, Solina. It might have knocked me out of commission for a while, too. Thorin held nothing back—he had no reason to. That's why he didn't want you there in the first place. He can't fight at full capacity if he has to worry that the by-blow could kill you."

"So you just left him?"

"No. I'm going back. You're staying here. Give me the hammer and the cuffs."

I glared at Baldur and opened my mouth to refuse, but he didn't give me the chance. He locked his arms around me. I struggled while he raided my pockets and pilfered Thorin's bracelets. If I really had wanted to stop him, I could have burned him, but deep down, Baldur and I both wanted the same thing: to give Thorin his weapons. A small voice urged me to let Baldur have his way. He stood a better chance of returning Mjölnir to Thorin than I did. Baldur grabbed the chain around my neck, and Mjölnir's lanyard broke free. I let out a scream of protest, but it did little good. Baldur was gone, and so was Thor's hammer.

"You're crazy if you think I'm just going to stand here and wring my hands and wait for you to come back and get me!"

But Baldur couldn't hear me anymore. The problem was, Baldur *was* crazy, at least a little bit. Maybe he really did think I would stand there. I moved out from the trees into a nearby clearing and spun around, searching the sky.

In the distance, a copse of black clouds disrupted the blue morning sky. Lightning crackled through their billowing darkness like glowing filaments in the world's biggest plasma globe. The display was beautiful and amazing, and Thorin was its maker and master. How could my trivial fire compare against something like that? *What a monumental ego I have, thinking he needed my help.* But the same moment that thought concluded, the lightning dispersed, crackling away like an ellipsis at the end of an unfinished sentence. The clouds faded, shedding their weight and magnitude until they resembled a flock of fluffy, harmless lambs. Maybe the fight had ended. Or maybe something had happened to Thorin.

Screw standing here and waiting. I couldn't judge distances. How far would I have to go to get back? A mile? Two? It didn't matter. I made up my mind to go, and I went, putting my heart and lung health to the ultimate cardiovascular test. I wasn't a runner, but adrenaline can do amazing things for the human body. It gives mothers the strength to raise cars off their trapped children. It gives soldiers the ability to hold out until backup arrives. It made my feet fly, gave them wings.

Mercury, eat your heart out.

CHAPTER THIRTY-FOUR

PERHAPS BALDUR HADN'T STRANDED ME as far away as it first seemed. Or maybe I really had flown—a little of my shooting-star power had blossomed, giving me the extra lift and speed I needed. The trip passed without awareness, like making it home from work without remembering anything about the drive and asking: *How did I get here?*

When I reached the battlefield, Thorin was still in the middle of the fight, swinging Mjölnir in a blur. Rubble piles littered the field around him—lifeless remains of golem bodies making their own burial cairns wherever they fell. A handful of stone men remained, keeping Thorin occupied as Rolf danced in and out with the sword, apparently recovered from its inert state.

Warlord indeed. I had lost track of time, and it seemed as though Thorin had fought for hours while maintaining an aggressive and relentless pace. How much longer would he last? Thorin's sweater showed singe marks, signs of Surtalogi's close encounters. A nasty wound over Thorin's chest peeked through a rip in the dark wool. Another slash had rent a hole in his side, over his ribs, but he fought as though the injuries didn't bother him. While I hated being the helpless heroine who stood on the sidelines while the hero did all the grunt work, I also understood the danger of being Thorin's stumbling block. I edged in closer, looking for an opportunity to help without getting in his way.

Baldur and I had lost physical contact, and I couldn't see him anymore because of our invisibility runes. He could have been standing a foot away, and I wouldn't have known. I grumbled curses at him while keeping my attention focused on Thorin. That probably explained why I didn't see Rolf's next trick until it was almost too late.

Only five or six golems remained, and one parted from the group, heading for Thorin. Thorin turned his back to me as he prepared to swing his hammer. A few yards separated us, but the space provided sufficient room for another golem to rise from his underground grave.

They're like cockroaches. They just keep coming.

Thorin demolished the stone creature in front of him, but that distraction held him long enough for the new creature to grab his ankle and throw him off balance. The air behind Thorin shimmered. Rolf appeared at Thorin's side, sword already swinging through the course of its strike. Surtalogi's fire spewed a rain of plasma sufficient to drown Thorin—instant incineration. Thorin never saw Rolf's attack, but I did, and I called on my flames in response. With no time to think, question, or doubt, I threw myself into the fray and raised my flames to maximum burn, shielding both Thorin and myself.

Rolf had seen the sword take my powers when I fought against Grim and probably knew if he kept Surtalogi focused on me long enough, the sword would drain me dry and render me useless.

The sword can have my fire. Just let me last long enough for Thorin to rally his counter attack. "I can't hold him off forever," I said. "Whatever you're going to do, you better do it fast."

Thorin's dark eyes reflected my flames, and he looked like a demon freshly released from Hell. "Sunshine? I told you not to come."

"You knew I wouldn't listen. Be grateful. I just saved your ass. Again."

Thorin roared something indeterminate, but he didn't stay to argue. He blipped out of sight, and a moment later, Surtalogi's flames disappeared. Rolf was splayed on the ground. Thorin kneeled over him, his hand wrapped round Rolf's throat, squeezing off his air supply. Thorin held Mjölnir poised overhead, only feet away from ensuring Rolf's death.

The remaining golems fell, one by one, as if crushed by an invisible hand—an invisible hand that no doubt belonged to Baldur.

As I retracted my flames, Rolf's gaze settled on me, and he wheezed a silent laugh. "Knew you'd show up," he croaked.

"You can see me?"

My ears popped, and Baldur appeared, visible, at my side. "That invisibility rune couldn't stand up against your fire *and* Surtalogi's flames," he said. "Not unless I made it a permanent part of your essence, and we didn't have time for that. Thought it'd be better to go with something temporary. I should have warned you."

"Doesn't matter anymore." I kept my gaze on Rolf. "It's over now. Rolf is defeated."

Another soundless laugh rocked Rolf's shoulders.

"What's so funny?" Thorin asked.

Rolf made a choking noise. Thorin released his grip enough to allow Rolf to speak, but he kept Mjölnir raised in a conspicuous threat. "See how she looks at you, God of Thunder. How she'd risk herself for you? If only she knew your true character. And the Allfather, so quick to give his support to the unworthy. It's a shame."

"What do you mean?" I asked.

"You want to know who I really am?" Rolf's gaze shifted to Thorin. "I told you that you would have to earn it. And, oh, how you have."

"Go on then," I said. "Cut the dramatics and tell us."

"Are you sure, Solina?" Rolf looked back at me. "Once said, it can never be taken back. It's like opening Pandora's Box. You can't close it again, but you'll wish you could."

"Say it," Thorin snarled. "But if you won't, I'll kill you and live with the disappointment of not knowing. I've gotten good at living with disappointment."

Rolf grinned again. "Don't say I didn't warn you." And with that, the face of the man whom I'd known as Rolf Lockhart melted away to reveal another, one even more familiar.

Everything ground to a halt, my breathing, my heartbeat—the entire world stopped spinning and fell off its axis. I couldn't have said a thing if the fate of every life on earth depended on it. Not that I needed to say anything.

Baldur said it for us all. "Val? Is it really you?"

CHAPTER THIRTY-FIVE

"VAL?" I SAID. HIS FAMILIAR blue gaze turned on me and cleared me of any doubt. Bile crawled up my throat. I coughed, trying to choke it back down. "How could you? How could it *be* you? Grim broke you in half."

Val twisted his lips into a wry smile. "There's more to me than meets the eye. Obviously."

"It's been you all along, hasn't it?" Thorin said. "I suspected, but I didn't want to. You are my cousin. How could you betray us?"

Val erupted with a cold, cruel laugh. It turned into a cough. He hacked, turned his head, and spat. His cold eyes turned back to Thorin, and he said, "I killed your cousin the day of the final battle in Asgard and took his place."

"If you are not Vali Odinson, who the hell else would you be?"

"I *am* Vali, but I am no son of Odin."

Thorin hesitated, the gears turning in his head. "Loki," he said. "Loki had a son."

"Loki had many sons," Val said. "Most did not survive."

My brain plugged back in and whirred to life, making connections, drawing conclusions. Loki was the trickster god of schemes, pranks, and deceptions—it explained Val's immense aptitude for deceit. It also meant he had some very problematic family relations.

"Helen is your aunt?" I asked. "Are you here to do her bidding, or was it your plan all along?"

Val's face sharpened into a look of hatred so severe I felt it in my bones. "I don't give a damn about Helen's ridiculous schemes. This has nothing to do with her."

"Then what is it? What do you want?"

"Revenge."

I blinked at him. "I don't understand."

"Why not? It's a language you speak so well. Someone takes your other half away from you, mercilessly murdering an innocent brother, and you'll do anything to make them pay. That's something you appreciate, right?"

My brow furrowed as I contemplated his words, and a recent memory bubbled up from the darker depths of my brain. "That was your brother I saw in your memory? The one the wolf was killing? But it wasn't Hodr because you're not Vali, son of Odin."

Val moved his head in a slight nod. "Now, Solina," he rasped. "Ask me who the wolf was."

Val's words were the current in an exposed wire that made my whole body buzz, muscles lock up, teeth grind together. *Don't want to ask. Think I already know, but wish I didn't. Wish I may, wish I might...* "No," I whispered, shaking my head.

"Rolf." A Nordic contraction meaning "notorious wolf."

"No," I repeated.

Time stopped while I processed. Then it all fell into place. I *had* read that legend. I *did* know that history. The rest of the story, the missing piece, was the ending to the tale Grim had told me in his office about the purpose behind Val's existence. If Vali had been the head on one side of the coin representing Odin's vengeance, then Loki was tails. As punishment for the trick Loki had played on Hodr—the blind god who had unknowingly killed Baldur because Loki set him up to do it—the Aesir bound and tortured Loki, burning him with acidic snake venom that dripped on him for eons. But that wasn't the worst part. Not by far.

"The Aesir turned me into that wolf," Val said. "Odin and his kin forced me to change into a rabid, mindless beast. They set me on my brother. His name was Narfi, and he was my twin. Just like Mani was your twin. I ripped Narfi's guts out, Solina. I had no idea what I was doing until it was over. The Aesir used my brother's entrails to bind my father so they could torture him."

Val hacked again and spat out another gob of saliva. "I woke to find my brother dead, his blood on my tongue, his flesh between my teeth."

I gasped and put my hand over my mouth. My stomach heaved—so did my heart. I turned aside and retched. Overdramatic? Not after the visions I had seen. Not after I had lost a beloved twin brother to a nearly identical modus operandi. The gods' ancient game of revenge never ended. Back and forth swung the finger of blame, taking out innocent lives, ruining families, and devastating guiltless individuals, all to satisfy some enormous primordial arrogance.

I wiped my mouth, burning and bitter with stomach acid, and glared at Thorin, but he refused to look at me. "Is it true?" I asked.

Thorin raised his chin and lowered it, a slight nod but undeniable affirmation. I buried my face in my hands and sobbed.

"You know what it's like to lose your twin, Solina," Val said. "But do you know what it's like, living with the knowledge that *you* were the one who killed him? I've wanted revenge for a very long time. And now I have it."

"And how is that?" Thorin asked. "You are at *my* mercy. I should have killed you already. I'll finish this and put you out of your misery." Thorin rose up, but I grabbed his hand and moved into his line of sight, capturing his gaze.

"No," I said. "Tell us, Val. Tell us how this is your revenge."

Val's eyes glittered as he stared at Thorin. His mouth curled up, not quite into a smile— it was too hard for that. "She knows who you really are, now, God of Thunder. She knows what you're capable of. We all do. My revenge is to see you care for someone other than yourself for the first time in eons and know that I was the one who took that away from you, and all I had to do was tell her the truth. Tell her who you really are and what you are capable of."

Val's gaze shifted to me. "Not so godly now, is he, Solina? He's as tainted as the rest of us."

"Val, you tried to kill me in San Diego," I said.

"No." He shook his head. "I scared you into running back to Thorin. Everything that's happened, has happened just as I planned."

"How is that possible?"

"Stupid, simple Val, right? Not so mighty as Thorin, not so pure as Baldur. How was I even considered a god? But I told you, Solina. I *know* everything. I *remember* everything." Val's attention turned to the sky.

Following his gaze, I looked up in time to see two massive black birds crash down on us from above—talons scratching, wings beating, beaks stabbing. I ducked and covered my head. Baldur cried out. Thorin yelled something, and thunder rumbled again in the distance. When I looked back up, Val had disappeared along with his birds. A pair of black feathers rested on the grass where Val had lain, and they reflected the sun in iridescent purples and greens, like the sheen on an oil puddle.

"The sword!" I said, as my brain chugged back to life. I jumped up and spun around, searching for it. Thorin stood up beside me, also scanning the ground.

Baldur stepped up and waved his hand in a calming gesture. "I secured it while Val was speechifying. It's safe."

I turned and surveyed the field—the quiet, mundane, rural field. It was empty, other than the strange rock piles. *Let the landowner try to figure that one out. Who am I kidding? Val probably* is *the landowner. He probably had this trap set for ages.* "You were clearheaded enough to think about the sword while Val was making the biggest confession of betrayal of the millennium?" I asked.

Baldur shrugged. "I survived living with Hela. Nothing much shocks me anymore."

"What the hell were those birds about? Val is suddenly Alfred Hitchcock?"

Baldur looked at Thorin, who returned his stare. They both nodded.

"Hugin and Munin," Baldur said. "Odin's ravens."

"Hugin and Muni—" I stopped midsentence when my lazy synapses made the connection. *How stupid can I be?* "Hugh Rabe and Joe Muniz. Val's roommates are Odin's ravens? What the hell?"

"What the hell, indeed," Baldur said. "It made some sense when we still knew Val to be the last surviving son of Odin's direct lineage. But he had convinced us the ravens' omniscient ways were lost after Ragnarok, and he was keeping them out of kindness and loyalty."

"Why didn't *you* inherit them?" I asked.

"I was in Hela's realm when Odin died," Baldur said. "I was in no state to take possession of his birds."

"So Val got them?"

"Vali, Son of Odin, got them. I'm not sure how Vali, Son of Loki, managed to take over their control. But he is the son of the Trickster. If he inherited half of Loki's skill, then many things are possible."

"So," I said, "somehow, he took control of the ravens when he killed Odin's son."

"Yes, it would seem so." Baldur furrowed his brow. He scratched his chin in a thoughtful gesture. "But I don't know how."

"It's not a question we have to answer right now," Thorin said. "We need to get moving before more trouble shows up."

I nodded but refused to meet Thorin's gaze, although his stare burned a hole in my forehead.

"I need to get back to New Breidablik," Baldur said. "I need to check on a couple of things. How about I meet you back at the rental cabin in an hour?"

"No—" I started, but Baldur blipped away without hearing the rest of my protest. *No, don't leave me alone with Thorin.*

A breeze danced past and caught my hair. I tucked the loose strands behind my ear, inhaled a deep breath, and turned to face Thorin. He held himself stiff. His jaw was hard from clenching his teeth together, but his eyes... I looked away, unable to bear the infinity in their depths—an eternity of everything he felt. It was too much.

"How are we going to get there?" I asked, my voice dry, my tone deadened. "One of your discreet rental cars is going to come pick you up? Out here, in the middle of nowhere?"

Thorin shook his head and stepped closer to me. "No, Sunshine."

"Don't call me that," I snapped and turned away, surprised by my own bitterness. "I'm sorry, I don't know where that came from."

"I do," Thorin said. "And I understand it."

Good thing one of us does. Everything inside me had gone numb, and I dreaded what would happen when it all thawed out. "Please," I said and raised a hand. "No sympathy from you. Not right now. Can we just... Can we just go?"

Thorin cleared his throat and caught my gaze. "It requires physical contact. Are you okay with that?"

"I thought only Baldur could take on a passenger."

"I can carry you when I have Mjölnir."

Val had said the ancient weapons amped up their power. Maybe that was the only thing he hadn't lied about.

I motioned to Thorin's injuries, to the oozing burn mark on his chest and ribs. "Are you sure you've got it in you?"

Thorin's nostrils flared, and his eyes narrowed. A growl rumbled in his throat.

"Fine." I lifted my arms in a way that looked like I was asking for a hug. "God forbid we do anything to bruise your ego."

Thorin stepped closer, took my hips between his hands, and said, "Hold on tight. It's a hell of a ride."

I wrapped my arms around his neck and said, "Then it's a good thing this ain't my first rodeo."

Snap crackle pop. We were gone.

CHAPTER THIRTY-SIX

THORIN SAID NOTHING WHEN WE arrived at the cabin. I went to the kitchen, hoping Baldur had left coffee in the pot that I could reheat in the microwave. Thorin went to his room, changed into a clean shirt, and returned to the living room. He crouched before the fireplace, stoked the coals, and brought the fire back to life, if for no other reason than to put his attention on something other than me. At least, that's what I figured. Knowing Thorin, he wasn't avoiding my glare out of shame or regret. More likely, he was struggling to control his emotions. I, however, remained numb.

Val's revelations had hurt me, and the wound ran deep, and raw, which explained why I had shut down everything inside me. That kind of injury was threatening to incapacitate me, and I couldn't afford a breakdown. My brother's best friend, a man I had taken into my heart as an intimate confidant, had exposed himself for a lying bastard of the grandest design—a manipulator on a scale so massive I barely comprehended it. From the start, I had worried Val might lie and use me to get something he wanted, but I'd never imagined anything like the scheme he'd constructed. How could I have guessed the magnitude of his betrayal?

However... I felt sorry for Val. I knew his pain and understood what it had driven him to do. I understood why.

And Thorin. *Oh, the gods, Thorin.* Val had undoubtedly wanted me to hate Thorin—hate him enough to leave him—but did I? I searched myself for animosity or disgust or loathing, but I only found numbness, as if Baldur's invisibility rune had reconstructed itself and taken up residence in my heart.

"You were there?" I stepped closer to Thorin, who lingered in a crouch before the fireplace. "You were one of the ones who did that to him?"

Thorin rose up to full height and turned to face me. I expected to see blackness in his eyes, but it wasn't there.

"Were you a part of turning Val into the beast?" I asked.

"It was thousands of years ago." He said it in a tired voice as if he knew it was insufficient but worth a try anyway.

"A million years wouldn't matter if I was an eternal being who was forced to kill my own brother."

Thorin raised his chin. His eyes hadn't gone dark, but he was still a proud man.

I shouldn't expect remorse from him.

"And what if I *was* there?"

Unconsciously, my hands balled at my sides. "Then I might put some blame on you for what Val has become."

"You pity him?"

"No. Not pity. But empathy? Yes. I can put myself in Val's shoes. I know what it would have done to me if I had woken to find I had killed Mani. If I had picked his flesh from my teeth. I couldn't have lived with it, and if I had, it would have made me a monster."

Thorin stepped closer to me and captured my gaze. An earnest light burned in his eyes. "You probably can't understand how beloved Baldur was to us. He was the epitome of what a god should be, and he made the rest of us feel we were all a little closer to the ideal we had reached for but failed. Baldur was our Christ, but his death didn't redeem our sins. It only made them lower and uglier. It made us *all* lower and uglier. Losing him..." Thorin shrugged and shook his head. He swallowed. "We would have burned the world ourselves if it would have stopped our hurting. We wanted Loki to feel our pain, to know the enormity of our loss and what he had cost us. It wasn't moral, it wasn't *right*, but ask me if I would do it again, Solina."

Thorin knitted his brows. "Ask me what I *wouldn't* do to avenge the death of my family. Ask me what horrors I *wouldn't* inflict on my enemy, on the one who would destroy someone I loved. Right or wrong is not a question that applies to those circumstances."

I snorted and deepened my voice in mimicry of a man's. "It was desperate times—we were desperate men."

Thorin huffed. "You're making jokes?"

"I'm trying to cope. Sometimes I do it gracelessly." I turned away from him and paced the living room. *Make him suffer a little. He deserves it. We're all about the revenge these days, right?* "People say revenge is prison and forgiveness is freedom."

"And have you forgiven Mani's killer?"

I stopped and turned to face Thorin. "I didn't have to forgive him. I killed him."

Thorin's eyes flashed. "Was I not due the same justice?"

"It's a bitter cycle. When does it end? How many of us will go down with that ship?"

"When Baldur died, I would have happily gone down with his ship."

"But you didn't."

Thorin shook his head. His posture had softened—perhaps he had caught a whiff of truce in my tone. "I survived, and I moved on. And that, in a way, is also a revenge."

"Do you think Helen Locke cares if I go on or not? Do you think it hurts her that I continue to live?"

"I think it does, yes." Thorin closed the remaining distance between us and peered into my face as if searching for something.

I inhaled his scent, lightning and rain. Tentatively, I took his hand, and the connection thawed me a little—touching him was like exposing the cold places inside me to sunlight. Our physical contact brought forth no visions, which maybe meant Thorin was keeping his thoughts fully in the present.

He squeezed my fingers and didn't quite smile, but the hardness in his face eased. "I think every day your heart continues to beat brings her a great deal of infuriation."

I sniffed. "Well, good. I think I'll go on with the heart beating and the air breathing and the getting on with life. I'd do it for no other reason than to be a thorn in her side."

Thorin chuckled, and his humor dispersed the worst of the acrimony between us. Things hadn't returned to normal, but I could move on. I could continue.

I retreated to my room and packed up my few measly belongings. Lost in the endless whirlpool of my thoughts, time passed quickly, and Baldur returned before I could wonder about him or worry about his return. His voice carried through my bedroom door as he talked to Thorin. I squared my shoulders, stiffened my spine, and went out to join them.

"Solina," Baldur said. "We need to plan our next steps. Staying at the cabin any longer is probably not safe."

I nodded. "I agree. And I know exactly what we need to do next."

Baldur's eyebrow arched. "Oh?"

"Kill that damned wolf," I said. "It all begins and ends with him, and we never should have lost sight of that. I've been thinking about it, and it's possible the Aerie has resources we can utilize. Maybe Skyla can convince the Valkyries to join the hunt. This is what they were made for. Skyla has been looking for a cause to unite them. Hunting Skoll—it's the perfect thing, the answer to their battle lust."

Baldur bit his lip against a smile. "Battle lust?"

"How long has it been since you've given them a purpose? They train and play fight and hold tight to their traditions, but there's no outlet for their aggression. The Aesir have squandered a powerful resource. We should have exploited them sooner."

"You think Skyla can lead them to a unified action?" Baldur asked, tactfully ignoring my *squandered* comment.

"I'm depending on it. We were driven apart by our own stubbornness, by fate and circumstance. It made us easy pickings. But we're back together... for the most part."

Val was gone, never to return, and I mourned him. I grieved the man my brother had loved, the man I had considered a dear, if deeply flawed, friend. The Val I'd thought I knew was merely a ghost of someone who had died eons before. I still felt his absence like a missing organ, but I hid my concern for Val in the same dark place I put all my other unhelpful emotions. "With the Valkyries behind us, it might be possible to end this thing. Once and for all."

"But you don't trust them," Baldur said.

"Not completely. But I trust Skyla, and we need their help." I turned and eyed Thorin. "I want to trust you too, know that you'll be at my back, be the wall everyone has to go through first if they want to get to me."

Thorin scowled. "Why don't you already believe that?"

"You've chosen Baldur over me too many times."

Thorin flinched. His gaze shifted to Baldur.

Baldur nodded. "It's true. I released you from your vows, but I still made demands of you." Baldur's gaze shifted to me. "Don't be too hard on Magni. There are thousands of years of allegiance between us. That's a lot of indoctrination to overcome in a short time. It won't happen again."

"Easy to say," I said, "now that you have Nina back. Swear to me that you'll make no more demands of Thorin's loyalty. Swear to me that when I need him, he'll be free to decide for himself."

Baldur nodded. "I swear it."

I turned to Thorin. "Swear that I am your only priority. Promise my well-being comes before anything or anyone else."

Thorin snarled. "I swear it, but only if you swear not to run headlong toward danger and ignore the counsel of those vowed to protect you."

I wasn't going to run headlong toward danger, but that wasn't the same as avoiding it altogether. And I was going to listen to Thorin's counsel, as well as Baldur and Skyla's. But I was ultimately going to make my own decisions. *I should be an attorney: there are no true mutual agreements, only the appearance of them.* "I swear it."

"If the Valkyries will come," Baldur said, "tell them to meet us at New Breidablik. If Vali Lokison truly has command of Odin's ravens, New Breidablik is the only place safe from their omniscience."

"How will we track Skoll from New Breidablik?" I asked.

"I'll reach out to my network," Baldur said. "They've been off the job since we found Nina, but I can put them on Helen's trail and, thereby, the wolf's."

Once we agreed on a course of action, we all made ready to withdraw to New Breidablik.

Out on the cabin's front porch, Baldur blipped away after casually saying, "See you back at the ranch."

I sucked in a breath and held it as Thorin stepped close. "Before we go one step further," he said, "there's something I need to do." He slipped Mjölnir from his pocket, slid the pendant free from its chain, and stuffed the hammer back into his pocket. He dangled the chain before my eyes as a hypnotist might.

"Put my leash back on?" I asked, already lifting my hair out of the way.

"After all that's happened, you would go without it?" Thorin leaned close. He slipped the chain around my neck and fastened the clasp. The gesture brought him intimately close as his fingers brushed against my neck. Like an afterimage burned on my retinas, the brief and ghostly likeness of a woman in a horse-drawn chariot appeared, racing across a field of blue. The vision might have meant Thorin was thinking of Sol, or it could have meant he was thinking of me. *Where does she end and I begin?*

"No." I fingered the necklace. "I don't mind it. I just wish I didn't need it."

Thorin studied me as he adjusted the chain to lie flush against my skin. He held my gaze for a moment. What did he see when he looked at me that way? What was he looking for? Thorin exhaled and shook his head, breaking the spell. "Things aren't going to be like they were before, are they?"

"I still believe in you, if that's what you're wondering."

And it was true. No matter my muddled emotions, I still believed in his powers and abilities. Nothing had stopped him from being the God of Thunder.

"But no, things aren't the same," I said. "Another layer of my naiveté has peeled away. If there was any innocence still living in me, I think it's gone now."

Thorin shook his head. "You are the sun, Solina. You may be wiser and harder, but nothing can take away your light."

Glad you think so. Me... I'm not so sure. "Neither of us is the same as we were before," I said. "And especially not to each other."

Thorin's breath caught. I was close enough to sense his reaction, and it felt like anticipation.

"It's not something I'm willing to define, yet. It's not the right time."

He eased his hands around my hips and drew me in. "You'll let me know when it is the right time?"

Karissa Laurel

I slid my arms around his neck and held him close—maybe a little closer than necessary. "You'll be the first to know."

Thorin tightened his grip on me. My ears popped, and the world vanished. Our movement through the æther mirrored the sensation of an ocean voyage in a horrible storm. My stomach lurched, my sense of up and down disappeared, and vertigo swirled my consciousness into a soupy mess. The experience took apart my world and stranded me in the unfamiliar and unknowable. Then Thorin curled himself around me, and he held me close. He was a steadying presence, the calm among the fury.

Val had said I opened Pandora's Box, and maybe he was right. But Pandora had closed the box before hope could escape. Did that mean she had doomed the world to hopelessness, or had she kept it safe so we'd know where to find it when we needed it most? I chose to believe the latter. I chose to believe we could win.

"Don't let me go," I whispered and tightened my grip on Thorin.

Thorin put his lips close to my ear, and despite the roaring winds, his reply cut through the deafening chaos. "I wouldn't dare."

ACKNOWLEDGMENTS

First thanks are for God and family. Nothing I've done would matter without faith, hope, and love.

To my beta readers, Jean Hobbs and Diana Carey, your friendship and advice is golden.

Thanks to Suzanne Warr, not just for your editorial guidance, but for going above and beyond with advice and mentorship and for letting me tag along on your coattails every once in a while.

Also thanks to Kelly Reed for trimming up, cleaning out, and polishing everything to a high glossy shine—and for getting my *Princess Bride* references.

To Mary Fan, Erica Lucke Dean, and Jaime Leigh: you've been one of the best parts of joining the Red Adept Publishing family. Thank you for kindness, friendship, and laughter.

Thanks to my earliest readers and fans, and especially those book bloggers who have been willing to take a chance on a new author. Bloggers grease the wheels that make the book world go round. We couldn't do it without you.

ABOUT THE AUTHOR

Karissa Laurel always dabbled in writing, but she also wanted to be a chef when she grew up. So she did. After years of working nights, weekends, and holidays, she burnt out and said, "Now what do I do?" She tried a bunch of other things, the most steady of those being a paralegal for state government, but nothing makes her as happy as writing. She has published several short stories and reads "slush" for a couple of short-story markets.

Karissa lives in North Carolina with her kid, her husband, the occasional in-law, and a very hairy husky. She loves to read and has a sweet tooth for speculative fiction. Sometimes her husband convinces her to put down the books and take the motorcycles out for a spin. When it snows, you'll find her on the slopes.

Karissa also paints and draws and harbors a grand delusion that she might finish a graphic novel someday.

www.ingramcontent.com/pod-product-compliance
Lightning Source LLC
Chambersburg PA
CBHW020252200626
46816CB00001BA/252